# Immortal Unchained

## LYNSAY SANDS

First published in Great Britain in 2017 by Gollancz
an imprint of the Orion Publishing Group Ltd
Carmelite House, 50 Victoria Embankment
London EC4Y 0DZ

An Hachette UK Company

1 3 5 7 9 10 8 6 4 2

A CIP catalogue record for this book is
available from the British Library.

ISBN 978 1 473 22153 6

Printed in Great Britain by
Clays Ltd, St Ives plc

MIX
Paper from
responsible sources
FSC® C104740

www.lynsaysands.net
www.orionbooks.co.uk
www.gollancz.co.uk

# Prologue

"I begin to think they are going to be late," Domitian murmured, hefting his duffle bag higher on his shoulder so that the microphone hidden in his sleeve would catch his words.

"Perhaps it is a sign." Lucian Argeneau's voice was surprisingly clear. The earpiece they'd given Domitian was so small that it was unseen once inserted, but the sound came through loud and crystal clear. "We should scrap this now and—"

"Still trying to talk me out of going, Uncle?" Domitian asked with amusement, and then suddenly impatient, added, "I do not know why you are so resistant to my doing this. Especially with Uncle Victor, Lucern, Decker, Nicholas, Aunt Eshe, Mirabeau La Roche, and Santo Notte now among the missing. I would think with all of them having been taken—"

"That is precisely why," Lucian growled. "This is dangerous. We have already lost several hunters, people armed and trained to handle situations like this. You, Domitian, are going in there unarmed, and you are *not* a hunter."

"True, but I was a warrior once. I can handle myself," Domitian argued. "Besides, none of your hunters were invited, I was."

"Yes, but was it because you are a chef and Dressler wants you to work for him? Or because you are an immortal he wants to add to his collection?"

"I told you. He does not know I am an immortal," Domitian said slowly and firmly, stressing each word. They'd had this conversation several times already, but it seemed they would have it again. "If Dressler knew, he could have taken me at any time. He has been a regular in my restaurant for five years. He obviously does not know."

"Or perhaps he did not wish to kidnap an immortal so close to home," Lucian countered. "It might have led us straight here to Venezuela."

Domitian shifted impatiently at the suggestion. "One immortal missing in Caracas would hardly have brought you here when so many have gone missing in the United States."

"Perhaps. Or perhaps we would have—"

"Is that helicopter headed this way?" Domitian interrupted, raising a hand to shield his eyes from the sun as he watched the vehicle approach. It was flying low and seemed to be headed straight for where he stood at the base of the large dock . . . which was where he'd been directed to wait for his ride. He'd expected a boat, but—

"Are those pontoons?" Lucian asked sharply in his ear.

Domitian knew that Lucian and the others wouldn't have as good a view from the small boat where they waited farther along the docks. On top of that, they were staying out of sight in the small cabin in the bow, which had only tiny windows that were glazed and screened. Their view would be highly obscured compared to his.

"Yes. The helicopter has pontoons," he confirmed, his gaze on the skids with the floatation devices affixed to them. It was fitted out to be an amphibious helicopter so that it could set down on water or land, which made Domitian suspect that this *was* his ride. Apparently he wasn't the only one to think that, he realized, wincing as a loud curse sounded in his ear.

"You are not to get on that helicopter!" Lucian ordered firmly. "Make an excuse. Tell them you have changed your mind. We did not plan for this. The boats out in the bay might lose the helicopter. Do you hear me?"

His thoughts racing, Domitian watched the helicopter slow and begin to drop by the end of the dock. To get on board or not was the question. If he said he had a fear of flying, Dressler might send a boat for him and then Lucian's men could follow from a safe distance to find the island. Then again, he might not. Dressler might suspect something was afoot and simply cancel the job offer altogether . . . and Domitian couldn't risk that. He had to get on that island. His life mate was there and could be in danger.

"Domitian? Can you hear me?" Lucian barked sharply, and then his voice faded as he asked someone else, "Is this thing working? Why is he not answering?"

"Perhaps the noise from the helicopter is drowning you out," another voice responded. Domitian was pretty sure that voice belonged to the young hunter Justin Bricker and was grateful for the suggestion. He would pretend it was true and he couldn't hear his uncle. He *was* getting on that helicopter. He might be risking his life doing it, but not getting on risked his chance of any kind of a happy future.

"Dammit! Domitian! Do not get on that helicopter! Domitian?"

Ignoring the voice in his ear, Domitian watched the helicopter set down, not on the water, but on the end of the dock. He then started forward.

"Domitian Argeneau!" Lucian's voice roared in his ear.

"It's Argenis, Uncle. Not Argeneau," Domitian reminded him gently before unobtrusively plucking the earpiece from his ear and tucking it into the front pocket of his tight jeans. It didn't matter what anyone said. He was going, Domitian thought as he watched the passenger door of the helicopter open.

Instinctively ducking, he rushed quickly under the rotors to the entrance. A man in a suit was waiting with his hand out to take his duffle bag. Domitian handed it over with a nod of thanks and then grasped the door frame and climbed in. The window seat was the only one available, so he settled into it and pulled the door closed without having to be told.

Domitian then started to turn to get a better look at the other men in the helicopter but stiffened in surprise as he felt a sudden sharp pain in the side of his neck. He lost consciousness almost at once.

# One

Sarita closed the book she'd been trying to read and tossed it impatiently aside. It was a horrible book. Or perhaps she just wasn't in the mood to read, she acknowledged with irritation, getting restlessly to her feet. As a police officer, her life at home in Canada was usually a busy one, full of activity and even urgency. But here . . . all this sitting around waiting to be able to visit her grandmother was beginning to fray on her nerves. Sarita was anxious to see for herself how her grandmother was doing after her accident. It was why she was here, after all. Instead, she'd spent her time since arriving in Venezuela, stuck on this island, alternating between pacing and trying to read books that simply couldn't hold her interest. It was driving her crazy, sitting here, waiting for Dr. Dressler to return to the island and instruct his men to transport her to the mainland. Unfortunately, he hadn't been here when she'd arrived, and they wouldn't take her there without his orders.

Clucking impatiently under her tongue, she left the library, her mouth tightening as her gaze slid to the two men standing guard inside the front double doors of the house. They stood one on either side, eyes straight ahead, faces expressionless, hands loosely at their sides within easy reach of the sidearms she knew each wore.

And that was the only thing they were doing right as far as she could tell. She'd been told the ridiculous level of security on the island was because kidnappings had become so rampant in Venezuela and "el Doctor" wanted to ensure his safety as well as that of his family, his employees, and visitors like her. But if that was the case, then he should have all of his security on the outside, watching for the approach of would-be kidnappers, not inside, watching the goings-on in the house. Although he had that too, she acknowledged. There were two men standing guard outside the double doors as well, and a dozen more walking the grounds as far as she could tell. "El Doctor" was obviously paranoid about kidnappings. But since her own mother had been kidnapped and killed when she was young, Sarita supposed she should probably appreciate his efforts to ensure their safety. Instead, she just found the men posted everywhere something else to be annoyed about today.

Knowing she was in a foul mood from a combination of boredom and frustration, Sarita turned on her heel and headed up the hall toward the kitchen. She'd get a drink and maybe one of Aleta's yummy cookies, and see if the cook had something for her to do to help pass the time. At that point, even something as mundane as washing dishes would be welcome . . . which told Sarita just how bored she was.

Grimacing at the depths to which she'd sunk after three short days of inactivity, Sarita pushed the kitchen door open and stepped inside. The rich aroma of something delicious rolled over her as she entered, and her nose twitched as she inhaled the scent. Spotting Aleta stirring a pot simmering on the range in the center of the island, she moved closer to peer at the contents with interest. There were chunks of vegetables and meat in a thick juice. It smelled like heaven.

*"Hola,"* Aleta greeted her softly, a shy smile curving her lips.

Sarita smiled at the woman. *"Hola.* That smells good. I swear, Aleta, you're an angel. Everything you make is delicious."

*"Gracias,"* Aleta said, flushing with pleasure.

"What is it?" Sarita asked, leaning across the island to inhale more deeply.

*"El estofado de ternera,"* she answered.

"Mmm," Sarita murmured, again inhaling the scent coming off the beef stew.

"Is not quite time for dinner, but it is ready," Aleta said, watching her practically drool over the pot. "If you are hungry, you can eat now."

"Oh, yes please," Sarita said at once.

Aleta chuckled at her eagerness. "Go out to the dining room and I will bring it in."

Sarita shook her head. "I can eat here. It would be nice to have some company," she added when Aleta frowned.

The woman's expression softened then and she nodded. "Here then. Sit down," she added, gesturing to the stools on the opposite side of the island from where she was cooking.

Sarita wanted to insist on getting her own food and drink, but suspected if she tried Aleta might change her mind about letting her eat in the kitchen. So she sank obediently onto one of the stools and watched as Aleta fetched her a bowl and spoon and served up the stew.

*"Que quieres tomar?"* Aleta asked as she set the bowl before her.

"Water is fine," Sarita answered and then said *"Agua"* as well. Aleta seemed to speak English well, but the way she slipped back into Spanish at times—as she had when she'd just asked what Sarita wanted to drink—suggested the cook might not be fully fluent in the language. She had no desire to embarrass the woman by making her admit it.

Picking up her spoon, Sarita scooped up some of the stew, blew on it briefly, and then slipped it into her mouth. It was as good as it smelled, better even, and she moaned with pleasure as the flavor burst on her tongue.

Chuckling, Aleta set a glass of water and a plate with a large *tequeno* on it next to her bowl, and then turned back to her stew.

Sarita picked up the fried breadstick with cheese inside and eagerly took a bite. She loved Aleta's *tequenos*. Honestly, she loved everything the woman had made for her since her arrival on the island three days earlier. Sarita was seriously considering trying to lure her away to Canada with a job. She was just trying to work out if she could afford it. Her apartment didn't have enough room to house the two of them. She'd need to buy a house, and then there was the whole immigration issue to worry about.

Sarita was just finishing her stew and *tequeno* when Aleta set her spoon aside again and retrieved a blender from the cup... ...set it on the counter, plugged it in, an... ...d to the refrigerator. A moment later she wa... ...ack to the counter with an armload of cleaned and precut greens and vegetables.

"What are you making now?" Sarita asked with curiosity as Aleta dropped a good portion of the vegetables into the blender and then moved to the pantry.

Aleta backed out of the pantry a moment later with a jar of some kind of powder. Carrying that to the blender, she murmured, "El Doctor's *bebida nutritive.*"

The doctor's nutrition drink, Sarita translated and stiffened on her stool as she watched Aleta measure out a portion of the powder. Voice sharp, she asked, "El Doctor's back?"

"Back?" Aleta frowned at the powder in her measuring cup and added a bit more, shaking it to level it out as she did. "Back from where? He has not gone anywhere for weeks. He is always down at the labs since he took the *ano sabatico.*"

Sabbatical, Sarita translated. Dr. Dressler had told her he was on sabbatical from the university when he'd called her about her grandmother's falling and injuring herself. And apparently he'd been spending all of his time since then down at his labs . . . not on the mainland as she'd been led to believe. After Dr. Dressler's call telling her about her grandmother's accident and his fears for her well-being since falls could be deadly for older women, Sarita had immediately booked a flight to Venezuela to check on her. She'd been met at the airport by the head of Dr. Dressler's security team and flown out here by helicopter only to learn that her grandmother was still in the hospital in Caracas and had not yet returned to the island. She'd immediately requested to be transported back to the mainland so that she could see her, but had been told that neither the boats nor the helicopter could be used without first gaining Dr. Dressler's permission and he was not here.

Sarita had assumed that meant he wasn't on the island and had been waiting impatiently for his return, but it seemed he was on the island, just not at the house. She frowned now at this news, furious that Dressler's man hadn't made that clear. Had she known, she could have sought out Dressler himself to get the needed permission, and been at her grandmother's bedside days ago.

Scowling, Sarita stood and quickly carried her empty bowl and plate to the sink.

"Leave it. I will do that," Aleta said when Sarita started to rinse them.

"*Gracias*," Sarita murmured rather than argue and turned off the tap. She'd finished rinsing them anyway. Turning to head for the door, she added, "And thank you for the dinner. It was delicious."

"*De nada*," Aleta said absently as she concentrated on her measuring.

Sarita was halfway up the hall before she recalled the men at the front door. Not wanting to be questioned and possibly stopped from going down to the labs, she turned as she reached the entry and jogged up the stairs that led to the second floor. Sarita moved quickly along the hall to the room she'd inhabited since arriving and slipped inside.

A cautious glance out the French doors in her room showed her that the sun was setting. In the dying light she could see men moving toward the house from every direction. While it had not quite been dinnertime when she'd arrived in the kitchen, it was nearly that time now and she was not the only one who appreciated Aleta's cooking.

She watched until all of the men had moved around the house and out of sight. They'd be heading to the door of the kitchen to fetch their food, she knew. It would leave a skeleton crew of two men at the front door as well as the men on the towers and at the gate to the fenced-in labs. Those men would then be relieved so they too could eat. Or perhaps food would be taken to them. Sarita had no idea, she'd never cared enough to find out.

She didn't really care now either, Sarita decided as she slid out onto the balcony. Finding the yard empty, she climbed over the balcony rail, lowered herself until she hung from the bottom of the white-painted metal, and then let herself drop lightly onto the terrace below. A little grunt slid from her lips as her bare feet slapped on the stone. After a quick glance around, she hurried along the side of the house to the front corner.

A quick peek around the corner showed Sarita that even the men at the front door had gone in search of their meal. She'd always assumed that because the men inside waited to eat in the second shift, that the men outside would too, but it seemed not. Pondering that, she broke away from the house and hurried across the lawn, heading for the path through the trees to the labs.

Sarita expected to be stopped at any moment, but she made it all the way to the tree line outside the fence without encountering anyone. Pausing just inside the trees, she eyed the fenced-in buildings that made up Dr. Dressler's labs. From the air the half a dozen long low buildings had made her think of army barracks.

Now, as her gaze slid over the towers on each corner of the high fence surrounding the buildings, she decided it looked more like a prison.

She looked at the men in the towers again, this time checking each one more carefully. Sarita couldn't be sure in the dying light, but it seemed to her that their attention was focused inside the fence rather than out. As if they were guarding against someone escaping rather than intruders. Thinking that could only be good for her, she straightened her shoulders and approached the gatehouse at the fence entrance.

Sarita prepared herself for a verbal battle as she crossed the short distance, expecting whoever was guarding the gate to refuse her entry. But she was determined that she would at least make them call Dr. Dressler out to the gate. She *would* get him to tell his men to take her to the mainland in either the helicopter or a boat so that she could see her grandmother. It was why she was here in Venezuela. And Sarita was pretty pissed about being made to cool her heels here on the island for three days when her grandmother was in a hospital on the mainland.

In the end, Sarita didn't have to argue with the man in the gatehouse. She walked up to the window, opened her mouth to explain herself, and then closed it without saying a word as she noticed that the blond man inside wasn't even looking her way. He was sitting with his back to the window and gate, earbuds in his ears as he watched a movie on the computer on the counter in front of him.

A porno, she saw as her gaze slid to the computer screen.

So much for security, Sarita thought dryly and glanced

to the gate. There was a large gate, presumably for vehicles, and a smaller one for people to pass through. Sarita walked to the smaller gate. When she found it wasn't even locked and opened easily, she shook her head with disgust and slipped through, then pulled it gently closed. She headed for the nearest building at a quick clip and was more than halfway to it before a shout sounded. It was followed by another, and then another as others heard the call and noticed her.

Sarita ignored them and kept going, but she did move a little faster. She made it to the door, and a glance around as she slipped inside showed her that while one or two men were climbing down the ladders on the towers, the man in the gatehouse still had his head down as he watched his porn. Apparently, he hadn't yet noticed anything amiss. She suspected he'd be in a heap of trouble for it.

Pulling the door closed, Sarita turned to survey the room she'd entered. It was a lab, all white with upper and lower metal cupboards on two walls, a large industrial refrigerator as well as a large industrial freezer along another and a desk against the last wall. Two small, wheeled tables sat a little distance apart in the center of the room, and those caught and held her attention at once.

Having trouble accepting what she was seeing, Sarita moved slowly across the room to the first table and stared down at the top half of the corpse lying strapped on it. It was a man who was probably about twenty-five. His hair was short and blond, his face handsome but bloodless, and his upper body was in perfect shape . . . except for the fact that it ended just below his belly button where he appeared to have been cut in half.

Sarita stared at him blankly, noting that there were a couple dozen metal straps rising out of the table, crossing over his body, and then disappearing through slots in the table surface. There was one across his forehead, and then at his throat, his shoulders, under his armpits, and another every couple of inches down his torso after that for the length of the table. There were also half a dozen smaller metal straps holding his arms down from his armpits to his wrists.

Sarita turned her head to peer at the second small table where the lower half of his body lay. A small towel was draped over his groin, and there were even more straps running over his lower body, with a great gaping wound where his body had been separated. It looked as if he'd been sawn in half like a tree.

As she studied the open wound on the lower half of the body, and the one on the upper body, Sarita had to wonder why she wasn't freaking out.

Probably because of the lack of blood, she thought . . . and because it didn't look real. Or perhaps because it reminded her of Body Worlds, an exhibition of preserved human bodies that showed the anatomy of the inner body. Her father had taken her to see it at the Ontario Science Centre back in 2005. This reminded her of it, a bloodless display of inner workings. It looked like one of those. It was obviously a cadaver from the university or something.

That made sense, Sarita thought. After all, Dr. Dressler was a professor at one of the universities in Venezuela. Mind you, universities didn't generally let professors take cadavers home that she knew of.

And why both halves of the body were strapped to the table like that was a complete mystery to her.

The sound of approaching voices caught her attention and Sarita turned her head toward the door as someone said, "I will handle it. You get back to your posts . . . and do your jobs this time."

The door opened then and an older man stepped inside. Dressed in dark pants and a white doctor's coat, Dr. Dressler was tall, with a full head of snow-white hair parted at the side and brushed away from his face in waves that suggested he was a little overdue for a haircut. He had a mustache and goatee to match, but his eyebrows were a mix of snow-white and a darker brown or black that suggested he'd been a dark-haired man when younger. The skin on his neck was saggy and a little crepey and his face had the wrinkles and lines age eventually carved in everyone's face, but they were much less pronounced than she would have expected from someone she knew to be in his eighties.

"Dr. Dressler?" she asked uncertainly, before glancing to the woman who followed him into the room. Also wearing dark pants and a doctor's white coat, she was much younger, perhaps in her thirties. Her hair was blond and pulled back in a tight bun, revealing a face that was untouched by makeup but still beautiful.

At least it would have been beautiful if she didn't have such a sour expression on her face, Sarita thought.

"Sarita, my dear. What a pleasure to finally meet you," Dr. Dressler said, drawing her attention back his way as he led the blonde across the room. He clasped her hands in his and used his hold to shift her to the side as he added, "Unfortunately, you have arrived at a rather inconvenient moment. This experiment is time sensitive, so please just stay here out of the way while we do our work and we shall talk afterward."

Staying by the wall where he'd urged her, Sarita watched silently as he then joined the blonde and helped her roll the two tables together so that the upper torso of the corpse met the lower torso perfectly.

"Fetch the blood, Asherah," Dr. Dressler ordered as he then moved to flip latches on each side of the tables where they joined, turning the two short tables into one long one.

The blonde immediately moved to a refrigerator at the end of one wall of cupboards and opened the door, revealing stacks of bagged blood inside.

Sarita stiffened in surprise. The bags looked like something you'd see in a hospital or blood bank, but the number of them was staggering. She would have guessed there were at least a hundred bags stacked on the refrigerator shelves. A ridiculous amount for anyone to have.

Asherah carried the bags to a wheeled tray of surgical instruments, dumped them on it, and rolled the tray up next to the table, then moved off to collect two IV stands without being told. The moment she set them next to the table, Dr. Dressler collected one of the bags of blood from the tray and began to set up one of the IVs. Hanging the bag of blood from the hook, he quickly affixed the tubing before inserting the needle in the corpse's left arm. Once finished he grabbed another bag of blood off the tray and dragged the second IV around to the right side of the body to do the same. He then glanced up expectantly.

Following his gaze, Sarita saw that Asherah had gone back to the cupboards to collect something else. She was now returning with what looked like a ball gag, but with more straps. There was also a funnel where the ball would be, she noted as Asherah got closer to the table.

"Two minutes," Dr. Dressler warned, eyeing his watch as Asherah strapped the harness into place, with the funnel in the corpse's mouth.

Asherah straightened and moved quickly back to the refrigerator to collect another half a dozen bags of blood. She dropped most of them on the wheeled tray with the others when she returned, but kept one and picked a scalpel from the surgical items on the tray before moving up to the table where it was joined. She peered down at where the two halves of the body were pressed tight together and simply waited, seemingly at the ready.

Shaking her head with bewilderment, Sarita asked, "What—?"

"Shh," Dr. Dressler hissed. "You'll understand in thirty seconds."

Sarita closed her mouth, but shook her head again at the madness she was witnessing. Offering indignities to a corpse was an indictable offense in Canada and what they were doing seemed to fit that description. Unfortunately, this was not Canada and she had no idea what the laws were here in Venezuela. She'd certainly be looking into it the first chance she got, though, Sarita decided.

"Time!" Dr. Dressler snapped and quickly opened the roller clamp on the IV next to him, before rushing around the table to do the same on the second IV. Blood immediately began to race down the tubes toward the corpse's arms, but Sarita hardly noticed that—she was too busy watching with horror as Asherah poked a hole in the bag of blood she held, and allowed the crimson liquid to gush out over the body where the two halves were now pressed together.

"Dear God," Sarita breathed with a disgust that only increased when Dr. Dressler now grabbed a second scalpel and another bag of blood off those remaining on the wheeled tray and punctured it over the corpse's face. Blood immediately began to flow into the funnel fixed in the corpse's mouth.

Clenching her fists, Sarita stood to the side, revulsion curling her stomach as she watched the pair's actions. She was starting to wish with all her heart that she was a police officer in Venezuela instead of Canada and could arrest the mad doctor and his equally crazy assistant. She had no idea what they thought they would achieve with this lunacy, but—

Sarita's thoughts died abruptly as the corpse's eyes suddenly popped open and he began to shriek. Or tried to. What came out was a raspy gurgle as he tried to scream around the liquid pouring down his throat. It forced some of the blood back out in a small spurt that splashed over Dr. Dressler.

"You forgot the tube, Asherah," Dr. Dressler accused harshly, but quickly added, "Don't stop what you're doing!"

Asherah had started to lift away the bag of blood she was holding over the wound at Dr. Dressler's first words, but stopped at once when he ordered her not to.

"Sarita, there should be a length of tube on the counter along the wall behind me. Fetch it for me," Dr. Dressler ordered sharply as he continued to let the blood pour down the throat of the man she'd thought was dead, but who was now screaming his head off and shooting the blood back out of his mouth as he did.

Stunned now by what was happening, Sarita did as asked, found the mentioned tubing and took it to

Dr. Dressler. When she reached his side though, he nodded toward the tray. "Grab another bag of blood."

Turning, she picked up the bag and offered it to him. He took it with one hand, waited a heartbeat for the one he already held to empty, then tossed it aside and moved the fresh bag over the mouth.

"Hold this," Dr. Dressler commanded once he'd punctured the new bag as he had the first.

Sarita hesitated, but then moved around to the opposite side of the table and took over holding the new bag of blood. Her hands were trembling, she noted, but she did her best to hold the bag steady and ground her teeth together as the corpse continued to scream, sending most of the blood shooting back up through and around the funnel and onto her and the doctor both now. But a moment later Dr. Dressler was feeding a tube through the funnel and down the man's throat. The tube, apart from ensuring the blood got to his stomach, also appeared to hamper his ability to scream. The moment several inches had been fed through the funnel, his screams stopped.

Quite sure the action was only adding to the man's pain, Sarita had to look away and shifted her gaze down to Asherah rather than watch. The assistant was tossing aside the first bag she'd cut open, but quickly grabbed and opened another over where his body was split in half. Sarita shook her head, unable to believe what was happening.

Dr. Dressler finished inserting the feeding tube, but didn't then take back the bag of blood she held as Sarita expected. Instead, he hung two fresh bags from the IV stands next to the ones already in use. It drew her attention to the fact that both bags were already half-empty. IVs usually didn't work that quickly in her experience. All she could think was that the catheter must be larger than the standard. She had no idea what it might be doing to the corpse's veins though.

The very thought made Sarita give her head a shake. The man obviously wasn't a corpse. Corpses didn't move and scream. But he *should* be a corpse. He'd been cut in half for God's sake. That thought kept running through her head as she held bag after bag over his mouth while Asherah did the same over his wound and Dr. Dressler manned the IVs and fetched fresh blood from the refrigerator as needed.

Sarita was holding her sixth bag and beginning to think this would go on forever when Asherah suddenly growled, "Time."

Dr. Dressler immediately glanced at his wristwatch, nodded, and then beamed at Sarita. "Very good. Asherah will clean up the worst of the blood, and then take over with that last bag you're holding. I have to make a note of the time and then we can talk."

He hurried away to the desk she'd noticed earlier, and Sarita turned her attention to Asherah as the woman reached under the table and retrieved some kind of nozzle. It was only when she pushed a lever and water began to run out over the midriff of the body that Sarita realized what it was.

Careful to keep her hand in place over the funnel, Sarita bent slightly to look under the table and saw that the top half of the table was fixed in place, only the bottom half was movable. Two pipes ran up one table leg, one pipe ending at a hose with the nozzle on the end, the other to a drain on this side of the table. Straightening again, she checked to be sure the bag of blood was still over the funnel, and then looked over to see that Asherah had already rinsed away most of the blood from the body.

Finding the spot where the upper body had been separated from the lower half, Sarita saw that they were now joined, with just an angry red scar where they had once been separated.

*"Madre de Dios,"* she breathed, unable to believe her eyes.

"Move."

Glancing around with surprise, she saw that Asherah had finished with the hose and moved up beside her. Even as she noted that, the woman took over holding the bag and urged her away. "El Doctor wants to talk to you."

Sarita stepped back, her eyes returning to the scar where the body had once been cut in half.

"Move," Asherah repeated coldly. "You are done here."

Noting the dislike on the woman's face, Sarita reluctantly turned to walk to the desk where Dr. Dressler was scribbling furiously in a notebook.

Apparently finished making his notes, he raised his head as she stopped in front of the desk, and he smiled at her widely as he stood up. "Thank you, Sarita. Your help was invaluable."

"What exactly did I help with?" Sarita asked with a frown as Dressler moved around his desk. "That man was dead."

"Not dead," he assured her, crossing the room to the cupboards and retrieving a couple of syringes before moving to the refrigerator. "And not a man."

Eyebrows rising, Sarita peered back to the table. "He looks like a man to me."

"Yes," he agreed, bending to retrieve two ampoules from the refrigerator. "But he's not. He is an immortal."

"Immortal?" Sarita asked, following him back to the table. When he didn't answer, but concentrated on preparing a shot for the man, she glanced to Asherah as she tossed the now empty blood bag away. When the woman then moved around to the wheeled tray and grabbed another bag of blood, Sarita thought she intended to keep feeding it into the funnel. Instead, she replaced one of the now empty IV bags before grabbing another bag and replacing the other as well.

"Immortals are scientifically evolved mortals," Dr. Dressler announced, drawing Sarita's attention back to him. "This man is full of bio-engineered nanos programmed to keep his body healthy."

Finished filling the syringe, he set the ampoule on the wheeled tray and then simply held the shot and peered down at the man he called an immortal as he explained, "These nanos fight disease, repair the ravages of sun and time, and—as you saw—repair injuries."

Sarita shifted her gaze back to where the body had once been separated, and was quite sure the scar was smaller and less angry-looking than it had been just moments ago.

"After enough blood there won't even be a scar," Dr. Dressler announced. "The blood is what powers the nanos you see. They apparently use it to replicate themselves as well as to make repairs and so on."

"Blood," Sarita murmured, glancing toward the empty blood bags now littering the floor.

"Yes, they need a lot of it when injured," he said with a nod. "But even if not fighting illness or repairing an injury, the nanos need more blood than their host bodies can produce to keep them young. The nanos have forced their host bodies to evolve to make up for that need. In effect, making them scientifically created vampires."

When Sarita turned to him with disbelief, he glanced to Asherah and said, "Show her."

Asherah unhooked the harness from around the man's head and began to slowly remove it, pulling the feeding tube out with it.

Sarita half expected the man to begin screaming again, but other than a weak moan he was silent. Once Asherah had set the harness and tube aside, she picked up one of the disposed blood bags and sliced it open, then wiped up the little bit of blood left inside. It amounted to a couple of drops at best, but she waved it under the man's nose and despite his seeming to be unconscious, two of his upper teeth shifted and slid down in his open mouth, becoming fangs.

Gasping, Sarita took a step back.

"It is fine. We are safe," Dr. Dressler assured her. "Although if those straps were leather instead of titanium it would be a different matter. Aside from giving them fangs, the nanos make their hosts incredibly strong and extremely fast. They also have astonishing night vision. And they can read and control minds," he added grimly, finally bending to inject the man with the shot he'd prepared as he said, "Which is why we have to keep them drugged."

"Them?" Sarita asked with a frown.

"There are eighteen here in my labs," Dr. Dressler said, straightening from giving the shot.

"Why?" Sarita asked with dismay as he put the used

shot on the wheeled tray and set about filling the second syringe. "Surely they're dangerous?"

"Not normally, no," he assured her. "As a rule they consume bagged blood. In fact, it's a law among their kind, now that blood banks exist. They are forbidden to bite us mere mortals."

Sarita relaxed a little. If they stuck to bagged blood that wasn't so bad.

"And even before blood banks, they apparently weren't allow to kill anyone they bit. It's how they've managed to live among us with no one the wiser all these millennia."

"Millennia?" Sarita narrowed her eyes on the doctor, but he merely shrugged.

"Apparently they were a people isolated from the rest of the world who advanced technologically much more quickly. The nanos were a result of one of those advancements." He pursed his lips and considered the man. "They claim their home was Atlantis, and that when it sank into the ocean, only those with the nanos survived and crawled out to join the rest of the world. They also say that in Atlantis they had doctors and hospitals as we do today, and were given blood transfusions to combat the nanos' need for extra blood. But when Atlantis fell it was an end to those transfusions. Technology in the rest of the world was far behind that in Atlantis, and the nanos forced fangs, speed, and the other abilities on them so that they could gain the extra blood they needed to survive."

Sarita surveyed the man on the table and shook her head. "If I'd passed him on the street, I never would have known he wasn't human."

"That's the beauty of it. He *is* human," Dr. Dressler assured her. "He and others like him have children and families and live, laugh, and love just like the rest of us. Only they get to do it longer and don't suffer illness while they do. He's no different than you or I except for those nanos. Without them, he would be merely mortal, and with them, *we* could be *immortal*."

Sarita stiffened, something in his voice as he said that last part disturbing her. "You cut him in half," she said slowly, putting it together in her head. "You want the nanos and cut him in half to try to get them."

"No," Dr. Dressler assured her. "That would be a waste. The nanos are programmed to remain in the host body. Even bleeding them dry doesn't work. The nanos apparently move into the organs and skin to avoid leaving with the blood. You might get a couple from your efforts, but those disintegrate quickly once out of the body."

Sarita was about to ask how he knew that, and how the man *had* got cut in half if he hadn't done it, when Dressler continued, "I know the nanos must be transferrable, though. They have to be for them to turn their life mates."

"Life mates?" she echoed, briefly distracted.

"Hmm." He nodded thoughtfully. "Apparently while immortals can read and control most mortals, there are a few instances when they can't. One is if the mortal is mad. Apparently, that makes it difficult. The other is if the mortal is a life mate to them. In fact, that is how they recognize a life mate."

Sarita opened her mouth to ask what a life mate was, but closed it again as he said, "Anyway, I didn't cut him in half in an effort to retrieve nanos. I did it as part of an experiment to see how long his upper and lower body could be separated and yet still repair itself if pressed back together. We started with thirty seconds, and have been working our way up from there. This time it was two hours. Of course you have to void them of blood before doing it or else the nanos try to use what blood they have to try to repair the body at once while separated. The two halves start to seal, the bottom half dying from lack of blood long before it finishes the job. But as long as there is no blood, it's as if the nanos force the body into a sort of stasis. Once you put the two halves back together and add blood though, they kick into action and heal the body. It works if you just cut off a finger, hand, foot, or limb too. And the faster you give them blood, the faster they heal."

"Dear God," Sarita breathed, peering down at the man on the table. She was horrified that Dr. Dressler had actually deliberately inflicted this kind of pain on a living, breathing human . . . vampire or not.

"I have made it my business to find out all I can about their kind but must confess I'm growing tired of this experiment. I think we'll move on to removing a limb and destroying it, and then see if the nanos can build a new limb in its place."

"You—" Sarita broke off in shock when he suddenly raised the second syringe he'd prepared and shoved it into her neck, pressing the plunger home. It happened so quickly she didn't get a chance to react or try to stop him. By the time she started to raise her hand, he was already pulling the needle out and setting it on the wheeled tray.

"Wh—?" She stared at him in horror, unable to form the question she was trying to ask. When she swayed on her feet, he caught her arm to steady her, and then glanced toward the ceiling as the sound of a loud engine reached them.

"That will be the helicopter returning with your life mate," Dr. Dressler murmured and then offered her a smile as he let her sink slowly to the floor. "The two of you are going to be a great help to me, Sarita. I can't tell you how much I appreciate it."

# TWO

Sarita stirred sleepily, slowly realizing she was on her back in bed. She never slept on her back. She was a side sleeper and always had been. Being on her back with her hands resting just below her breasts . . . well, frankly it made her think of her father in his coffin.

Grimacing as that thought pulled her the rest of the way from sleep, Sarita promptly turned onto her side and let her eyes open. She then froze for a heartbeat before jerking to a sitting position in bed.

"What the hell?" she muttered, staring around at the alien room.

It was not her bedroom in her sunny little apartment in Toronto, Ontario. This room was decorated all in white. It was also at least three times the size of her room at home. Three large ceiling fans hung overhead, spinning in a desultory fashion and stirring up a nice soft breeze, and they, along with the three sets of French doors that lined the wall to her left seemed to parcel off each section of the room without the need for walls. In front of the doors at the far end, a couch, loveseat, and two chairs made up a sitting area, all were wicker with white cushions. In front of the middle set of doors was a small, glass-topped wicker dining table for two. The final set of French doors was right next to the bed she was sitting in, which was a sea of white bedclothes. Sarita had never seen a bed so big. It was bigger than king-sized, certainly. It was also terribly romantic with gossamer white curtains pulled back to drape at each post of the four-poster bed.

All in all, it looked like she'd been dumped in the middle of an advertisement for a honeymoon retreat in a tropical paradise, Sarita thought, peering out at the plants and palm trees she could see through the doors next to the bed. There was a stone floored terrace just outside the doors, but beyond that was a wall of jungle that would offer privacy to any honeymooners making use of the four-poster. It was a lovely room, and a lovely setup . . . but she had no idea how she'd got there or what she was doing there.

Pushing the soft white sheets aside, Sarita slipped her feet to the hardwood floor on the same side as the French doors, and then noticed the white nightgown she was wearing and paused to finger it with bewilderment. This was definitely not hers. She was the kind of gal who slept in an overlarge T-shirt and cotton panties. This too was straight out of an advertisement for honeymooning in paradise. Spaghetti straps dropped down to make up a piped and gathered neckline that barely reached above her nipples, and even then didn't cover them well. The material was thin and sheer, offering cover to her breasts only because of the way the material gathered there. The silky material wasn't presently gathered on her legs, however, and she could clearly see her tan legs through it and even the mole on her upper right thigh.

Standing abruptly, Sarita glanced around, relieved when she spotted a robe draped over a wicker chest at the foot of the bed. She hadn't noticed it on her first scan of the room. Moving to the end of the bed, she snatched up the material and quickly shrugged her arms into it. A grimace claimed her lips, though, as she wrapped it around front and used the sash to tie it closed. The robe was as light and sheer as the night-gown, the neckline piped and gathered too and just as low as the neckline on the gown. They were obviously a set but weren't meant for covering anything.

Muttering under her breath, Sarita took another look around the room in search of actual clothing, prefer-ably her own. But there was no sign of luggage or even drawers that might hold her possessions.

Aside from the French doors leading outside, there were also three solid wood doors in the room, all painted white to match the walls. One of the doors was in the wall opposite the bed, beyond the wicker furni-ture. For some reason Sarita suspected it was the one that led out into the rest of the house or hotel this room was in. She turned away from it for now, unwilling to leave the room dressed as she was.

Her gaze slid between the other two remaining doors. Both were in the wall the bed butted up against, one on either side of it, in fact. The one on the side she stood on was open, and Sarita found herself looking into a large white bathroom.

Moving to the doorway, she glanced around and saw

that the honeymoon theme continued here with a tub built for two and a large glass-walled shower you could have fit most normal-sized bathrooms into . . . or two people having crazy monkey sex. There was also a long white marble counter with two sinks, a separate smaller counter with a chair and large lighted mirror for doing makeup, and a door leading to an entirely separate small room that turned out to hold nothing but a toilet and a bidet.

Sarita peered at them and was suddenly aware that she had to relieve herself. Sighing, she quickly slipped inside to use the facilities, her mind racing. A plethora of questions were chasing each other through her mind. Unfortunately, she had no answers and her mind was just running around in circles in her head. Where was she? What had happened? How had she got here? Whose clothes were these? And how had she got into them?

Sarita wondered about that as she noted that even the panties she wore weren't her own. A silky white thong was the only thing under the nightgown. Sarita did not wear thongs. She'd tried them once because they were so sexy-looking, but hadn't been able to bear the feeling of having a constant wedgie. What the hell was going on? That seemed to be the question that kept drumming through her head. The last thing she remembered . . .

Actually, her memory was pretty fuzzy just now. She had some vague recollection of a lab and a corpse and some nonsense about vampires, but it was all so disjointed and surreal in her mind that she felt sure it was some fragmented nightmare she'd had. She also had something in her mind about worry for her grandmother, but, again, it was so fragmented and fuzzy she wasn't sure whether it was real or a dream. For all she knew, what was happening right now was a dream too. Certainly she couldn't afford a vacation in a place like this.

Panic tried to climb up inside her, but Sarita forced it down. She was a police officer, trained to control her automatic responses and assess situations before deciding the best way to respond to them. So . . . she would assess, Sarita decided firmly as she finished in the water closet.

Stepping back out into the large bathroom, she caught a glimpse of herself in the mirror over the sinks. The sight made her blink. Her black hair fell in wild abandon around her face and over her shoulders. It and her tan skin were an amazing contrast to the sheer white, flowing gown and robe. She looked like she'd stepped out of a gothic novel . . . or a porno, she thought with dismay, noting how her tan skin and the white thong she wore were revealed through the sheer cloth as she moved. Fortunately, the way the material gathered at the neckline helped hide her breasts . . . mostly.

Clucking her tongue with irritation, Sarita quickly washed and dried her hands, using the soap and fluffy white towels provided. Their presence made her start opening drawers and cupboards in the bathroom to see what they held. She found loads of soap, shampoo, conditioner, towels, and washcloths in the cupboards under the sink.

Lifting the makeup tabletop next, she found more cosmetics than a woman could use in a lifetime. There seemed to be every shade of lipstick, blush, and eye shadow ever created, all brand-new and with their wrapping intact. There were also various eyeliners, mascara, tweezers, nail files, and clippers, and so forth in the same packaged state, along with a hair dryer, several different curling irons, from flat to huge curls, and hairspray as well as various hairbrushes and combs. Basically, anything a woman might need to make herself pretty for any occasion.

Sarita stood still for a moment, simply staring at what was available as she tried to understand what all of this meant. The sheer sexy nightgown, the makeup, the big bed . . .

"No," she muttered and then let the makeup tabletop drop as she whirled away to hurry out of the bathroom. The bedroom was still empty—that was all Sarita noticed as she rushed around the bed to the door on the other side of it. Her breath left her on a relieved sigh as she opened that one to find a walk-in closet stuffed with clothes and shoes.

Thank God! She could put on some real clothes and go find out where the hell she was and what was going on, Sarita thought. Her relief was short-lived, however. Within moments she was standing in the middle of the closet, forcing herself to breathe slowly.

The confusion that had assailed her on first waking had given way to anger as she'd gone through the closet. There wasn't a scrap of her own clothing here, or at least, nothing she recognized as her own. Every single item hanging up was a negligee or nightie. There were various colors and lengths, from short skimpy blue baby dolls to long see-through crimson peignoirs, but every hanging item of clothing was some revealing nightwear suitable only for a honeymoon.

As for the drawers, they were full of thongs, stockings, and bikinis. There wasn't even one bra. And those shoes she'd noticed on first entering? They were all stilettos, a rainbow selection of them, one to match every peignoir hanging up. They were sexy as hell and useless in her current situation.

Letting her breath out slowly, Sarita turned and moved back into the bedroom and then paused, unsure what her next move should be. Her gaze slid to the door she suspected led into the rest of the building . . . and possibly to answers, but Sarita found herself moving away from it. She had no idea what was beyond that door and after discovering all the negligees and baby dolls in the closet, she wasn't sure she wanted whatever answers were waiting for her. But staying where she was didn't seem a good idea either, Sarita decided as she bumped up against something and turned to stare down at the bed.

Her gaze slid reluctantly to the unknown door again, but then quickly shifted to the French doors instead. At least there she could see what she was stepping out into, Sarita thought and moved around the foot of the bed to the first of the three sets of French doors. Pausing, she peered out at the terrace and jungle, and then glanced as far to each side as she could from her position.

The terrace stretched out in both directions, left and right, the jungle bordering its length like a privacy fence. She also saw that there was wicker furniture outside, but she didn't see any people around.

Sarita reached for the handle of the right door and turned it carefully, trying to be as quiet as possible. Once it unlatched, she eased it open and then poked her head out far enough to get a better look around. There wasn't really much more to see than that the terrace ran around both corners of the building. Sarita couldn't tell what might lie around the corner of the building to her left, but to her right she spotted the rounded end of an in-ground pool sticking out just past the building.

After a brief trip back to the bedroom to unplug and snatch up the bedside lamp, Sarita slipped out onto the terrace and began to creep along the cold stone tiles toward the right. She slowed as she passed the last set of French doors of her room and neared another set. Hand tightening on the lamp, she leaned forward just enough to peek inside.

Her gaze slid over a large open living room. It stretched the entire length of this end of the building. Again there were ceiling fans, hardwood floors, and white walls, but there were also throw rugs, and pillows adding splashes of color. The furniture was of the large overstuffed variety rather than the wicker used in the room she'd woken up in. The room was empty of any human inhabitant.

Relaxing a little, Sarita continued to the corner of the building to survey the pool and its surroundings. The jungle bordered this area too, running around the teardrop-shaped pool and back on the other side of the building. There was a waterfall at the top end of the teardrop where water spilled lazily over rocks stacked twelve feet high before dropping into the pool. It was beautiful.

Unfortunately, she wasn't in a position to enjoy it, so Sarita moved along the terrace to the next corner of the building. This one led to the front of the house, where the jungle fell away, leaving sand to border the terrace and run twenty or thirty feet down to the shore and an empty dock. She looked out at the ocean briefly and then considered the solid front double doors of the house under the shady porch before turning to retrace her steps to the open door of the bedroom.

Sarita didn't stop there, but continued on to the next

corner to peer around it. More terrace and French doors awaited but there was no sign of an actual person. Sarita moved to another set of French doors and repeated her cautious peeking routine. What she found this time appeared to be an office, also uninhabited. Her gaze slid over a dark wood desk and bookshelf-lined walls, and then she continued on to a small window. Knowing this would be a new room; she slowed and peeked cautiously through the high window at . . . another bathroom. Much smaller than the one off the bedroom, it was just a toilet and sink.

A guest bathroom, she supposed, and moved cautiously forward to the first of two sets of French doors beyond the bathroom. Sarita wasn't surprised when the first set of doors gave her a view of a kitchen, while the second revealed a dining area. She *was* surprised however that both rooms were just as empty as the rest of the house.

Pausing at the front corner on this side of the house, Sarita stared out over the sand and water again and then frowned and peered at the front doors. None of this was making sense. She was dressed for sex in the middle of a honeymoon paradise, but there didn't seem to be anyone here but her.

Unless there was a second floor, Sarita thought suddenly. She hadn't seen any stairs in her exploration, but . . .

Sarita walked quickly out onto the beach and then swung back to peer at the house. No second floor. She was alone. Which made absolutely no sense at all. Despite her embarrassing state of undress, she still would have preferred to find someone who could have explained things to her . . . like why she was here, and where here was.

Shaking her head, Sarita turned away from the house and next made her way out to the dock. She walked out onto the end of it and peered first one way and then the other along the beach, noting that it didn't stretch far on either side before curving away. So this house was on a tip of the island, or some body of land, she reasoned and glanced down, noticing what appeared to be brand-new rope on two of the dock posts. One on the post at the very tip of the dock, and one on the second one from shore, they were a good ten or fifteen feet apart, suggesting the boat that usually docked here wasn't a large one.

Sarita turned to look at the house. There was nothing but jungle around the building, no sign of a road. It could only be accessed by water. But there was no sign of a boat and she appeared to be the only person here.

For now.

That last thought had her heading for the house again, this time moving quickly. She appeared to be alone. But someone had brought her here. The empty dock suggested that whoever that was had left for some reason. But they hadn't just dumped her in a house in the middle of nowhere for no reason. They would certainly be back and she needed to prepare herself for that. She needed to find a weapon or a phone or something to help get her out of this situation.

Whatever this situation was, Sarita thought grimly. Considering all the negligees and skimpy swimsuits she'd found, and that they were the only form of covering available, she suspected sex had something to do with her presence here. If that was the case . . . well, Sarita had no intention of being anybody's sex slave.

Mouth tightening, she used the front doors to enter the house. The entry was a large area between the dining room and living room. She could see into both rooms from there and quickly ascertained that they were as empty as they'd appeared from outside. After a hesitation, she turned into the dining room. It held a large glass-topped table and six chairs. There was a large vase in the center of the dining table with a huge, riotous bouquet of flowers. Sarita barely gave the flowers a glance as she continued on through the large arched entrance separating the dining room from the kitchen.

The kitchen seemed the most likely place to find a better weapon, so Sarita started there and was surprised to find she didn't have to search every drawer and cupboard to obtain one. There was a wooden block on the island with a set of chef's knives in it. Long sharp knives, short sharp knives, and a cleaver were on display.

Setting the lamp on the kitchen counter, Sarita moved to the wooden block and pulled out the butcher knife. After testing the feel of it in her hand, she set it on the island and pulled out two of the steak knives as well, thinking they would be good for throwing. Jerking up the ridiculous robe and nightgown, she slid the two blades under the strap of the thong. When the strap held and wasn't dragged down by the weight of the knives, she grabbed two more and added them. They did pull a bit at the strap, but it stayed up, so she let the frothy white material fall back into place and snatched up the butcher knife again.

Okay, she was armed. Now what? Find a place to hide where she could ambush her captor on his return? Or—

Phone! Sarita thought suddenly, and clucked her tongue with irritation as she recalled her earlier intention to find one. A quick glance around the kitchen didn't reveal a phone, so she moved back through the dining room to the living room, but a survey of that room proved there wasn't one there either.

Fingers crossed, she used the door from the living room to slip into the office and walked to the desk. Sarita wasn't terribly surprised not to find one there either. It had been a bit much to hope for, she supposed. Kidnapped and left alone with weapons *and* a phone? Not likely. She was lucky the knives were even available, or that she'd been left alone, Sarita thought and frowned. Really, what kind of kidnapper kidnapped you and then left you alone with weapons so readily available? You'd think he would have cleared out anything and everything she might use to defend herself. Unless whoever it was hadn't expected her to wake up so soon from whatever drug they'd given her, she thought. Or perhaps they'd been unexpectedly delayed in returning. Maybe she'd got lucky and their boat had blown up.

That would be karma, Sarita thought and was smiling at the idea when she noticed the envelope leaning up against the desk lamp. Smile fading as she saw that her name was on it, she snatched it up and started to sit in the desk chair only to be pointedly reminded of the knives she'd sheathed in the strap of the thong she wore. Literally. A quick poke from a couple of the blades was enough to make her straighten and decide to remain standing.

The envelope wasn't sealed. Setting down the butcher knife, Sarita lifted the flap and pulled out the letter inside, then unfolded and read the message on the fine vellum paper.

*Dear Sarita,*
  *Your clothing was blood encrusted. Asherah cleaned you up and put you to bed.*

Sarita sagged against the desk as those first words sent memories washing over her. Dr. Dressler's lab. The poor man cut in half. Dr. Dressler and the woman arriving. Blood splashing over her as that poor immortal tried to scream and—Immortals? Bio-engineered nanos? Her head spun briefly as everything Dressler had told her washed back into her mind, and then she recalled the shot he'd given her in the neck.

"Bastard," she muttered with a disgust that was directed at herself as much as him. While it seemed obvious he was a scumbag, she should have been more alert. She should have noticed the movement when he'd reached out to inject her, and she should have batted his hand away or something.

Taking a deep breath, she counted to three and reminded herself that she wasn't Wonder Woman. No one was. She did the best she could and regret was a waste of energy that could be directed toward more useful endeavors.

"Right," she muttered. "Let's get on with it."
Raising the letter, she started again.

*Dear Sarita,*

*Your clothes were blood encrusted and ruined. Asherah cleaned you up and put you to bed.*

*It occurred to me once you'd lost consciousness that I didn't explain the importance of your being a life mate. From what I can gather it appears a life mate is chosen by the nanos in their host, and are rare creatures that the immortal cannot read or control, and can live happily with throughout his or her life. They are also few and far between. Some immortals apparently wait centuries or even millennia to find theirs. While some have been fortunate enough to find one, lose them, and later, usually much later, find another, there are other immortals who never find even one life mate. So life mates are valued more than any-thing else in an immortal's life.*

*It seems immortals—like gibbons or wolves—mate for life. Not because of any moral standard, but quite simply because another mate would not satisfy their needs. What I've been told is that life mates suit each other in every way, and that life mate sex is like no other—powerful and over-whelming to the point where both parties faint or pass out at the end. I suspect that the nanos must cause this by releasing a rush of the relevant hor-mones.*

*I also understand that life mates find each other irresistible, and in fact often spend weeks or even months in bed on first meeting. I tell you this so that you know there is no reason to believe I will think less of you if you find yourself doing*

*the same thing, or even let the man bed you on
your first meeting. I expect that.*

Sarita snorted at the comment. She didn't give a crap
what a whackjob like Dressler thought of her. She'd
sleep with whoever she wanted whenever she wanted.
Although, frankly, she wasn't a one-night-stand kind of
gal or one likely to "drop trou" on first meeting someone either. Sarita's father had been an old-fashioned
type of man; he'd also been overprotective and insisted
on meeting every male she'd ever dated. She knew
without a doubt that he'd given every one of them the
*"hell hath no fury like a father whose baby has been
groped by some horny teen"* speech, quickly followed
by the *"I have a big backyard to bury you in"* speech.
She was lucky she'd got laid at all.

Shaking her head, Sarita turned her attention back to
the letter, quickly finding where she'd left off.

"Yada yada first meeting," she murmured as she
found the spot.

*Now, do not be alarmed. You are in the home
my wife and I first inhabited on moving to Venezuela. We lived there for a year as we waited
for our house on the island to be built. I had it
renovated and updated some months ago in an-
ticipation of this eventuality. I hope you find it
comfortable and to your liking.*

*Everything there has been supplied for your
use.*

*The refrigerator and cupboards in the kitchen
are stocked full of food and will be refilled as*

*necessary. The wine rack in the dining room is full of vintages I thought you might enjoy.*

Sarita's mouth tightened. It was sounding like he expected she would be there for a very long time. He had another think coming.

*You have met your life mate, although it was long enough ago that you may not recall. Apparently you were thirteen when you first entered his restaurant in Caracas. He recognized that you were his life mate, but was gentleman enough not to claim you while so young. Instead, he decided to let you live your life and grow up first and put a private detective on your tail who, for the last fifteen years, has fed him monthly reports on your life.*

"What?" Sarita gasped with dismay. Thirteen? That's how old she was when her mother died. It was also when she and her father had moved to Canada. She tried to think of any restaurants they'd visited here in Venezuela before moving to Canada, but it had been fifteen years. Besides, with the trauma of what had happened to her mother, that year was kind of a blur in her memory anyway.

Sighing, she glanced back to the letter, reading the part about this life mate's *deciding* to *let* her live her life and grow up. Big of him, she thought with disgust. As if she didn't have a say in it? As for putting a private detective on her tail for the last *fifteen years* . . . well, that was just creepy. Stalkerish even. But just because

Dressler said it, didn't mean it was true. Not once in fifteen years had she noticed anyone tailing her around town or anything, and she was a cop, trained to observe things.

Sarita frowned briefly, but then continued on with the letter. "Yada yada, reports on your life . . . there it is."

*His name is Domitian Argenis. He is below.*

"Below what?" Sarita muttered, and then read the next line.

*I left the refrigerator downstairs stocked with blood for him.*
*For your own safety, I suggest you wait for him to wake up, feed him at least four bags of blood, and ensure he understands that you are not responsible for his being chained to the table, and that you are a victim and as helpless as he—*

"Helpless my ass," Sarita growled.

*—before you unchain him.*
*Good luck. I expect to learn a lot from your stay at my home away from home.*

*Dr. Dressler*

"*Before I unchain him?*" she muttered with disbelief. Some poor guy was chained in the basement? At least she assumed he was in the basement. "El Doctor" had said he was below and then mentioned a refrigerator in the basement, so she was guessing below was the basement.

"But where the hell is the basement?" Sarita muttered, scowling at the letter for not adding that bit of information. She hadn't seen stairs anywhere in her tour of the house.

Dropping the letter, Sarita started around the desk, thinking she'd have to go through the house again. But she paused as she noticed a bookshelf at an angle in the opposite corner of the room. The edge of it was out an inch or so past the shelf next to it.

Eyes narrowing, Sarita walked over to the bookshelves, grasped the side of the one sticking out and pulled.

"Eureka," she murmured as the shelf swung out like a door. "Hidden doors. Just what I should have expected from Dr. Whackjob."

Stepping into the opening left behind, Sarita eyed the set of stairs leading down into darkness and scowled. "Cozy."

A glance to the wall on either side did not reveal a light switch. Feeling along the wall on either side of the door frame itself didn't either. It seemed she was expected to creep down blindly into the dark like an idiot.

Sarita stared briefly into the black hole, wondering about the man chained up down there. She wasn't buying this life mate business Dressler had written about, but she was curious to find out what this supposed life mate looked like.

With her luck, he'd be some cross-eyed drooler with a cowlick, Sarita thought and then shrugged. Whatever. It didn't matter. She wasn't interested in being some vampire's vampiress. She *was* curious to see him, though. But there was no way in hell that she was creeping down into that darkness without some sort of light.

Spinning away from the hidden entrance, Sarita headed back to the kitchen to search for a flashlight. But, of course, there didn't appear to be one.

Slamming the last cupboard door with an irritated bang, she hesitated, and then sighed and moved to the drawer beside the sink. Opening it, she retrieved the box of matches she'd spotted there during her search. It was one of those big boxes of wooden matches with a striking strip on the side, and it was full, she noted, opening the box.

Taking them with her, Sarita walked out to the living room. She had a vague recollection of spotting candles in here on one of her trips through and—

"Aha!" she said with triumph, hurrying to the fireplace mantel where there were four large candles in holders lined up with some sort of brass decoration in the middle as the centerpiece. Snatching up one of the candles, she returned to the office.

Setting the candleholder on the desk, Sarita quickly lit it, and then tucked a couple of extra matches between her lips just in case her candle went out. She then snatched the candleholder and her butcher knife and headed for the secret door.

The stairs were tight and steep she discovered with the first step, and Sarita caught up as much of the cloth of the nightgown as she could in the hand holding the knife and raised it above her knees. She would never admit this, but she had been known to be a bit clumsy at times, and tangling her feet in the gown and taking a fall was not something she wanted to experience.

Sarita took a couple more steps, candle held out in

front of her, and squinted against the flame while trying to see beyond it. She then slowed as a scene from an old black-and-white movie she'd once seen came to mind. A lone woman in a long white nightgown descending stairs into darkness with only a candle to light her way. Meanwhile the evil Dracula waited in the darkness below, ready to pounce on her.

*Yeah, good one, Sarita. The perfect thing to think of at this moment,* she reprimanded herself mentally as she continued down. Her Dracula was supposed to be chained up down there, but what if he'd got loose?

Sarita quickly pushed that thought away as unhelpful and continued down. She couldn't see any more than a couple steps ahead, and didn't need old movies to help her imagine what lay ahead. Still, other scenes from movies were suddenly sliding through her mind. All of them were just different versions of that one scene in every horror movie where the stupid chick did something incredibly idiotic that got her stabbed or horribly beheaded.

That thought made Sarita stop abruptly on the stairs as she realized she really was being like that idiot broad from every horror movie. The big-haired twit with large bouncy boobs and no brains usually in something skimpy and—Cripes! *She* had big hair, big boobs, and was wearing a see-through negligee! She *was* that girl!

Nah, her hair was long, not really big. It wasn't curled to within an inch of its life and hair-sprayed to death. And yeah, she had big boobs, but that was hardly her fault. They were natural not bought, and truly, her large breasts had been the bane of her existence since they'd popped out on her chest when she was thirteen. Their presence had not gone unnoticed by the boys in her school and what had followed was teasing, taunt-ing, and attempts to cop a feel by the more skeevy of her schoolmates. They were the reason behind her first punching a male in the face. She had punched many more since then, both on and off the job, which was why her partner at work called her Rock'em Sock'em Reyes, or just RSR for short.

Sarita smiled crookedly at the thought of Jackson, her patrol partner. He was a good guy. Newly married and madly in love with his wife, he often treated her like a little sister. He was the closest thing she had to family now and just thinking of him made her straighten her shoulders. Big-boobed twit or not, she was going down there. Besides, unlike the idiot chicks in movies, she was armed with more than double Ds. She had a knife and knew how to use it. Mind you her gun would have been more reassuring, but . . . Whatever, Sarita thought as she stepped down onto a cold hard floor and paused.

She stood still for a moment, just listening, but there was no slight shuffling as someone moved in the dark-ness, no hiss of a vampire about to launch himself on her.

Nothing, she thought, and let go of the breath she'd been holding to suck a draft of fresh air into her eager lungs.

Okay, not so fresh, she corrected herself, wrinkling her nose at the stale, damp scent that assailed her. The basement definitely had a moldy odor to it. Sarita shifted one bare foot along the floor and then lowered the candle until she could see that it was indeed con-crete and not simply hard packed earth.

Straightening, she glanced around, hoping her eyes might have adjusted enough for her to make out something in the dark. They hadn't, though, so she shuffled forward several feet until the candlelight revealed a wall with a door in it. Releasing the hold she'd had on her gown, she reached for the doorknob.

The clank of metal on metal as the knife handle banged against the knob made her wince, but Sarita turned it and pushed the door open.

The candle flickered wildly in the draft created by the opening door. Terrified it would go out, Sarita instinctively drew it closer to her chest and raised her butcher-knife-holding-hand to try to shelter the flame. She didn't know if that helped, but after a moment the candlelight settled again and she let out the breath she'd been holding on a relieved sigh that blew the damned thing out.

"Crap!" Sarita muttered into the darkness, nearly spitting out the two matches she'd placed between her lips. Reaching up instinctively to remove them, she poked herself in the cheek with the butcher knife and was so startled she dropped the candle, holder and all. Sarita then immediately froze as the dark seemed to crowd in on her, sending a prickly sensation along her skin.

Trying to ignore it, Sarita took a deep breath and reasoned with herself. The candle had gone out and she'd dropped it and now it was dark. Not a big problem. She had matches. She'd light one, find the candle, and light it again. *Boom*, problem solved, she told herself.

The minute Sarita reached up with her now-empty candle hand and took one of the matches from her mouth she felt a little better. Even the match would give off light. All she had to do was strike it on something. It would light and she'd use it to find the candle. Everything would be fine, Sarita reasoned . . . except that she hadn't brought the matchbox with its striking strip on the side.

Not a problem, she told herself again, the concrete floor was rough, and she could use that. It sounded easy enough. Unfortunately, Sarita had forgotten the knives tucked into her thong. She was reminded forcefully of them when she dropped quickly into a kneeling position and the knives stabbed into her skin, her hunched position pressing her stomach against the top of them and basically forcing them into her legs.

The match in her mouth was spat out on a curse as Sarita quickly straightened again. Ignoring that for now, she felt the top of her thighs to see how much damage she'd done to herself. But it was dark, and the cloth of the nightgown and robe didn't help any.

Muttering over her stupidity, she yanked up the material of both gown and robe and felt around again. Sarita's fingers encountered what she assumed was blood on the front of her upper legs, but there didn't seem to be too-too much of it. At least it wasn't gushing or anything, so she didn't think she'd done herself too much damage. Which was a relief.

Sighing, Sarita put the hilt of the butcher knife between her teeth to hold it, caught the material of the gown and robe between her chin and chest and used both hands to retrieve the knives from her thong. She then raised her chin, letting the material drop back into place and took the butcher knife out of her mouth as she considered her options. She only had two—find the matches or at least one of them, light it, and find and light the candle, or go back upstairs and retrieve another candle and more matches.

Sarita glanced over her shoulder toward the stairs, relieved to see the light spilling down from the open door above. Actually, now that the candle was out, her eyes were adjusting and she could see a little more than she had with it. Or maybe it was because the light wasn't between herself and what she was trying to see. Whatever the case, she could see darker shapes in the gloom around her. And what looked like a long chain or string dangling from the ceiling at the foot of the stairs.

Forgetting about the matches and candle, Sarita crossed back to the stairs, caught all of her knives between one hand and her chest, then reached up to feel the item with her free fingers. It was a string with a tiny bell-shaped weight on the end. She gave it a tug and then squeezed her eyes shut when a click was accompanied by an explosion of light in the room. Easing her eyes cautiously open after a moment, she saw that the source of light was a bare bulb in a fixture on the ceiling.

Lowering her head, Sarita turned to peer around at what appeared to be a storage area. Old wicker furniture was stacked along the wall to her right, and several boxes filled the space on the left, the stairs were in front of her, and—

Sarita turned and stared at the opposite wall where more items and boxes were stacked on either side of the door she'd opened. The light didn't reach far into the next room, but she could see the corner of a metal counter just inside. She could also see her candle and its holder lying in the doorway with the matches not far away.

Sarita crossed the small space, set her knives on the counter just inside the door and knelt to gather the dropped items. She collected the matches and set them and the candle on the holder, picked it up, and started to get back to her feet, but she paused as she looked at the room before her.

Enough light was spilling through the doorway that she could make out shapes, and one in particular had caught her attention. There was a table in the center of the room . . . and there was a body on it. Sarita immediately thought of the last man she'd found on a table. Well, two tables really, at least at first.

Stomach clenching, she straightened slowly and reached blindly to the side with her free hand to feel along the wall for a light switch. Her fingers encountered a cool metal upper cupboard, and then just below that she found what she thought was a light switch. Relieved, Sarita flicked it upward, and was blinded all over again when overhead florescent lights buzzed to life at least ten times brighter than the room with one bald bulb.

Blinking rapidly, she caught snapshots of the room as she tried to force her eyes to adjust more quickly. Blink. The lab was very similar to the lab in the fenced-in area on the island. Blink. There was the metal table in the center of the room to her left. Blink. There *was* someone on the table. Blink. He was unmoving and naked and— Blink. Damn he was hot.

# Three

Sarita wasn't sure just how long she stood in that doorway gaping at the man on the table. But he was worthy of the time given. Because he was definitely not a cross-eyed drooler with a cowlick.

Well, actually, his eyes were closed and he was unconscious so she couldn't be positive about the cross-eyed drooler part, but frankly, with a body like that, she could overlook a few flaws, Sarita thought and then blinked and gave herself a slap.

"Snap out of it," she muttered. "He's a vampire . . . scientific or not. And if Dressler was telling the truth, he's been having you followed around for years like some creepy perv," she added for good measure, because really, that bothered her. It wasn't that she trusted Dressler and what he said all that much, but really, why would he lie about something like that? Still . . . how could she have been tailed by a private detective for fifteen years and not have known it? Crazy. Impossible. "God, look at that chest."

Sarita rolled her eyes as that last part slipped out. She had no idea where it had come from. But seriously, he had an amazing chest. At least what she could see of it above the chains that were wrapped around both the table and his body from just below his elbow to his upper thighs. It was a lot of chain.

There was also an intravenous catheter taped to his inner elbow on this side, she noted. And strong, muscular legs were revealed below the chain skirt, tapering down to nice calves before chains began again at his ankles, covering several inches and then stopping at his feet.

Dr. Dressler had mentioned that these immortals were stronger than mortals, but this just seemed like overkill, Sarita thought and finally started forward. She stopped after only a couple of steps when she realized she was still carrying the candle. Pausing, she swung back to set it on the counter by the door, making a mental note not to forget it when they went back upstairs. They might need it again.

That thought gave her pause. When *they* went back upstairs? *They* might need it? Was she really planning to free the naked vampire on the table? Originally she'd just been curious to see him. She hadn't intended to free him necessarily. Now though . . .

Turning back to face the room, Sarita let her gaze drift over the chains binding the man. He was supposed to be stronger, faster, and whatnot. He might come in useful in helping her get out of this place. And yeah, he was a vampire, but he had also been drugged and dropped here by Dr. Dressler just as she had. They had a common enemy. What was that old saying? The enemy of mine enemy is my friend?

*Damned right I'm unchaining him!*

*Maybe*, Sarita added, moving back to the table.

She glanced over the chains, but not seeing the end of it anywhere on top, started to bend to check under the table, only to pause as she spotted a drop of blood on the floor. Straightening again, she looked more closely at the chain around his lower arm. It was just above where the spot of blood was on the floor and she, at first, thought he must be wounded under all that chain. A more thorough examination didn't reveal any evidence of blood on the table or chain, though.

Perplexed, Sarita glanced back down to the floor again to see that there were now two drops of blood, side by—

Three, she corrected as she stepped back, revealing another drop lying between where her feet had been.

She was the one bleeding, Sarita realized and quickly began to tug up the material of the negligee and robe she wore. She'd forgotten all about stabbing herself with the knives earlier. Her worries about getting the candle lit and being able to see again had pushed it from her mind. That worry was gone now, though. She had lots of light and took the opportunity to get a better look at the wounds.

A grimace claimed her lips once she got her nightgown and robe out of the way and could see the four slices along the tops of her thighs. Two of them were very shallow and already scabbed over with dry blood. Two, one on each leg, were bleeding freely. Not a lot, but enough that blood was dribbling down her legs in slow rivulets.

She'd clean them up and bandage them later, Sarita decided as she let the gown and robe drop back into place. They weren't so deep as to be a major concern, but cuts could get infected and that was more likely in the tropics than anywhere else. It wasn't just spiders and slithery creatures that thrived here. Bacteria enjoyed the wet, hot climate too.

Assuring herself that she'd tend to them the first chance she got, Sarita peered at the face of the man again and then reached out to gently pat his cheeks in the hope of waking him. There was no reaction at all, not even a stirring, so she tried again, patting his cheek more firmly. When that had no effect either, she flat out slapped him. Nothing.

Leaning over him, Sarita pressed a thumb against his eyelid and pulled it open. The man's eye was the most beautiful blue she'd seen in her life. Seriously, it was gorgeous, as blue as the sky on a sunny day, but with streaks of silver shot through that almost seemed to shimmer. She was so taken with the color that it took a moment for her to remember why she'd opened his eye in the first place, but then Sarita forced her attention to the pupil and nodded solemnly.

"Drugged," she muttered, releasing his eyelid and turning to look at the intravenous bag. His being immortal and all, she'd assumed it was an empty bag of blood. Now she saw that there was an inch of clear liquid still in the bag. Well, mostly clear, she noted, narrowing her eyes at the milky quality of the liquid inside.

Not just saline then, Sarita thought.

Turning her attention to the catheter in his arm, she ripped the tape away and slid the apparatus out. She let it drop to swing free next to the table, and then gave the insertion point a quick look to be sure all was well. A bead of blood had bubbled to the surface, but when she brushed it away Sarita couldn't even see a pinpoint to show her where the needle had gone in. He healed that quickly.

Shrugging, she released his arm and peered at his face again, wondering how long it would take for the drugs to wear off. Probably a while, she decided and debated what to do next.

Sarita glanced around the room, spotted the refrigerator along the wall to her right, and walked over to open it. Blood. Lots of it. Not as much as had been in the refrigerator she'd seen in Dr. Dressler's torture chamber, but a good thirty or forty bags.

Another sign that Dressler expected them to be here a while, Sarita thought and felt her mouth flatten. That was not going to happen. She was getting out of there as quickly as she could. She had things to do. She had to find her grandmother, and that could be a problem in itself. She hadn't seen her in Dressler's house or in the labs, but that didn't mean she wasn't there. Certainly, Sarita no longer trusted that the man had told her the truth when he'd called with the news that her grandmother had been injured in a fall. Wherever she was, Sarita had to find her and get her away from the crazy old geezer the woman had worked for since before Sarita was born. And then she fully intended to report the bastard to the Venezuelan police and see that charges were laid against him before she went home to her little apartment and her job. She'd have to take her grandmother with her, Sarita thought now. The woman would have nowhere to go here.

Her mind immediately crowded with worries about

how she could do that. Would she need a visitor's visa? How did you go about getting one? Did her grand-mother even have a passport?

Shoving those concerns away for now, Sarita pushed the refrigerator door closed and turned to lean against it as she considered how to get away from this place. Dr. Dressler had said in the letter that this was where he and his wife had lived as they'd waited for the house on the island to be built. She supposed that meant this house was on the mainland. That was something at least. There was a dock and no road so they were obvi-ously on the coast and a good distance from the nearest village or town.

They'd have to walk out, Sarita supposed. Try to find help. Hopefully they wouldn't have to travel too far to find it. But there were plenty of provisions here that they could take with them just in case it took them a while to find civilization.

Sarita didn't like the idea of having to walk out of there dressed as she was, though, or in any of the ri-diculous concoctions in the closet upstairs. Which was probably why that was all there was available to her. Dr. Dressler had probably hoped that would keep her here.

"Not gonna happen," Sarita muttered and pushed away from the refrigerator to walk out into the next room. She'd quickly check the boxes while she was waiting for sleeping Dracula there to wake up. Maybe she'd find something useful, like old clothes. They'd probably stink of mold or mothballs, but she could deal with that, and at least she'd have some protection against being eaten alive by bugs.

Stopping by the boxes along the one wall, Sarita

began opening them. The first appeared to be stuffed with plain brown paper, but when she grabbed a handful and pulled it out, it unraveled and something tumbled to the ground and shattered.

Frowning, Sarita stepped back and peered at the broken china on the floor. A teacup, she realized, spotting a delicate handle still attached to a broken bit of china. The box was full of china, she realized after feeling the paper-wrapped items still inside. Setting that box aside, she moved on to the next, but it too held china, as did the third. The fourth box had a bunch of old board games in it. The next two boxes had books. Most were paperbacks, old romances and pulp fiction, nothing that would be helpful to clothe herself or the man in the next room.

Sarita barely had the thought when a jangling noise drew her head sharply around. Recognizing it as the sound of chains clanging against each other, she forgot about the boxes and turned to rush for the door. Unfortunately, while she'd been conscious of the broken teacup on the floor and been careful to avoid the shards of porcelain while she'd searched the boxes, she didn't think of them as she turned to sprint for the door. At least, not until a sharp pain had her gasping and reaching for the nearest box for balance as she jerked her foot up off the floor. The box didn't offer much stability. The minute her fingers brushed it, the damned thing and the two boxes it rested on toppled away, crashing to the floor.

Holding her sore foot off the floor, Sarita stared at the sea of broken glass now covering the ground between her and the door and couldn't hold back the explosive string of curses that slipped from her lips.

Domitian had just woken up and realized he was
chained to a table when someone began calling their
duck. At least he thought they were calling a duck. His
thinking was a little slow and fuzzy, his vision blurry,
and his hearing might be off too, but he was sure what
he heard was "Duck! Duckity duck duck duck! Duck!"

Although why anyone would name their duck Duck
was beyond him, and really, no animal would answer
to the fury in that voice, he thought. And then another
"Duck" rent the air, only this time he realized it wasn't
*duck* he was hearing at all, but *fu—*

"You're awake!"

Domitian turned his head and stared blankly at the
vision standing in the doorway. And she *was* a vision.
Long dark hair tumbled over the woman's shoulders,
flowing out behind her, and beautiful dark eyes peered
at him over her presently puckered lips as she peered at
him with displeasure. He wondered over her expression
briefly, but then she began to hop forward, the movement causing the long, sheer flowing gown she wore to
play peek-a-boo with the tiny white panties and beautiful olive skin it was doing a poor job of hiding.

Damn, the woman was a gorgeous little bundle. Short,
curvy with large breasts and in the most sinful nightgown
it had been his pleasure to see, Domitian decided, letting
his gaze slide over the see-through white gown with red
ribbons. It was almost enough to make him forget he already had a life mate, he thought as he watched her breasts
bounce with every hop.

*Hop?* he thought suddenly. Yes, she was hopping,
Domitian reassured himself as she continued forward.
It was not a result of whatever had left him so fuzzy-
headed where he lay. The woman was hopping on one

foot and leaving a trail of blood on the concrete floor as she made her way to him.

"I didn't expect you to wake up so soon," she said as she reached the side of the table and grasped it to balance herself. Her eyes slid over his face. "I only took out the IV maybe ten minutes ago. I figured you might be under for another hour or better."

"IV?" Domitian queried, his voice surprisingly gruff. His throat was dry and scratchy. His head hurt too. He was obviously dehydrated and in need of fluids, he thought as he tried to ignore the scent of blood coming from the woman, but it was hard to ignore and made his stomach rumble.

"Yeah." She reached to the side and dragged an IV stand with an almost empty bag hanging from it closer so that he could see it. "Dr. Dressler left you all trussed up here on a saline drip with a little something extra added to keep you in la-la land. I took it out when I got down here."

Releasing the IV, she turned and hopped away.

Domitian immediately turned and tilted his head, trying to see where she was going. She hopped to a refrigerator behind him. He saw her open the door, but couldn't see why until she let the door slide closed and turned to hop back, now with half a dozen bags of blood in her arms. His eyes widened incredulously.

"What is that for?" he asked warily.

"For you," she said, her tone all business. Reaching the table, she dropped the bags on the metal surface next to him. "You're an immortal."

It wasn't a question. She sounded pretty sure and Domitian's eyebrows rose. He wasn't used to mortals knowing about his kind, but she was somehow connected to Dr. Dressler, who knew. Which was a damned shame, he decided, his gaze locking on her breasts as he saw that her activity had made the cloth of her gown gather between them, leaving the lovely full globes as good as bare with just a veil of sheer cloth over them.

Domitian had a terrible urge to reach out and touch them, but the chains restrained him . . . which was a good thing, he told himself with a frown. He had a life mate, or would once he claimed his Sarita. He had no business noticing other women's breasts.

"You work with Dressler?" he asked and scowled at both the possibility and the fact that the words didn't come out as strong as he would have liked. Damn, his throat was dry and sore. He needed blood.

"The hell I do," the woman growled, sounding insulted at the suggestion as she turned and hopped away toward the door.

She picked up something and turned, but it wasn't until she was halfway back that he saw that what she'd gone to fetch was a long butcher knife. And she was hopping around with it, apparently oblivious to the fact that she could skewer herself with it if she fell. Not a rocket scientist then, he thought dryly.

"Dressler's a whacked-out sadist," she huffed out as she reached the table again and picked up one of the bags. "He drugged and dropped me here too."

Domitian frowned. "Why would he—?" The words stopped on a gurgle as she suddenly held the bag over his mouth and punctured it with the knife, sending a torrent of the thick liquid splashing into his open mouth and onto his face.

Swallowing the mouthful he'd first got, he turned his head to the side to avoid the flow and snapped, "What the hell are you doing?" as the liquid now continued to pour out over the side of his head.

"Trying to feed you," she said with exasperation. Catching him firmly by the chin, she tried to force his head back to its original position. "Open your mouth."

Domitian resisted at first, but then conscious of the wasted blood, let his head roll back and opened his mouth for the blood to flow in. The liquid was running too swiftly though. He tried to keep up with it, but ended up choking and coughing, sending a good portion of the liquid shooting out over the woman's face and chest.

"You guys are messy eaters," she muttered with disgust, tossing the bag aside the moment it was empty and reaching for another.

Domitian ground his teeth and growled, "This is not how we feed."

"Oh?" She stopped with the bag and knife over his mouth and raised an eyebrow. "How do you feed, then?"

"Unchain me and I will feed myself," he said at once.

That brought a snort from her luscious lips. "Yeah, right, buddy. *If* I unchain you, it isn't gonna happen until you've had at least four bags of this stuff. I have no intention of being your breakfast."

Domitian scowled. "We do not feed on—"

"Yeah, yeah," she interrupted. "You have rules against feeding off mortals and yada yada. Well, forgive me, but I'm a cop and know a lot of rule breakers. I have no intention of taking chances here. So tell me how to feed you properly or I'm gonna slice this bag like I did the last one and feed you that way."

They glared at each other briefly and then Domitian sighed. "I let my teeth out and you pop the bag to them," he said grimly, and then reluctantly cautioned, "But not too hard or the bag will rupture and splash everywhere. And not too lightly or my teeth won't puncture it."

"Right. Not too hard, and not too light," she said with a roll of the eyes. And then she lowered the knife and said, "Okay, so get your fangs out. We don't have all day here."

Domitian spared a moment to glare at her. He had no idea who she was, but she was definitely a bossy bit of goods . . . and ridiculously sexy in that damned night-gown. Cursing under his breath, he opened his mouth. His fangs had been trying to slide out since she'd entered the room, bringing the scent of blood with her, but he'd forced them to stay where they were. Now he let them slide forward. The woman watched with fascination, and then slapped the bag to his mouth.

They both released a relieved little sigh when it landed properly, sliding onto his fangs without burst-ing. Domitian relaxed then, his gaze sliding over her as he waited for his fangs to drain the bag. There were splashes of blood on her cheek and neck now, but it pretty much coated her pretty breasts both above the gown's neckline as well as through the frail cloth itself. He found himself wishing he could lick it away for her. The thought was a rather shocking one for a man who hadn't thought about sex in centuries, at least not in regards to anyone but the life mate out there waiting for him to claim her.

Shocking enough in fact to clear Domitian's thinking a bit and make him realize that he should have taken control of the woman and made her unchain him the moment she'd entered the room. That had his gaze rising to her forehead so that he could focus on her thoughts and take control.

Only he couldn't.

Coming up against a blank wall in her mind, Domitian regathered himself and tried again, but it was no good. He couldn't read this woman.

For a moment Domitian was too shocked to think anything, but then his brain began to screech.

*Dear God! She was another life mate! After all these millennia alone, he now had two women to choose from; his sweet little Sarita and this . . .* creature.

Domitian's gaze skated to her breasts again as a surfeit of possibilities began to fill his mind. The most interesting one was the thought of two life mates in his bed. He had some trouble picturing his sweet Sarita naked and in his bed at that moment, but he could see this one there, her hair a wild mass on the pillow, her eyes sleepy with desire, her mouth open on a moan rather than pursed with irritation or displeasure and her breasts glistening with blood as they were now.

If the bag hadn't been in the way, Domitian would have licked his lips as he gazed at them. They were lovely. Large and full like ripe melons waiting to be plucked from the vine. And her nipples, he breathed out slowly through his nose as he focused on her nipples, noticing that they were growing hard before his eyes.

Curious, he glanced back to her face and saw that while he'd been ogling her, her own eyes had been busy traveling down his body. They were now focused on the chains across his groin.

"Are you wearing anything under that chain skirt of yours?" she asked suddenly, her voice slightly husky.

Apparently not pleased by that, she scowled and lifted her gaze back to his face. "Are you?"

Domitian merely peered at her over the bag in his mouth. It was hard to speak with a mouthful of bag.

Seeming to realize that, she said, "Blink once for yes and twice for no."

Unsure of the answer, he stared back unblinking.

"I'll take that as an I don't know," she announced dryly and ripped the now-empty bag away.

"What's your name?" Domitian managed to get out just before she slapped another full one to his teeth.

She arched her eyebrows at him. "You should know. You're the one who's had a private detective following me around for *fifteen years.*"

Domitian stilled at this irritated announcement, his eyes examining her face. Sarita? No it couldn't be, he thought. But now that he was looking at her face and not her breasts, or the rest of her body in that seductive nightgown she was wearing, there was something . . .

As she'd said, the private detective he'd hired had been sending him monthly reports for fifteen years. The reports had told him what she was doing and with whom. He'd read about her doing well in school, her taking martial arts, her part-time jobs as a teenager, and the large group of friends she'd had. He'd been proud as could be when she finished high school and went on to university to get a bachelor's degree in criminology. He'd always planned to wait until she'd grown up and worked at her chosen career for two years before going to claim her. So, when she'd graduated, he'd started to plan his trip to Canada, where he'd intended to arrange to "bump into her" and then woo her as she deserved. But then Sarita had applied to and been accepted into the police college. At the time he'd been disappointed at the delay in his being able to claim her. But he'd stuck to his guns and waited.

She was well worth the wait, Domitian decided as his gaze slid over her again.

While the reports he'd received had been pretty thorough, even at first mentioning the boys she had dated, the one thing they had not included was pictures of Sarita. That had been by Domitian's choice. He had wanted her to experience a little life before he claimed her, and it had been easier for him to resist doing that so long as he thought of her as the child she'd been when he'd first seen her in his restaurant. Domitian had feared he might not be able to resist going to her sooner if he got pictures of her at eighteen, nineteen, or twenty. So in his mind she'd remained the skinny, flat-chested child he'd first met, and while he'd often imagined what she might look like now, none of his imaginings had equaled the seductive and lush woman bending over him, feeding him blood. Damn, she'd grown up fine.

So, not two life mates, Domitian realized, and wasn't at all disappointed. Fantasies aside, it would be difficult to please two immortal life mates in bed when you passed out after pleasuring the first. Besides, he could only turn one and would have had to choose between them if there were two.

Now he didn't have to, Domitian thought, his eyes drifting back to her breasts. God he couldn't wait to get his hands on them. He would feast on them, lick the blood away, and suck those perfect little pebbles between his lips, lash them with his tongue, and nip at the buds as he thrust into her and—

The clank of chains drew his attention from her

breasts and Domitian peered down to see that he'd definitely been affected by his thoughts. He'd managed to work himself up to the point that he now had an erection pressing against the chains across his groin. He hadn't thought there was a lot of give in the chains, but judging by the bulge now noticeable between his legs he supposed there must be.

Apparently he wasn't the only one to notice his present state. Sarita said dryly, "If you have enough blood to spare it for erections, you've definitely had enough."

Domitian shifted his gaze back to her, his eyes getting caught on her jiggling breasts as she tossed the empty bag aside.

Sarita turned back, scowling when she saw where he was looking and snapped, "Hey! Eyes up here, buddy!"

He jerked his eyes up to meet hers, and she scowled and shook her head. "Look, we have to get something straight here. Dressler said we're life mates or some such thing and mentioned a bunch of twaddle about great sex and yada yada, but I'm not interested. Got it? There will be no kissy kissy, gropey gropey . . . or sex. *Entender? No sexo!*"

Domitian bit his lip to hold back the laugh that wanted to escape him. He suspected she wouldn't see what was so amusing here, but really, he'd imagined their first meeting repeatedly over the last fifteen years. But not once in any of them had she been a feisty little bit of goods in a sexy-as-hell see-through gown telling him *"no sexo!"*

"Got it?" she repeated.

Domitian nodded mildly, allowing a smile to curve his lips. "As you wish."

Sarita's eyes narrowed, his words hitting on some

memory in the back of her head. When she couldn't access it, she just let it go and straightened to prop her hand on her hips as she looked him over. Reluctant concern entering her expression, she asked, "How are you feeling?"

Domitian couldn't hide his surprise at the seeming change in attitude.

"I mean are you full or what?" she explained, and then apparently not wanting him to think she was actually concerned about his health, added, "Full enough not to bite me if I unchain you?"

"I will not bite you," Domitian assured her solemnly, and then just because he felt quite sure it would annoy her, he added, "until you ask me."

"Yeah, well that'll be when hell freezes over then," Sarita muttered and suddenly ducked out of sight.

Startled, Domitian lifted his head and strained against the chains to glance over the side of the table, relaxing when he saw that she'd merely dropped to sit cross-legged on the floor so that she could examine the chains under the table. But he frowned when he noticed the smears of blood on the floor where she'd been standing. And those red ribbons he'd thought were part of the gown? They were crimson rivulets of blood trailing from her upper thighs down, he saw.

Domitian had just opened his mouth to ask if she was all right when she announced, "There's a padlock holding the chains together."

"Are you—?"

"It's okay. It's a number lock padlock," she growled.

Forgetting his question, Domitian let himself lie flat again and asked, "Why is that okay?"

"It's one of those padlocks with four number wheels

on it. You have to enter the right numbers to open it," she explained and he heard her moving around and the jangle of chain.

"And that's good because?" His tone was dry this time. It didn't sound all that good to him. If the padlock was on the top of the chains around his waist, he could have just broken it and got himself free. But not being able to reach it made that a problem and he knew without a doubt she wouldn't have the strength to simply break it herself.

"It's good because I had a boyfriend in high school who showed me how to crack these suckers," she informed him. "I think he was trying to impress me," Sarita continued dryly. "But really, all it did was convince me that he'd be one of the guys I'd have to arrest one day when I became a cop, and that I should never use these kind of padlocks again. At the time, I had one for my bike," she explained absently, and then added irritably, "You'd think Dressler would have left the combination in his letter."

"Hmm," Domitian murmured, but he was wondering if the boyfriend in question was one he'd received reports on. After her first couple of boyfriends in high school, he'd told the private detective not to bother reporting on them in future. While he'd wanted her to grow up and have all the usual experiences a young woman had, Domitian had found he had a terrible jealous streak. Every mention of a spotty teenage mortal taking her to a dance or film had made him want to get on a plane and go claim her. Fortunately, he'd restrained himself.

"So," he said when the silence drew out with just the

clanging of chains, "you wanted to be a police officer even in high school?"

"Since I was thirteen," she answered, her voice growing husky and sad.

Domitian merely grunted. Thirteen was when her mother had died. He didn't doubt for a minute that was the reason she'd decided to become a police officer. It was a subject that obviously still hurt her, though, and he found he didn't like her sad. He preferred his "feisty Sarita," so, knowing it would annoy her, he suggested, "Perhaps you should look around and see if he left a combination somewhere here in this room."

"I don't need a combination," she ground out with obvious irritation. "All you have to do is pull firmly on the shackle and spin each of the wheels from the farthest one out, to the one nearest the shackle. As each wheel hits the right number, it locks in place and the shackle slides out a bit and you move on to the next. It's easy and—" she gave a hoot of success and then finished "—done!"

Her fist flew up with the removed lock in it and then Sarita popped back into view. Her air was triumphant, but he didn't miss the wince that crossed her face as she straightened next to him. A determined expression took over almost before he'd registered the pain, and she quickly began to unravel the chain from around him and the table.

"I'm not sure where we are," Sarita said as she worked, drawing the end of the chain across his body, letting it drop under the table and then reaching across him to grab the now-longer length of chain and pull it across him again. "Dressler said it was his first home here in Venezuela. Where he and his wife lived while they waited for their island house to be built. We're on the coast, but I'm not sure where, and there's no road access, just a dock and no boat. We're going to have to walk out of here to find help."

"You're bleeding," Domitian said the minute she stopped speaking. "He hurt you?"

"What?" She paused in removing the chain to look down at herself. Her gaze stopped on her bloody chest and she shook her head. "You're the one who got me all bloody. While I was feeding you. Remember?" she said, trying to prod his memory.

"Not your beautiful breasts," he said solemnly, and was surprised to see her flush and appear a little flustered. Apparently, she was not used to compliments like that. A situation Domitian intended to change. "I was referring to your shapely legs and feet."

When she peered down at herself again, he craned his head to get another look at her blood-streaked lower body and feet.

Sarita scowled at her injuries and shook her head again as she returned to unraveling the chain. "That wasn't Dressler."

"Then what happened?" Domitian asked at once.

"I stepped on broken glass," Sarita said with a shrug as she drew the chain across his body again and let it drop.

That explained the bloody footprints and her hopping, he acknowledged. But—"What about the blood on your legs?"

Sarita was silent so long he didn't think she was going to answer, but finally she grimaced and admitted, "I stabbed myself with steak knives."

*"What?"* he asked with disbelief. "Why?"

"Well, I didn't do it on purpose," she said with irritation. "It was an accident."

"How the hell do you accidentally stab yourself with a steak knife?" Domitian asked with disbelief.

"Four steak knives actually. Well, a paring knife and three steak knives," Sarita corrected and then explained, "I had them tucked into my thong, forgot about them, bent to pick up something, and—" She ended with a shrug, and then suddenly stopped working to glance toward the door. In the next moment she'd grabbed the knife she'd set on the table and started to hop away toward the door.

"What are you doing?" Domitian asked with concern. "Stop that, you will hurt yourself. Finish unchaining me and I will see to your wounds."

"You aren't seeing to anything," she assured him sharply. "And I'm just getting my knives in case you go getting ideas once you're unchained."

"Do not be ridiculous," he growled, and then watched with dismay as Sarita reached the counter by the door and began to gather several knives off the metal surface. No doubt the paring knife and three steak knives she'd mentioned. Much to his dismay, she clutched them by the handles, pressed close to her chest along with the butcher knife, and began to hop back to the table.

"Stop!" Domitian bellowed with horror, visions of her falling and stabbing herself dancing in his head.

"Stop yourself," Sarita barked continuing forward.

It was all too much for Domitian. Positive she was about to tumble to the floor and impale herself on all five of the damned knives, he sat up abruptly, snapping the remaining chain surrounding him. Some part of his mind noted that he hadn't been left completely naked, he still had his boxers on. But most of his concentration as he lunged off the table was on getting to his life mate before the foolish woman killed herself with those damned knives.

Sarita released a startled curse when he swept her off her feet and pressed her to his hard chest. But she didn't protest, merely clutched her knives against her bosom, and scowled up at him as he carried her out of the room.

# Four

Domitian carried Sarita upstairs before slowing and then it was only to look around the office they were now in. The moment he spotted the open door into what appeared to be a living room, he headed that way, only to stop once through it.

"A bathroom?" he asked.

Instead of answering, Sarita glowered at him and demanded, "Put me down."

Snorting at the suggestion, Domitian glanced around again. This time he spotted a door farther along the wall and instinctively headed that way. He didn't bother to ask Sarita to turn the doorknob for him when he reached it. Half-suspecting she'd refuse anyway, he released the hold he had on her legs and reached out to open it himself, leaving her weight to balance on his arm without his hand to hold her in place. It only took a second and then he was carrying her into the room.

As his gaze slid over the sitting area, table for two, and bed, Domitian at first thought he'd made the wrong choice. His footsteps slowed, but then he spotted the long counter with double sinks through the door to the right of the bed. He continued forward more quickly now, carrying her into an opulent white bathroom and right up to the sink counter where he set her down between the two sinks.

Sarita hadn't said a word since demanding to be put down. She'd merely glowered at him, her hands tight around her knives, her expression suggesting she'd like to plunge the lot of them into his face.

Half-afraid she'd do just that, he tried for a soothing tone. "I will not harm you."

A snort slid from her lips and her fingers tightened around the knives. "Damned right you won't."

"I am just going to remove the glass from your foot and tend to your injuries," Domitian continued, ignoring her rude response. Raising his eyebrows, he asked, "Okay?"

"I can do it myself," she snapped.

"It will be easier if I do it," Domitian argued and dropped to kneel in front of her. He took her foot in hand to examine it.

"It's the other one," Sarita said at once, her tone dry and sharp.

"Of course," he muttered and quickly switched feet. Raising it so he could better see the bottom, Domitian tried to concentrate on the job at hand and ignore the sweet smell of her blood. It was hard, though, when all he wanted to do was lick if off her, and that desire had nothing to do with hunger, at least not the hunger for blood. He'd had enough blood to fight whatever had been used up trying to combat the drugs he'd been given. His hunger now was purely for the woman before him. She was independent and feisty and sexy as hell sitting there in that damned gown.

His eyes wandered from Sarita's bloody foot to the trails of blood on her legs and followed one up under the gossamer cloth of her nightgown. It led all the way up her calf to her thigh, and up it to the sliced skin just below the strap of the thong she wore.

She may as well be wearing only the thong for all the protection the gown offered, he thought with disgruntlement. But he found himself licking his lips as his gaze slid between the blood trails and that pure white triangle of cloth, the only thing preventing him from having a perfect view of her—

"There are tweezers in the makeup table."

Domitian's eyes immediately shot to her face and he could tell she'd noticed where he'd been looking.

"I will tend to the cuts after I see to the foot," he announced as if that's what had held his attention. He suspected she wouldn't fall for the ruse, though. His voice had been raspy with a desire he couldn't hide.

Domitian set her foot down and stood to move to the makeup table she'd mentioned. A quick search produced tweezers still in their packaging, which he broke open as he moved back to Sarita.

"I will try not to hurt you," Domitian promised as he knelt in front of her and reclaimed her foot.

Sarita merely nodded, but he couldn't help noticing the way her hands tightened around those knives of hers again. It made him release her foot and straighten.

"What are you doing now?" she asked suspiciously.

"I would rather not be stabbed should I inadvertently

hurt you while removing the glass," Domitian said simply and then waited.

When Sarita stared at him suspiciously, not setting down the knives, he found a little exasperation of his own.

"They are really quite useless to you as a weapon anyway. It would not kill me if you stabbed me."

"Maybe, but I bet it still hurts," she said grimly.

"Yes. Which is why I would rather avoid it," Domitian said pointedly, and then added stiffly, "You are my life mate, Sarita. Dr. Dressler may not have told you this, but an immortal would never willingly harm a life mate. However, unless you want to continue to hop around like a crazed bunny, I need to get that glass out of your foot, and may unintentionally hurt you doing so. I do not wish to be stabbed for my efforts. Please put the knives down."

Sarita scowled, glanced down at the weapons she held, and then sighed and set them on the counter next to her with obvious reluctance.

"Thank you," he said softly, and set down the tweezers to pick up the knives and quickly move them to the other side of the sink and out of her reach. When he then went to grab the tweezers again, they were gone.

Sarita had them, Domitian saw. She had also raised her injured foot to rest on her other knee so that she could see the bottom of it. Smiling at him widely, she shrugged. "No need to thank me. I couldn't hold them and take the glass out at the same time anyway."

Domitian opened his mouth, but then simply closed it again and leaned against the counter next to her. Waiting. There were three pieces of white porcelain in her foot, one large piece and two smaller. She could manage the large piece, but he knew the smaller ones were going to be difficult and painful to remove, which was why he'd suggested removing her knives.

Ignoring him, Sarita plucked out the larger of the three pieces first as he'd expected. She then turned her attention to the small pieces just visible under the skin and Domitian winced as she began to poke around the no-doubt tender flesh, trying to force the glass to the surface.

"Let me help," Domitian said, straightening when she sucked in a hissing breath of pain.

"I don't need help," Sarita said stubbornly and continued to poke and dig, causing herself unnecessary pain.

Losing patience with her, Domitian snatched the tweezers from her hand and knelt in front of her again. "Give me your foot."

"No," she growled. "Give me back the tweezers."

"No," he responded at once, and then took a breath before saying in a more reasonable tone, "I have better eyesight. I can remove it quickly. Let me help you."

For a moment he thought she'd refuse, but then Sarita released a pent-up sigh, and snapped, "Fine," as if she were doing him a favor and stuck out her foot. She then crossed her arms and glared at him.

Domitian found a smile creeping across his face at her attitude and quickly ducked his head to examine her foot so she wouldn't see it.

Apparently he hadn't been quick enough, however, because she growled, "Go ahead and snicker, fang boy, but you walked right through a floor full of that broken china on your way up here and I get to dig at your feet next."

"Why do I get the feeling you would enjoy causing me pain?" Domitian asked wryly, leaning in to remove the first small piece of glass from her foot. She hadn't responded by the time he removed the glass, so after tapping the tweezers on the edge of the sink to remove the fragment, he asked mildly, "What have I done to make you so angry?"

A glance up showed her looking dissatisfied and as mulish as a twelve-year-old boy. When he simply held on to her foot firmly, and waited for her answer, Sarita finally shrugged unhappily. "I don't like the idea that someone has been following me around for fifteen years."

"Ah." Domitian turned his attention back to her foot. "I apologize for that. But I did not wish to disrupt your life by insinuating myself into it while you were so young. I wanted you to have a normal childhood and experience everything other girls do—school, friends, even boyfriends," he added, his mouth tightening around the word. "However, I didn't wish to lose track of you either. I wanted to be able to approach you once you were old enough and woo you in the normal fashion. But I needed to know where you were when the time came, so I hired a private detective."

"That's all?" she asked suspiciously.

Domitian shrugged as he worked on the last sliver. "Pretty much. I got monthly reports letting me know that you were alive and well. Sometimes they included little details like the school you attended, or that you had friends and were attending parties and dances or whatnot. But I told him not to give me names or to be too intrusive in gaining his information."

"Why?" Sarita asked, sounding a little more curious and less angry.

"Because I did not wish to know who you were dating," he admitted gruffly.

"Why?" she repeated with real interest now.

Domitian raised his head and peered at her briefly, but then admitted, "Because you have been mine since the moment you entered my restaurant with your father at thirteen and I realized I could not read you," he admitted solemnly.

Sarita's eyes widened slightly at this announcement and the possessive way he said it and she was suddenly aware of both his hands curved around her heel, and his breath blowing softly over her foot. Swallowing, she closed her eyes and struggled not to curl her toes as Domitian returned to his efforts, adding, "I did not want to know another male might be kissing you."

Sarita bit her lower lip and dug her fingernails into her hands as she not only felt his words breathed across her toes, but suddenly had an image in her mind of this man kissing her, his arms tight around her, his fingers pulling her head back, his hips grinding against her as his tongue swept through her mouth. Frightened by the wave of need that rolled over her, Sarita forced her eyes open, banishing the image.

"Or caressing your luscious breasts," Domitian continued. His fingers shifted, brushing over the sensitive skin of her instep, but it was Sarita's breasts that tingled in response. Her nipples even hardened as if he was doing what he was speaking about and she closed her eyes briefly again, only to be assailed by a sudden vision of Domitian peeling her nightgown down away from her breasts and covering them with his hands.

"Or stripping your clothes away and exploring your hidden depths with his lips and tongue and body."

Sarita shook her head and forced her eyes open to see that his gaze was sliding along her leg, following an invisible path to her core. It was just a look, but she could almost feel his touch there, and she foolishly closed her eyes again as a shudder ran through her. This time the vision that filled her mind was of his kneeling between her legs, tugging her forward until she perched on the edge of the counter and then kissing a trail up one thigh to the strip of white cloth between her legs.

"Oh God," Sarita gasped, startling herself. She blinked her eyes open with confusion just in time to see Domitian getting to his feet and setting the tweezers on the counter.

"All done," he said lightly, turning back to her. "That was not so bad, was it?"

Sarita stared at him blankly, her body throbbing with need, and then raised a hand to her forehead and shook her head. "I don't—"

She closed her eyes again and sucked in a breath as the imaginary Domitian was immediately there, tugging the silky cloth of the thong aside and burying his head between her thighs so that his tongue could rasp across her sensitive flesh.

"Sarita? Are you all right?"

She opened her eyes to find that Domitian had bent toward her as he asked the question. His face was directly in front of hers, his lips just inches away, his breath sliding over her lips and setting them tingling too.

Growling, Sarita caught him around the neck and tried to pull him closer, wanting—no, needing—to kiss him. But Domitian resisted and reminded her, "You said n—"

"Shut up and kiss me," Sarita snapped, and much to

her relief he did. His mouth immediately shot down to cover hers, his tongue sweeping out to slide between her lips just as it had in her mind moments earlier.

His kiss was hot and deep and so sweet that she almost didn't notice his hands sliding under her bottom and lifting her as he straightened. She did wrap her legs around his hips, though, when his hands shifted to her upper legs and he urged them up and apart. Sarita groaned into his mouth as their groins rubbed against each other, the action sending a wave of liquid fire rolling through her body.

Trembling in its wake, Sarita kissed him desperately and shifted her hips to bring about the sensation again. She felt Domitian's hand tugging at the neckline of her robe and gown and briefly broke their kiss to lean back enough to allow him access. She then watched as he quickly tugged the material of both items down, freeing her breasts. Her nipples were hard and excited, eager to be touched, and Sarita breathed "yes" on a groan when his hand covered one. But she then tightened her arms around his neck and pressed forward, trapping his hand there as she covered his mouth again, silently demanding another kiss.

Domitian answered the call, whipping her into a frenzy with his tongue even as he squeezed her behind and the breast he held. When he then caught her nipple between thumb and finger and rolled and pinched it gently, she cried out into his mouth and broke their kiss to throw her head back as she arched into the caress. She also tightened her legs around his hips and shifted, grinding against the hardness that had grown between them.

Domitian's response was a string of curses through

clenched teeth, and then she felt the edge of the cold counter under her bottom.

Blinking in surprise, Sarita stared at him with confusion, and then uttered a startled gasp as he dropped to his knees before her and simply tore off the hated white thong she wore. When he then buried his face between her thighs, Sarita cried out, her feet slapping against the front of the cupboards and her arms moving back so that she could brace herself on the countertop as she arched, her butt partially lifting off the counter as he set to work.

Domitian didn't just rasp his tongue across her flesh as he had in her imaginings, he devoured her. Holding her legs firmly apart, he used teeth and tongue and lips as he explored every inch of her most sensitive flesh.

Within seconds Sarita was lost. Legs thrashing where he held them pinned open, bottom bouncing, she clawed at his head and shoulders and moaned over and over. And every time she moaned, Domitian groaned in response, his mouth vibrating against her skin and increasing her pleasure twofold and then twofold again.

Just when Sarita was sure she couldn't stand a moment more, Domitian broke off what he was doing, and stood up between her legs. He jerked his boxers down, freeing a truly impressive erection, and then clasped her by the hips and thrust into her.

Sarita wasn't sure what she'd expected, but it wasn't to explode into orgasm with just that first thrust. But she did. She dug her nails into his shoulders and threw her head back on a long scream as wave after wave of pleasure exploded over and around her, drenching her in it, drowning her, until it finally pulled her down with it into the soothing darkness that waited beyond consciousness.

Domitian woke on the bathroom floor with Sarita draped across his chest. He didn't remember passing out and falling back, taking her with him, but he must have. He reached up to feel his head. There was no cut or bump, but there was dried blood. He'd obviously taken a good head banging as he hit the floor. It made him glad he hadn't been awake for it.

Domitian peered down at the top of Sarita's head, glad she had landed on top of him. He never would have forgiven himself if she'd got hurt. Life mate sex could be damned dangerous for a mortal, at least when it ended, and was therefore best performed only on soft surfaces. He knew that, but had got carried away in the moment.

Next time he'd take more care, Domitian vowed silently, and ran a hand gently over Sarita's hair. She'd been even more passionate and responsive than he'd expected when he'd sent those images out to her of what he wanted to do to her. Domitian had merely hoped they would excite her and soften her attitude toward him, so he'd been more than surprised by her reaction. Pleasantly surprised, but surprised. The woman was a powder keg of passion.

And she was his, Domitian thought with satisfaction. Finally, his patience had been rewarded and he was here with his life mate in his arms and all was right with the world.

Well, not all, he thought suddenly as he looked around the room.

Domitian hadn't been thinking very clearly since waking up chained to the table in the basement. He'd like to blame it on whatever drug had been used to keep him asleep, but he knew that wasn't the case. He'd been suffering a bad case of life mate–head; the inability to think past his desire to possess the woman presently lying unconscious on his chest. It had passed for now, but he knew it would be back, and probably at the most inopportune time. Which meant he had to think while he could, and now that he was doing that, several questions were coming to mind.

Where the hell were they?

And why were they there?

His gaze dropped to Sarita and Domitian had a vague recollection of her saying something about Dressler drugging and dropping her here too. Why? What was the man up to? Why had he kidnapped them and then put them together in this house? For that matter, why had he kidnapped all those other immortals? Were they each in other houses, wondering the same thing?

Domitian didn't know, but he was pretty sure that as pleasant as things were at that moment, whatever plans Dressler had for him and Sarita didn't include an ending he would like. They needed to get out of there.

And he needed blood, Domitian thought, becoming aware of the gnawing in his stomach.

Glancing down to Sarita, he gave her a gentle shake to wake her. When that had no effect, he eased her gently off him and to the side to lie on the cold tile, then got quickly to his feet and bent to scoop her up off the floor. She didn't even stir as he carried her into the bedroom and set her in the bed.

Domitian stared down at her for a minute, taking in her sweet face in repose. You'd never guess how prickly and stubborn she could be from how she looked now, he thought wryly. And then his gaze slid down to her body and his thoughts turned to her passion. Her breasts were still exposed above the neckline he'd tugged under them, showing that her nipples were no longer hard. And her legs had fallen open a bit when he'd set her down, leaving a perfect view of what he'd been so eager to taste.

Domitian licked his lips, suddenly hungry to taste her again. He almost did just that, almost crawled onto the bed with her to lick away the dried blood as he'd wanted to do earlier and then taste her essence. It was the licking away the dried blood that kept him from climbing into bed for round two. Domitian would have had no compunction about licking fresh blood from her body should she have freshly cut herself, but dried blood was something else. It was just nasty. Even thinking about doing that told him how much he needed to feed.

Sighing with regret, Domitian turned away and left the room to make his way to the office and downstairs. It wasn't until he reached the bottom of the stairs that he recalled the glass everywhere.

Domitian paused, briefly considering just walking through it again, but that and his head wound were the reason he needed blood again so soon. The nanos had forced the glass from his foot as he'd knelt to remove her splinters. They had also repaired the small cuts from the china as well as his head injury and now needed more blood. There was no sense adding to their need.

Turning on his heel, he returned upstairs to fetch a broom and dustpan from the kitchen.

Sarita stretched happily and rolled onto her back in bed. She felt great. Awesome. Incredible. She hadn't felt this good in a long time, if ever, and she owed it all to—

Her eyes blinked open and she stared blankly up at her own reflection. It told her that she was alone in the bed, but—*Dear God, the ceiling is mirrored above the open bed frame!* How tacky was that? And how had she not noticed *that* when she'd woken up here earlier?

Obviously, she hadn't looked up. Tilting her head, Sarita wondered what it would have been like to have watched her and Domitian having sex. Probably not that great, she decided. Watching herself writhe and moan while Domitian had done the things he'd done . . . well, frankly, it would have taken her right out of the moment.

Which would have been a shame, because she hadn't had her pipes cleaned like that in a heck of a long time, Sarita thought with a grin and then quickly groaned and closed her eyes.

"Snap out of it," she ordered herself grimly, but it wasn't easy. He was *sooo* hot, and man, she'd never experienced sex like that, hadn't even imagined it was possible. Unfortunately, her Catholic upbringing was warring with the woman she'd grown into, an independent female cop who had no qualms about going after what she wanted. It was all leaving Sarita an extremely confused woman. One part of her brain was telling her she had been very naughty and should head to the nearest priest for confession. The other part was suggesting if she was going to have to do penance anyway, she really should find Domitian and jump him again.

Dear God, she'd really done that! Sarita shook her head at her reflection with dismay. After her grand lecture to him that there would be no kissy, kissy, gropey, gropey and *no sexo*, she'd gone ahead and started it herself! *She'd* kissed *him*.

Oh, the shame! Oh, the humiliation! Oh . . . she wanted to do it again.

Opening her eyes, Sarita met her gaze in the reflection above and said solemnly, "You are obviously a very confused woman."

And God, what a mess she was, Sarita thought as she noted the dried blood everywhere. It was on her face, her chest, her hands, legs, and feet. And her nightgown? That was a tangle around her waist leaving everything else bare.

She looked like a two-bit whore whose last John had been a slasher.

"Ugh," Sarita said with disgust and forced herself from the bed. She needed a shower and a good stiff drink. Alternately, she needed a shower and a good stiff Domitian, she thought. And then she shook her head.

"You are incorrigible, Sarita Reyes," she muttered to herself as she headed into the bathroom. "Your father is up there somewhere in heaven, his head hung low with disappointment and shame, and all you can think about is . . ."

Sarita stopped talking to herself as she reached the shower and quickly turned on the taps. But her thoughts didn't stop there, because all she was thinking about as she fetched a towel, shampoo, and soap was just how mind-blowing and hot sex with Domitian had been.

Dressler had said life mate sex was like no other and she couldn't agree more. He'd also said it was overwhelming and stuff, and he hadn't been kidding. If what she had experienced was all due to those nanos he'd mentioned, then damn! They were one fine invention and she was all for them, Sarita thought as she stripped off the ruined nightgown and robe and stepped into the shower to begin shampooing her hair.

Unfortunately, or perhaps fortunately, thoughts of Dressler were enough to dampen her wayward desires and Sarita's mind turned instead to what El Doctor wanted as she rinsed the shampoo from her hair. Why had he put her there with Domitian? Sarita wondered as she began quickly scrubbing the soap over her body, removing the dried blood.

In the letter he'd said he hoped to learn a lot from her stay here. What exactly was it he hoped to learn? He'd already known about life mate sex, so that wasn't it. Unless he had cameras here and hoped to see it for himself.

Sarita stiffened at that thought, and then raised her head and turned in the shower. She spotted one almost at once. It was in the corner of the shower, recessed in the wall, but a tiny lens was just visible if you were looking for it.

Resisting the urge to cover her private bits, Sarita lowered her head, turned her back to the corner, and then stepped under the spray to rinse off. The moment she'd finished, though, she turned off the water and grabbed the towel she'd collected. Rather than dry herself with it, she simply wrapped it around herself toga-style.

Sarita glanced around the bathroom as she stepped out of the shower, spotting three more camera lenses as she did. There was one in each of the other three corners of the room.

"Nice," she hissed under her breath.

Pretending not to have seen them, Sarita walked over and snatched up a hand towel off the rack to dry her hair as much as possible, then ran a quick brush through it before slipping out of the room.

A stop in the closet proved that it wasn't magic and hadn't suddenly produced real clothes for her. Heaving a resigned sigh, she went through what was available and chose a short, red-and-black lace-and-satin night-gown that at least had substance to its very short skirt.

"And that's all it has," Sarita grumbled once she had it on and saw that the lace top showed as much as it hid. She could clearly see the outline of her breasts, but at least a couple of strategically placed lace flowers mostly hid her nipples. Shaking her head, she didn't bother with shoes, but hurried out of the bedroom in search of Domitian.

A search of the living room, dining room, and kitchen did not turn up Domitian. Though, she did spot more cameras, four in every room. She should have checked the bedroom too, but now supposed she needn't bother. If the bathroom wasn't sacred, the bedroom definitely wouldn't be.

The office was empty too but also had cameras, Sarita noted as she rushed through it to make her way quickly downstairs. She didn't, however, spot any in the room at the bottom of the stairs. Probably because the walls were stone and cameras couldn't be recessed in them. Possibly also because the room was unpleasant, damp, and smelly. He wouldn't imagine they'd do anything there.

Sarita was halfway across the floor before she noticed that the glass had all been cleaned up, but barely gave it a thought as she hurried into the abandoned lab.

"Domitian." She scowled when she spotted him by the refrigerator. She'd started to worry that he'd been removed while she'd slept, and here he was chowing down on more blood, she thought with irritation as he removed an empty bag of blood from his mouth. The last of four, she saw, counting the empty bags already on the counter.

*"Mi Corazon,"* Domitian greeted with a smile as he tossed the empty bag next to the others and moved to meet her. As he walked his eyes dropped with appreciation down over the nightgown she wore.

Noting that his blue eyes grew more silver with each step and recalling that they'd burned a brilliant silver as he'd made love to her upstairs, Sarita began to back warily away. Putting her hand up, she said *no* firmly, her gaze skating around to find the cameras in the corners. Not in the walls this time, but recessed in the trim on top of the upper cupboards.

Eyebrows rising, Domitian paused and Sarita hesitated. She wanted to talk to him about Dressler and why they were there, but not around the cameras. She didn't doubt for a minute that they recorded audio as well as video, and she didn't want Dressler knowing what they were talking about.

"Not here," Sarita said finally, and then tried on a

pouty moue for the cameras that she suspected looked more like a grimace and said, "The floor is too hard."

"Ah," Domitian breathed, moving forward again. The silver had receded a bit in his eyes at her *no* but came surging back now, and Sarita's body responded, producing liquid like Pavlov's salivating dogs. Only her salivating was much lower and warmer.

"Come. We will go upstairs," Domitian breathed, slipping his arm around her and urging her toward the door.

"Yes," she muttered, unable to resist leaning into him as his hand ran down her side from her waist to her hip and lower, before sliding up under her nightgown to clasp one round cheek. It was only then Sarita realized she'd forgotten to hunt for a thong to wear under the skimpy gown.

"Oh boy," she breathed, and then slipped away from his caressing hand and stepped determinedly in front of him as they reached the bottom of the stairs. Whispering so the cameras in the other room wouldn't pick up her words, she said, "We need to talk,"

Misunderstanding her whispering, Domitian stiffened at once and glanced up the stairs. "Is someone here?"

"No," Sarita assured him, patting his chest reassuringly. At least it started out a reassuring pat, but turned into a pawing pat. He had such a lovely chest she just couldn't resist touching it.

"*Mi tresoro?* What is it?" he asked softly. Unfortunately, he also clasped her arms and then ran his fingers lightly up and down them as he waited.

The simple touch was very distracting and Sarita found herself shivering as it sent tingles slipping through her again. She didn't even really notice herself inching closer to him until her nipples brushed against his chest through the lace top of her nightgown. Already semi-hard, they turned to stone then as excitement raced through her, and a little *ahhh* slid from her lips.

"Ah, Sarita. *Besame*," Domitian breathed the demand that she kiss him, his head lowering toward her.

"No!" She turned her head abruptly away, scowling again with irritation at how distracting the damned man was. It was bad enough fending him off without her own body betraying her like this. "No kissing. I need to talk to you," Sarita added quietly. "We have to get out of here."

"*Si*," he agreed. "Talk. I will listen." Domitian began kissing her cheek, since that was all that was available to him, and then trailing his lips to her ear.

Sarita snapped her mouth closed to keep from moaning at the sensations his actions sent washing through her. She raised her hands to his shoulders, intending to push him back. Instead, she found herself clutching at him and arching as he nibbled on her tender lobe.

"*Mi Amante*," Domitian breathed, his arms slipping around to cup her behind and lift her up against him so that he could pepper kisses down her throat. "*Tu eres la mujer mas bella que he visto. Tue eres mi luz en la oscuridad.*"

*You are the most beautiful woman I have ever seen. You are my light in the dark,* Sarita translated in her head and then shook it to try to force the love words out and concentrate. "I really—we need to talk," she said breathlessly.

"*Si*," he breathed, easing her back to her feet. "Talk."

"Good," Sarita said with relief and tried to gather her thoughts again.

"I like this nightgown," Domitian murmured, one hand rising to toy with a nipple through the lace.

"That's not very helpful," Sarita growled as he caught the excited tip through the cloth and pinched it between thumb and finger. When his other hand then slid under the skirt of the nightgown again and clasped her bottom, Sarita was sure she was lost . . . until his fingers began a lazy meander around in front and along the top of her tender thigh. It was the first time she'd felt pain since cutting it. All she could think was that he'd unintentionally caught the skin of the cut and pulled it slightly. Whatever had happened, it was enough to help her fight off her attraction to him and pull back. When Domitian tried to follow, she slapped him sharply across the face and hissed, "Snap out of it! We have to talk about Dressler."

# Five

Domitian gave his head a shake and peered down at the little spitfire in front of him. Her face was flushed with desire, her lips full from his kisses, but her eyes were on fire with fury, passion, and despair. It was the despair that reached through his surprise and anger at her slapping him and brought on immediate calm.

They were in a tenuous position and needed to find a way out. The desire and need they were both obviously experiencing was playing havoc with their ability to do so, and they *were* both suffering under that desire and need. He could see it in Sarita's face. But she was trying to fight it while he had followed his growing erection across the room, thinking only of plowing it deep into the woman presently trying to come up with a way to save them both.

Letting his hands drop away, Domitian straightened and took one slow step back. He nodded and then, voice flat, said, "You are right. We should talk."

He saw regret flicker briefly across her face, but Sarita took a small step back and simply asked, "Do you know why we were kidnapped?"

After a hesitation, he said, "I was kidnapped because I am immortal. Dressler has been collecting immortals for the last couple of years."

"Do you see any other immortals here?" she asked dryly and then pointed out, "And I'm not immortal."

Domitian shook his head slowly, and then eyed her with curiosity and asked, "You have some idea why we are both here?"

Sarita sighed, and nodded unhappily. "Dressler has been experimenting on the immortals he took."

"Experimenting how?" Domitian asked at once with concern.

"I only know about one experiment, but it was absolutely awful," Sarita said grimly and quickly told him about the experiment she'd interrupted and then inadvertently helped with.

"At the end he explained about the nanos that made your kind immortal, and mentioned that my life mate was coming." She frowned and then added, "Before that though, he said he'd made it his business to find out everything he could about your kind. I'm quite sure this experiment was just one of many. I wouldn't be surprised if every one of the immortals he has is strapped to a table with different limbs or pieces missing. The man is sick."

"*Madre de Dios,*" Domitian breathed. His stomach was now churning at the thought of what the one immortal Sarita had seen had suffered and what the others might even now be going through. The worse part was he knew some of those immortals. Hell, he was related to four of them. Glancing at her sharply, he asked, "What color eyes did the man you saw have?"

She appeared surprised at the question, but then thought briefly before saying, "He only opened his eyes once and it was quick, but I remember thinking they were the most beautiful silver-green eyes I'd ever seen."

"Green," Domitian breathed with relief.

"What is it?" Sarita asked with a frown. "Do you know one of the immortals on the island?"

He wasn't surprised she'd guessed that. The woman was smart and a police officer. She was probably trained to put clues together.

"*Si*. Or at least I know five men who have gone missing and suspect they are on the island," he admitted, but he didn't mention that one was his uncle Victor and another three were his cousins Lucern, Nicholas, and Decker. The fifth man, Santo Notte, was related only by marriage and very loosely at that. He also didn't mention his aunt by marriage, Eshe Argeneau, or her partner Mirabeau La Roche.

"I'm sorry," she said solemnly and Domitian winced as her words made him realize that while none of his relatives could be the man cut in half, they were probably being subjected to other, equally horrible experiments as she'd suggested.

Concern and guilt battled within Domitian as he realized that while his relatives were suffering unknown horrors, he'd been dropped into a tropical paradise and was mating with his life mate. Shaking his head, he paced away, and then returned, growling, "Why am I here? Why am I not in a lab being cut up? Why is he not experimenting on me?"

"I think he is," Sarita said quietly.

Domitian stopped midstep and whirled on her. "What?"

She shrugged and gestured to the nightgown she wore and pointed out, "He put us here in this honeymoon haven, left only skimpy gowns for me and boxers for you, along with lots of food, wine, blood for you, and a *very* big bed."

"*Si?*" he said, not seeing how that could be an experiment.

"He said he'd made it his business to learn everything about immortals," Sarita pointed out. "I think that must include seeing firsthand the life mate sex he's heard about. There are cameras all over this place. At least inside. I didn't look to see if there are any outside."

She frowned briefly and then shrugged. "I suspect this is part one of the experiment—watching us mate in a natural habitat. The next part is probably to force us to mate in a lab with electrodes all over us to measure heart rate and whatnot, and then take blood tests before, during, and after to check for hormone levels and such."

"*El es el Diablo,*" Domitian breathed with horror.

Suffering the physical pain this man was likely putting the others through was bad enough, but while Sarita tried to hide it, he could see that the idea that someone had filmed and watched their private moments upset her. He couldn't imagine how being forced to perform sexually in a lab with electrodes and whatnot would affect the petite woman before him. And he wouldn't have it, Domitian thought grimly. They would not be making love again until they were away from here and safe.

"Of course," Sarita said now, a scowl on her face, "he could have taken our blood after we . . . you know . . .

banged upstairs in the bathroom," she said, flushing a bit. "I lost consciousness. He said that happens, but I woke up in bed instead of on the floor and he could have—"

"I moved you to the bed when I woke up," Domitian assured her and then said stiffly, "And we did not *bang*, we made love."

Her eyebrows rose slightly. "I'm pretty sure you have to love someone for it to be making love, and I don't love you. I don't even know you."

Domitian knew he shouldn't be hurt by her words, but he was. It reminded him that while he'd known for a decade and a half that she was his life mate and had followed her life, coming to admire, respect, and care for her over the years, she'd never even heard his name until just hours earlier. He put that issue aside for now as another cropped up in his mind. "Wait, this cannot be an experiment. There is no way Dressler could know that you are my life mate."

"He does," Sarita assured him. "He told me in the lab, and then he talked about how hot life mate sex is and stuff in the letter he left."

"The letter. Where is it?" Domitian asked at once.

"It's on the desk in the office," she admitted, but caught his arm as he turned toward the stairs and reminded him in a quiet voice, "There are cameras everywhere up there, and in the lab down here too. We need to watch what we do and say."

Domitian's expression tightened. Giving a short nod, he caught her hand and led her back upstairs.

The letter was on the desk where she'd left it. Domitian urged her into the desk chair, and then settled on the corner of the desk and quickly read the message.

Unlike her, he only paused to comment once while reading it and that was to curse.

"What?" Sarita asked curiously.

"He knows my name," Domitian said on a sigh.

"Okay," she said, narrowing her eyes. "Was he not supposed to?"

He shook his head. "I have lived under the name Diego Villanueva for the last five years, and that was the name he hired me under."

"Hired you?" Sarita asked with surprise.

"*Si.*" Domitian supposed she'd assumed that he'd just been abducted off the street or something like the others, so he explained, "Dressler has been offering me a job for years and I always refused. But when this kidnapping business was tracked to him, I accepted his offer. The bastard played me from the start," he added grimly. "He knew my real name all along."

"What job did he hire you for?"

"Chef at his home on the island."

Sarita nodded slowly. "Yeah, he played you. Aleta is the cook there and she's amazing. He wouldn't replace her," she said with certainty.

"I am a master chef, trained at all the best European schools," Domitian said a little stiffly.

Sarita shrugged that away as if all his training and skills were of little import and then asked curiously, "So why have you been living under the name Diego Villanueva for five years?"

"Immortals live a long time and do not age. We have to move every ten years to avoid mortals noticing."

"Ah," she murmured with understanding. "What was your name before Diego?"

"My true name, Domitian Argenis," he answered

promptly. "And when I leave here I will be Domitian again. Diego the chef has left the restaurant and moved on to greener pastures."

"And no one will recognize that Diego is Domitian?" Sarita asked dubiously.

Smiling faintly, he explained, "I have several restaurants. I will not return to the same one. The manager there will continue managing and reporting to me for another ten years and I will move on to another restaurant or start a new one."

"Right," Sarita murmured and then turned the subject back to where it had started and asked, "So how do you think he knew about me and this life mate business then?"

Frowning, Domitian turned his attention back to the letter and read the rest, but mostly it was just Dressler saying he hoped to learn a lot from their stay in his "home away from home" before he signed off.

Domitian shifted his gaze back up the letter to the part about Sarita being his life mate and that while she didn't know him, they had met when she was thirteen and he'd kept track of her ever since using a private detective. The man seemed to know everything regarding him and Sarita, he noticed with bewilderment.

"I do not know how Dressler knows," Domitian said finally, tossing the letter on the desktop. Meeting her gaze he assured her, "I told no one you were my life mate."

"What about this private detective you hired?" she asked. "Could he have—?"

"No," Domitian said at once. "He is mortal. He knows nothing about immortals and life mates and I did not educate him in the matter."

Sarita accepted that, but then tilted her head and asked, "So what reason did you give the detective for why you were having me followed?"

"Ah." Domitian shifted uncomfortably, grimaced and then admitted, "I told him that your mother was my sister, but that your father and I had a falling out and he would not let me see my only living blood relative anymore. I said I wanted him to keep track of you so that once you were an adult and could make your own decisions I could contact you and you could decide whether you wished to see me or not."

That seemed to shock Sarita. Eyes wide with disbelief, she asked, "You told him you were my *uncle*?"

"Well, I could hardly tell him the truth," Domitian pointed out, defensively. Scowling, he added, "I do not see why it would bother you anyway."

"Hmmm, I don't know," she said dryly. "Why would it bother me for people to think I was playing patty cake with my uncle?"

"Patty cake?" he asked with bewilderment.

"Bumping fuzzies," she said and when he still looked blank added, "Shaboink."

Domitian just shook his head with bewilderment. He had no idea what she was talking about.

"Never mind," Sarita muttered and then sighed and pointed out, "Anyway, we still don't know how Dressler knew you thought I was your life mate."

"I do not *think* you are my life mate, I *know* it," he said firmly. "And you should know it too after what happened in the bathroom."

"Yeah, yeah, it was mind-blowing sex and I fainted," she admitted. "Whatever. That still doesn't explain how Dressler knew."

"No, it does not," he admitted and pondered that briefly and then shook his head. "I have no idea how he found out."

"Well, I guess we can ask him when he comes to get us for part two of the experiment."

Domitian peered at her silently. While her words were light and slightly sarcastic, he could see the fear in her eyes. She was terrified they would not escape and would be forced to take this experiment, if that's what it was, to the next level. He wasn't going to let that happen, however.

"I think we need a swim to relax," he announced suddenly, catching her by the arm and urging her toward the door. He actually got Sarita halfway across the room before she jerked her arm free and spun on him.

"A swim? Are you kidding me?" she demanded.

"I think better after a swim," Domitian said mildly, but jerked his eyes toward the nearest camera as he added, "Trust me. Go get changed and I will fetch towels."

Judging by the way Sarita suddenly calmed and turned toward the door, she'd got his message. "Fine. I'll meet you by the pool."

"Yes," he breathed with relief and waited until she left. Domitian then said, "Towels," and turned toward the French doors. He slid out onto the side terrace and headed for the French doors to the kitchen. A quick glance ahead, and another back the way he'd come as he slid into the kitchen proved that there were no cameras mounted on the side wall of the house.

All Domitian could find in the half bathroom off the kitchen were a couple of hand towels. Shrugging, he took them, and then slipped back outside through the French doors again. He walked around the house to the pool so that he could check the front of the house and the side the pool was on as well. No cameras outside then, he noted as he paused and glanced along the back of the house where the bedroom and en suite bathroom were.

That was something, at least, Domitian decided and carried the towels over to drop them on one of the lounge chairs. At least they could talk out here without the fear of being listened to. It was why he'd suggested a swim. Also, a quick dunk in the cold pool would hopefully help keep their minds on track if they got distracted from their objective.

That thought in mind, Domitian walked over and dipped a toe in the water to test the temperature.

"How is it?"

Glancing around he saw Sarita approaching in a hanky torn into three tiny triangles that were taped over her important bits. At least that's what it looked like. The bikini bottom had less material than the thong she'd worn earlier, and the bits of cloth over her breasts barely covered her nipples let alone her breasts.

"*Dios,*" Domitian breathed and thought with horror that Dressler was a diabolical bastard.

Sarita slowed as she noted Domitian's expression. The bathing suit she had on, if it could be called that, was the biggest one available. Not big in size—they were all her size—but this one had offered the most material, covering more than the others would have. It still covered very little.

Sarita kept in shape for work. She did a hundred sit-ups and push-ups every morning and night, and then did an hour of cardio every evening after dinner to stay fit and in good running order to chase down perps. She was extremely fit.

Unfortunately, she also liked to eat, and the combination left her fit but still overly curvy. She had thighs
and hips she felt were too big and a muffin top that
made her groan with despair. However, her body was
her body and after a quick grimace on seeing herself in
the bikini and noting what it exposed, she'd shrugged
and headed out with her head held high.

Now, on spotting the horror on Domitian's face,
though, Sarita narrowed her eyes and stopped, almost
daring him to say something insulting about how she
looked in the swimsuit.

She didn't have long to wait.

"How is a man to think with his woman looking like
this?" Domitian exploded, waving at her as if she were
a nightmare. "Look at you! Your beautiful breasts over-
flowing those little patches of cloth. You might as well
not even be wearing the top! And those little straps that
make up the bottoms. They just draw the eye to your
luscious hips and your shapely legs. *Oh Dios!* Your
legs! I just want to lick and kiss my way up their gorgeous length. No! I want to lick and kiss every part of
your beautiful body, and then—" He broke off, almost
gasping, and then turned and plunged into the pool to
start swimming toward the waterfall.

Sarita stared after him rather blankly, her mind slow
to understand what she'd just heard. She'd thought him
horrified because of how she looked, and he was, but
not in the way she'd expected. Good God, the things he
wanted to do to her. Domitian would give good phone
sex—that was for sure. His words alone had left her
standing there wet and aching for the pleasure she already knew he could give her. And she couldn't do a

damned thing about it. They had to work out a plan to get off this island, and she was guessing that was why Domitian had suggested the "swim." He had been thinking that there were no cameras here.

She glanced around the pool, eyeing the forest suspiciously. There could be cameras in there that they couldn't see. It didn't matter, however. Being overheard was the main concern and the sound of the waterfall would cover any conversation they had so long as they kept it down. The problem was controlling themselves long enough to talk and come up with an idea to get out of there, and that was starting to seem impossible.

"God, I need a drink," Sarita muttered and glanced over her shoulder toward the house, but turned back quickly at the sound of splashing.

Domitian had surfaced after one lap and was now walking up the pool stairs, the water falling away with each step to reveal his gorgeous shoulders, his wide chest, his flat stomach, and—

Good God, he'd said she might as well not be wearing the top, but he might as well take off his boxers. Soaking wet, they clung to him like a second skin, and were doing nothing to hide the amazing erection he was sporting. It was pointed straight at her, and he was following it she noted, taking a wary step back.

"I need you, *mi Corazon*," Domitian said helplessly.

"No," Sarita said firmly, taking another step back. "We need to figure out how we're going to get out of here."

"We will walk out at nightfall," he announced, continuing forward.

"But how? If Dressler knows we're trying to leave,

he could send men after us. Hell, there could be a fence around this place a mile into the woods where his men are waiting to stop us."

"We will worry about that after I make love to you," Domitian assured her soothingly. "But now . . ." He shook his head helplessly, and gestured toward his penis. "I cannot think like this, *querida*. I need you. I need to fondle and kiss your sweet breasts and suckle your nipples with my lips. I need to feel and taste your wet heat on my tongue, and then bury myself in your warm, hot body and feel you squeeze and milk me as I thrust into you until we both scream our pleasure."

"We'll faint," Sarita protested weakly, continuing to move back.

"*Si*, but it is only midafternoon, we have time."

"The cameras," she protested with a little more strength, and her face went grim as she recalled them. Her voicing that worry had been a desperate attempt, but now that they were in her head, they were an issue. She had no desire to be a porn star for the likes of El Doctor.

"The cameras are inside. We are outside," he said gently.

"There might be cameras out here," Sarita pointed out stubbornly, not backing up anymore, but staying put and crossing her arms forbiddingly. "But even if there aren't, we could be seen by the cameras in the living room."

Domitian paused, a frown furrowing his brow as he considered the problem and then he brightened. "The pool."

"We'd drown when we passed out at the end. At least I would," she pointed out.

"Oh, *si*," he muttered and considered the problem

again, and then said, "Come. I have an idea." Catching her arm, Domitian turned and tugged her to the nearest lounge chair where he released her and dropped to sit halfway up, his legs on either side and feet flat on the stones that made up the terrace floor.

"What are you—?" she began with confusion and then gasped with surprise when he caught her by the upper legs, turned her, and tugged her down to sit in the V his legs made.

"There. See?" Domitian murmured, brushing her hair out of the way so that he could press kisses along her neck.

"No, I don't see," Sarita muttered, trying to get back up.

"All the cameras in the living room see is my back," he whispered by her ear before giving it a nip.

"True," she said and her attempts to remove his hands from her waist and get up weakened a bit, but only a bit before she said, "What if there are cameras in the trees?"

"They will see nothing I promise. Watch."

Sarita had no idea what she was supposed to watch until one of his hands left her waist. She glanced around curiously to see that he'd reached behind him to retrieve a . . . towel? She blinked at the tiny hand towel and shook her head. "*Those* are the towels you brought for us?"

"It was all I could find in the small bathroom off the kitchen," Domitian said with a shrug and opened the towel to rest it on her chest and stomach. Sarita stared down at it with bewilderment until he slid one hand under the towel, and then up under the ridiculously tiny bathing suit top she wore.

Gasping, she pressed back against him with her

shoulders while her chest arched upward into the palm that suddenly covered her breast.

"You see? No one will see anything."

Sarita gave a breathless laugh. Her voice was equally breathless as she writhed between his chest and fondling hand and gasped, "So you're . . . just going . . . to grope me . . . to orgasm."

"Oh, much more than that, *mi amor*," he assured her, sounding a little breathless himself, and then his other hand slid under the towel and down between the cloth of the bikini bottom to cup her between the legs.

Sarita jumped in his arms and gasped as he slid a finger smoothly inside her.

"Much more," Domitian assured her on a groan as his thumb began to slide around the nub above where his finger was plundering her.

Sarita groaned in response, but started to shake her head. Turning to try to glare at him, she said, "You can't—"

Her protest ended abruptly when his mouth covered hers, his tongue slipping in to silence her own.

Sarita shuddered, her hips moving of their own accord to the dance he was leading, her tongue tangling with his. She lifted one hand to cover his where it remained at her breast, encouraging him as he began to pluck at and toy with the nipple of first one breast and then the other. The combination of everything he was doing was driving her to a fever pitch. Whoever said making out and just hitting first, second, and third base without making it to fourth wasn't very satisfying, had obviously never had an immortal life mate running those bases. The man was driving her wild. One more minute of this and she would—

Sarita's thoughts died abruptly as he slid a second finger in to join the first and her body went off like a rocket. Grabbing for his hands, she tore her mouth away to cry out, vaguely aware that he was shouting as well, and then sunset came early for her as Sarita's mind shut down.

She woke up some time later to find herself reclining on Domitian Argenis's chest as he ran his fingers lazily up and down her arms. He might be a great lover, but he made for a lumpy bed, she decided and immediately sat up. This time he hadn't carried her to the bed. They were still on the lounge chair by the pool.

Sarita caught the hand towel as it started to fall, but on checking to see that her bathing suit was in place and covering as much as it had before this little side excursion, she let the towel drop away and turned to scowl at Domitian as he sat up. "That wasn't fair."

His eyebrows rose in question. "What, *mi amor*?"

"First you made a meal out of me in the bathroom and now you . . ."

"Pleasured you?" he suggested.

Sarita flushed and turned away. "Yeah, that, here. Meanwhile, you haven't got a thing from it," she muttered, and tried to stand up, only to have him catch her shoulder and keep her on the seat.

"*Si, mi Corazon*. I have."

"What?" she asked with disbelief. "You—"

"I got great pleasure from both joinings."

Sarita clucked her tongue with irritation and tried to remove his hand from her shoulder so she could get up. "There was no joining. Well, I suppose there was for half a second the first time," she added dryly. "But there was no joining this last time. You just—" Her words died abruptly as Domitian released her shoulder to slide down to catch her hand and drag it back to cover the front of his boxers. He was already semierect, or perhaps still semi-erect, she guessed, but at her touch, began to grow. Sarita didn't notice at first, she had frozen, shocked and confused by the excitement and pleasure that jolted through her the moment her hand touched him.

"That is how we joined," Domitian said, his voice gravelly with passion.

Sarita turned slightly on the end of the lounge chair to look at him, and then glanced to where her hand was touching him as her movement accidentally shifted her hand, sending another thrill of pleasure through her.

"It is called shared pleasure," he said, growling now. "It is something only life mates enjoy." Covering her hand to keep it still, Domitian added, "I felt every moment of your pleasure, experiencing it as if it were my own. And at the end, my shout of pleasure joined yours and we both lost consciousness."

"Really?" She glanced to his face with interest.

"*Si*. Really."

"That's a pretty nifty perk," Sarita admitted, and slid her hand inside his boxers to pull him out. He was surprisingly sensitive, she found. Just doing that had jolt after jolt of pleasure riding through her.

Domitian bit back a groan and tried to remove her hand. "*Si*. Now let go, turn around, and let me—"

"No," she said, shifting to kneel on the concrete in front of the chair instead, never releasing her hold on him as she did.

Domitian groaned, but then caught her hand to stop

her and asked, *"No?"* with bewilderment. "But I want to touch you."

"Too bad," Sarita said with a shrug. Offering him a wicked smiled, she added, "You've already done that. And I've always wanted to know how good I was at BJs."

"BJ? That is—Ah yes, that is what I thought it was," he said faintly as she leaned onto the end of the lounge chair and took him into her mouth.

Startled by the tsunami of pleasure that swept through her then, Sarita closed her eyes and nearly bit him, but managed to stop herself at the last moment. Once she felt she was prepared for what was going to come, Sarita began to move her mouth over him, moaning along with Domitian as pleasure immediately began rushing through her again. The vibration from her moan merely added to the pleasure, causing her to moan again, which brought on more pleasure and more moaning. It was like a circle without end, the pleasure building and building with each go-round until she could barely breathe.

*"Madre de Dios*, you are good," Domitian gasped, his butt rising off the seat slightly as he tried to follow her mouth.

Sarita couldn't agree more. Literally, she couldn't agree with him with her mouth full. But she was rather impressed with herself as she drove them both crazy with her lips, teeth, and tongue. She was vaguely aware of Domitian tangling his hands in her hair and clutching her head a moment later. Sarita knew he was saying things, but he wasn't making much sense. Beautiful words in Spanish were followed by the filthiest demands, but she didn't pay them much attention. She was listening to her own body's dictates, applying more pressure now, moving faster, slowing, speeding up, nipping lightly to increase the pleasure she was experiencing. And the entire time, Sarita was moaning, her body trembling on that very edge of the freedom release offered her, and then . . . *bang*! Something snapped and pleasure shot to every corner of her body, filling her and blocking out the light as she sighed and slid into unconsciousness.

# Six

Sarita woke up this time to find her head on Domitian's thigh and his exhausted member passed out in front of her.

It was a heck of a thing to wake up to, she thought wryly as she eased carefully away from him to sit up on the stone floor at the end of the lounger. He was still asleep this time, she noted, which was kind of weird. Domitian had woken up first the last two times today, she thought, and she glanced along his body to his face to see that not only was he still unconscious, but he was also extremely pale.

Sarita glanced up toward the sun and frowned as she tried to figure out what time it was. The sun was making its downward journey, but was still high in the sky so she supposed it must be mid to late afternoon, somewhere between 2 and 4 P.M.

That realization was somewhat staggering. She hadn't even know Domitian a full day yet. It felt like forever.

And really, how stupid was the man to be messing about out here with her where he would pass out under the hot sun? Not once, but twice, mind you. This life mate sex obviously made idiots of its victims. And had it really not even been twenty-four hours since Dressler had knocked her out in his lab with that shot? *Really?* It felt like a week.

Sighing, she got to her feet and then paused in surprise as a wave of dizziness swept over her. Domitian wasn't the only one who'd had too much sun, apparently. While Sarita had grown up in Venezuela, she wasn't used to such concentrated sun and for so long anymore.

She probably needed water, Sarita told herself. She would get some before she went down to get blood for Domitian. She glanced down at him and changed her mind. He looked like death warmed over. She'd get the blood first and then fetch water for herself, she decided, moving cautiously away from the lounge chair and toward the house.

Sarita felt better the moment she stepped inside the shaded house. It was a good twenty degrees cooler than it was outside, the ceiling fans turning slowly and pushing the cooler air around. She actually shivered at the difference as she pulled the door closed and headed for the office and the hidden door to the basement.

Her gaze swept the boxes in the room at the foot of the stairs as she passed through it, and Sarita recalled that she hadn't finished her search of them. She'd return to do that after getting blood for Domitian, she decided as she continued into the old lab to retrieve the blood.

Sarita had four bags in her arms and was backing out of the refrigerator when she felt something brush her elbow. Glancing to the refrigerator door, she saw that there was a piece of tape sticking out with a bit of paper on the end. It looked like something had been taped there but had been torn off.

Letting the door close, Sarita glanced around and spotted a balled-up piece of paper on the floor. Curious, she carried the blood bags to the table and set them down, then hurried back to pick up and smooth out the paper. On one side there were four numbers and Sarita grimaced as she recognized them. They made up the combination for the numbered padlock she'd had to pick to free Domitian.

It seemed Dressler had left the combination after all. He'd probably put it in the refrigerator to make sure she did feed Domitian the blood before she freed him. Too bad he hadn't put it on the bags where she might have noticed it rather than taping it to the inside of the door where she'd overlooked it.

"Men," she muttered to herself, and in the next moment silently apologized to men in general for the insult. Dressler was a monster not a man.

There were a couple of words under the numbers and she read them with interest.

*This combination is for you to use to free Domitian AFTER YOU FEED HIM AT LEAST FOUR BAGS OF BLOOD. However, the letter inside is for him. Please be sure he reads it.*

It was a piece of paper, not an envelope, but it still had the crease where it had been folded in half, closing the letter to Domitian inside when taped to the door. Eyebrows rising, Sarita turned the paper over and read the message on the other side.

*Domitian Argenis,*

*This blood is clean and unsullied. It is safe to consume. I offer it as a way to ensure you do not hurt our little Sarita. I know how important life mates are to your kind.*

*Obviously there is something I want from you. I will contact you soon to let you know what that is. In the meantime, please enjoy my home away from home.*

                                        *Dr. Dressler*

Sarita read the note at least three times before balling it up and tossing it on the floor where she'd found it. The message didn't really say much. The blood was obviously fine. At least it hadn't harmed Domitian, although, frankly, she hadn't even considered that it might not be fine.

And Domitian had already told her that life mates were important to an immortal. As for the "obviously he wanted something from Domitian" part, that wasn't really news either. They'd already decided he'd put them there for a reason. But that line troubled her anyway. As did the mention that he would contact Domitian soon to let him know what that something was. He didn't say he'd contact them, just Domitian.

Frowning, Sarita gathered up the blood she'd come down for and headed back upstairs. She was crossing the living room to the doors to the terrace before she realized what she found most bothersome about the letter. It was the fact that Domitian hadn't mentioned it to her.

Why was that? she wondered, pausing by the doors.

Several possibilities filled her mind. Perhaps he had thought it would upset her, which suggested he thought her weak. Or perhaps he hadn't told her because he didn't want her to know Dressler was going to contact him somehow. Or perhaps because he'd already contacted him and told him what he wanted. Perhaps Dressler had told him about the cameras and that he wanted them to have sex. Maybe he'd promised Domitian freedom or something if he performed often and enthusiastically.

Sarita glanced to where Domitian still lay, apparently unconscious on the lounge chair. She briefly considered not taking the blood out to him. She even considered leaving him out there in the sun to fry, grabbing several bottles of water from the refrigerator upstairs, and trying to leave right now on her own. But then she pushed the door open, stepped out, and kicked it closed before walking to the lounge chair.

One glance was enough to ascertain that Domitian was still unconscious and incapable of feeding himself. Sarita dumped the bags of blood on the chair next to his body and then gave him a good slap to try to wake him up so he could feed. When that had no effect, she straightened to consider what she should do.

After a moment, Sarita hurried back into the house and through the living room and bedroom to the en suite bathroom where she retrieved one of the steak knives still lying on the counter. She then fetched a large bath towel as well before hurrying back out to the pool.

Moving quickly now, she covered Domitian with the bath towel from the neck down to prevent further damage from the sun, then grabbed a bag of blood and held it over his mouth. Sarita was raising the knife to puncture the bag when she recalled what Asherah had done in the lab to bring on the immortal's fangs. Pausing, she set the bag down and punctured the tip of her finger instead. It was just a small jab, enough to bring on a bead of blood that she then waved under Domitian's nose.

His nose twitched, and then his mouth fell open and she watched as two of his upper teeth shifted and then slid down, becoming pointy little fangs. Sarita stared at them for a minute, marveling that they looked just like normal teeth when in their resting position, but then she grabbed the bag of blood again and popped it to his fangs. Once she was sure it was fixed in place, cradled in his open mouth, she let go and slowly removed her hand, ready to grab it again if it rolled or shifted and fell off. When that didn't happen, Sarita straightened with a sigh and then left him there and went back inside to get her water. She was quite sure he'd wake up before the first bag was empty and would be able to then feed himself the rest of the bags she'd left him. It hadn't seemed to take much for the corpse guy to come sputtering back to life and he'd apparently been drained.

The bottled water was ice cold when Sarita pulled it from the refrigerator. Hot as she was, she didn't open it at once, but instead pressed it against her forehead and then her cheeks, sighing as it cooled her heated flesh. When she finally opened it and began to drink, she gulped half of it down in one go. Sarita then tossed the cap in the sink and grabbed a second bottle from the refrigerator to take with her before heading for the basement again. She was determined she would finish her search of those boxes this time . . . and the cupboards in the old lab too.

Actually, perhaps she'd start in the lab, Sarita thought suddenly. There might be an old lab coat stashed away in one of the drawers or cupboards that she could wear when she left this place. Even an apron would cover more than anything in the closet upstairs did.

Heck, if there were curtains on any of the windows here, she'd be sewing herself a gown a la *Gone with the Wind*, Sarita thought dryly and then paused at the bottom of the stairs as she thought of the sheets on the bed. She wouldn't even have to sew that, she could just wrap it around herself toga style.

Sarita almost turned to run back upstairs, but then continued on into the lab. It would only take a minute to check the cupboards for a lab coat, and that would be much less cumbersome than the large sheet from the bed.

She started her search with the cupboards along the wall next to the door, quickly opening and closing cupboards and drawers one after the other as she walked along. All Sarita found was dusty old—and probably outdated—lab equipment, a couple of pencils, a stapler, an empty whiskey bottle, and blank notepads.

Disappointed with her results, she moved on to the floor-to-ceiling cupboards along the wall with the refrigerator and freezer. The first cupboard was an old broom closet with a tin dustpan and a broom and mop, both disintegrating with age. The other two cupboards were empty except for hooks, which had no doubt at one time held lab coats.

Sarita almost gave up her search then to go out to the waiting boxes in the next room. But she'd been trained to be thorough in a search, so she continued on to the row of upper and lower cupboards along the wall opposite the door. She didn't expect to find anything of much interest in these cupboards either, though, so was startled to open the first door and find herself staring at several large liquid-filled jars with bizarre shapes floating in them.

Sarita eyed them briefly with bewilderment, and then stepped forward and picked up the center jar of three on the lower shelf. She then drew it closer to her face to examine the contents. For one whole minute she had no idea what she was looking at. Her mind simply couldn't make sense of what she was seeing.

Here was a tiny fist. Here a tiny foot attached to what could be a tiny, malformed leg. Here another tiny foot with a perfect leg, and between the two a tail of some sort. A fish tail, Sarita realized, turning the jar slowly until she could see the head of the bent figure. But instead of a baby's head, some kind of large insect head peered out at her through the clear glass. The sight so startled her that Sarita nearly lost her grip on the jar.

Tightening her fingers at the last moment, she caught the lid of the jar, then quickly set it on the counter and backed away, her instinct to get as far away as possible from the monstrosity.

Sarita stopped after just a couple steps, however, her gaze sliding to the other jars in the cupboard. There were two rows of three, or had been before she'd removed the one she'd just set on the counter. Now her gaze slid over the other jars with a sort of sick fascination. Each held a mutant fetus, what she presumed were partially human babies with atrocious deformities or mutations. There was a perfectly formed fetus with skin that made her think of a salamander. One with a misshapen head and what looked like fur running down its back. Another with no limbs, just a head and trunk, the skin so see-through the organs inside were visible, though those didn't appear to be quite right. Another fetus was almost perfectly formed, but with only four toes and fingers and those sporting long curved claws. The last was just a jellied mass with nothing human about it.

"Dear God," Sarita breathed. She stared at the jars on display for a moment, her stomach turning, and then moved almost without thinking to the next cupboard and opened that door as well, and then the next and the next and the next. Her gorge rose with each door she opened and each set of six jars revealed, until Sarita was gagging on her horror and disgust as she opened the last.

Covering her mouth, she backed away then and simply stared at the varied monstrosities on display, hardly aware of the silent tears spilling from her eyes and running down her cheeks.

These were not naturally occurring malformations. They couldn't be. She was sure they had been engineered. Human DNA spliced with various animal and fish DNA to create atrocities she'd never imagined could exist. It was horrifying. She couldn't imagine how it had been done. What kind of sick psycho could do something so monstrous?

Dressler seemed the obvious answer. It seemed immortals weren't the only thing he liked to experiment on. He liked to play with human DNA too. The real question was why? Why would he do this? What did he hope to get from it?

Footsteps coming down the stairs in the next room caught her ear, and Sarita quickly dashed her tears away. She wasn't a crier by nature. She'd only cried three times in her life; when her mother died, when her grandfather died, and when her father died. Her tears now were an aberration, and one she wasn't willing to share with anyone.

"Sarita?"

Taking a deep breath to steady herself, she turned to see Domitian crossing the room toward her.

"I woke up and you were not—" He paused halfway across the room, concern suddenly flooding his face. "What is wrong? Have you been crying?"

"No," Sarita snapped, and then rolled her eyes with irritation. So much for her attempt to look normal, she thought, but added in a calmer voice, "There is nothing wrong. I was just . . ." She turned, gesturing to the open cupboards and frowning at the jars.

"Ah . . ." Domitian continued forward to stand at her side, his face grim as he looked over the jars. "I saw them earlier."

"I didn't," Sarita responded, her voice hollow.

"Then this must have been a shock," he murmured, slipping a comforting arm around her shoulder.

Sarita didn't respond. She also remained stiff under his arm, unable to relax. It wasn't because of the jars, though. It was that damned letter and his not telling her about it, and her worry that Dressler already had contacted Domitian somehow.

"My uncle said that one of Dressler's men mentioned a host of creatures on the island," Domitian announced now. "Fish people and bird people, and a centaur I think."

"What?" she asked with disbelief, but then she glanced back to the fetus with the fish tail between its legs before letting her eyes slide over the other mutations. She shook her head. "I didn't see anything like that on the island."

"Perhaps they are kept in the labs you mentioned," Domitian suggested.

Sarita nodded slowly. "There were several buildings. I only saw the front room of the first building, though. I suppose he could have had any number of people and things locked up there."

"Speaking of locked up, Dressler did leave you the combination to the padlock on my chains," Domitian announced suddenly.

Sarita stiffened up just a bit more. "Oh?"

"*Si*. It is around here somewhere." He glanced around the floor briefly. "It was taped on the inside of the refrigerator door. It had the combination on the outside and a brief note on the inside saying the blood was unsullied and he would contact us later to tell us what he wanted from us."

Turning back, Domitian grimaced and admitted, "I meant to tell you about it, but when you came down in that little red-and-black nightgown I am afraid I forgot. I can find it, though, if you want to read it. I think I tossed it on the floor somewhere."

"No," she breathed and felt herself relax. He'd meant to tell her and got distracted. That was all. He hadn't been hiding anything from her.

"He is a monster."

Sarita glanced to Domitian to see that his attention was on the jars again. She peered at them herself, and felt a lump forming in her throat. These creatures Dressler's man had mentioned must be his successes, the mutations that had survived. Fish people and bird people, and a centaur? Why would he create such beings? What kind of life could they have in this world? Not that he was allowing them out into the world. At least she hadn't encountered any while on the island. She wouldn't be surprised if they were locked up in his labs, probably being dissected and experimented on just like the immortals.

Suddenly unable to bear it anymore, Sarita stepped forward and closed the cupboard door in front of them. The moment she did, Domitian began to close the others to the left of it and she started to do the same to the ones on the right.

"We have to leave here," Domitian said quietly as they worked together.

"Yes," she said simply.

Once the last door was closed, he moved back to clasp her arms and turned her to face him. Peering down at her solemnly, he said, "Thank you. For the blood. And for covering me. For taking care of me."

"It was nothing," Sarita said, shrugging his hands as well as his words away and turning to lead the way out of the room. And it really had been nothing. It certainly hadn't been taking proper care of him in her book. That would have included staying to feed him bag after bag until he woke up and then making sure he was okay. Not just popping one to his fangs and leaving. But she'd been too angry to do that, angry and suspicious about the letter and his not telling her about it.

No, that wasn't the truth, Sarita acknowledged. She *had* been angry, but it had been because his not telling her about the letter had frightened her. She'd feared what it might mean. She'd thought they were a team trying to escape together up to that point, but the letter had raised doubt in her, and fear. Most anger was based in fear, she knew.

"The sun will be setting soon. I think we should collect some bottled water and some canned goods and leave as soon as possible," Domitian said quietly once they were out of the old lab.

Sarita paused and turned back to point out, "He'll see what we are doing on the cameras and might send men to hunt us down."

"There is nothing we can do about that. We will just have to be quick about gathering things and hope to get out before he can get men here to stop us," he said firmly.

When Sarita frowned and looked uncertain, he pointed out, "We either take a chance and leave now, or wait here for whatever he has in store for us next. What do you prefer?"

"Leave now," she said without hesitation. Putting it that way rather made it obvious that it was the only choice.

Domitian smiled and relaxed a bit. "I am glad to hear it. I was not happy at the thought of having to knock you out and drag you out of here like a caveman."

Sarita snorted and turned to start upstairs, saying, "Knock me out? In your dreams."

"Trust me, in my dreams knocking you out is the last thing I would do to you," Domitian assured her, following. "Unless you count—"

"Don't say it. Don't even think about it," Sarita warned, knowing he was thinking about their postcoital faints.

"It is difficult not to think about it when I am following your perfect behind up the stairs in that ridiculous swimsuit," Domitian assured her. "Why do bikinis no longer have a back on them? Why even wear them at all, if all it is, is a strip of cloth up the crack of your bottom leaving your cheeks on display?" he complained, and then added, "Do not mistake me, it is a beautiful behind you have, but most distracting and—"

"Domitian?" Sarita interrupted as she stepped off the stairs and into the office.

"*Si?*" he asked.

"Stop looking at my butt," she ordered firmly.

He remained silent as they left the office, but as they entered the living room, murmured, "As you wish."

The words made Sarita whip around to eye him suspiciously. The last time he'd said that was in response to her lecture about no kissy, kissy, no gropey, gropey, and *no sexo*. And look how that had ended. She suspected the man wasn't as agreeable as he'd like her to believe, and that "as you wish" from him didn't mean what it would from everyone else. She just hadn't figured out what it did mean from him yet.

"Why do you not go take a shower and change into something a little less distracting? I will prepare a picnic for us while you do and we can eat out on the beach," Domitian said loudly, adding a wink in case she didn't understand that he was trying to buy them some time before Dressler would realize they were making an escape attempt.

"Sounds good," Sarita said just as loudly, but turned toward the kitchen instead, adding, "I'll just grab the first aid kit so I can put some antiseptic on the cuts on my legs after I shower."

"There is a first aid kit?" Domitian asked, following her.

Sarita nodded. She'd spotted it on one of her earlier

searches through the kitchen. There was a sewing kit too, and she decided she'd take that to the bathroom with her as well. Sewing a sheet onto herself might be the only way for her to have something that would help her cover up against mosquitos and the other bugs here. She wasn't running through the jungle in a bikini or one of those ridiculous negligees.

"All set?" Domitian asked when she straightened from collecting both kits.

"Yes." Sarita headed for the door adding, "Can you throw some bottled water in the picnic too? I'm pretty dehydrated after spending all afternoon in the sun."

"My pleasure," Domitian said, but he was beaming at her, and she knew he was pleased she'd just given him an excuse to pack the water. It might help keep Dressler from realizing too quickly what they were up to. She could only hope, anyway, Sarita thought.

The moment she stepped out of the kitchen, Sarita's mind turned to what they might need for this escape. The problem was they hadn't discussed how they meant to travel. Did he plan for them to traipse through the jungle or follow the beach?

Following the beach away from here would be easiest and probably safest, at least from whatever animals, reptiles, and insects might inhabit the jungle. On the other hand it left them out in the open and exposed should Dressler realize what they were up to and send men to search for them along the shoreline.

Then again, while heading straight out into the jungle might make for a shorter trip and one where they were less likely to be found again by their kidnapper, it also meant they might be walking into unknown peril. Sarita had lived in the city as a child here, she and her parents living in Caracas before moving to Canada. She had no idea what animals could be found in the jungle around this house, but knew there were tigers and jaguars in Venezuela's Amazonian jungle as well as bushmaster snakes. Yeah, the jungle didn't sound a good bet to her.

Hurrying back through the bedroom to the bathroom, Sarita turned on the shower taps and then went to fetch towels. She meant to grab one, but quickly changed her mind and grabbed four instead, tossing three on the makeup table before taking the other with her to sling over the shower. It had occurred to her that the large towels could come in handy. They could be useful just as towels, but could also be used to bundle everything up in and carry slung over their shoulders like Santa's sack. That was the reason for two of them. The third one was because she was considering turning it into a toga rather than using a sheet. The towels were quite big and should reach well below her knees. They were also thick, offering more protection from bugs and snakes. But aside from that it would demand the least effort. She could wear a swimsuit, wrap the towel around herself and then use one of the large safety pins in the sewing kit to pin the towel closed. She could even use a second one to secure it to her bikini top so that there would be no risk of the towel dropping and tripping her up.

Satisfied with that idea, Sarita stripped off her bikini and stepped quickly under the water.

She took care in washing the cuts along her upper legs as well as those on her feet. And was careful to scrub every last inch of her body to be sure she removed every trace of the dried blood she'd missed during her earlier shower. She even shampooed her hair again to ensure she removed any drops of blood that may have splattered there. With all of that, it still didn't take her more than three or four minutes to shower.

Turning off the water, Sarita tugged the towel off the panel where she'd placed it. She scrubbed her hair with it to dry it as much as possible and then simply wrapped it around herself, toga-style. Grabbing the other three towels as well as both the first aid and emergency sewing kits, she then left the bathroom.

Sarita entered the closet a moment later and quickly went through the swimsuits in the drawers again. She retrieved and donned the most decent of the remaining bikinis, a black number that she hadn't noticed earlier. It actually had more than a thong back unlike most of the others, and the top actually looked like it might at least cover her nipples.

She opened the first aid kit next, considered the contents, and then set to work smearing her injuries with antiseptic cream. Once that was done, she slapped a fabric bandage over each wound, including the ones on her feet.

Satisfied she'd done all she could, Sarita set the first aid kit next to the sewing kit and grabbed one of the large towels. She wrapped it around herself, and then opened the sewing kit to retrieve a couple of the large safety pins to pin the towel into place.

Satisfied, she then turned her attention to the shoes in the closet.

# Seven

Domitian closed the last box along the wall and shoved it away with irritation. He'd come downstairs to finish searching the boxes and see if he could find anything to wear besides the boxers he presently had on. It was a sensible idea. He could hardly go traipsing into the jungle in just boxers. Well, really he could, but Sarita couldn't in a negligee and high heels, and she had mentioned that those were the only clothes available to her here besides bikinis.

Unfortunately his search had turned up nothing. Not only were there no clothes in the crumbling old boxes in the room at the bottom of the stairs, but there wasn't anything else they might use when they left this place either.

Turning away from the boxes, Domitian started for the stairs. He would check on Sarita and see if she was nearly ready. He had set out some things in the kitchen for their supposed picnic, but they would need more than he had out. He just didn't want to bring the rest out until Sarita was ready to go. The more time they had to get as far away as they could from the cottage before Dressler sent his men out to stop them, the better.

He headed to the kitchen first, hoping she might be done with her shower and waiting for him there. Domitian didn't find Sarita, but he did find proof of her recent presence. It looked as if someone had ransacked the place and he was quite sure that neither Dressler nor any of his men were responsible for it the moment his gaze slid over towels, canned food, and a first aid kit.

That was all he bothered to catalog before hurrying to the bedroom. They had to get moving. If Dressler was watching the camera feed, all that stuff on the island would tip him to the fact that a simple picnic wasn't their intention.

A muffled thudding reached Domitian's ears long before he reached the bedroom. Frowning at the sound, he pushed through the door and spotted Sarita almost immediately. There was a closet to the left of the bed that he hadn't noticed before. The door was open and Sarita was sitting on the floor, wrapped in a towel . . . trying to beat a shoe to death with a . . . can opener?

Slowing, Domitian walked to the door and peered down at her.

"Hi," she said, not bothering to glance up.

"Hi yourself," he responded. "What are you doing?"

"Trying to get the heel off this shoe," she answered, and then gave the heel another whack with the can opener before explaining, "I'd rather not go traipsing through the jungle barefoot if we have to go that way."

Sarita paused to examine the shoe she'd been pounding. "The leather feels soft. It might flatten out a bit with a little wear. I just need to get the heel off—"

Her words died as Domitian bent, plucked the shoe from her hand and snapped the heel off with little effort.

"Huh," Sarita muttered, taking the shoe when he handed it back. Pursing her lips, she examined it briefly and then muttered "Thank you" as he bent to pick up the second shoe and snapped off its heel as well.

"We have to go," he said, offering her a hand to get up.

"Yeah. I know." Ignoring his hand, she got to her feet and moved past him into the bedroom. Grabbing two large bath towels off the bed in passing, she led the way to the door.

Domitian followed, his gaze on her legs below the towel she had wrapped around her body. She'd obviously taken a shower as suggested. Her hair was still wet, he noted.

"I gathered together some things we might need before I thought of the shoes," Sarita announced as she led him through the living room.

"That would not be the pile of stuff on the island in the kitchen would it?" Domitian asked with a frown.

"Yes. I thought we could load it all into these two towels and carry it Santa-style." She held up the bath towels she'd grabbed as she spoke.

"Santa-style?" Domitian echoed with bewilderment. What the hell was Santa-style?

"Like a sack," she explained. "We put the items in the middle, gather the ends, and hoist them over our shoulders to carry them."

"Dear God," he muttered with dismay.

"What?" Sarita asked over her shoulder and he could

hear amusement in her voice. "You're a big strong guy. You could probably carry it all by yourself if you had to."

"Yes, but Sarita, we cannot possibly drag everything you have piled in the kitchen with us," he said reasonably. "I do not think everything will even fit in two towels. We would probably need six to fit it all. Surely we do not need all of it?"

They had reached the kitchen by then and Sarita considered the stack of items on the island and snatched up a pile of towels. Tossing them onto the stove, she said, "I suppose we don't need those. The supersized bath towels can do double duty as Santa sacks and towels if necessary."

Domitian raised his eyebrows. That was all she didn't think they'd need? His gaze swept the stack of items and he picked up a plastic box about the size of a ream of paper. "What about this?"

"It's a sewing kit," she explained, taking it away from him and setting it back on the island with the other items.

"You intend to get in a little sewing around the campfire at night?" he asked dryly.

"Not me, but those boxers of yours look kind of flimsy. Catch them on a branch or something else and you might be as good as naked if we don't have something to sew them up," she pointed out, and then shrugged and added, "But I was thinking more along the lines that the sewing kit might come in handy if one of us gets badly injured and needs sewing up. The first aid kit has antiseptic and bandages and such, but nothing to close a deep wound."

That gave Domitian pause. Considering the cuts in her upper legs and the glass in her foot, Sarita was proving almost more dangerous to herself than Dressler was so far. If she continued as she was going, he might very well have to sew up some wound or other at some point. Still, they could just take a spool of thread and a needle. It wasn't necessary to drag the whole sewing kit along with them, he thought and was about to say so when Sarita spoke up again.

"Besides, while it's larger than I'd like, it's a nice flat surface and might come in handy for cleaning fish on, or setting things on that we don't want to get dirty, like bandages. *And*," she added, picking it up again and hefting it. "It's pretty light, so won't add to the weight."

"Very well." Domitian gave in. Her arguments were actually pretty good, but there was still way too much for them to be carting around, so he turned to the island and snatched up a pile of white cloth, only to frown as it unraveled and he recognized it. "Is this your nightgown?"

"It *was* the nightgown I was wearing," Sarita corrected, apparently unwilling to claim it as her own. Picking up a second ball of cloth, she said, "And this is the robe I was wearing. But—" she pulled the hem of the robe over her head and grinned at him through the gossamer material, "—now they're mosquito netting to keep the bugs out while we sleep. I washed the blood out of both of them," Sarita added and then examined the material as she removed it and pronounced, "They're both almost dry already."

It was actually a pretty clever idea, but Domitian didn't say so. He was troubled by the fact that she seemed to think they would have to walk for more than a day to find civilization and help. Or perhaps he was more distressed that he couldn't assure her that wouldn't be the case. Turning to the items on the island, he pulled out a racket next and pursed his lips as he spun it in his hand.

"A tennis racket? Really?" Domitian shook his head. "Where did you even find it?"

"It's a badminton racket," she corrected, taking it from him. "And I found it in one of the wicker storage boxes on the terrace. There was a badminton net too and I considered bringing that, but it's far too big and bulky, so I decided that the racket and stockings would do instead."

"Do for what?" he asked with bewilderment.

"As a fishing net," she said as if that should be obvious. When he merely stared at her blankly, Sarita sighed with exasperation and picked up one of a pair of stockings. Holding the racket up, she explained, "We slice out the strings of the racket so it's a hoop, loop the top of the stocking over the hoop and sew it on, and voila, a net to catch fish." Peering at the silky cloth Sarita smiled wryly and added, "A shame they aren't fishnet stockings, huh?"

Domitian smiled faintly at her joke, but merely said, "That is brilliant." He took a moment to enjoy the satisfaction his compliment brought to her face, but then asked quietly, "But you have canned food and water here too. Do you really think we will need to find fish for supper? Just how long do you think it is going to take us to find help?"

Sarita's pleasure faded at once. Turning back to the island, she set the racket and stockings down and then quietly admitted, "I don't know. But Venezuela's coastline is more than 1,700 miles long. A lot of it is inhabited, but not all, and there are at least four national parks along the coast too that aren't inhabited. I really don't think Dressler would have put us here if it was close to help. Do you?"

"No," Domitian acknowledged solemnly. He'd planned to just pack up Sarita and a few items and charge out of here like a bull charging a red cape. He hadn't considered that it might take longer than he hoped to reach help. Now he considered that and realized this might be more dangerous than he'd first thought. He hadn't considered the effects of trekking for days through the woods without blood to top himself up, or that he might become dangerous to Sarita if that happened. And that was just as a result of the passage of time. It didn't take into account the exertion of the trek, the effects of the heat and sun, or the possibility of injury. Any of those could quickly leave him in serious need of blood and dangerous.

Once those issues were factored in, Domitian began to wonder if this was such a good idea. But they really had no choice.

"Right," he said aloud, straightening and turning on his heel.

"Where are you going?" Sarita asked with surprise.

"I shall be right back," he said instead of answering. "But then we are going to sort through every last item here and get rid of anything that is not absolutely necessary. We cannot possibly take all of this with us."

Domitian didn't wait for her response but made his way quickly to the office and then down into the basement. He'd top up before leaving. Not too much, the nanos would just work to get it out of his system. But Domitian wanted to start out with as much blood in his system as he could safely consume to ensure he lasted as long as possible. He didn't want to harm Sarita.

Trying to distract himself from that worry, Domitian started running through a mental list of the items he'd taken note of upstairs, trying to decide what they could leave behind.

"What time do you think it is?"

Domitian glanced toward Sarita, his mouth twisting with displeasure when he saw how she was flagging under the weight of the "Santa sack" she carried over her shoulder. Despite his determination that they wouldn't take everything she'd collected, in the end they had.

Oh, he'd tried to whittle down the contents, but Sarita had a reason for every item she'd chosen, and her reasons were good. At least they sounded good when she explained them. So they'd ended up piling everything onto the two towels and then gathered the ends making a "Santa sack" each.

While Sarita had teased earlier that he was a big strong guy and could probably carry all of it on his own, her bag was as big, bulky, and heavy as his was. He had tried to take the heavier items in his own bag to lighten her load, but she had refused to allow it, insisting on dividing the items evenly between them and carrying "her share."

The woman was stubborn as a mule, Domitian thought but found his mouth curving into a slight smile at the knowledge. He kind of liked that about her. Oh, not that she was stubborn, really, so much as that she wasn't acting like an entitled princess, expecting him to take care of her and carry the load alone. He liked that she was independent and determined to take care of herself. Still, he hated to see her struggling under the weight of her Santa sack when he could easily carry both without much effort. The problem was finding a way to get her to let him take more of the burden. She was proud and independent. It was tricky.

"Domitian?"

"Hmm?" He dragged his mind from his thoughts and glanced at her face inquisitively.

"What time do you think it is?" she asked, sounding a little annoyed that she had to repeat the question.

Domitian turned his gaze to the darkening sky overhead. In Caracas, the sun rose between five minutes to six and about ten or twelve minutes after six every morning, but it set eight minutes after six pretty much every night. He didn't think the house they'd been put in could be far from Caracas if the doctor had lived in it while first teaching at the university. Shrugging, he said, "Probably a little before six o'clock."

"Dinnertime," Sarita muttered.

Domitian frowned. They'd only been walking for about an hour, but while they'd started out at a quick clip, Sarita had begun to fall behind a bit after the first half hour. It had surprised him. She was a fit woman. But then she was carrying that ridiculously heavy Santa sack. And trudging through the sand took more energy than walking on the hard-packed earth of the jungle would have.

Domitian had wanted to take the jungle route initially, but had quickly changed his mind. It wasn't because of Sarita's argument that they could get lost too easily in the jungle, where they wouldn't be able to see the sun's position to ensure they traveled in a straight line, or that it was likely to be full of poisonous snakes and other dangerous animals. It was more because she didn't have any proper clothes or shoes.

Domitian had been a little stunned when he'd suggested she go dress before they leave and she'd announced that she *was* dressed. And then she'd pointed out that she had the bikini on underneath, that she'd pinned the towel to it, and that it certainly covered her more decently than any of the nighties in the walk-in closet would. He supposed it did. Although he suspected one of the long negligees, while sheer, would have at least protected more of her from insect bites. And that was the only reason he thought that perhaps she should have worn one of those instead. It had absolutely nothing to do with the fact that he was recalling, and missing, the view he'd had of her breasts, stomach, and thighs, not to mention the sexy little thong she'd had on under the gauzy white nightgown he'd seen her in. At least that's what he told himself, but even he wasn't buying it.

As for shoes, even without the heels, the ones she'd chosen made walking awkward for her. The leather may have seemed softer and more likely to flatten out than the other shoes she'd had to choose from, but the soles were not flat. The shoes had retained their form, only now without the heel to offer its little bit of support. The moment she'd put them on and staggered across the kitchen, Domitian's mind had been made up. She couldn't possibly wear the shoes as they were. They would have to take the beach. At least at the start. He planned to soak the shoes in the sea for a while on their first stop to see if he couldn't flatten them out after that for her. In the meantime, he hadn't been willing to risk the jungle with her barefoot. So they'd set out along the beach, determined to keep an eye peeled for approaching boats in case Dressler sent men after them.

Now, though, her comment that it was dinnertime made Domitian glance to Sarita with concern and ask, "When did you last eat?"

Sarita was silent for a minute, and then reluctantly admitted, "Supper last night. If it was last night that Dressler drugged me."

Cursing, Domitian turned to head for the trees that bordered the beach.

"What are you—Hey!" Sarita protested when he snatched her "Santa sack" in passing and slung it over his shoulder with his own makeshift bag.

It said a lot that Sarita didn't protest further, but trudged along after him. That alone told him that she must be on her last leg.

As an immortal Domitian didn't have to eat so long as he consumed blood. Sarita, however, had to eat for energy, and while he'd fed countless times that day and even taken in extra blood before they'd left, Sarita hadn't eaten at all.

He hadn't seen her drink anything today either, Domitian thought with a frown. Here she'd taken care of him, fetched him blood and popped it to his mouth when she woke up on the terrace and he still slept, and he hadn't bothered to even ask if she'd eaten. And he was a chef!

Upset at himself for his lack of consideration, Domitian glared at Sarita when she dropped to sit on the sand with a weary sigh.

"It was foolish of you to go without food," he growled, though he was more upset at himself than her.

"I often do foolish things," Sarita informed him, not

sounding concerned. "It's part of my charm. My father used to say so," she added, and flopped back to lie in the sand.

"He did, did he?" Domitian asked, a reluctant smile tugging at his lips and forcing his anger back. Setting down the bags and dropping to sit next to her, he began going through their contents in search of something healthy for her to eat.

"Yes," Sarita assured him and suddenly sat up to lean past him and snatch a can from the pile of items in the nearest bag. Waving it in front of his face, she added, "Besides, you haven't eaten either."

"No, I have not," Domitian agreed. The difference was he didn't need food if there was blood available. There wasn't blood available to him right now, however, and eating would reduce the amount of blood he would need. Not by that much, but every little bit helped when you were without. Besides, it would lighten the load in their sacks if they ate some of it, but Domitian frowned as he read the label on the can she was waving at him. "Canned fruit?"

"Nourishment and liquid too," she said simply and dropped the can in his lap before reaching for another as well as the can opener. Sarita made quick work of opening her own can, and then handed him the opener and sat back to begin picking fruit out of the metal tin and popping it in her mouth.

Domitian watched her briefly, but then opened his own can and began to eat the fruit inside. It actually wasn't bad, considering, he decided. It wasn't that good either, though.

"So, you are a chef," Sarita commented after they'd eaten in silence for a few moments.

Catching the wistful tone in her voice, Domitian glanced over to see her eyeing the label on her can with dissatisfaction. It seemed she wasn't completely happy with her meal. He couldn't blame her, Domitian decided as he chewed a piece of what he thought might be peach. The can label said mixed fruit, but while the pieces inside were of varying shapes and colors they all seemed to taste the same. He should have made her a meal before they'd left the house, he thought. Something hearty and filling and as delicious as he found her. He would like to cook for Sarita, Domitian thought. He wanted to satisfy all her appetites. Unfortunately, at the moment they didn't have the time for him to satisfy even one.

Deciding to distract them both from what they couldn't have, Domitian picked another piece of fruit out of his can, and commented idly, "Dr. Dressler is your grandmother's employer?"

"Yeah. She's worked for him for . . . God, I don't even know how long it's been," Sarita admitted and then tilted her head skyward and tried to work it out aloud. "Forty-some years, at least," she guessed finally. "My father was a little boy when she started to work for Dr. Dressler," Sarita said. "She apparently worked for him and his wife for eight or nine months before leaving my father and grandfather to move to the island."

"So she lived at home and came here to the house where we were placed at first, and then once they moved to the island she left your grandfather to live on the island permanently?" Domitian asked with interest. This was news to him. The reports from his private detective had only covered the fact that her grandmother still lived in Venezuela, worked for Dr. Dressler, and that Sarita wrote to the woman weekly. It hadn't covered the history of the grandmother. That hadn't been important to Domitian. At least, not until his uncle had arrived in Venezuela with several hunters in tow, claiming Dressler was behind the recent rash of immortals that had gone missing.

"Yes. Well, I don't know if it was just for the job. Maybe my grandfather was abusive or something. I don't know the whole story. It's the one thing Grandmother is reticent about. But, Dad—" she shook her head sadly "—he never forgave her for abandoning them. She apparently tried calling to speak to him, but he wouldn't take the calls, so she started sending weekly letters that he tore up and threw out."

Domitian's eyebrows rose. "Then how did you end up in contact with her?"

"My mother," Sarita said simply.

"How?" he asked. "Did she insist you write her?"

"No." She frowned at the suggestion, and explained, "Grandmother didn't know that Father was throwing out her letters. She must have suspected when she never got a reply, but she kept writing anyway and was still sending weekly letters when he and my mother married. Mom said he never mentioned the letters to her while they were courting, and when the first one arrived after their wedding, she was the only one home to receive it."

"She said she didn't think much of it until she gave it to Dad and he just tore it up and threw it in the garbage, and then left the room. She said he was grumpy the rest of the evening, which was unusual for him, and then was fine after that until the next letter about a week later, and the next. Mother said four letters came in four weeks that he just tore up and threw out, and each was followed by a night where he was angry and miserable to live with. By that fourth letter she'd had enough. She waited until he had slammed from the room as usual, retrieved the letter, and hid it away.

"After he left for work the next morning, she fetched the letter. Then she sat down at the table, taped it back together, and read it. She was shocked when she realized it was from his mother. There had only ever been my grandfather in my father's life since she'd known him and Father had always refused to talk about his mother, so Mom had assumed Grandmother was dead and talking about her was just too painful for him."

Sarita fell silent for a minute and picked up her can again to pluck another piece of fruit out of it. After chewing and swallowing, she shook her head and said, "I don't know what was in that first letter, but my mother decided to write her back herself. Her first note was just to let my grandmother know who she was and that Dad didn't read her letters, but just ripped them up and threw them out."

Sarita smiled faintly. "Mom said she was just hoping that once the woman knew she was wasting her time writing, she'd stop sending letters and upsetting Dad. But a week later another letter arrived, this time addressed to her."

"Whatever was in that letter apparently touched my mom," Sarita said solemnly. "She answered it and every week another letter came addressed to her, and every week my mother answered. She told Grandmother about herself, my father, their life together, and then about me when I was born. She said Dad never asked if he'd received his weekly letter, and she never explained why he wasn't getting them anymore. It became the only secret she ever kept from him."

"When did you find out about the letters?" Domitian asked when she fell silent.

"I was about eleven," Sarita said with a small reminiscent smile that fascinated Domitian. It suggested a softer side to her she seemed determined to keep hidden most of the time.

"I was snooping and came across a box stuffed full of letters," Sarita explained. "Mother had kept every one in case my father ever had a change of heart and wanted contact with his mother. He could read the letters. Instead, I found and read a bunch of them before she caught me. Mother explained how she had come to correspond with Grandmother and made me swear not to tell my father. It became our secret then."

"And you started to write her too," he suggested, but Sarita shook her head.

"No." She peered down into her can of fruit, and swallowed, before saying gruffly, "That didn't happen until my mother died when I was thirteen. When the first letter arrived from Grandmother after that, I wrote her to explain that mother was dead and could not answer her letters anymore. The next letter was addressed to me. We've been writing ever since."

"And your father never knew?" Domitian asked.

"Are you kidding?" she asked with dry amusement. "That man knew everything. He pretended not to know though."

"What makes you think that? Perhaps he did not know."

Sarita shook her head. "There were many times when he got to the mail before Mom or I could. He must have seen the letters. He would have recognized the handwriting, but he never said anything."

"Hmm," Domitian murmured, but asked, "Did your mother ever take you to meet her?"

"No." Sarita shook her head. "Grandmother never left the island or invited us to it."

"Until now," he said.

Sarita frowned now, her lips pursing as she shook her head again. "Actually, she didn't invite me this time either. Dr. Dressler did."

Domitian stilled.

"Dressler called me last weekend," she explained. "He introduced himself as Grandmother's employer, said she'd taken a tumble on the stairs and hurt herself. He said he was concerned. She was older and injuries like hers could lead to complications in the elderly. He felt that a visit from me might help perk her up and ensure her recovery. He asked me to come to the island to surprise her." Sighing, she added, "I had two weeks of vacation coming up. I asked for it off and was on a flight two days later."

"So you got to the island . . . three days ago?" he guessed.

"Four," she corrected. "He called Saturday. I flew out Monday, and then wasted three days kicking up my heels before Dressler knocked me out and brought me here. Today would be the fourth day since I flew here to Venezuela. Unless I was unconscious more than just overnight as I assumed when I woke up here, this is Friday."

Domitian nodded. It had been Thursday when he'd gone to meet the helicopter that he'd thought was to take him to the island. She was probably right that it was Friday. Unless, as she'd said, he too had been unconscious for more than just a night. Pushing that worry away, he asked, "Did you think it odd that it was Dr. Dressler who invited you and not your grandmother?"

"Yeah." Sarita nodded and then shook her head and said, "But no. I thought she'd taken a bad spill and was weak and sick. I thought it was good of him to call me," she added bitterly.

They were both silent for a minute and then she said thoughtfully, "You know, my grandmother rarely mentioned Dr. Dressler in her letters, but when she did it seemed obvious she didn't care for him at all and didn't consider him an "honorable man" as she put it. I should have realized there was something up when he called. Barring that, I should have realized at the airport, or when I got to the island."

"Why at the airport?" Domitian asked with curiosity.

"Because when I landed here I didn't even go through customs," Sarita told him grimly. "We landed on the tarmac. They rolled up one of those portable stair thingies for us to disembark, and when I got to the bottom of the stairs, this big beefy guy in a suit stepped in front of me. He asked if I was Sarita Reyes. I said yes I was and, while everyone else continued into the airport and to customs, he just took my arm and steered me to this jeep. My luggage was already waiting there," she added, and when Domitian's eyebrows rose, she explained, "My seat was on the back of the plane. I was one of the last to disembark. Everyone's luggage was out and on this big metal shelf on wheels on the tarmac when I came out. Well, except my luggage, which, as I said, was already in the jeep."

When he nodded, she continued. "Anyway, the minute the big beefy guy had me in the jeep, it took off and drove farther down the tarmac to where a helicopter was waiting. Big Beefy Guy loaded me and my luggage in, plopped himself down beside me, and we took off and flew to the island. I didn't go through customs or immigration or *anything*," she said and then shook her head. "Jeez, I knew crime and corruption were bad here, but seriously, skipping customs and immigration? Who does that?"

Domitian merely shook his head and didn't bother mentioning that immortals did that on a regular basis. It wasn't germane to the conversation. Besides, Dressler was not immortal, although he had several at his disposal. Immortals he'd kidnapped. Perhaps the man had coerced one of them to handle things at the airport, he thought. If not, it must have cost him a lot of money to ensure Sarita's arrival in Venezuela wasn't recorded. That didn't suggest that his plans for her included her leaving, he thought with concern.

"Anyway, once we got to the island, Big Beefy Guy ordered two men to bring the luggage and then showed me up to my room. I thanked him and asked when I could see my grandmother and he said she wasn't on the island. She was in the hospital on the mainland. But would be home soon."

"I am surprised you didn't demand to go to the mainland to see her," Domitian commented.

"I did," Sarita said grimly. "But Big Beefy Guy said he couldn't authorize that—he said that I would have to wait for Dr. Dressler to return. He was the only one who could give permission for use of the helicopter or boat to take me to the mainland. In the meantime, I should just relax and *enjoy my stay,*" Sarita finished with disgust.

"That must have been frustrating," Domitian murmured.

"Yeah, you could call it that," Sarita said dryly. "Actually, I was super P.O.'d. Especially when I found out that Big Beefy Guy had misled me. He made it sound like Dr. Dressler wasn't on the island and there was no way to contact him. Meantime, Dressler was there on the island all along, just down at his labs."

"How did you find that out?" Domitian asked.

"Aleta."

"The cook?" he asked, recognizing the name.

Sarita nodded and quickly told him about her early dinner in the kitchen and Aleta's having made El Doctor's nutrition drink. "That's when I snuck down to the labs and saw the immortal cut in half."

They were both silent for a minute, and then Sarita frowned and said, "You know, my grandmother started out as a cook and housekeeper for the Dresslers, but as she got older they brought in more help. She mentioned that someone was hired to cook, and then later someone to help with cleaning house, and I got the feeling that now she's more a companion to Mrs. Dressler."

*"Si?"* Domitian murmured, wondering where she was going with this.

"But none of the names matched up," Sarita said now. "I mean, I can't remember the name she mentioned—it was only the once—but I'm pretty sure the cook she named wasn't Aleta."

"Perhaps the first girl left and was replaced with this Aleta and your grandmother just didn't mention it," Domitian suggested.

"Yeah, that's what I thought too, but she also only mentioned one girl being brought in to help with house-keeping and there were at least three at the house," Sarita continued. "And before you say it, yes I know they might have hired more help over the years that Grandmother didn't mention, but on top of that, I didn't once encounter Mrs. Dressler or their son even once while I was there."

"Son?" Domitian asked with surprise. His uncle hadn't mentioned that Dressler had a son.

"Hmm . . ." Sarita nodded solemnly. "Grandmother mentioned him several times over the years. I got the feeling she thought he was the perfect son. His name is Thorondor."

"Thorondor?" Domitian asked, wincing over the un-usual name. Life would be hell for a boy with a name like that. Children could be cruel.

Sarita shrugged. "I guess Mrs. Dressler was a Tol-kien fan. They call him Thorne for short."

Domitian nodded, but suggested, "Perhaps this Thorne and his mother are staying in their apartment on the mainland so that Mrs. Dressler could visit your grand-mother daily." He knew his uncle had sent men to check the apartment on the mainland and found it empty. But Mrs. Dressler and this Thorne fellow could have been at the hospital at the time, he supposed.

"I didn't know they had an apartment on the main-land," Sarita said slowly. "I did think maybe she was on the mainland, though, to visit Grandmother, but . . ."

"But?" he prompted.

She hesitated, and then admitted, "During the three days I was on the island, I wandered pretty much ev-erywhere in that house. Every door was open except for Dr. Dressler's office door and I looked into every room I could." Shaking her head solemnly, she added, "There was no sign of Mrs. Dressler or Thorne. I didn't see either of them, and there were no pictures or personal items to suggest either they or my grandmother ever lived there. Every room, even what was obviously the master bedroom was . . ." Sarita frowned, searching for the words to explain what she'd found. "They all looked unlived in. They were like empty hotel rooms. Furnished and ready for occupancy, but unused at the moment."

"And when I asked Aleta where Dr. Dressler's wife and son were, she just gave me this blank look as if she'd never heard that he had a wife. Then Big Beefy Guy came into the kitchen and told me to stop bothering the staff with questions that were none of my business. He suggested I go out in the garden or otherwise amuse myself."

Domitian shook his head, not sure what to say, or even what to make of this information. He'd never really given Senora Dressler much thought. Ensuring his life mate was safe and finding out the location of the island as well as what Dr. Dressler was up to had been his only concerns when he'd agreed to go.

"As we were walking here I started to wonder if Mrs. Dressler, Thorne, and my grandmother didn't live in the small house," she added thoughtfully.

"The small house?" Domitian asked at once. "What small house? You never mentioned a small house."

"It never came up," Sarita said with a shrug.

"It is up now. Explain," he requested firmly.

She seemed amused by his stiff voice, but said, "When we flew in on the helicopter I got to see the whole island. The fenced-in area with the labs was on the tip of the island as we approached, there was a bit of jungle and then the big house came next with an open area around it. After that there was a large expanse of jungle, but at the very tip of the far end of the island there was a smaller house on the beach with a pool beside it."

"A small house with a pool?" Domitian asked, straightening from where he'd relaxed back against the base of a palm tree. His voice sharp, he added, "Like the house we just left?"

"Yeah. I considered that myself as we were walking," Sarita admitted, sounding unconcerned. "But then I thought about not encountering Mrs. Dressler or her son at the big house and decided they—and my grandmother—probably live in the little house instead. I mean, who would want to live with Dressler? The man's a monster.

"Of course," she added with a frown. "Now that I know about the apartment, I suppose that could be where they are. The big house could be like a cottage. Where they usually stay on the weekends and in the summer when Dressler isn't teaching. That could explain the hotel air to the place." Following that through, Sarita continued slowly, "But if they normally stay in the big house and just aren't there now because they returned to the mainland to stay close to Grandmother, then the little house isn't where they live . . . which means it *could* be the little house that we woke up in after being drugged."

Domitian couldn't have been more stunned if she'd pulled a hammer out from under the towel she was wearing and suddenly hit him with it. For a minute his thoughts were in such chaos, he couldn't even hold on to one.

He'd rushed them out of the house to get her as far away as possible to somewhere she'd be safe from Dressler, and instead might be walking her straight into his arms.

Cursing under his breath, he leapt to his feet.

"Where are you going?" Sarita asked with alarm, getting up as well.

"It is okay. I just want to go a little farther along the beach and see if you are right and we are still on the island," he said reassuringly.

"But what if you're seen?" she asked with concern.

"I will be careful. But I have to see if you are right, *mi Corazon*. If we are on Dressler's island then we have to find a way off it, and quickly. And walking up to the house and asking for a ride is not the way to go about it. Just sit and rest for a bit. I will be back before you know it," he said and then turned and hurried away before she could argue further.

Sarita watched until Domitian followed the curving beach out of sight, and then turned to glance out toward the water. She'd been keeping an eye out for anyone approaching in a boat as they walked, and even if they were on the island with the house and labs as she suspected, she still had to because water was the only way to approach the house.

From the helicopter, Sarita had thought she'd spotted a road disappearing into the jungle in the direction of the little house, but if that's where they were, apparently it didn't go all the way to it. They'd double-checked before setting out and hadn't found even so much as a dirt path to walk on.

Movement out of the corner of her eye drew Sarita's head quickly around, but she relaxed when she spotted Domitian jogging toward her. Her first reaction was relief, until she noted the vexed expression on his face.

"What's wrong?" she asked as he stopped and simply gathered the ends of first one towel and then the other.

Domitian didn't really answer her question. He merely slung both Santa sacks over his shoulder as he straightened. Turning back the way he'd come, he then said, "Come with me," and started walking at a quick clip.

Sarita frowned and hurried after him, but his legs were longer, allowing him to take larger strides. The shifting sand underfoot didn't help either. It had made walking difficult even when they'd been moving at the slower pace they'd settled into on leaving the house, which was why they'd moved down to walk in the wet and more solid surf despite the risk of being spotted by an approaching boat. Domitian had matched his stride to hers then so as not to leave her behind, but he wasn't now. He seemed to be in the grip of some strong emotion and eager to get to where he was taking her, so Sarita bit back her protest at his speed and tried to move a little more quickly.

With her focus on Domitian and keeping up with him, Sarita didn't notice the dock at first when it appeared before them. Or anything else really, until he stopped and turned back to peer at her.

Slowing, Sarita took in his inscrutable expression and finally glanced around at their surroundings. Her heart stuttered with anxiety when she spotted the dock a little ahead on their left, and her head quickly jerked to the right even as her feet stopped moving altogether, but then she just gaped at the house above the beach.

Sarita didn't know what she was expecting to see. The dock was much smaller than the one in front of Dr. Dressler's house. Still, the last thing she expected was to find herself peering at the same house she'd woken up in that morning, and which they'd left behind a little more than an hour ago.

"But—" She glanced back the way they'd come, briefly wondering if they'd somehow got turned around and come back the way they'd left, but even as she did it, she knew that wasn't what had happened. She had been wrong. This wasn't Dr. Dressler's island. At least not the one where the houses and labs were. It was a different, much smaller island . . . and they'd just walked all the way around it and right back to the house they'd been trying to escape.

# Eight

Sarita surfaced in the pool and ran her hands over her hair, pushing the water back along the soaking strands and away from her face. Letting her hands drop into the water, she then peered toward the waterfall with a little sigh. It was as beautiful at night as it had been during the day. There were lights in the pool as well as along the edges of the waterfall. They were also on the house, brightening the terrace. So, even at night it was a truly beautiful spot, a little bit of paradise in the middle of the ocean.

Too bad it was like that Eagles' song, Sarita thought, you could never leave. At least, that's how it seemed to her, because as far as she could tell, they were stuck there.

Sighing again, she leaned back to float in the water and stared up at the night sky overhead. By her guess, perhaps half an hour had passed since Domitian had led her to the beach in front of the house. After getting over her shock at finding herself there again and realizing the ramifications, Sarita had glanced at Domitian. He'd noted her expression and then had turned silently and led her back into the house.

They hadn't said a word to each other since. Domitian had simply set down the bags on the floor in the entry and then had disappeared into the office. Sarita had briefly considered unpacking the bags and putting everything away, but then had thought, *Why bother?*

She'd headed for the bedroom and the bathroom beyond. Their excursion, short as it had been, had left her hot and sweaty and covered with sand; a shower had seemed a good idea. But once she'd got there, she'd simply stood in the bathroom and looked around at the opulent setting, her stomach churning. It was part of a prison. A pretty prison, but a prison just the same and Sarita suddenly couldn't bear even being inside.

Turning, she'd retraced her steps and made her way back out to the living room where the pool had caught her eye. The cool water had seemed to be calling out to her, offering to soothe her stressed body. The next thing Sarita knew she was moving to the doors. By the time she'd reached them, she had undone the two pins fastening the towel to her bathing suit top. She'd opened the door and stepped out to walk to the edge of the pool, undoing the last pin, the one that kept the towel closed, as she went. Then she'd simply let the pins and towel drop and made a shallow dive into the pool.

Now she lay in the cooling water, surrounded by the soothing sounds of nature. The whisper of the breeze through the trees of the jungle surrounding the pool. The twitter of night birds. The splash of water traveling over the rock waterfall at one end of the pool . . .

It should have been a little slice of heaven—instead, it was a kind of hell.

"Sarita?"

Straightening in the water, she turned toward the house, spotting Domitian at once. He'd come out of the dining room and was moving through the living room toward the door to the bedroom as he searched for her. She called out to him and he paused at once and glanced her way.

Spotting her through the glass doors, Domitian used the one she'd left open and slipped outside to stand by the pool. He then just stared at her.

Sarita stared back, wondering why he'd gone to the office.

"Are you okay?" he asked finally.

"As okay as a cockroach in a Roach Motel," she said sarcastically. When confusion covered his face, she realized he wouldn't understand the reference and explained, "They are cockroach traps. The cockroach goes in, but is caught and can't get back out."

Domitian didn't smile at her poor joke. Expression serious he said, "We are not trapped, Sarita. I promise I will get you off this island and take you somewhere safe."

"You shouldn't make promises you can't keep."

"I can keep it," he assured her.

"You're forgetting that Dr. Dressler could be back at any moment. He could be pulling up to the dock in a boat right now," she pointed out.

"He will not come here so soon," Domitian assured her.

"You can't know that," she said.

"His letter said he had this house renovated and up-dated for just this eventuality," he reminded her and pointed out, "He would hardly go to that trouble and expense for one day's use."

"True," Sarita said thoughtfully. She'd forgotten about that part of the letter. "But why did he do it? What the hell does he want from us?" she asked, and heard the frustration in her own voice.

"I do not know," Domitian admitted, and then announced, "I made us a meal."

Sarita almost snapped that she wasn't hungry, but she actually was, and taking out her temper on him would not get her the answers she wanted. Shaking her head, she moved to the stairs and walked out of the pool.

Domitian was waiting with a towel held open.

"Thank you," Sarita murmured, when he wrapped it around her shoulders. Clutching the ends under her chin, she moved past him, saying, "I'll just go change. I'll be quick."

If he responded, she didn't hear it as she hurried back inside.

Two minutes later, Sarita had removed the damp towel Domitian had wrapped around her and was glancing from it to the somewhat lacking wardrobe that was available to her. She briefly considered pulling on a dry swimsuit and pinning a fresh towel to it, one that wasn't damp, but really all the remaining swimsuits had thong bottoms that were just plain uncomfortable. She wasn't eager to wear any of them. Besides, the towel she'd worn as a toga that day was a dirty heap by the pool, the one she'd just removed was damp and would be uncomfortable, and between their using them after showers and swimming, and her raiding them to carry their items, the stack of towels was shrinking quickly. They'd soon be out of clean towels if she kept using them as clothing.

Dropping the damp one, she turned resolutely to the clothing supplied to her and wondered with disgust who had picked all these ridiculous nightgowns. Muttering under her breath, she settled on a black one with a short, sheer skirt, but lace on the top that would mostly cover her breasts. She'd have to wear a thong with it for it to be anywhere near decent, but the top was what Domitian would see sitting at the table and that was her main concern. Most of the other gowns were sheer there too.

She pulled it on quickly, found a black thong, donned it with a grimace and then hurried into the bathroom to run a brush through her wet hair. Her gaze slid briefly to the makeup table as she did, but then slid away. This wasn't a date. The last thing she needed was to make herself attractive. They already had trouble keeping their hands off each other and she didn't want to end up splayed on the dining room table and howling for the cameras as Domitian—

Sarita cut that thought off quickly as she felt heat pool in her groin. Honestly, she was like a bitch in heat around the man. Just thinking about him made her . . .

Rather than finish the thought, she threw the brush on the counter and hurried from the room.

Domitian was in the dining room, standing behind a chair that he politely pulled out for her when she entered.

Sarita glanced at his face as she approached, caught the way his eyes started to glow that strange silver as his gaze slid over her latest ensemble and just managed not to shake her head as she took her seat. Much to her relief, Domitian didn't so much as touch her shoulder, but eased her chair in and then immediately moved around to claim the seat opposite.

Sarita glanced down at her plate and then stopped and said with surprise, *"Lomito en salsa de mango!"*

*"Si."* Domitian smiled faintly when she glanced to him with amazement. "It is what you ordered each of the three times you were in my restaurant, so when I saw we had the ingredients to make it, I did."

Sarita smiled crookedly. "Well, now I know which restaurant you own. Buena Vida was my father's favorite. But expensive—it was only for special occasions," she said with a reminiscent smile. "Before my mother died, Papa took her there every year on their anniversary. The first time I got to go was the night before we moved to Canada. He wanted 'our last meal in Venezuela to be memorable,' as he put it, so he took me there."

She smiled faintly, and then her expression turned sober and she said, "We went again five years ago when Grandfather died. We came back to arrange the funeral and see him buried, and the night before we left for home, Papa took me there again . . . the last time I was there was two years ago when Papa—" Much to Sarita's horror her voice cracked, and she bowed her head quickly and stared through eyes suddenly glazed with tears at the sirloin in mango salsa on her plate.

"When your father died and you brought him home to be buried between your mother and grandfather," Domitian finished for her solemnly.

Sarita nodded once, but was concentrating on her breathing. She was taking in repeated deep breaths that she then let out slowly, the whole time thinking, *Dammit, I never cry!*

"You ate in my restaurant the night before you flew back to Canada," he added. "This time alone."

Sarita closed her eyes as that last word cut through her. *Alone.*

She'd thought she'd lost everything when her mother died and her father moved her away from her friends and grandfather to live in Canada. But Sarita hadn't felt truly alone until the day her father had a heart attack and left this earth. Oh, she still had the friends she'd made in Canada, and the other cadets who had been in police training with her at the time. But she alone had flown home to Venezuela with her father's body, and she alone had seen him buried.

Even her grandmother hadn't been there, which was Sarita's fault. It had all happened so quickly and there had been so much to do to arrange to fly her father's body back to Caracas as well as make the funeral arrangements long distance that she hadn't thought to contact her grandmother until the morning of the funeral. By then it was too late. She hadn't had a phone number for the woman then. They'd only ever written. So she'd seen her father buried, and then she'd written and mailed a letter to her grandmother with the news of his death. That night she'd followed tradition and eaten at her father's favorite restaurant, alone.

"I wanted so much to comfort you that night," Domitian confided quietly and then admitted, "I got the latest report from my detective just that morning. I knew your father had died and that you had flown home with his body to see him buried. The moment I got the lone order for *Lomito en salsa de mango* I looked out. I could not see your face, you were sitting with your back to the kitchen, but I knew it was you. You looked so lost and alone sitting there all by yourself. It was a struggle for me not to go to you."

"Why didn't you?" she asked, her voice sharper than she'd intended. But she had really needed comfort that night. Sarita raised her head to peer at him through watery eyes.

"To you I was a stranger," he said simply. "You would not have wanted comfort from me. And had the natural attraction between life mates overwhelmed us, I feared you would hate yourself for whatever happened between us at such a tragic time."

Sarita gave a short nod of understanding, then peered down at her plate and breathed out slowly again. Sirloin in mango salsa. She would never look at it again without thinking of her father . . . and she simply couldn't eat it.

"I'm sorry," she murmured, pushing her chair back. "I think I just want to go to bed."

Domitian didn't protest or point out that he'd worked hard to make the meal that she wasn't eating. He simply murmured in understanding and let her go. Sarita was quite sure he couldn't know how much she appreciated that.

Sarita wasn't sure how long she'd been asleep or even what woke her up, but suddenly her eyes were open and she was staring into the dark, listening to a soft rustling sound somewhere at the bottom of the bed. Ears straining, she tried to figure out what it was without giving away that she was awake. When she couldn't, she reached slowly for the bedside lamp, only to pause as her hand encountered material.

Frowning, Sarita slid her hand first to the left and

then to the right, but the material appeared to be hanging there like a wall. Easing silently up the bed a bit, she ran her hand along the cloth until she found the end, and then reached around it, felt for the lamp on the other side and turned it on.

Of course, she was immediately blinded by the light, but her eyes quickly adjusted and Sarita noted the wall of white cloth along the side of the bed, hanging from the top frame. Another ran along the bottom as well and Domitian stood on a chair, even now affixing a third swath of white cloth along the frame on the opposite side of the bed.

"Sheets?" she asked with amusement.

"*Si.*" Domitian continued his work, stepping off the chair and onto the edge of the bed to string the cloth farther along the frame without having to move the chair now that she was awake.

Sarita watched the play of muscles in his arms and chest until she noted that she had an interesting view up the bottom of his boxers from her position. Clearing a suddenly full throat, she asked hopefully, "Are we going to have sex?"

"No."

"No?" Sarita squawked with disbelief. "Why not? What's all this for then?" she asked, gesturing toward the curtain of sheets now nearly surrounding the bed. She'd assumed it was so they could have sex without worrying about the cameras in the room capturing it . . . *Apparently not*, Sarita thought and scowled at him.

Domitian chuckled at her outrage as he continued his work, moving farther up the edge of the bed until she could have reached out and touched him. "First it's '*no sexo!'* Now it's *'What? No sexo?'"* Glancing at her, he arched an eyebrow. "I have plans for you, you will see."

"Hmm." Sarita muttered, but resisted the urge to touch him and sat up in the bed. She shifted back to lean against the headboard, but didn't bother tugging the sheets up to cover her lap despite the fact that she was now nude under the sheer black nightgown. The last thing Sarita had done before climbing under the sheets and duvet was to strip away the latest hated thong she'd donned earlier to wear under it. They really were uncomfortable. She wouldn't have been able to sleep with it on. Now, she was as good as naked to him from just under the breasts down.

"Oh," Domitian sighed. "You are going to make this difficult, *si?*"

"I don't know what you're talking about," she said with a shrug, straightening her shoulders and thrusting her breasts out as she pretended to examine her nails.

Domitian chuckled under his breath but continued to work. It seemed to take forever for him to finish, though, mostly because he kept casting furtive glances over her rather than paying attention to what he was doing.

"Finally."

Sarita glanced up at that to see that the sheet now reached all the way to the wall on this side as well, and frowned when she noticed that he was now outside it. She was about to lean over and tug the sheet aside to see what he was doing when he did it himself.

Pulling the sheet back with one hand, he climbed in to join her, balancing a tray on his other hand like an expert waiter.

"What's this?" she asked with interest as he let the sheet slip closed again and settled cross-legged next to her.

"Food. You must eat," Domitian said firmly. "You have had little more than a couple of pieces of fruit all day."

"Oh." Sarita peered with interest over the tray he set on the bed between them. There was a selection of meats and cheese, crackers, olives, two glasses of juice, and one glass of wine.

"Who gets the wine?" she asked suspiciously.

"You," he answered easily. "Wine is no good for us."

"Us being immortals?" she asked with interest.

Nodding, Domitian picked up an olive and popped it into his mouth.

"How is it no good for you?" Sarita asked at once, picking up a cracker and piling cheese and meat on it.

"The only effect it has on us is to make the nanos work hard to remove the alcohol from our system. It means consuming more blood."

Sarita wrinkled her nose at that, placed a cracker on top of the meat and cheese, making a mini sandwich and ate half of it in one bite. Flakes of cracker immediately sprinkled down on her breasts and thighs and she made a face. Thinking they were going to have crumbs in bed, she raised a hand to brush away the ones on her chest, but Domitian caught her hand.

"I will lick them off later," he assured her, urging her hand down.

A slow smile spreading her lips, Sarita said with satisfaction, "So there will be *sexo* later."

"No," Domitian answered promptly and built a cheese, meat, and cracker sandwich for himself.

Sarita stared at him for a moment, half confused and half annoyed, but then just shook her head and popped the second half of her own cracker sandwich into her mouth. She was hungry. More like starved really. She would worry about the "sex or no sex" thing later.

They ate in silence for a bit, and then Sarita glanced at Domitian and said, "So you're a chef with your own restaurant. Why would you accept a job cooking for Dressler?"

Domitian blew a breath out and shrugged. "It is a long story."

"Yeah, well, it doesn't look like we're going anywhere for a while, so spill."

Nodding, he said, "Several immortals have gone missing from the United States over the last couple of years. No one noticed at first, because it was only one or two and they were spaced far apart. But the number has grown and the time between kidnappings grew shorter recently and it was noticed."

Sarita's eyebrows rose slightly, but she nodded to encourage him to continue.

"I knew that my uncle had the Rogue Hunters looking into it from a phone conversation I had with Drina, and—"

"Who's Drina?" Sarita asked sharply, surprised at the different emotions whipping through her at the mention of another woman. Possessiveness, worry, and even jealousy were suddenly tugging at her emotions, which was kind of unexpected for Sarita since she wasn't clear on her own feelings for the man.

"My sister," he explained gently. "She is a Rogue Hunter in Canada. She used to live and work in Spain where my family lives, but found her life mate recently. Since he lived in Canada, and Uncle needed more Rogue Hunters there, she moved to be with her mate."

"You have family?" she asked, unable to hide her surprise.

Domitian arched his eyebrows. "You thought I had been hatched?"

"No, of course not. I just—" Shaking her head at her own stupidity, Sarita said, "Dr. Dressler mentioned that your kind were like us, with families and everything, but I guess I just—I mean Dracula didn't have family, you know? I guess I just keep mixing you up with him." Seeing from his expression that she'd managed to insult him, she quickly said, "I'll try not to do that. So what are Rogue Hunters?"

Domitian stared at her narrow-eyed for a moment, but then slowly relaxed and explained, "Basically, they are the police for immortals. They hunt rogue immortals, those who are breaking our laws and feeding on or harming mortals, or turning them in numbers, and so on."

Her eyebrows rose. "You have your own police force?"

"Well, mortal police could not manage our kind what with our ability to read and control minds," he pointed out gently.

"Right. Dr. Dressler mentioned that you guys were able to do that," she said with a frown. Tilting her head, she added, "But he said you couldn't read or control me?"

"No. It is how I knew you were my life mate," he said solemnly.

Unwilling to talk about that, Sarita lowered her eyes and tried to think of something to say that would steer the topic away from this life mate business. She wasn't sure how she felt about the man sitting across from her. He was sexy as hell, and she'd never had sex like they shared, but really he was still a stranger to her . . . and he was different. Not mortal.

Sarita was no longer horrified by the fact that he was a vampire. Or perhaps it was closer to the truth to say she'd stopped worrying about that for now. However, while she needed to work with him to get off this island, Sarita wasn't sure she would be able to accept what he was once that was done. She certainly wasn't ready to think about what he might want from her or if she could give it.

"So is your uncle the head of these immortal police then?" she asked, finally, as that question occurred to her.

"*Si*. But no," Domitian said and grinned at the face she made in reaction to the confusing answer. Taking pity on her, he explained, "A man named Garrett Mortimer is supposed to be the head of the Rogue Hunters, but he answers to Uncle Lucian who was never good at delegating."

"So two cooks in the kitchen?" Sarita suggested.

He smiled with appreciation at her choice of words and nodded.

"Why does this Mortimer guy have to answer to your uncle? Who is he?"

"My uncle Lucian is the head of the North American Council of Immortals. They make the laws, and basically govern our people there. He also used to run the hunters before he put Mortimer in charge of them."

"Right, okay." Sarita nodded, sure she understood the basics now. "So, your uncle had this Mortimer guy put his Rogue Hunters on the job."

"*Si*. They were to find out if the disappearances were connected and, if so, who was behind them. Immortals were disappearing from several areas, but the last three disappeared from bars in Texas, so they concentrated there and hunters and volunteers were sent out to act as bait. But something went wrong. A couple weeks ago two of the volunteers—twin brothers I understand— were kidnapped together."

"Twins," Sarita murmured recalling Dr. Dressler's "experiment." Scientists had a thing for twins and experiments, didn't they? She couldn't even imagine what he was doing to them. Maybe cutting them in half and then seeing if once blood was applied Twin A's bottom half would reattach itself to Twin B's upper half and vice versa? The very thought made her shudder with disgust.

"Fortunately, both men escaped," Domitian added finally, and would never know how close he came to getting punched for not saying so right away and sparing Sarita her distressing imaginings.

"A handful of Dressler's men died," he continued obliviously, "but not before our people found out some vital information. One, the intent was to fly the two captured men to Caracas, and then on to an island, and two, that the man in charge was a Dr. Dressler."

Sarita nodded.

"So Uncle Lucian rounded up as many Rogue Hunters as he felt he could spare and flew down here to try to find Dressler. They quickly realized that he was a university professor here in Venezuela. But he must have caught wind that they were coming, or perhaps he suspected they might when he didn't hear from his men, because by the time the hunters landed in Caracas, Dr. Dressler had gone on sabbatical."

"During their first week here, all they were able to

learn was that Dressler had both an apartment in the city where he stayed while teaching at the university, and a residence on an island somewhere that he went to on weekends and during summer break. No one seemed to know the name of the island, though, or where it was, although it was mentioned that he had a helicopter as well as several boats that he used to get back and forth. So Uncle Lucian decided they would have to check every island within five hundred miles of Caracas."

Sarita blinked and asked with disbelief, "Five hundred?"

Domitian shrugged. "He was being conservative in the hopes of speeding up the hunt."

"You think five hundred miles is *conservative*?" she asked with a disbelieving laugh.

*"Si,"* he assured her. "The apartment in the city might have been necessary only for the nights he had evening classes. But it may also have been because the island was too far to travel to and from daily so that the island house was like a cottage would be to an American or Canadian. Helicopters can travel at speeds of one hundred and forty miles an hour. Five hundred miles would only take three and a half hours or a little more to travel to."

"Hmm," she murmured with a nod. A couple of guys at work had cottages up north in the Muskokas, a good three-hour drive away or more depending on traffic and coffee stops. One of them had invited a bunch of their coworkers out to the cottage one weekend last summer. Sarita had been one of those invited and she'd been chatting with the people in the neighboring cottage. They lived farther south and drove five hours to reach their cottage every weekend. Driving up Friday night and leaving Sunday afternoon. If the island house *was* used as a cottage for Dr. Dressler, three or four hours wouldn't be that far to go she supposed.

"Anyway," Domitian continued, "Uncle Lucian divided the areas up into four quadrants and sent two teams of two hunters out to each."

"What happened?" she asked at once when he paused.

"Nothing at first," he answered. "They were using boats, not helicopters, in the hopes of making a stealthy approach, but it was a lot of area to cover."

"And?" Sarita prompted when he fell silent.

"The third day two teams from two different quadrants did not report in," Domitian admitted solemnly. "Two women, Eshe, my aunt by marriage, and Mirabeau La Roche McGraw made up one team, and my cousins Decker and Nicholas made up the second team."

"Oh," Sarita breathed softly. She'd known he knew some of the missing immortals but hadn't realized they were family, and she asked, "Your aunt and cousins are Rogue Hunters too like your sister?"

"*Si,*" Domitian murmured, and then cleared his throat and continued, "Anyway, when the two teams didn't turn up by dawn, Uncle Lucian tried to have their phones tracked, but they must have been disabled. So he pulled everyone off the other two quadrants, and split them up between the two quadrants the teams had gone missing from. But now they were looking for the missing hunters as well as the island Dressler owns."

"Did he check the land registry office?" Sarita asked and then frowned. "That's what it's called in Canada, I don't remember what it is called here, if I ever even knew, but they must have some record of who buys what properties."

Domitian nodded. "They checked. There is no property listed to a Ramsey Dressler in Venezuela."

"Ramsey," Sarita muttered. She'd never known Dr. Dressler's first name. Her grandmother had never mentioned it. Shaking her head, she said, "He must have used another name then."

"*Si*, that is what is suspected, but we have no idea what name he might have used."

"Right," Sarita breathed. "So, I gather from the fact that Dressler is still out here torturing people with his experiments that they didn't find the island?"

"No, and another four hunters went missing. This time one from each team of two."

"What?" she asked with amazement. "How?"

Domitian shrugged helplessly. "No one knows. With each team it was the same story. The other hunter was there, and then suddenly was not."

Sarita stared at him blankly and then shook her head. "Well, the ones who came back had to have seen or heard *something*. They were on boats, right?"

"*Si*, but the hunters who returned were all piloting the boats. In each case they said they were skimming through the water, glanced around to say something to their partner, and they were gone. They did not hear or see anything to suggest a struggle. And whatever happened was quick. In two cases the missing man was holding a conversation with the pilot when it happened. They said something, the pilot responded, glanced back to them, and they were not there."

"Oh, that's just spooky," Sarita declared after a moment.

*"Si,"* Domitian murmured.

"None of them were related to you this time, were they?" she asked with concern.

Domitian nodded slowly. "My uncle Victor, and Lucern, another cousin, were among those taken. My sister, Drina, was on one of the teams, but fortunately, she was piloting the boat. She returned, but the man partnered with her, a man named Santo Notte, did not."

"Your sister is here in Venezuela?"

*"Si.* Uncle Lucian called in all the Rogue Hunters in North America after my aunt and cousins went missing. There are several civilians down here now too trying to help, which has Uncle Lucian furious," he added wryly.

"Why would that upset him?" Sarita asked with surprise.

"Because he's lost so many hunters who are skilled and trained for situations like this. He considers it far too dangerous to have nonhunters here and fears they will just be cannon fodder."

"But he let you help," she pointed out.

"Actually, he refused my help when I first offered it," Domitian admitted with a crooked smile, and explained, "When I learned he and the others had flown in, I went directly to the villas they'd rented and offered to help, but he said no, it was too dangerous and I was not a hunter." He shrugged. "So I returned to my restaurant and helped the only way I could."

"Food?" she guessed at once.

Domitian nodded. "I cooked large batches of food four or five times a day and sent it to the villa."

"I'm sure they appreciated that," she assured him.

He shrugged, and continued, "I offered my assistance

again when my aunt and cousins went missing, but again was refused."

Sarita reached out and covered his hand sympathetically. He seemed perfectly calm about it all, but she could sense the frustration and anger simmering under the surface at not being allowed to help search for his missing family members.

Domitian stared at her hand briefly, then turned his own over and clasped her fingers gently, his shoulders relaxing somewhat.

"So," she said, clearing her throat, "what changed? Why did he let you help in the end?"

"You," Domitian said squeezing her fingers lightly.

"Me?" she asked with surprise.

"*Si,*" he said solemnly. "Dressler has been a regular in my restaurant for at least two years and has offered me a job as his personal chef every couple of months during that time. But two days ago, he called and offered it again. This time, though, he mentioned that Sarita, the granddaughter of one of his employees, was coming for a visit and he wished to offer her more than the slop his regular cook served."

"Aleta doesn't serve slop," Sarita said, snatching her hand away and scowling at him for the insult to the woman.

"He said it, not me," Domitian assured her solemnly. "And now that I know he knew all along that you are my life mate, I am sure it was just an excuse to mention your name and let me know you were here."

"Oh . . . yeah, it probably was," she said, relaxing.

"Anyway," Domitian continued, "I could hardly refuse the offer this time, not when I knew you were on the island and quite possibly in danger. So I accepted the job—as Dressler no doubt expected—and then I went straight to the villa to give Lucian the news." He smiled wryly. "I expected him to be pleased. After all, Dressler had no idea I was an immortal so I would not be in danger, and my uncle could have my phone tracked and find out where the island was."

"I gather he didn't see things that way?"

"Hell no. According to him I was throwing myself in harm's way. Dressler probably *did* know I was an immortal, and this was just a trap to add another one to his collection, and Dressler would incapacitate my phone and myself quickly to prevent their following. Which he was right about as it turns out," Domitian said on a sigh.

"And yet he let you come," she said.

Domitian snorted. "He had no choice. This is South America, the North American council has no power here or over me. Once I pointed that out, he had no choice and started making plans on how best to track me and keep me safe and so on."

Sarita nodded, but was now frowning as she considered what he'd said and then asked, "I'm surprised that wasn't a problem."

"What?" Domitian asked.

"Well, this isn't North America," she pointed out.

"No," he agreed.

"Mortal police can get pretty testy about jurisdiction and whatnot," she said with a grimace. "Don't the South American Council mind that your uncle has come into their jurisdiction in pursuit of a perp? Or did your uncle contact them and coordinate with them on this operation?"

Domitian made a face, and then admitted, "Actually, I assumed they knew, but when we were on the way to the docks, a call came from the villa that the South American Council were there and wanted to see him. Uncle Lucian just said he'd be back soon and hung up, but one of the men, Justin Bricker, said, 'Uh-oh. They've found out we're here.'"

"Hmm." Sarita bit her lip. If immortals were anything like mortals, she suspected there might be a mini turf war happening on the mainland about now and wondered what that looked like between vampires. A duel at dusk with stakes? Shaking her head, she reached for another cracker, intending to make another cracker sandwich, only to pause as she realized they were all gone. They'd eaten every last crumb of food from the tray Domitian had brought as they'd talked. There wasn't even an olive left.

"Time for dessert," Domitian announced, grabbing the tray and slipping quickly out of their sheet-wrapped cocoon. When he didn't reappear again right away, Sarita frowned and crawled across the bed to tug the sheet aside and see what he was doing.

Setting the tray aside and stripping off his boxers maybe? she thought hopefully. He would make a lovely dessert. But when Sarita looked out she saw that the room was empty. Domitian had left.

Releasing the sheet, she dropped back to lie on the bed with disappointment. The man was sending mixed messages. Saying no he didn't plan to have sex with her, and then saying he'd lick the crumbs off her later. Now he had apparently gone off to find them dessert. She had no idea what he had planned.

# Nine

Domitian cut the last profiterole in half, filled it with ice cream like the others, and then retrieved the chocolate sauce he'd left to stay warm on the range. Tipping the pan, he drizzled it slowly over the profiteroles he'd arranged on the plate, and then set the plate on the tray with the wine and small dessert plates. He took a moment to go over the items on the tray, making sure he had everything, and then picked it up and headed back to the bedroom.

Sarita had chosen bananas flamée as her dessert the three times she'd eaten at his restaurant, but after her reaction to the sirloin in mango salsa, he wasn't making the mistake of serving her the dessert she usually ordered too. He was hoping the profiteroles would be better received.

"More wine?" Sarita asked with amusement as he pulled the sheet aside and climbed back into their cocoon.

"It is a muscat, perfect with profiteroles, but I made cappuccinos too. You can have one or both as you wish." He settled on the bed and let the sheet drop back into place as he set the tray on the bed between them.

"Profiteroles?" she asked with interest and leaned over to look at them. Her eyes widened. "Did you *make* these?"

"Of course," he said with amusement.

"I've never had freshly made profiteroles," she confessed. "I've had the frozen ones they sell at the grocery stores in Canada, but—"

"Garbage," he assured her as he slid two onto a small plate and offered them to her with a fork. "These will be much better."

Sarita smiled slightly at his bragging as she took the plate and fork. She cut off a piece of ice cream–filled profiterole and slid it into her mouth as Domitian busied himself pouring her a glass of the muscat before pushing the sheet aside and leaning to set the wine bottle on the bedside table and out of the way.

"Mmmmmmmmm."

Domitian let the sheet drop back into place and turned to smile at Sarita as she moaned over her first bite of profiterole. "Good?"

Sarita nodded and swallowed. "Oh yeah. Heavenly," she assured him. "You're a keeper."

"I am glad to hear you say that," Domitian said solemnly, and recognized the moment when she realized what she'd said by how she stilled and then flushed with embarrassment. When Sarita followed that up by gulping down a mouthful of wine, Domitian sighed to himself and picked up his own plate to eat.

The woman hadn't yet accepted that they were life

mates, and he knew he shouldn't rush her, but couldn't help himself. He had waited more than two millennia to find his life mate. Fifteen years ago he had found her, but had forced himself to wait for her to grow up and become her own woman. The plan had been to wait until she had worked for a couple years in her chosen profession and then find and woo her, but Dressler had cut some time off that goal with his actions. Still, to his mind, Domitian had been incredibly patient. However, it seemed he would have to be patient a bit longer. He could do it. One did not live this long without learning patience. But that didn't mean he would enjoy it.

Glancing at Sarita, he noted the tight, uncomfortable expression on her face and sighed inwardly. The woman was as closed up as a turtle in its shell. He needed to open her up a bit before she would even see the possibilities before her. Swallowing the bit of profiterole in his mouth, he said, "Tell me about yourself."

Sarita glanced up with surprise, and then arched an eyebrow. "I would have thought your private detective had told you everything there was to know."

Domitian shook his head. "Those were just cold hard facts written on pristine white paper. I want to know more than the facts. I want to know you," he said firmly. "I want to see the past through your eyes. The present too. I want to know your dreams, your wishes, your heart. I wanted to know the real Sarita, not the facts behind her existence."

Sarita stared at him wide eyed for a moment, and then lowered her head and peered down at the ice cream melting and sliding out of her profiteroles. She was silent for so long he began to think she wasn't going to respond at all, but then she said, "I had a pretty normal childhood until I was thirteen."

Domitian exhaled slowly, realizing only then that he'd been holding his breath, unsure she would respond to his request.

Sarita shrugged. "Happy loving parents, good in school, lots of friends, and a grandfather who spoiled me rotten and who I adored . . . and then my mother was kidnapped."

She took a bite of profiterole and ice cream, chewed, and swallowed and then chased it with a sip of wine before adding, "Although, I suppose that was pretty normal too when you think about it. Kidnapping in Venezuela is practically a national pastime and there were more than a couple of kids in my school who knew someone who had been kidnapped."

Domitian nodded solemnly. Kidnapping had become rampant in Venezuela. It was visited on everyone, the rich, the middle class, and even the poor. In fact, it was so commonplace that people had begun forming groups with friends, coworkers, and neighbors, joining together to put money into funds to pay off kidnappers and get back the loved ones of the people in their groups.

"My father loved my mother dearly and did everything the kidnappers told him to do. He didn't contact the police, he didn't tell anyone, and he gathered together the demanded money and went to the meeting place they instructed him to, to deliver it. He'd expected my mother to be there and to be exchanged for the money, but they told him it didn't work that way. That once they were safely away and sure that the *policia* weren't there somewhere waiting to jump them, they would send my mother to him."

"But they did not," Domitian said softly, sorry he'd made her relive this sad part of her life.

"Oh, they did," she assured him, and then added bitterly, "in pieces."

Domitian winced. The kidnapping had happened three months before he'd met Sarita and learned he couldn't read her. The detective he'd hired had mentioned in his first report that her mother had died in a kidnapping gone wrong, and her father was moving her out of the country because of that, but hadn't given specifics. Domitian hadn't asked for any.

"I am sorry," he said softly.

Sarita acknowledged his words with a nod and turned her gaze back to her plate as she scooped up another bite of profiterole. After swallowing, she said, "After my mother's death, my father was afraid the same thing would happen to me, and decided he had to get me out of Venezuela. He worked for the Royal Bank of Canada here. He was the assistant manager at their branch office in Caracas and, with the bank manager's help, was able to get a transfer to a branch in Canada." Her expression turned thoughtful. "I think the bank helped to speed up the paperwork needed for us to move, visas and whatnot. It still seemed to take a while, though, several months I think."

She paused, apparently trying to recall, and then shrugged. "Anyway, off we went to Canada. We settled in a little town just south of Toronto where it would be easy for my father to commute into the city to his new bank. Fortunately, it was summer and school was out. Well, for everyone else," she added wryly. "My father wanted me to get a good start once school began, and he wanted me to be able to protect myself, so he signed me up for martial arts two nights a week, and then hired me a teacher to teach me English. I spent that first summer learning English eight hours a day, every day. It was English, English, English with the occasional martial arts break at night."

"Your father found a teacher willing to work seven days a week?" he asked with amusement.

"Oh no, the teacher only taught me during the weekdays, my father taught me on Saturday and Sunday . . . and usually for a couple of hours on weeknights after work. My whole life was mostly English. By the time school started, I was sick to death of contractions and the order of adjectives and nouns." She rolled her eyes and then sighed and shrugged. "But I had learned enough that I was able to go to a normal high school."

"Were you already in high school at thirteen?" he asked. It seemed young to him.

"Fourteen," she corrected. "My birthday is—"

"July seventh," Domitian finished for her with a nod. "Yes, of course. You would have been fourteen by the time school started."

"Right," she said slowly, eyeballing him. "Your private dick would have told you my birth date."

"Yes," he said simply.

"Hmm," she muttered, and then continued, "Anyway, my life was pretty normal again after that. High school dances, going to the mall with friends, bush parties, making—"

"Excuse me," he interrupted. "Bush parties? This is what?"

Sarita shrugged. "Just what it sounds like, parties in the bush."

Domitian pursed his lips briefly and then said, "That would be a very small party."

"Heck no, tons of kids went. Like I said, it was a small town. There wasn't much to do unless you drove to the city, and the first two years of high school there was no driving anywhere. But even after my friends and I all started turning sixteen and getting our licenses, none of our parents were willing to let us take the family car into the city. I don't think anyone's did really. The older kids were at the bush parties too."

"In a bush?" he asked with disbelief. "Lots of you? In a bush?"

"Yes," she said, not seeming to understand his confusion, and then her eyes widened. "Not the bush like a plant, not *arbusto*. Bush like a small woodland area or forest, *bosque*."

"Ah . . ." Domitian nodded, a wry smile curving his lips. "I learned English centuries ago and still cannot get it right. I am impressed you mastered it in a summer."

"I wouldn't say I mastered it that summer," she assured him, seeming amused. "I still struggled my first year of high school, but I knew enough to get by. Besides, you speak English perfectly. New words and terms or slang pop up all the time. Even speaking it daily it's hard to keep up sometimes. The kids are always coming up with something I've never heard before."

Domitian smiled softly. She was trying to make him feel better as if he might feel stupid that he'd made a mistake. His self-esteem wasn't that weak, but it was sweet of her to be concerned for him.

"Anyway, like I say, everything was pretty normal after that. I finished high school, went to university to get a criminology degree, went through police training, and—" she shrugged "—now I'm living the dream."

Domitian's eyebrows rose at the tinge of sarcasm in her voice. "Your dream was not to be a police officer?"

Sarita made a face. "Yeah, it was, but—" she shook her head "—I wanted to be a police officer to *help* people. To make sure no one else lost their mother the way I did. Instead, I'm scraping drunks up off the sidewalk, stopping speeders, and arresting shoplifters. And none of them take responsibility for why they're in trouble. Do they just say, 'Thank you, Officer, for not leaving me to freeze to death on the sidewalk' or 'Sorry, Officer, you're right. I was speeding' and take their ticket or whatever? No. They're always trying to give excuses. The drunk we pick up every night like clockwork never drinks too much, someone must have roofied him. The speeder was unfamiliar with the road and thought the speed limit was higher, or their speedometer must not be working, or everyone else was doing it, or they were speeding because they had to pee. And the shoplifter? Oh no, they weren't shoplifting, they just absentmindedly dropped it in their purse or pants and forgot to pay."

She puffed out a breath of exasperation. "And when those excuses that we've already heard a hundred times don't work? Then they start cursing and shouting at us, and kicking out at us and struggling so that we have to wrestle them to the car. And the whole time they're yelling at their friends to videotape this. 'It's abuse! It's abuse!'

"It gets pretty fricking depressing at times, I gotta tell you. I became a police officer to help people, but they don't want the help when it's directed at them. Oh yeah, they're happy when it's directed at someone else but—For instance, a couple months ago Jackson and I pulled this guy over for speeding and weaving. He—"

"Speeding and weaving?" Domitian interrupted. "I understand speeding, but by weaving you do not mean—?"

"Weaving all over the road," she explained.

"Ah." Domitian nodded. "Sorry. Proceed."

"So, he blows over the limit and—I mean on the breathalyzer," she stopped to explain. "It reads how much alcohol they have in their system."

Domitian nodded.

"Right, so he blows over the legal limit, and then freaks out when we arrest him. Starts cussing us out and even took a swing at Jackson. Fine. Nothing new there, right?"

Apparently it was a rhetorical question, because she went on, "Fast forward to two weeks ago. We're called to a traffic accident. This cute little six-year-old was hit crossing the road from her house to her neighbor's across the street. Turns out the driver was speeding and over the limit."

"And it is the man you arrested two months earlier," Domitian guessed.

"No. *He's* the kid's father. *This* drunk is a neighbor. But the father, who let the kid cross that busy street without supervision, and who wanted to kill us both just a month and a half earlier for arresting *him* for doing the same thing, *and on the same damned street*, starts shouting at us now about how we don't do our jobs and stop speeders and drunk drivers in his area.

"Ack!" she exclaimed with disgust. "I wanted to plow the guy. But no, I had to be polite and take his abuse. And the whole time he's yelling at me, I'm trying to comfort the little girl with a shattered pelvis and broken leg as we wait for the ambulance."

When she sat back with a little exasperated grunt, Domitian said gently, "It sounds a very thankless job."

"It is," she assured him, and then added, "And it isn't."

"Which is it?" he asked with a faint smile.

Sarita smiled crookedly back. "Sometimes you can make a difference and really help someone. And sometimes they even appreciate it, and those days—" she blew out a long breath "—those days make up for all the crap days. But man, they are few and far between. I've only been on the job for a year and already feel like I've aged ten. Seeing the things people do to each other?" She shook her head sadly. "Sometimes I'm ashamed to be human."

They were both silent for a minute. Sarita was peering thoughtfully down into her cappuccino cup. He was peering just as thoughtfully at her, thinking that her job sounded incredibly thankless and stressful. Most police officers no doubt got into it because they wanted to help people. But he suspected the things she'd described probably wore them down pretty quickly. He didn't like the idea of her being worn down. And he wondered how much of the hard outer shell she presented to the world had been there before she'd become an officer. Perhaps they trained them to be that way. She was expected to be strong on the job, and in control in emergency situations. It would mean being tough he supposed.

Once he'd persuaded her to be his life mate, perhaps he should talk to her about changing her career and—

Domitian stopped his thoughts there and gave his

head a little shake. If all he'd wanted was a Barbie doll to do as he thought best, he might as well have picked any mortal who caught his fancy. But part of the reason life mates were so special was because they could not be controlled. And the entire reason he'd left Sarita to grow up rather than claim her when he'd found her while so young was so she could grow into her own woman and hopefully wouldn't be led by him.

No. He wouldn't try to convince her to change her career. He would let her make her own decisions and simply support her in those decisions the best he could.

Sarita drank the last of her cappuccino, and set the cup back on the tray with a little sigh, then straightened her shoulders and glanced at Domitian. Judging by his expression, she'd depressed him as much as herself with her little rant. Time to change the tune of this conversation, she decided and said, "So, that's me. Your turn. Let's hear about you."

Domitian jerked his head up and eyed her with surprise. "Me?"

She chuckled at his expression, and then teased, "What? A pretty boy like you has never had a gal want to stare into your dreamy eyes and hear all about your life?"

"Not that I recall," he said with a smile.

Sarita snorted with disbelief. "Yeah right."

"I am telling you the truth," he assured her.

Sarita eyed him suspiciously, and then arched an eyebrow. "So what do you do on dates then? I mean most people at least tell a little about themselves."

"I do not date."

"Right," Sarita said slowly and then shook her head. "Sorry buddy, no one gets as talented as you are in the bedroom, or should I say bathroom and lounge chair," she added dryly before finishing, "without a couple thousand sexual experiences under their belt."

"Ah." Domitian murmured, and then shrugged mildly. "I have had sex, of course."

"Of course. You just didn't bother to first talk to the women you bedded," she said with disbelief and then sat up straight as she realized that was how it had gone with her. She hadn't known a damned thing about him other than his name and that he was an immortal when she'd jumped him in the bathroom.

"I undoubtedly did speak to the women I bedded as you so charmingly put it," he said with amusement. "However, it was so long ago I don't recall if they asked about my life first."

That was sufficiently distracting to pull Sarita away from fretting over what she feared might be considered slutty behavior, and she eyed him now, wondering how long it had been since he'd slept with a woman. He was immortal—he could be two, maybe even three hundred years old. Had it been ten years? Twenty? Maybe even fifty years since he'd slept with a woman? As her father used to say, the only way to know was to ask, so she did.

"How long has it been since you slept with a woman? Before me," she added quickly in case he tried to avoid the answer by naming the incident on the lounge.

"Hmm." Domitian tipped his head, apparently having to think back a bit to remember, and then he nodded and said, "I believe it was when Auletes succeeded Alexander II."

Out of cappuccino but still thirsty, Sarita had just

reached over to pick up the glass of wine he'd poured for her. Straightening with it in hand, she glanced to him with confusion. "Who? What now?"

"Sorry," Domitian said with a wry shrug. "I should have said when Ptolemy XII Neos Dionysos succeeded Ptolemy XI Alexander II as King of Egypt."

Sarita stared blankly, and then simply said, "Huh?"

Domitian frowned and offered, "Neos Dionysos was also known as Auletes or Nothos, does that help?"

"Are you kidding me? Hell no, it doesn't help! What are you talking about?" she asked with exasperation. "Egypt has presidents not kings, and right now it's some guy named el Sissy or something."

"El-Sisi," he corrected with amusement. "And yes, they have presidents now, but the leaders were kings when I lived there. Or Pharaohs."

"Pharaohs?" she gasped. "Seriously? *Pharaohs?*"

"*Si.*" He nodded, seeming fascinated with the expressions flittering across her face.

"But Pharaohs are—That was back before—Christ, you—"

"*Si*, pharaohs reigned before Christ," he said with a nod. "Then the Romans invaded in about 30 B.C. and they carried the title of emperor for—What is the matter? Are you all right? Why are you gulping your wine?" he asked with concern.

Sarita just shook her head and downed the rest of the wine in her once-full glass. By the time she finished, she was gasping for air. Setting the empty glass on the tray, she gave her head a shake and then glared at Domitian for a minute as she regained her breath, before saying, "Please do not tell me that you are trying to tell me that—you're telling me—"

"Concentrate, *mi Corazon*," he encouraged. "You can get it out."

"You are *not* telling me that you were born in 30 B.C.," she said firmly.

"No," Domitian agreed, turning to tug the sheet aside and grab the wine bottle off the bedside table.

"Thank God," Sarita muttered, her body relaxing.

"Thirty B.C. is when I last enjoyed copulation with a female . . . other than yourself of course," he explained, letting the sheet drop back into place and turning with the bottle. "I was *born* in 260 B.C."

"No, you weren't," she said at once.

"*Si*, I was," he assured her and began to pour more wine into her glass.

"No, you—Just give me the bottle," she muttered and snatched it from his hand when he stopped pouring and glanced to her with surprise at the request. Ignoring that, Sarita raised the bottle to her lips to drink straight from it.

"The detective I hired did not mention a drinking problem," Domitian said dryly as he watched her chug.

Sarita glared at him around the bottle, but then stopped chugging and lowered it. She held on to it, though, and simply stared at him for several moments.

Ignoring her, Domitian slid another profiterole onto a plate and offered it to her.

Sarita was so annoyed with him she almost refused out of principle. But the profiteroles were so good, and it wasn't their fault she was annoyed with him. It seemed unfair to take out her anger on them so she took the plate, muttering a very short "Thank you."

"*De nada*," Domitian murmured, watching her cut off a large piece of profiterole and pop it in her mouth.

In her irritation, she wasn't paying much attention to what she was doing and the piece was much larger than she'd intended. Not dangerously so, but it meant a lot of chewing and moving food around in her mouth before swallowing to be sure she didn't choke. The entire time she did, Sarita glared at Domitian.

"I do not understand your distress," he said as he watched her chew. "You said that Dressler had explained about the nanos and our being immortal and such."

Sarita swallowed the food in her mouth, took a drink of wine from the bottle to clear her throat, and then nodded. "Yes. Immortal. But I was thinking—you know—a hundred years old, maybe two . . . *not* two *thousand!*"

"Two thousand, two hundred and—"

"Oh my God!" The words exploded from Sarita's mouth and her eyes went as big as saucers. "Two thousand years?"

"Two thousand, two hundred and—"

"In Egypt?" She interrupted his second attempt to give her his exact age.

"*Si.* I lived in Egypt two thousand, two hundred and—"

"So you wore those little white skirts and stuff?"

"What I wore was a shendyt not a skirt," he said stiffly.

"If that means little white skirt, that's what I'm talking about," she said with a grin and then started to raise the bottle to her lips again, but stopped as a thought occurred to her. "Were you still there when the Romans took over?"

"*Si.*"

"Oh God!" Sarita gulped down some more wine, and then lowered the bottle to say, "Please don't tell me you had to trade in your skirt for those ridiculous long togas and those silly-looking leafy things they wore on their heads."

"I fear so," Domitian said with amusement as she raised the bottle again for another chug. "Although as a gladiator, I had to wear a subligaculum and—"

"Oh my God! You were a gladiator?" she asked the minute she could get the bottle down and swallow what she'd taken in. "Oh, I bet you were super hot as a gladiator."

"Er . . ." Domitian said, unsure how to respond to that. He had a healthy ego, but it seemed kind of egotistical to agree with her that he had looked hot in his subligaculum.

"Tell me what it was like?"

"Wearing a sublig—?"

"No, no," she interrupted. "What was it like being a gladiator?"

Domitian shrugged. "Up early, good food, hard training, the most amazing massages I have enjoyed in my life, and—"

"Wait, wait," Sarita said with a frown. "You're a vampire."

"Immortal," he corrected stiffly.

"Whatever," she said, waving one hand. "But as a gladiator you'd have to be out in the sun all—"

"No. I can control minds, remember?" he said gently. "I just made sure our *doctores* always placed me in the shade for practice."

"Doctors decided where you would fight?" Sarita asked with surprise.

"Not doctors, *doctores*," Domitian corrected her gently. "It is what the trainers were called."

"Oh." She shrugged. "Okay, so you got to train in

the shade, but you couldn't gladiate in the shade. That would have been out in the coliseum, in the open."

"*Si*, but each gladiator only had to fight three or four times a year, five at the most," he said with a shrug.

"What?" she gasped with disbelief.

Grinning Domitian nodded. "*Si*. The rest of the time it was just good food, training, massages, baths, and willing women. Life was good."

"Hmm. Sure," Sarita muttered, suddenly seeming annoyed. "If that's all you want from life."

"I was young then," Domitian said with amusement. "It *was* all I wanted from life."

"Um, no," she said dryly. "You said Rome conquered Egypt in 30 B.C., so if you were born in 260 B.C. you were . . . er, let's see, we have to go backward, right, so two hundred and thirty minus thirty . . . two hundred and thirty years old," she said, and then arched an eyebrow at him. "Two hundred and thirty years old is not young."

"Actually, I was only one hundred and fifty. I was a gladiator in 110 B.C. while I still enjoyed food and sex," he explained. "And it was in Rome, not Egypt that I was a gladiator."

"Oh," Sarita frowned. "For some reason I thought you were born in Egypt."

"I was. My family was from Egypt, and I lived and worked there for my first thirty years."

"Worked as what?" she asked curiously.

"I was trained to be a *sesh*—a scribe," Domitian explained. "That was what my mother wanted me to be, and I did try, but it was terribly boring to me and when I was about twenty-five I ran off to be a soldier. I thought that would surely be more interesting, and it was at times, but in peacetime it was just hard labor, helping to move stones for pyramids and such. I only stayed with it for five years or so."

"Really? You helped build a pyramid?" Sarita asked with fascination.

Domitian smiled faintly at the question. "I think calling what I did 'helping to build a pyramid' a bit of an overstatement. I helped move a few large blocks, but that was about it, and it was backbreaking work, even for an immortal," he assured her. "Anyway, I soon grew tired of that and landed in Ostia, where I was a *urinatores* for a decade."

"Er, what is a urinator?" Sarita asked, wrinkling her nose.

"*Urinatores*," he said on a laugh. "A salvage diver. We dove down as far as thirty meters with nothing but a diving bell with air trapped in it that we could breathe out of as we worked. Once it ran out we had to surface and trap fresh air to go back down. A dangerous job for mortals, but not for me, which is why I made out so well monetarily."

"From there I landed in China where I ended up becoming a *praegustator* for a decade for Emperor Qin Shi Huang. I pretasted food to test it for poison," Domitian explained, and then added, "Another very dangerous job had I been mortal since the emperor wasn't well liked. But I was immortal, so . . ." He shrugged. "I was well paid while there, which is part of the reason I stayed a full decade, but it was also because I found I quite liked food."

"You didn't like it before that?" she asked with amusement.

"Oh, yes. Well, sometimes. Soldiers did not exactly

eat gourmet meals, and I was not much of a cook myself so my time as a *urinatores* was not very educational in that regard, but the emperor had proper cooks and he did like his food. And so did I. The food there was new and different. I decided I wanted to travel around and try food from other cultures. So, despite being offered a great deal of coin to stay, I left and started my wandering, looking to try different foods and such. At least until I started to lose my taste for food."

"When was that?" she asked at once.

Domitian sighed and thought back. "I guess it started when I was about a hundred and eighty or so. I began to eat less and less frequently, and five years later at the celebration of Ptolemy XII's accession was the last time I actually enjoyed food."

"And the last time you had sex," she said.

Domitian nodded. "The two appetites often dwindle away together."

"Why?" she asked at once.

Domitian shrugged helplessly. "It happens to all immortals eventually. I actually held on to my appetites longer than some of my kind. I think because I traveled around and tried various and exotic foods."

"And various and exotic women?" she suggested sourly.

*"Si,"* he said unapologetically, and then added, "All of whom are long dead and turned to dust so no longer worth your jealousy."

"I'm not jealous!" Sarita protested at once, but wasn't sure she was telling the truth. She'd certainly felt the pinch of something as she'd brought up his exotic women. *Damn, I am jealous*, she realized and took another drink from her bottle.

Lowering it, she squinted at him and asked, "So what else did you do besides urinating and gladiorating?"

*"Urinatores,"* Domitian corrected on a laugh, and then added, "I do not think *gladiorating* is a word."

"Eh . . ." Sarita waved that away with unconcern. "So, what else did you do?" she demanded.

Domitian shrugged. "Once I lost my appetites, I bounced between farming, traveling as a trade merchant, and opening and running pubs or hostels, with the occasional mercenary work thrown in to keep practiced in defense."

"What kind of mercenary work?"

"I was a dragoon for a while," he said after thinking for a moment.

"What? You guys suck blood *and* blow fire?"

"Dragoon, not dragon," he said on a laugh. "A dragoon is a musketeer on horseback."

"Ooooh," Sarita breathed, impressed. "Musketeers are cool. I bet you were hot with long hair and those froufrou hats."

"Froufrou hats?" he asked, sounding affronted.

"Well, you know, with the wide brim and the feathers all poking out of it," she said, waving her hands around her head to show him what she meant. "Most guys wouldn't be able to carry it off, but I bet you did. Just like I bet you carried off that Egyptian skirt thing nicely too."

When Domitian merely stared at her with a bemused expression, Sarita asked, "Were you ever a pirate? I could see you as a pirate. All tight black pants and billowy shirt and long sword."

Domitian nodded slowly. *"Si.* As it happens I did do a brief stint as a pirate."

"No!" Sarita breathed with amazement. "Oh, you were *naughty*!"

"In my defense it was only for a year or so to aid my sister, Alexandrina. She was short a couple men on her ship, so I put in with her for a while to help out."

"Your sister was a pirate captain?" she asked, eyes wide.

"Well, technically, Drina was a privateer," Domitian admitted.

"Ah, pirating with permission," Sarita said, nodding wisely, and then asked, "Any other jobs that were exciting? Were you ever a knight?"

"I was knighted three or four times," he admitted, and then explained, "In a different country each time."

"What else?" she asked.

Domitian shook his head apologetically. "I am afraid there is nothing else of much note I have done. Other than that, I farmed, and—Oh, I almost forgot, I was a Bow Street Runner for a while. They were—"

"I know what Bow Street Runners were," Sarita interrupted on a laugh. "I'm a police officer, and those guys—well, I had a teacher who considered them London's first professional police force." She smiled. "So that means, you were a sop too at one time."

"I think you mean cop," Domitian said with amusement. "Yes, I guess I was or was as good as, and I think you are tipsy."

"Me? Never," she assured him. "I don't drink."

"Which would explain why you might be tipsy now," he said dryly, taking the half full bottle from her lap and pushing the sheet aside briefly to set the bottle on the bedside table again.

"I'm sure I don't know why you'd think that," Sarita said, sitting up straight on the bed and trying for a serious face, which just made her want to giggle.

"I think that—" Domitian let the sheet fall into place as he turned back to face her again "—because you are laughing and smiling and completely relaxed. I suspect those are three things you do not often allow yourself to do."

"Oh, so now you're saying I'm a stick in the mud too," she accused teasingly.

"Never," he said solemnly. "But I am saying that you have a beautiful smile and if a glass or two of wine makes you relax enough to share it with me, then I think I shall serve you wine at every meal."

Sarita swallowed, her smile wavering. Sobriety dropping around her like a cape, she said, "I don't want to eat any more meals here, Domitian."

After a hesitation, he leaned forward and cupped the back of her head to draw her close so that he could whisper, "Just two or three more meals here, *mi Corazon*. I plan to get us both off this island tomorrow night."

"Tomorrow?" she asked with surprise. Drawing back slightly, she peered at his face as he nodded. "How?"

The word was barely a whisper, but he heard and drew her back to say, "I am going to swim for the mainland."

Her eyes widened with shock. "You're going to leave me here alone?"

"Hush," Domitian whispered and placed his forehead on hers. "No, *mi tesoro*, I would never do that. I will take you with me . . . on my back."

Sarita gaped at him briefly, and then opened her

mouth to tell him just how crazy an idea that was. But Domitian trapped the words before they could even be formed by simply kissing her.

Startled, Sarita raised her hands to push him away, determined to tell him his plan was completely insane. But by the time her fingers reached his shoulders the thought was lost and she found herself clinging to him as she kissed him back.

Domitian's arms closed around her at once, his hands spreading on her back and pulling her tightly to his chest, molding her upper body to his. Sarita groaned into his mouth and shifted to her knees to move closer. The action put her at the same height as he was sitting, she noted and then was distracted when his hands slid under the sheer black nightgown and skimmed up her legs.

When one hand cupped her bottom and the other slid up to brush teasingly between her legs, Sarita gasped and broke the kiss.

"You have been driving me mad with this all night, *mi Corazon*," Domitian growled, releasing her bottom to tug at the sheer cloth of her nightgown. "Take it off for me. I would lick and suckle your breasts."

Sarita groaned as the hand between her legs teased her again, and then quickly caught at the material of the nightie and tugged it up and off. It wasn't even over her head before Domitian closed his mouth on one excited nipple and began to draw as his fingers stopped teasing and slid smoothly along the warm, damp flesh between her legs.

"Oh!" Sarita gasped, tossing the nightgown aside. Clutching at his shoulders, she panted, "I thought you . . . said . . . *no sexo*."

Letting her nipple slip loose he raised his head to meet her gaze and agreed, "*No sexo*. But I will make love to you."

Sarita's eyes widened, but she went willingly when he eased her back to lie on the bed.

# Ten

Sarita woke up abruptly and with the certain knowledge that she had to get up at once and visit the bathroom. Too much wine was her personal assessment of the situation. The good news was at least her head didn't hurt, she thought and glanced around to see that Domitian was unconscious on the bed next to her.

Smiling, she started to sit up, but paused as she realized that his arm was across her waist. Sarita carefully lifted his hand up and to the side so she could sit up. The man didn't even stir as she crawled to the top of the mattress to tug the sheet aside and get out of bed. Letting it drop back into place, she hurried into the adjoining bathroom.

She snatched up a bath towel on her way in, tossed it over the shower's glass panel and then reached in to work the taps. Leaving them on to allow the water to warm, she then slid into the water closet to handle more pressing issues.

Moments later, feeling much relieved, Sarita left the water closet to check the temperature of the shower. The water was perfect and she stepped under it with a little sigh that died in her throat as she tipped her head back and spotted the camera lens.

Mouth tightening, Sarita lowered her head and pretty much raced through her shower after that. She then turned off the water and quickly wrapped the towel around herself sarong-style as she got out. Moving to the counter she ran a brush through her damp hair and brushed her teeth as she debated whether to go back to sleep or not. Sarita wasn't tired anymore, but if they really were going to try to leave the island that night, she should probably sleep as much as possible today.

Grimacing, she met her gaze in the mirror and shook her head slightly. There was just no way they were going to be able to swim to the mainland. First, they had no idea what direction the mainland was. Secondly, there were sharks and other predators out there in the ocean, and she didn't fancy playing Jonah in the belly of a whale. And then there was the distance. She hadn't seen even a hint of land in any direction as they'd walked around the island. They could be ten miles from the mainland or a hundred. Neither of them had any idea.

No. Sarita just couldn't see swimming for the mainland. But maybe they could build a raft or something. Turning off the taps, she dried her hands and then leaned against the counter to think. They might not be able to leave tonight if they went by raft, but at least there was a better chance of surviving.

How long would it take to build a raft? She pondered that now. Cut down some trees, tie them together using sheets maybe. Make some kind of shelter to keep Domitian out of the sun, and make some paddles or something so they didn't end up getting pulled out to sea by currents.

That thought was alarming enough that Sarita pushed away from the counter and moved back into the bedroom. She glanced toward the bed, but all there was to see was the sheet wall Domitian had created. Leaving him to sleep, she slipped into the walk-in closet and grabbed another swimsuit to put on under her towel. Once she was as decently dressed as she was able in this place, Sarita headed for the office with its shelves of books.

When she didn't know something, Sarita researched it. At home she would have been checking the internet, Googling "how to make a sturdy raft" and "how to navigate unknown waters by the stars" and "what you should take if you expect to be stranded on the ocean." Unfortunately, there was no internet here. Hopefully the office had something useful on one of its many bookshelves.

It didn't take Sarita long to see that the books in the office wouldn't be much help. There were a couple of shelves of novels, but the rest were old scientific journals on genomes and DNA splicing and whatnot. If she'd wanted to create one of the poor creatures in the jars in the basement, she probably would have been all set, Sarita thought grimly. But there wasn't a single book that looked like it could tell her how to navigate by the stars or build a raft.

She was turning away with frustration when her gaze landed on one of the novels on the shelf, an old classic, *Robinson Crusoe*. Figuring it was better than nothing and might have at least one or two useful bits of information, Sarita grabbed it, cursing when the book next to it tumbled off the shelf and fell to the floor.

Muttering under her breath, she bent to pick it up, reading the title as she straightened. It was *The Hobbit* by J.R.R. Tolkien, Sarita saw, and there was a bit of paper sticking out at the top. Curious, Sarita opened the book and stared at the folded pages inside. It looked like a letter. Carrying everything to the desk, she set the books down, settled on the chair and opened the letter.

*Dear Margaret,*

*Sorry this letter is so long in coming, but life has been a bit chaotic of late. And I apologize but this will be a short letter because it's nearly bedtime and Ramsey will be home soon.*

*First the good news; Ramsey and I are expecting our first child! Oh, Maggie, I wish I could have told you this face-to-face. I know you'd be as happy for me as I am about it, and we'd be hopping up and down and squealing like schoolgirls.*

*I did try to convince Ramsey to bring me home for a visit so I could tell you this in person. Sadly, he says there is just no way we can make it back to England before the baby is born. As disappointed as I am, I know he's right. There is so much to do!*

*I mentioned in my last letter that we were living in a charming little house on its own island, but that we were looking for a larger home nearby.*

*We found several nice houses, but none of them seemed to have everything Ramsey needed, so he determined to build a new house instead, and bought a nearby empty island.*

*The new island is five times bigger than the little one we're now living on and, as far as I can tell, Ramsey is having a house built that is also five times bigger. He's building labs too, which is good if it means he won't have to stay at the university so late working in the labs there.*

*Fortunately, the new island is only half an hour away in the little fishing boat Ramsey purchased to motor back and forth. Well, it is when he pilots it anyway. I'm afraid I don't go as fast as he does and it takes forty or forty-five minutes if I'm alone. I prefer it when Ramsey takes me, but he's so busy preparing his classes and overseeing his student's labs that most of the decisions about the new house have fallen to me. That means that more often than not I have to make the trip myself to meet up with the contractor on the bigger island.*

*The big island isn't visible from the little island except on the clearest of days and even then it's nothing more than a shadow on the horizon, easily missed if you didn't know it was there. You can't imagine how nervous I was about piloting the boat my first time alone. I was sure I would miss the island and end up out in the middle of the ocean and out of gas. But Ramsey was so sweet and encouraging about it. He was sure I could do it, and did everything possible to make it easier for me. He marked the boat's compass at a point just between the twenty and thirty degree points and said to keep the boat headed in that direction and I would reach the island fine. And he was right! I could and did do it, and was ever so proud of myself afterward. Mind you, I still prefer him at the helm, but needs must and in this case we need the house done and ready before the baby comes and if it were left to him that would never happen.*

*Speaking of that, Maggie, I don't mean to complain, and I know he has to work, but I just didn't realize how much time Ramsey's work would take up. Most of the time I'm left alone out here on this little island with no one but our maid, Mrs. Reyes, to talk to and I'm afraid she doesn't know much English. On top of that, she is only here during the day when I often am not. Ramsey pays a local fisherman to bring her out and take her back to the mainland every night and some days I see her only in passing as she arrives and I leave or vice versa. But the nights are lonely. Ramsey often doesn't return from the mainland until bedtime and then he's too exhausted to do more than grunt "goodnight." It makes me long for home. I miss you so. I miss all my family and friends and I miss England. This isn't nearly the exciting adventure I thought it would be when I agreed to marry him and move here. But I'm hoping everything will change once the house is done and the baby is here. Then he can work in his own lab and spend time with the baby and me. I'm sure things will improve then. In the meantime, I—*

Sarita lowered the letter with a frown. It ended there, rather abruptly too, obviously midthought. She supposed Dressler had arrived home from the university then and Mrs. Dressler had probably shoved the unfinished letter in the book, intending to finish it later, but never getting back around to it.

Slipping the pages back into the book, Sarita closed it and tapped her fingers on the cover, her mind churning.

Domitian rolled over and reached for Sarita, but found only sheets. Frowning, he opened his eyes and peered around the cocooned bed. He was alone. Turning onto his back, he stared up at the ceiling, only to find it was himself he was looking at. The ceiling was mirrored.

Damn, he hadn't known that was there, Domitian thought and examined his reflection. His short hair was spiked in spots, probably from Sarita pulling on it last night, but other than that there was nothing much to see. The scratches and hickies he was quite sure she'd given him were gone now, the nanos having erased every trace of what had happened in that bed last night, three times.

Well, unless you counted the mess the bed itself was in, he supposed. The duvet was gone, probably lying somewhere on the floor next to the bed, and the upper sheet was bunched up at the bottom of the bed. As for the lower sheet, it had come off on both upper corners and curled in toward his head and shoulders. That was all there was to see. Now if Sarita was there, he would have had a perfect morning view. He could kiss her awake and then if he laid on his side next to her, he could watch her face in the mirror as he caressed her body and gave her pleasure.

That idea was rather appealing, Domitian decided, sitting up. He'd take a shower, brush his teeth, run downstairs for a quick blood top-up, and then find Sarita and lure her back to bed.

It was a solid plan, and worked right up to the point where it came to luring Sarita back to bed. Domitian showered, used the razor he found in the drawer to shave, and then brushed his teeth before heading downstairs to suck back some blood. He heard banging from the kitchen as he passed through the living room from the bedroom door to the office door, and wondered what Sarita was doing but didn't stop to check. After draining four bags, he went back up, though, and straight to the kitchen, his nose twitching. There was a heavy stench of something burning in the air, and his footsteps slowed warily as he passed through the dining room to the kitchen.

"There you are!" Sarita greeted him in a tone he would have said was a cross between "I'm super annoyed and trying not to show it" and "June Cleaver's got nothing on me" good cheer. In other words, it was super fake and tinged with the threat of violence. One glance around the chaos in the kitchen told him why. His Sarita was brilliant, beautiful, sexy, and he was sure she had many talents . . . but cooking obviously wasn't one of them, he decided as she announced, "I made us breakfast."

"*Si*. I see that," Domitian murmured, his gaze sliding over burned toast, bacon that was raw on the ends and burned in the middle, and eggs so underdone the tops of the whites were clear. No, the woman could not cook, he thought and sat down in the chair at the island when she indicated it, determined to eat every last bite if it killed him.

"I'm not as good a cook as you," Sarita announced as she settled next to him. "But you made me dinner last night, so I thought I'd handle breakfast." Shrugging, she confessed, "Breakfast for me is usually cereal or toaster strudels, though, and they didn't have those here, so I did the best I could."

It was such an unapologetic apology that Domitian was hard pressed not to chuckle. The woman had no problem acknowledging her few flaws or failings and even seemed to accept having some as inevitable. He really liked that about her. Too many people tried to be perfect at everything, or made excuses for not being perfect. Sarita just shrugged as if to say "I did my best. Take it or leave it."

He was more than happy to take it, Domitian decided and picked up his knife and fork, then paused to glance at Sarita when she began to make choking, gagging sounds.

"Oh God," she muttered after spitting out the piece of toast and egg she'd apparently combined to put in her mouth. "Oh, ick. No, put those down." She slapped at his hands, making him put down his fork and knife, then snatched up both her plate and his and stood to carry them around the island, saying, "We can't eat this. It's awful. Those eggs are *raw*." Opening the cupboard under the sink, she tossed both meals into the garbage, plates and all, and kicked the door closed with a shudder. "Ugh. I hate raw eggs."

Exasperated, Sarita walked to the refrigerator, opened

it to peer inside, and asked, "How about a cheese sandwich instead? I can manage that."

Shaking his head, Domitian stood and walked up behind her to catch her by the shoulders and urge her back toward the chair she'd just left. "How about you sit down and relax and I make breakfast?"

"Oh, but you cooked last night," she protested. "I could try again. Maybe French toast or something. That's just toast dipped in eggs and milk then fried, right? Although, I'll have to see if they provided any maple syrup here first. Do you guys get maple syrup down here or is that a Canadian thing? I don't recall ever having it when we lived here."

Sarita had escaped his loose hold and made a dash for the cupboards, but he caught her and turned her back toward the stools at the island. "Sit. It will be my pleasure to cook for you. I enjoy it. In fact you are the reason I learned to cook."

"What?" she asked with surprise, dropping onto the chair and turning to look at him.

"It is true," Domitian assured her, opening the refrigerator to pull out more bacon and eggs. "If you will recall, I lost my appetites back—"

"Before Christ was born," Sarita finished for him dryly. "Yeah, I remember." Frowning now, she said, "Speaking of which, if you didn't eat before meeting me, why did you own a restaurant?"

"I like them," he said simply. "It is where people go to celebrate happy events. Besides, I do not only own restaurants. I have a couple of hotels and a nightclub too. In fact, prior to encountering you I had always spent more time overseeing the nightclub than at any of the restaurants. I usually left those up to the managers I hired to run them."

"So why were you at the restaurant the night my father took me?" she asked curiously.

"That was pure luck," he assured her as he pulled out a clean frying pan and set it on the range. "The previous manager had left rather abruptly due to health issues. That was not the lucky part," he added dryly, before continuing. "The lucky part was that I hired a replacement for him, but had to train him myself. And then you walked in." Smiling, he shook his head. "Suddenly I was much more interested in the food than in the management end of the business. Meeting you reawakened my appetites," he explained.

"All your appetites?" she asked, her eyebrows rising. She'd only been thirteen. Surely his interest in sex hadn't—

"All of them," he admitted solemnly as he began to lay the strips of bacon in the pan one after another. Turning the flame on under the frying pan, he added, "Of course, there was nothing to do about the reappearance of my physical desire. You were far too young. But food . . ." He shook his head. "Not only did I rediscover my delight in it, but I found I had a great desire to learn to cook the meal you ate that first time. You seemed to enjoy it so, and I wanted to be able to make it for you. So I had our chef teach me how to make it, and found I enjoyed cooking as much as eating."

"So you learned to cook?" she asked, watching him turn the bacon.

"*Si.* I hired a manager to oversee all the businesses for me and flew to Europe to attend the best culinary schools available. I spent ten years training."

"Ten?" Sarita squawked with surprise as he turned the bacon.

"*Si*. I had time to fill while I waited for you to grow up," he said with a shrug. "And I wanted to learn it all. I wanted to be able to make anything your heart desired. I wanted to ply you with delicacies no one else could."

"Ten years," she said thoughtfully. "Were you here then the second time we ate at your restaurant? The night before we returned home after Grandfather's funeral?"

"*Si*. I had returned just three weeks before," Domitian admitted and smiled as he recalled that day. "You cannot imagine how shocked I was when my manager came to tell me someone had asked him to thank the chef for such a lovely meal and I glanced out to see you and your father just making your way to the door to leave my restaurant."

"Your private detective hadn't told you I was here in Venezuela?" Sarita asked a bit archly.

Domitian shook his head. "His report came the day after you left. Which," he added, "was probably a good thing in the end."

"Why was it a good thing?" she asked with amusement.

"Because you were no longer a child," he said wryly. "You were twenty-three, a fully grown woman." He dropped some butter in the empty pan to melt and began cracking eggs into a bowl as he recalled the wash of emotion and desire that had rolled over him at just knowing she was near. "You were leaving, your back was to me, and I could not see your face. For a moment, I just stared at your back, hoping you would turn so that I could see your face. But you did not. Once the door closed behind you I did not think, I just rushed after you. But it was a busy night and there seemed to be a waiter or customer in my way every couple of feet. By the time I got outside you and your father were gone.

"I struggled that night," Domitian admitted solemnly. "When I first found you at thirteen, I had determined I would not claim you until you had worked at your chosen career for at least two years. At the time you returned to my restaurant you had returned to university to get your master's degree in criminology after taking only one year off to work."

"My father had paid my way through university to get my bachelor degree, but I felt I should pay my own way for my master's, so I worked for a year to get the money together and continued to work while getting my master's," Sarita explained softly.

*"Si . . ."* Domitian nodded as he eased the raw eggs from the bowl onto the second frying pan. Glancing to her then he grinned and said, "You cannot know how sorry I was to learn you had chosen a career that needed such long schooling. Although," Domitian added dryly, casting her the stink eye. "I understand a master's degree is not necessary to become a police officer, so you took longer than absolutely necessary."

Sarita laughed at his expression and shrugged. "I want to be a detective someday. So I went for a master's in criminology with a minor in psychology."

"And then it took forever to get accepted to the police force," he said grimly.

"Yes, there's a pretty lengthy selection process," she admitted. "There are three stages of assessment with tests and whatnot at each stage. It takes a while, and then once you're accepted, you still have to go to the police college for training."

"*Si*. I know this," Domitian assured her. "I found it out when I learned what you wanted to do. I was trying to judge how long it would be before I could come and woo you," he admitted, and then shook his head. "However, when I saw you that night in my restaurant, my good intentions flew out of the window, and if I had caught up to you, my noble plans would have been meaningless."

"Noble, huh?" Sarita asked with amusement.

Glancing up from the bacon he was turning again, Domitian eyed her seriously. "Believe me, waiting was noble. A sacrifice. I had already waited more than two thousand years to find you when I first saw you. They seemed to me to pass so slowly, but these past fifteen years?" He shook his head. "They seemed longer than the two thousand that came before."

Turning, he pushed the button to start the bread toasting and then grabbed two plates and butter. As he set them next to the toaster, Domitian admitted, "I searched for you that night. I called every hotel in the city looking for where you and your father were staying."

"We stayed in my grandfather's apartment," Sarita said softly.

"*Si*. That was also in the report I got the next day, but by then you were on a plane back to Canada." He fetched another plate, lined it with paper towel and shifted the bacon strips from the pan to the plate one at a time. "I forced myself to calm down then. I told myself it was fate making sure I stuck to my original plan, and I would wait until you had graduated and worked two years in your field."

Domitian glanced over to see Sarita watching him with an indefinable expression. She looked serious, but her expression was uncharacteristically soft at the same time. Wondering what she was thinking, he set the plate of bacon before her and turned his attention to removing the now perfect sunny-side-up eggs to two plates.

"And when I came for my father's funeral?" Sarita asked, walking around the island to begin buttering the toast when it popped.

Domitian almost sighed inwardly. He'd planned on skipping that trip, not wanting to upset her as talk of her father had last night, but it seemed fate was pushing them that way anyway, so he admitted, "I struggled then too, but a little less. You were in the police college. Once done I would only have to wait two years to come woo you."

"So, you were planning to come to Canada this summer?" she asked with curiosity.

"I already have the plane ticket," he admitted with a shrug. Turning off the heat under both frying pans, Domitian carried the plates with the eggs on them around to set on the island in front of their seats.

"And how did you plan to approach me?" Sarita asked, following with the toast.

Domitian held her chair for her as she sat down and set the toast on the island, then claimed his own seat before turning to her and saying solemnly, "I was going to walk up to you and say, 'My name is Domitian Argenis . . . You are my life mate . . . Prepare to be loved.'"

Sarita blinked at him several times, and then recognition bloomed on her face, and she cried, *The Princess Bride!*"

"*Si*." Domitian grinned, pleased she recognized it.

"As you wish!" she said suddenly and shook her head. "I knew it reminded me of something when you said that, I just . . ." Sarita shook her head. "I can't believe I didn't pick up on it at once. I love that old movie. It's a classic."

"It is not that old," he protested.

"It was made before I was born," she said dryly.

"*Si*, but you are still young," Domitian said, and she grinned.

"Yeah, and I always will be to you . . . because you're *so old*," Sarita taunted.

"You do enjoy reminding me of that," he said wryly.

"Hey," she said with a shrug. "I find amusement where I can. Life is short."

"It does not have to be," he said solemnly.

Sarita had turned back to her plate, but seemed to freeze at his words. The moment she did, Domitian could have kicked himself for saying them. It was too soon. He was rushing her and would scare her off if he wasn't careful.

"Orange juice," he said abruptly, and got up to go fetch glasses and the juice.

"Domitian."

He just managed not to hunch his shoulders as if against a blow as he heard the solemn tone to her voice. Forcing himself to remain calm and relaxed, he smiled at her inquisitively as he carried the glasses and orange juice back to his seat, trying not to look like he knew she was going to say something that would alarm him. *"Si, mi tresoro?"*

"I've enjoyed our time together," Sarita started carefully, and he heard the *but* coming before she said,

"But once we are off this island and I'm sure my grandmother is safe, I am returning to my job and home in Canada."

Domitian forced himself to nod mildly. "*Si*. And I will follow."

She frowned. "You'd follow me to Canada?"

He shrugged. "I have family there. It would be nice to be closer to my sister."

Her eyes widened incredulously. "You mean you'd *move* there? But what about your restaurants and—?"

"*Mi Corazon*," he interrupted gently, "you are my life mate. I will not rush you. I will remain patient and give you the time you need, but I will follow you to Canada and woo you as you deserve."

He saw Sarita's throat move as she swallowed, but then she turned her face down to her plate and he wasn't sure how she was taking his words. Domitian supposed he'd hoped she'd throw her arms around his neck and declare him the most wonderful man in the world and vow to be his. He knew that was a ridiculous hope, however. Life never went that easily.

They ate in a mostly companionable silence, and then cleaned up together. Domitian was about to finally get to his plan to lure her to the bedroom when she suddenly took his hand and led him from the kitchen. Thinking he wouldn't need to lure her to the bedroom and that she was leading him there instead, he followed easily. However, he frowned with confusion when instead of turning toward the bedroom, Sarita instead led him across the living room and outside.

"Er . . . Sarita?" Domitian asked finally as she tugged him toward the pool. "What are we doing?"

"We're going in the pool," she announced, releasing

him to reach up and undo the towel wrapped around her torso. Letting it drop to the ground, she stepped over it and dove into the water.

Domitian stared after her with bemusement for a minute, his mind frozen on the view he'd got of her in the tiny, pale pink bikini she was wearing today. It was smaller even than the white one he'd first seen her in and contrasted beautifully with her tan skin.

"Hey! Come on. Hurry up."

Blinking, he forced the image of Sarita that was still frozen in his mind's eye away and peered at the real woman to see that she was by the waterfall and appeared to be waiting for him. That was when he got the idea she might want to talk about something that she didn't want overheard by the cameras. Kicking himself into action, he walked to the edge of the pool, dove in, and swam toward her, surfacing just a foot or so in front of her.

"I was thinking when I woke up," Sarita announced.

"Okay," Domitian said warily and waited.

"Well, we have no idea where we are and no clue what direction to go in to get to the mainland," she pointed out. "And the ocean is full of sharks and whales and other unfriendlies."

"Unfriendlies?" he asked with amusement.

Sarita shrugged, "I just didn't want to say creatures that want to eat us," she admitted with a crooked smile. "Anyway, the point is I got thinking that maybe we need a raft, and maybe there'd be something in one of the books in the office that could help with this escape of ours, so I went and took a look. There wasn't really," she added quickly. "I mean the closest thing I found to useful was Daniel Defoe's *Robinson Crusoe*. But—"

"Sarita," he interrupted gently. "It will be fine. We may not know where we are, but it has to be north of Venezuela, so if we go south we will find the mainland."

"Yeah, but we have no idea which way is north and which way south," she said at once.

Domitian raised an arm and pointed toward the front of the house and the dock. "That way is south."

She blinked, glanced in the direction he was pointing and then turned back to him and raised her eyebrows in question.

"I am more than two thousand years old, *mi Corazon*. I learned long ago how to navigate by the stars."

"Oh." Sarita looked nonplussed, and then glanced toward the beach again, but followed that by turning to peer toward the jungle behind the house. "So north would be that way."

"*Si,*" he agreed patiently.

"Okay, well see, that's good to know, because the big island is north of this island," she announced.

Domitian stiffened. "I thought you did not know where this island was? Yesterday you thought we might *be* on the big island."

"I found a letter," Sarita said, suddenly practically bursting with excitement. "It was from Mrs. Dressler to a friend of hers back in England, and she was saying that they were living on this island but building a new bigger home on an island not far from here. Half an hour by one of those little fishing boats with an outboard motor. Well, half an hour when Dr. Dressler piloted it, but forty-five minutes when she did," she corrected herself. "Elizabeth Dressler said she was nervous about driving it there on her own, but he marked the compass at a point between twenty and thirty degrees north and said to keep the boat heading that way and she would reach the island."

"That is good news, *mi Corazon*," Domitian said smiling at her widely. "It means when we get to the mainland, we can tell my uncle where the island is."

Sarita frowned at him. "Yeah, but I was thinking . . ."

"What were you thinking?" he asked, wary again.

"Look, I don't especially want to go to the island, but—"

"No," Domitian interrupted firmly. "I am not taking you anywhere near that island. The idea is to get you as far from Dressler as possible, not to deliver you and myself into his arms."

"I know," Sarita said with understanding. "But just listen to me. I was awake for the helicopter ride to the island and it was quite a long ride. Unfortunately, I didn't check my watch when we left and arrived, but I'm guessing it was a good hour, and the helicopter wasn't puttering along like a fishing boat, it was going really fast. I don't think we can make it to the mainland."

"I can swim for a very long time," he assured her.

"Pulling me?" she asked. "Because I suspect you'll have to. At least part of the way. I can swim, but not all night and day. And that's the other thing," Sarita added. "What if it does take twenty-four hours or something to get there? You're the one who said five hundred miles was your uncle's *conservative* estimate of where the island might be. You aren't swimming that far in a night. We'll be swimming during daylight too, without blood for you to top up on. I don't particularly want to be a walking blood bank."

Domitian frowned. "We do not have to make it to the mainland. I am sure we will encounter another island—"

"What if we don't?" Sarita asked. "And what if we are attacked by a shark? What if you're injured?"

He was more concerned about *her* being injured by a shark, but before he could say so, she added, "Without blood to help you heal, you might be more dangerous to me than a shark."

Domitian opened his mouth to assure her he would never harm her, but paused as he realized he couldn't make that promise. If he were badly injured in a shark attack . . . Well, immortals had been known to lose their heads and attack mortals in that state. The nanos could cause terrible agony and a blood lust when they needed blood. Sarita might be right. He could be more dangerous to her than a shark in that case.

"And then there's my grandmother," she said now.

Domitian focused on her with confusion. "Your grandmother is on the mainland."

"Do you really believe that?" Sarita asked dryly. "Think about it. Dressler wanted us both here for some reason, and he is the one who called and told me that my grandmother needed me. What are the chances that she just *happened* to fall down the stairs and hurt herself at the exact time when he apparently wanted us here? Hmm?"

Domitian shook his head. That hadn't occurred to him. "But you said she wasn't on the island. We thought perhaps they live on the mainland in the apartment and use the island house as a cottage."

"I said there was no sign that she lived in the *big* house," Sarita said firmly. "But I was thinking about Grandmother's letters, and according to everything she's ever written me, she definitely lives on the island with Mrs. Dressler and her son year round. I'm pretty sure Dressler is the only one who stays in that apartment in town. They have to be in the little house. There is nowhere else that they could be."

"Okay," he said reassuringly. "We will give that news to my uncle and they can be sure to—Why are you shaking your head?" he interrupted himself to ask, but suspected he already knew why.

"I am not going to the mainland," she announced, proving he had known why after all. "I don't think we'll make it if we head that way. And I'm not leaving my grandmother stuck out there on that island with Dr. Demento while I follow you to my death in the middle of the ocean."

"Sarita," Domitian said patiently.

"I'm not," she said firmly. "But I won't stop you if you want to try it. Your chances are probably better without me to slow you down. You might even make it. And I'll even tell you everything I know about the big island so you can tell your uncle."

"And what then? You will try to make it to the big island by yourself?" he asked with disbelief, and then said grimly, "I don't recall any of the reports I got saying you were suicidal."

"I'm not," she assured him. "And while I'm not a marathon swimmer, I did take lessons as a kid, and I'm a good floater. I can swim, then float for a while to rest, then swim again."

"Sarita," he said, running a hand wearily through his wet hair.

"It's closer than the mainland," she pointed out firmly. "I know I can't make the mainland, but the island is closer. I'm sure I can manage getting there, and I don't even have to build a raft. There are some blow-up lounge mattresses in one of the wicker chests that will do for a shorter journey."

Domitian scowled. "I think you probably could reach the big island, but we would be swimming directly into Dressler's waiting arms."

"We?" she asked.

"Well, I am not letting you swim anywhere on your own. There are sharks out there," he said gruffly.

Sarita smiled widely, but then responded to his comment about swimming directly into Dressler's arms. "El Doctor and his men will be watching for boats, not someone swimming to the island."

Domitian considered that.

"Actually, this might work out better all the way around. After we check the little house on the north end of the island to make sure my grandmother is okay, we can sneak around and find out all we need to know to help your uncle and his Rogue Hunters attack the island."

"*Si,*" he agreed. "But how do we get that information to him?"

Sarita shrugged. "There is a phone in the big house. If there isn't one in the little house, then we can sneak into the big house and use that one. We could call your uncle, give him the location and all the pertinent info, and coordinate with him."

"Coordinate?" Domitian asked with alarm.

"Yes. Find out what time he expects to attack the island so we can help. We can even try to get in and free the kidnapped immortals so they can help from on the island," she added thoughtfully.

"No," Domitian said firmly. "You will wait some-where safe while I—"

"Domitian," Sarita interrupted patiently.

"*Si?*" he asked warily.

"Please don't go all Ramsay on me."

"Ramsey?" he squawked, seriously insulted. "I am nothing like Dressler."

"Gordon Ramsay, not Ramsey Dressler," she said dryly. "I know you're a chef, but that doesn't give you leave to go all Gordon Ramsay and start trying to boss me around," she explained. "I'm a police officer, trained for confrontation, and I've also studied martial arts since I was thirteen. As I mentioned, that was the first thing Dad signed me up for in Canada. Of the two of us, I'm more equipped to deal with this."

"I am more than a chef," he said indignantly. "I have been a warrior, a knight, a pirate. I can handle myself in battle, Sarita," he finished stiffly.

"Oh yeah. I guess you can help then," she said, turn-ing to head for the stairs. "Come on, we should get as much sleep as we can today so we're well rested to-night."

Domitian turned, but didn't start moving right away. Instead, he stared after her with suspicion, wondering how his trying to protect her had somehow turned into his having to justify his involvement in the battle that would come.

She'd turned the tables on him, he realized. And quite neatly too. And was now prancing off thinking he was going to let her risk herself by helping on the island.

"Sarita," Domitian said sharply. "We need to—" He'd meant to say they needed to discuss this further, but his voice died in his throat when she reached back to undo the top of her bikini and let it drop into the water as she mounted the stairs.

Turning once she stood on the terrace, Sarita faced him. Her hands were on her hips and her head was held high and proud, he noted before his gaze fell to her beautiful bare breasts. God, he loved her body.

"Hurry, Domitian. You need to make love to me so I can sleep," she said huskily. "I think we should stay in bed all day to be sure we are well rested for later."

He was across the pool and out, scooping her into his arms before she quite finished the last word.

"As you wish," Domitian growled as he strode toward the house.

# Eleven

Eyes narrowing, Sarita scanned the island in the distance, looking for any movement that might tell her someone was patrolling the beach and might notice their approach when they got closer. In truth, she wasn't worried about Domitian being seen, he was mostly under water with only his head bobbing up once in a while as he took in air.

Sarita, however, was presently lying on her stomach on an inflatable pool lounger and was much more visible. She knew they'd have to pop the mattress and let it sink soon, but that was okay with her. She hadn't really wanted to bring it anyway. She would have taken it willingly if she'd been trying to reach the island alone, just for safety's sake. But with Domitian to help her, she hadn't expected to need it. She'd insisted she could alternate swimming and floating and make the distance without the air mattress when he'd brought it up as they ate their last meal on the island in the cocooned bed. He'd insisted they bring it, however, arguing that her resting would slow them down and they needed to reach the island before dawn. With the lounger, she could rest on it when she wearied and he could tow her as he swam.

Sarita had given in and retrieved the air mattress from the wicker chest where she'd seen it earlier. Leaving Domitian to blow it up by the pool, she'd gone to collect scissors, and had taken them with her to the bedroom. She'd made the rope to pull the air mattress in the privacy of the cocooned bed in the hopes of not giving away what they were up to any earlier than necessary. It was the sheets actually on the bed she'd used, cutting thin strips that she'd then braided together. Fortunately, it hadn't taken too long. Still it had been later than they'd wanted when they'd taken the mattress and rope and headed for the beach.

Unfortunately, as Sarita had feared, she'd spent a good portion of the trip on the air mattress. Oh, she'd swum more than half the distance under her own steam, but Domitian was a much faster swimmer than her and she'd found herself having to climb onto the mattress to rest more often than she'd liked. It was humiliating each time he'd noticed her flagging and had relegated her to the mattress to be towed along like a sick whale pulled out to deeper water by a boat.

That thought made Sarita cast a quick glance around at the moonlit water for any sign of a shark or anything. They'd been fortunate and not encountered anything like that so far, but how long could their luck hold out?

Movement below her made Sarita glance down through the clear plastic window in the center of the lounger's headrest. She half expected to see the shadow of a fish swimming along under her. She'd seen that once or twice in the bright moonlight, the darker shadow of a fish in the dark water, or even a flash of color if it was right beneath the mattress. This time, though, she was shocked to see a human figure swimming past under the mattress. She saw the clear outline of a head, chest, and arms moving quickly through the water headed toward Domitian.

Cursing, Sarita immediately lunged off the mattress after the figure.

Domitian was just thinking they were getting close enough to the island that they should stop, pop the air mattress, and leave it behind when the makeshift rope tied around his waist suddenly seemed to go slack. Stopping, he turned swiftly in the water to look back and saw that while the lounger was still there, Sarita was gone.

Frowning, he quickly reached under water, grabbed the rope at his waist and gave it a tug. Pain seared his back as the cloth dug in before the makeshift rope snapped, but he ignored it and dove under water. The ocean was dark, but Domitian had no problem spotting Sarita some fifteen feet away. Still, it took him a second to accept that she appeared to be struggling with something. Not something, *someone*, he realized. It was a man, and he was dragging Sarita down deeper in the water and away from the air she needed to survive.

Growling in his throat, Domitian shot forward, swimming hard to reach them as quickly as possible. Sarita couldn't survive long under water without air. She already appeared to be flagging while the man showed no signs of having the same problem. Swimming up behind the man, Domitian didn't even hesitate, he simply snapped his neck, then caught Sarita by the arm and kicked for the surface, pulling her with him.

He'd feared she was unconscious on first grabbing her, but Sarita started coughing and sputtering the moment her head broke from the water. It was music to his ears. Relief racing through him, Domitian dragged her to the air mattress, and lifted her to lie across it, then held on to it with one hand as he patted her back to help her spit up the water she'd swallowed.

"Are you okay?" he asked with concern as she gasped for air.

Sarita nodded, but simply continued to suck in great drafts of air. When she'd recovered enough to speak, she turned a stark face to him and gasped, "His face."

Domitian frowned, and then glanced around for the man, but he hadn't floated to the surface. A sliver of concern slipping through him, he said, "Wait here," and released the mattress to dive under water again. He spotted the man right away, motionless in the water where he'd left him some fifteen feet away.

Bewildered, he swam to the figure and stopped to look him over. While Domitian was having to work hard to keep from rising to the surface thanks to the air in his lungs, the dead man was just floating there about ten feet below the surface, neither sinking nor floating upward. He appeared dead, though.

Catching one of the man's hands, Domitian kicked for the surface, dragging the body behind. He wasn't surprised to see that Sarita hadn't listened, hadn't rested on the lounger as he'd instructed. She was halfway between him and the mattress, looking around worriedly when he broke the surface and pulled the man up next to him.

"There was something wrong with his face," she told him, swimming closer to peer at the man now lying facedown between them. "And he seemed to be breathing under water."

Domitian nodded and pulled the man closer. It was as he started to turn him in the water that he noticed something behind the man's ear. Pausing, he pulled the ear forward to get a better view.

"They look kind of like gills," Sarita said with amazement, stopping next to him.

"Yes," Domitian muttered, running a finger along one of the six four-inch flaps that ran around the man's ear and curved down his neck.

"Does he have a tail too or just legs?" Sarita asked tightly, no doubt thinking of the fetuses in the jars back at the lab. "I couldn't tell while we were struggling."

"Legs," he answered.

"His fingers are webbed, though."

Domitian glanced to the hand she was looking at and saw that the skin between the fingers was indeed webbed.

"Probably his feet too," Sarita said thoughtfully, releasing his hand. "He was moving pretty fast in the water. If I'd been any slower I wouldn't have got him. As it is, I barely dove in quick enough to grab his foot as it whipped by."

"*You* attacked *him*?" he asked with surprise. He'd assumed the man had pulled her off the mattress.

Sarita nodded. "I saw him swim under the mattress. He was heading for you at speed. I was sure he was going to attack you so I dove in and grabbed him. It wasn't until he jerked around that I saw the knife," she added with a grimace and then glanced to the man. "He could have stabbed me right then, but didn't."

Domitian turned his gaze back to the man as well, wondering if he'd allowed his worry for Sarita to make him kill someone who had really meant them no harm.

"He seemed to be trying to half drown me, though," Sarita added. "Yet he wasn't overly rough while he did it." She frowned and then glanced to Domitian and said, "Dr. Dressler still needs something from us. Perhaps he's given orders that if we came around they weren't to harm me, but could do whatever was necessary to subdue you because you'll heal. Maybe he wasn't really trying to kill me, just weaken me to make me easier to handle."

Domitian nodded and relaxed a little. Sarita was probably right about that. Dressler would know by now that they hadn't just gone for a swim in the ocean and were headed somewhere. He would have warned his people to keep an eye out in case they somehow ended up near the island. Which meant there were probably other hybrids like this one in the water.

"We have to move," Domitian said, releasing the man and taking Sarita's arm to urge her back toward the air mattress.

"I wanted to see his face," she protested. "What I could see of it while we were struggling seemed odd."

"No time. There could be others out here," he pointed out grimly. "We need to move."

"Oh, yes of course," Sarita murmured and stopped trying to turn back.

When she started to swim, Domitian released her and followed the rest of the distance to the air mattress.

"We should pop the lounger," she said as they stopped next to it. "I can swim from here."

Domitian merely nodded, let his fangs slide out and bit down into the mattress. But he was wishing it was a bag of blood. His body had used up a lot of energy to get this far and keep his body heat high. He was starting to cramp with the need for blood.

"Handy," Sarita said with a wry smile as she watched him puncture the mattress twice more to speed up the release of air.

Domitian grunted. "Let's go," he said softly. They'd both instinctively been talking quietly. Voices carried across water.

Sarita nodded and struck out at a steady pace he could have easily outstripped, but didn't. They still had a distance to go to get to the island and then they had to make their way around to the north end. It was better to go at a steady medium pace than to go fast and wear Sarita out. Besides, he wanted to keep an eye out for any more gilled people that might be out there with them. Fortunately, they needn't rush. Either the big island wasn't as far from the little island as he'd thought, or they'd made good time. By his guess it was still a good couple hours until dawn.

Sarita kept expecting Domitian to overtake her and surge ahead to urge them to a faster pace, but he didn't. He stayed behind her as they approached and then swam around the island where Dressler had his labs. They were just turning to curve around the end of the island where the little house she'd seen should be when

Sarita realized why he hadn't overtaken her. He was watching her back in case there were more gilled creatures out there like the one now floating in the water on the other side of the island. Which was nice, but there was no one watching him and she twisted her head and glanced back toward him as she turned her face up out of the water to get her next breath. It was something she'd done every other breath since they'd left the air mattress behind, and he was there just as he had been each time she'd checked. But this time, he was swimming sidestroke instead of freestyle, obviously watching for her to look back, she thought when he noticed her looking and stopped swimming to gesture at her to stop as well.

Sarita obeyed at once and turned in the water to face him. As she waited for him to move up next to her, she cast a glance toward shore. They were much closer now than the last time she'd tried to scan the island. Back then it had been little more than a black blob with lights shining out from behind black shadows here and there. But they'd cut in closer as soon as they reached the end of the island, and in the dark shadows, she could make out the general shape of the beach and where the jungle that bordered it started. She couldn't see the house yet, but suspected they were close.

"Am I right in guessing the house is just around that cliff?" Domitian asked in a hushed voice as he paused beside her to tread water.

Sarita glanced to the outcropping he was talking about and nodded her head. "I think so."

"Then I think we should go ashore here and move through the trees instead of approaching by water."

Sarita glanced along the beach. There might be someone in the trees inside the jungle, but it was easy to see that the beach at least was empty. The same couldn't be said for the water around them. There could be a dozen gilled creatures hovering nearby under the surface, watching them, and they wouldn't know it until they were attacked. She nodded.

"I will follow you," Domitian said, glancing around the calm surface of the ocean.

Turning, Sarita struck out for shore, actually relieved to be able to do so. She stayed fit for her job, but while she hadn't had to swim the entire way like Domitian had tonight, it was obvious to her that she wouldn't have been able to. By her guess, she'd only been swimming for an hour or a little more since they'd left the mattress, and not quickly, yet was trembling from the effort. Those nanos obviously made Domitian and others of his kind superhuman.

The thought made her worry about how he was doing on that count. Were his nanos using up blood like crazy to keep up his speed and stamina? Was he now in need of blood? She had no idea what they would do if that was the case. They'd left the blood supply back on the island. Although, she knew there was a large refrigerator full of it in Dressler's lab. The problem was getting to it.

The first scrape of sand against her fingertips as she performed her next stroke made Sarita push those worries from her mind and lift her head from the water to look around. They were still quite a distance from where the water lapped at the beach, but it seemed it was shallow here, she realized as her feet drifted down to touch the sand her fingers just had.

Sarita stood up in the water and staggered to the

side before catching herself. Sighing, she stood still for a minute, surveying the trees as she gave her legs a moment of rest before forcing them to move.

"Are you all right?" Domitian asked in a voice that was almost a whisper as he waded up beside her.

Sarita nodded. "Just checking to be sure there's no one in the trees," she said softly.

Nodding, Domitian surveyed them himself. When he let out a little breath and relaxed a moment later, she knew that he hadn't seen anything. Since his eyes were undoubtedly better than hers thanks to those nanos, Sarita gave up looking as well and started forward. With every step she took she was sure her legs were going to give out, but they held her up and carried her to shore.

"Let us move up by the trees and sit down," Domitian suggested, taking her arm to urge her forward. "I think we should rest for a minute before we continue on. I want you able to run if there is trouble when we get to the house."

"What kind of trouble are you thinking there might be?" Sarita asked with a frown, briefly forgetting her shaky legs.

Domitian shook his head. "Could be anything—guards on the house, guards inside the house. Or your grandmother might not even be here. Dressler might have given the house to his head of security as part of his income."

Sarita considered the possibility, but shook her head. "That can't be. My grandmother and Mrs. Dressler have to live somewhere here on the island. And other than this house and the big house, all there is are the labs."

"I am sure you are right," Domitian said mildly. "I

just want to be sure you can move fast if you have to. Now sit down and rest your muscles."

Sarita glanced around to see that they'd walked all the way to the edge of the jungle while she was distracted. Relieved, she dropped to sit in the sand facing the water and drew her knees up to rest her arms on top of them. Resting her chin on her crossed arms, she peered out toward the horizon, noting that it was lightening. Dawn wasn't that far away. They couldn't rest long and should be inside before the sun brightened the sky and made them easily visible. There might be guards here.

"I will be right back."

Sarita glanced up with a start, but before she could ask where he was going, Domitian had slipped into the trees and disappeared.

"Probably going to the bathroom," she told herself in a mutter and glanced nervously along the shore, watching for anything moving. There was nothing that she could see.

Sighing, Sarita turned to scan the spot where Domitian had disappeared. Not seeing anything, she shifted her gaze back along the shore again to give it another quick once-over and then repeated the two actions, looking for Domitian, then checking the silent beach. Sarita had just done that for about the twentieth time and was looking along the shore when a crackling sound brought her head sharply around toward the trees behind her.

Sarita peered into the dark mass of trees, straining to see and thought she saw branches moving in a tree behind and to the left of her. And then a sound behind her on the right had her turning her head sharply to look that way. She sagged with relief when she saw it was Domitian slipping back out of the woods.

"Come," he whispered, holding a hand down to her.

Sarita took his hand and allowed him to haul her to her feet. Her legs were no longer trembling, but her muscles protested at being forced to move again so soon. Ignoring that, she followed Domitian into the jungle, asking, "Shouldn't we use the beach?"

"It is shorter this way," he replied quietly.

Sarita nodded to herself as she forced her legs to follow him up a winding path. He hadn't gone to relieve himself in the woods then, but had been checking out the house to be sure it was safe to approach. The man seemed to forget she was a police officer and could take care of herself. They'd have to talk about that some time, she thought, and then glanced up and leaned to the side, trying to see how much farther they had to walk. Her calf muscles were burning like crazy.

Unable to see around Domitian's wide chest and shoulders, Sarita simply put her head down and continued forward, reciting song lyrics in her head as she went as a way to distract herself. It worked so well that she was completely unprepared when Domitian suddenly stopped. She plowed right into his back, nearly knocking him over.

"Woah," he whispered, reaching back to steady her as he regained his own balance.

"Sorry," Sarita muttered and clasped his arm to lean out and try to peer around him again. This time she managed the feat, and her eyes widened as she saw that they were there. A small English-style cottage sat not ten feet in front of them. Two stories, it was cross-gabled with steeply pitched roofs and tall, narrow, lattice windows. Her gaze slid over the chimney and gabled entry and she nodded solemnly. "Oh yeah, Mrs. Dressler lives here."

"What makes you say that?" Domitian asked in a whisper.

"She was missing England in her letter, and this is definitely a little bit of England in the middle of the tropics," Sarita pointed out. "It looks like it could have been scooped up out of the Cotswolds and dropped here or something."

He nodded agreement. "Yes, I suppose it does."

"Come on . . ." Sarita started to move around him, but he caught her arm.

"Wait," Domitian rasped, pulling her close to his side. "What is the plan?"

"We knock on the door and ask to see my grand-mother," she said simply.

"Just like that?" he asked with disbelief. "What if Dressler has some of his security detail in there?"

Sarita glanced at the cottage again and shook her head. "It's too small for that. My guess is there are three tiny bedrooms upstairs, a living room, bathroom, kitchen, and dining room downstairs. There can't be much more than that," she said with certainty.

"I did not say his men had to be living there," Domitian said grimly. "What if they are posted at the doors?"

Sarita sighed with exasperation, but supposed it wasn't impossible. "Okay, we'll look in the windows first and then knock on the door if there's no sign of Dressler's goons."

"And if there are goons in there?" Domitian asked.

"Then we come back here and make another plan," she said patiently. "Come on."

He didn't stop her this time when she started toward the house, but did mutter, "You are entirely too used to being a police officer."

Sarita scowled at him over her shoulder. "What does that mean?"

"It means you seem to think you can just walk up to the door and knock and no one will take a shot at you or anything."

"I agreed to check the windows, didn't I?" Sarita pointed out. "Besides, I suspect Dressler needs us alive for whatever nasty little experiment he has in mind for us, so we aren't likely to be shot. Now hush or we'll wake someone up before we want to," she warned, slowing as they approached the front window on this side of the house.

"Too late for that, children. Do come in. We're all awake."

Sarita stiffened and peered at the window as the voice of what she thought was an old woman drifted out to them. Only then did she see that the window was open. Mouth tightening, she peered in at the dark shapes inside.

"The door is unlocked," the voice said now and Sarita thought it was coming from a chair across the room where she could just make out what looked like a seated figure. The voice was definitely an old woman's and it had an English accent to it.

"Mrs. Dressler?" she asked.

"Yes, dear. And you are Maria's granddaughter, Sarita. Come in, dear, she'll be down in a minute."

Sarita turned at once and moved around the corner to the front of the house. Domitian was hard on her heels. When she got to it, the front door wasn't just unlocked, it was half-open. They both slowed cautiously as they entered. Sarita half expected someone to leap out and attack them, but nothing happened and she paused a couple of steps inside to glance around. They were in a tiny entry. A door on her left led into a small kitchen cast in shadows from a light that had been turned on in the room behind it. A set of stairs were directly in front of them, leading to the second floor, a narrow hall led past the stairs to a door at the back of the house, and a door on their right led into a small sitting room.

"Come in," Mrs. Dressler said again, sounding a bit impatient now. "And close the door, dear. Ramsey has a man stationed on the beach, and if he sees the door open he might decide to investigate."

Sarita turned back, but Domitian was already closing the door.

"The guard on the beach is also the reason we can't turn on any lights yet. So we'll just have to sit in the dark and talk until the sun rises," Mrs. Dressler added now as Domitian took Sarita's arm and led her into the room. While she couldn't see a thing in the unlighted space, he seemed to have no trouble navigating the dark. But then Dressler had mentioned night vision as one of the improvements the nanos gave their hosts, she recalled.

"Your eyes are glowing, young man," Mrs. Dressler said quietly. "Are you one of the hybrids my husband created and enjoys torturing?"

"No," Domitian murmured and Sarita glanced around to see that his eyes were indeed glowing. Rather like a cat's did at night, she thought. But that didn't disturb her as much as the fact that the woman's question suggested she knew what Dressler had been up to all these years.

Sarita had rather hoped that wasn't the case. She'd been hoping Mrs. Dressler and her grandmother had been both ignorant and innocent all these years, and that was why they'd never turned him in or done anything to stop him. It seemed that wasn't the case, though, and it worried her that their lack of action might make them accessories. They might even approve of his actions, she thought now and turned back toward the chair where Mrs. Dressler sat. Using her best constable's voice, Sarita asked, "So you know what your husband has been doing, ma'am?"

"Oh, yes, child. I know better than anyone what that bastard is up to."

Sarita relaxed a little. There was no way to mistake the tone in Mrs. Dressler's voice as anything but loathing. The woman hated her husband and didn't approve of what he was doing. It didn't get her, or Sarita's grandmother, off the hook for not trying to stop it. But at least they weren't accomplices.

"This way," Domitian said quietly, taking her hand now and leading her the rest of the way to what turned out to be a couch. When he sat and tugged at her hand, Sarita settled next to him and squinted toward the woman in the chair across from them, but couldn't make out much more than a silhouette.

"You said my grandmother was coming?" she asked politely.

"Yes. My son went to wake her after he got me up and about," Mrs. Dressler said softly. "That was just before you started chattering outside the window. She won't be too long. But not too quick either, I should imagine," she said wryly, and pointed out, "We're not as spry as we used to be."

"Of course," Sarita murmured and then just sat there like a bump on a log, completely at a loss as to what to say. The situation seemed somewhat surreal to her in that moment. Fortunately, Elizabeth Dressler didn't appear to have the same problem.

"My son thinks the pair of you swam here," she announced abruptly. "Is he right?"

"Yes," Sarita answered.

"Where from?" Mrs. Dressler asked at once.

"From the little island you first lived on when you moved here from England," Sarita admitted.

"All that way?" she asked with amazement.

"Yes," Sarita assured her and then admitted, "Well, really Domitian swam all that way, I spent a good deal of the night lounging around on an air mattress, watching him do all the work."

"And tackling men with gills who planned to stab me from behind," Domitian put in at once, apparently not appreciating the picture she'd just painted of herself as a useless female.

"Ah. One of Ramsey's hybrids," Elizabeth said and sounded weary now. "Most of them are victims who want nothing more than to be left alone. But some suffer a sort of syndrome—What do they call it when kidnap victims start to side with their kidnappers?" she asked, a frown evident in her voice.

"Stockholm syndrome, I think," Sarita murmured.

"Yes. That's it," Mrs. Dressler said at once. "Well, some of his hybrids suffer from a version of that and simply live to serve him. They are extremely dangerous," she warned. "Like Charles Manson's followers, they would do anything for him, even kill. Bear that in mind."

Sarita opened her mouth to say she would, only to close it and glance around as she heard a creak from upstairs.

"That is your grandmother leaving her room. She will be down here soon," Elizabeth commented and then added, "I feel I should warn you . . . she will not be pleased that you are here."

"What?" Sarita asked sharply, her head jerking back toward her. "Why not?"

"Because you have stumbled right into the heart of hell here, child," Mrs. Dressler said unhappily. "People that come to this island rarely leave. At least not alive. My husband sees to that."

"And you allow it?" Domitian asked, his voice deep in the darkness.

"Allow?" Mrs. Dressler asked with dry amusement. "I have nothing to do with it. I am as much a victim and prisoner as those poor hybrids he's created. So is Maria."

Sarita's eyes were beginning to adjust, or perhaps it was just growing lighter in the room as the sun crept closer to the horizon, but she was quite sure she saw Mrs. Dressler's head turn her way as she added, "Did you really believe your grandmother wanted to abandon the husband and young son she loved more than life itself? Or that she wouldn't have done anything to meet her only grandchild? No," she said firmly. "She had no choice. Her one joy all these years has been the letters first from your mother and then from you. These last fifteen years, she has consoled herself with the knowledge that you were at least safe in Canada, far away from this horror. So," she added grimly, "no, she will definitely not be pleased that you are here. Neither am I, for that matter."

"You?" Sarita asked with surprise. "Why would you care?"

"Your grandmother was kind enough to share her letters with me, Sarita. First your mother's, and then yours when your mother died. She'd read them to me and then write you back, speaking her response aloud as she wrote and I would often suggest she mention this or that. It made me feel a part of it," she admitted. "Those letters have been the only bright spot in a very dark world for both of us over these many years. I've come to feel I know you as well as your grandmother does. I've grown to care for you. And it breaks my heart to see you sitting here on this island within Ramsey's reach."

"Elizabeth?"

Sarita glanced behind her at that call and heard someone shuffling down the stairs.

"In the sitting room, dear," Mrs. Dressler called softly.

"Thorne said there was someone here to see me. Who could—Why are you sitting in the dark?" The question was accompanied by a click and light suddenly burst from overhead.

Blinking, Sarita stood and turned to look at her grandmother for the first time in her life. What she saw was an elderly woman in a cotton nightgown and a fluffy white robe that she was clutching to her throat. She had silver-white hair, startled dark brown eyes, and a kind, wrinkled face that was presently filled with confusion.

"Who are you?" she asked uncertainly, her hand tightening on the bit of robe she clutched at her throat as she glanced to Mrs. Dressler. "She looks like—"

"Yes, Maria. It's Sarita," Mrs. Dressler said, sounding sad.

"What?" the woman said with bewilderment and turned back to Sarita, who nodded.

"*Si, abuela.* It's me," she said almost apologetically.

"Sarita?" she asked, her voice high. She took a couple of unsteady steps into the room and then just collapsed.

# Twelve

Sarita rushed around the couch toward her grandmother, but Domitian was faster. He even managed to get there and catch her grandmother before she hit the floor, saving her what would undoubtedly have been a good knock to the head. The moment he scooped the fragile old lady up into his arms, her eyes fluttered open.

Grandmother peered around with confusion, but her gaze sharpened as it landed on the face of the man in whose arms she lay, and she demanded, "Who are you?"

Sarita moved closer, drawing her attention and offered a reassuring smile. "It's okay, *abuela*. He's my . . ." She hesitated and then finished with "friend," frowning even as she said the weak word. It should fit, but Domitian had already become more than that to her. The problem was she wasn't sure what that more was.

"Sarita, dear, turn out the light before Ramsey's man sees it," Mrs. Dressler ordered.

She glanced toward the woman, and then stepped over to the wall and flicked off the light her grandmother had just turned on. But a vision of Elizabeth Dressler was burned into the back of her eyes as she did. The woman was in a wheelchair, not a seat, and there was a terrible scar down the side of her face. A face that otherwise seemed familiar to Sarita despite never having seen her before even in pictures. While she'd sent pictures every time they were requested by her grandmother—which was several times a year—when Sarita had requested one in return she'd been told her grandmother didn't have a camera.

"Set me down. I can stand!"

Sarita bit her lip at her grandmother's cantankerous order and turned to look to where the two had been before the lights went out again, but she couldn't see a darned thing. She was completely blind now after the intrusion of the bright light. Her eyes needed to adjust again, she supposed, and then frowned as she realized Domitian hadn't responded to the demand and her grandmother hadn't repeated it, yet she could hear movement. Guessing he'd used some of that mind control business to soothe her grandmother and prevent further protest, he was probably now carrying her around to set her on the couch. Sarita decided to find her own way back to the couch.

Reaching forward tentatively and finding nothing in her path, she moved forward, sure the back of the couch wasn't far away.

"Look out the window, Thorne dear, and be sure your father's man didn't notice the light going on and off. He might come to investigate," Elizabeth Dressler murmured and Sarita stilled, her ears straining for the sounds of movement. She hadn't seen anyone else in the room when the lights had gone on, but she hadn't really looked anywhere but at her grandmother and Mrs. Dressler.

Something brushed against her arm, and Sarita stiffened and turned her head. She smelled a hint of sea breeze and jungle and then a shadow moved in front of the window to the left of the front door, and she caught her breath at the misshapen silhouette revealed. Instead of a head and shoulders, it looked like Thorne had three heads, or a head and two humps, she thought. She glanced around with surprise when someone touched her arm.

"This way," Domitian said softly, drawing her to the right and in front of the couch again. He steered her along the couch and then urged her to sit. "Your *abuela* is on your left."

"Thank you," Sarita murmured as she settled on the cushions and then felt a hand on her arm. Knowing it was her grandmother reaching for her, she covered the hand with her own, but glanced back to the window only to see that the silhouette was gone.

"He doesn't appear to have noticed anything amiss," a voice as deep as Domitian's announced near where Mrs. Dressler sat.

"What are you doing here, Chiquita?" her grandmother asked unhappily as Sarita felt Domitian settle on the couch next to her.

"I came for you," Sarita said apologetically, squeezing her grandmother's hand in the darkness.

"Oh, such a good girl," her grandmother crooned sadly and Sarita caught a whiff of roses and then found herself pulled into the soft embrace of a much shorter and rounder woman as she added, "But I don't understand. Why?"

Sarita hugged her back, closing her eyes as a wave of emotion rolled over her. It had been two years since she'd had the love and comfort of family. Forcing back the overwhelming feelings, she cleared her throat and explained, "Dr. Dressler called and said you fell and hurt yourself."

"Fell?" her grandmother asked, pulling back as if she were trying to see her face to verify she'd heard her right.

Since Sarita couldn't see her grandmother, she doubted very much that the old woman could see her, so she said, "Yes. He said he was worried that there could be complications and felt my visiting might help you get through this."

"But I haven't fallen," Maria Reyes said with a confusion that soon turned to vexation as she added, "The old *bastardo*! What is he up to now?"

"Nothing good, I'm sure," Elizabeth Dressler said wearily and then asked, "But if he invited you to the island, why did you have to swim from the little island?"

"You were on the little island?" her grandmother asked.

*"Si,"* Sarita answered, squeezing her hand and then said, "I was here first. When I arrived I was told you were in the hospital and would be back on the island soon and I should wait. But the third day I was here, he knocked me out and I woke up on the little island with Domitian. We think we were supposed to be part of some kind of experiment," she admitted, but didn't explain that she thought it had to do with sex. It was her grandmother after all.

"Then you *are* one of the hybrids," Elizabeth Dressler growled, sounding furious. "And you were probably privy to what was going on the whole time."

Sarita stilled, at first thinking she meant her, but then the woman added, "What did Ramsey want you to do to our Sarita?" The question had barely ended before she snapped, "Thorne, restrain him."

"No," Sarita barked, practically throwing herself across Domitian's lap. "He's not with Dressler, he's here to catch him."

"What?" Mrs. Dressler gasped.

There was suddenly absolute silence in the room as if everyone had frozen and Sarita frowned with frustration, wishing there was some light so she could see where everyone was and what they were doing. Especially Thorne.

Hoping the stillness meant they would listen and leave Domitian alone, Sarita straightened to sit next to him again and explained, "People have been going missing from North America. Enough that it was noticed, and a—" she hesitated and then said "—a special policing team was put together to find out who was taking them, why, and where they were taken to. This team tracked the disappearances to Caracas and Dr. Dressler, but by the time they got here, Dressler had taken a sabbatical from the university and retreated to the island. They were able to find out he had an island, but not where it was. Apparently there's no record of his owning an island."

"He bought it under my maiden name," Mrs. Dressler said. "Elizabeth Salter. I didn't understand why at the time, but it was probably for just this sort of eventuality. The man is always thinking ten steps ahead of everyone else," she finished bitterly.

"Oh," Sarita breathed and glanced instinctively to Domitian. She couldn't see his expression, but when he squeezed her hand, she turned back. "Well, they didn't catch that, so sent teams out in boats to scout the islands. But eight of their people went missing during the searches and they were no closer to finding the island, so Domitian agreed to accept a job from Dressler to be a chef on the island to help them locate it. The plan was for them to track his phone to find the island, but Dressler didn't really want Domitian for the chef job. That was apparently just bait to get him here. The moment he got on the helicopter to fly here, he was knocked out. He was then dumped on the little island with me. That was the day before yesterday. Or maybe it was the day before that now," she added uncertainly, exhaustion slowing her thinking. Finally she stopped trying to work out the day count and simply said, "This is the third morning since both of us woke up on the island."

There was silence for a minute and then Thorne asked, "This special police force is going to storm the island?"

It was hard to tell if he was glad or concerned, Thorne's voice seemed to hold both emotions and again Sarita wished the light was better so she could see his face. As the sun rose, lighting in the room slowly got brighter, but it was still full of shadows and Thorne seemed to be in the darkest shadow in the room.

"They want to," she said firmly. "But they can't until they figure out where it is. As I say, they were hoping to track Domitian's phone, but Dressler must have destroyed or disabled it or they'd already have stormed the island, taken Dressler into custody, and freed the people he's taken."

"But why would El Doctor put you on the little island with this man, Chiquita?" her grandmother asked.

"Probably to harvest eggs," Mrs. Dressler said grimly, saving Sarita having to answer.

"He wouldn't need the man for that. Just Sarita," Thorne said, and the familiarity with which he used her name startled her. He spoke her name as if he had known her for years. But then, perhaps he too had been there for the letter readings, she thought. Perhaps like Mrs. Dressler he felt he knew her from her writings.

A crooked smile claimed her lips. It seemed like everyone in this room knew all about her life and had known of her and felt connected to her for years, Domitian with his private detective reports, and the rest of them from her letters. She was the only one who didn't or hadn't known much in return. She hadn't known about Domitian at all, and other than mentioning their names, her grandmother hadn't said much about Thorne or Elizabeth Dressler, and hadn't revealed much about herself either . . . like that she'd been a prisoner here all these years.

"Perhaps he was hoping for some fertilized eggs," Mrs. Dressler said into the silence.

"He couldn't have expected my little Sarita to have sex with a stranger," her grandmother protested at once. "She's a good girl."

Sarita winced at those words, and felt Domitian squeezing her hand gently.

"I wouldn't put it past Ramsey to have put drugs in whatever food and water he supplied to get whatever he wanted," Elizabeth said gently in response and then turned her head back toward Sarita and Domitian and added, "It's good you left the little island. Whatever reason he had for putting you there could not be good. But why come here?" she asked almost plaintively. "This is even less safe for you than the little island."

"That is my fault," Sarita admitted. "Domitian wanted to swim for the mainland, but I found a half-written letter from you, Mrs. Dressler, to someone named Margaret. It was tucked in a book in the office. In it you mentioned that this island was about half an hour or forty-five minutes north of the little island by fishing boat. That seemed manageable, whereas we weren't sure how far the mainland was.

"Besides, I was worried about you, Grandmother," Sarita said, addressing the woman next to her. "I saw one of his experiments in that lab of his, and after Dressler knocked me out, and then I learned about all the people he's been taking and experimenting on, I was worried about you. I thought this way we could check to be sure you were all right, get the exact co-ordinates for the island from you, use your phone to call the mainland, and pass along the information. And now I can tell them to be cautious, that there are hybrids and humans who are not on Dressler's side, but some who are."

"Oh, Chiquita . . ." Maria Reyes squeezed her hand firmly with one of her own, and patted it with her other. "We have no phone. El Doctor would not trust us with one. We could not even seal any letters we sent from the island. They had to go through him and he read them first."

Sarita wasn't terribly surprised by this. It actually explained the odd tone of the letters over the years. They were affectionate yet reserved at the same time.

A curse from Domitian brought her from her thoughts

and Sarita turned his way and assured him, "It is all right. There is a phone in the big house."

"Are you sure?" he asked with concern.

"Yes. The office door was open one day and I rushed to it thinking Dr. Dressler must be back, but Big Beefy Guy was inside talking on a phone."

Rather than relax at this news, she could actually see him frown. The room was getting lighter quickly. In fact, she could see him well enough to notice that he was extremely pale.

"Getting into the house might be tricky," he said now with concern. "I do not like your taking that risk. I will do it myself and—"

"Yeah right," Sarita said and snorted rudely at the suggestion. "Not gonna happen. Besides, it isn't *that* risky. Dressler's security is a joke," she assured him. "All we have to do is wait until dinnertime and we can practically walk in."

Domitian shook his head. "I do not want you taking that risk."

"And I am not going to be left behind like some helpless creature who can't take care of herself," she snapped impatiently. Honestly! She was trained for this stuff. Well, not exactly *this* stuff, Sarita acknowledged, but she wasn't some—

"Perhaps it would be better to try to steal a boat," Domitian said now. "That way we could take every one in this room and get them safely away from the island before the raid." Glancing to where Thorne stood hidden in the shadows, he asked, "He has more than one boat here, *si*?"

"Yes," Thorne answered. "But the keys are kept elsewhere and he keeps both the keys and the boats well guarded. He makes sure that no one can leave the island without his say so. As for the security on the house," he added and Sarita thought his head turned slightly her way. "While most of the men leave their posts at dinner-time. There are still some on duty, and the cameras do not turn off. They are on all day every day. The minute you entered the house someone would know."

Sarita pursed her lips as she considered the situation and then said, "His office has French doors. We'd have to go in that way. I could barricade the doors to the hall while you made the call. You'd have to be quick, just tell them the island is owned by Elizabeth Salter, and warn them to be prepared for a large security force and then get off. Hopefully that way we can get out before they stop us."

"And if we don't?" Domitian asked solemnly.

"Then we get caught and hold on until help comes," she said with a shrug.

"You don't seem to understand," Thorne said now. "The cameras are everywhere around the house, labs, and dock. They are also in trees on the border of the jungle so that Dressler can see every inch of shoreline and yard."

Sarita stiffened and looked to Domitian with alarm. "He'll know we're here then."

"No," Thorne said, drawing her gaze his way again. "Fortunately for you I couldn't sleep last night and was out . . . walking. I noticed you in the ocean long before you neared shore and took care of the cameras on the cove where you came out."

"Took care of them how?" Domitian asked.

"I snapped a branch above one, so that it hung in front of it obscuring its view. No doubt they'll send someone out to check on it, but hopefully they'll just assume an animal landed on the branch and snapped it."

"You said you took care of *them*," Domitian pointed out.

"I positioned myself in front of the other one until you left the cove," Thorne admitted reluctantly. "They won't think much of my being there."

"In the tree?" Sarita asked, recalling the sounds she'd heard and the moving branches in the tree. If this man had caused it, he was one hell of a tree climber, she thought. The branches she'd seen move had been at the top, some thirty feet in the air at least.

Thorne grunted in the affirmative and then added, "There are no cameras in the jungle itself, just in the trees along the border. There were at one time but they kept getting damaged or destroyed by animals, so Dressler didn't bother replacing them. He felt watching the approach to the jungle was sufficient. So once the two of you had started up the hill, I hurried ahead to wake mother and warn her you were coming. Once I had her situated out here, I took care of the cameras along the side and front of the house as well, and then went up to wake Maria."

"Will he not think it odd that all the cameras on the front and side of the house were destroyed?" Domitian asked, a frown in his voice.

"No. I destroy them regularly," Thorne said with a shrug.

"And Ramsey repairs them regularly," Mrs. Dressler added dryly. "It is a silent battle of wills between Thorne and his father."

"Do not call him my father," Thorne said stiffly. "He is a sperm donor, nothing else."

"Wait," Sarita said now, sitting up straight and trying to pierce the shadows around Thorne with her eyes as she asked, "How did you know who we were, or that we were headed here to the house?"

"You were talking when you came out of the water," he said with unconcern. "But even if you hadn't mentioned wanting to see your grandmother, I would have recognized you at once from your pictures," he said quietly. "Except for the color and style of your bathing suit, you could have stepped out of the one you sent Maria of you and your friends at the beach celebrating your getting into the police college."

"Right," Sarita said and sagged back on the couch, reminded of the skimpy suit she was wearing. She was suddenly grateful the light wasn't that great in here. Forgetting that her grandmother had already seen her, she said, "Don't have a heart attack when you see my swimsuit, *abuela*. It wasn't my choice, it was what Dressler left at the house for me." She grimaced and added, "Although I suppose I shouldn't complain—at least I had a change of clothes, even if I don't care for how revealing they are. Poor Domitian has been wearing the same boxers for three days."

"Oh dear, well we can do something about that at least," Elizabeth Dressler said, and suddenly wheeled her chair around the couch and toward the kitchen. "Come along Sarita, Maria, we'll raid my closet and see if we can't find something a little more suitable."

Sarita stood when her grandmother did, but glanced uncertainly to Domitian.

"Thorne," Mrs. Dressler said then. "Will you see if you have something Sarita's 'friend' can wear?"

"Of course," he murmured.

Mrs. Dressler nodded with satisfaction and then smiled at Sarita's grandmother when she took up position behind her chair and began to wheel her from the room. "Thank you, Maria," she murmured and then said again, "Come along, Sarita."

"Go. I will be fine," Domitian said when she still hesitated.

Nodding, Sarita turned to follow the two women. It turned out she'd been wrong. There might be three bedrooms upstairs, but the room she'd assumed would be a dining room turned out to be Mrs. Dressler's bedroom on the main floor. Still, Sarita suspected it had originally been a dining room, but had been converted to accommodate the elderly woman in her wheelchair.

"Here we are. Now, let's see . . ."

Mrs. Dressler's words drew her attention to the closet the woman had opened. It was a good size, running the length of the room, but the clothes all hung high enough that there was no way the woman could reach them. Sarita had just decided her grandmother must fetch the clothes she wanted for her, when Mrs. Dressler snatched up a long rod hanging amid the clothes and used the hook on the end to lift down a lightweight cotton peasant blouse.

"What about this?" she asked, holding it out to Sarita.

"It's beautiful," Sarita assured her, taking the top.

"Oh, yes that would look lovely on you, Chiquita," her grandmother said happily. "I have just the skirt for you to wear with it. And it is new, I just finished making it. Wait here and I will fetch it."

Sarita watched the little woman hurry from the room with a smile that faded slowly as she thought of what Mrs. Dressler had said earlier. Turning back to the woman, she said, "You suggested you were all prisoners here. Including my grandmother?"

"Yes," the woman said simply.

"Why?" she asked with a frown. "From what I understand when she was first employed by you, Grandmother came to work in the mornings and was allowed to leave at night. At least she did while you lived on the little island. Why did that not continue here?"

"It did for the first couple weeks after we moved here to the big house," Mrs. Dressler said, hanging her hooked pole from the clothes rod again. Sitting back in her seat then, she sighed and added, "But then I went into early labor with Thorne." Mouth tightening, she explained, "I had made arrangements to move to the mainland for the last month of my pregnancy in case there were complications. Ramsey was going to fly me out the next day, but suddenly I was in the throes of it. What I didn't know then was that Ramsey had no intention of letting me have my son on the mainland and had put something into my drink at lunch to induce labor."

Sarita's eyebrows rose at that. She was surprised he'd take the risk with his own child. If complications had occurred he might have lost both his wife and child.

Huffing out an angry breath, Mrs. Dressler continued, "I should have realized something was amiss when he cancelled his classes for the day and was home in the middle of the week. He said it was because he wanted to spend time with me, and I thought it was sweet and even fortunate that he was there when I started having contractions. I hurried to him, sure he'd put me in the helicopter and fly me straight to the mainland, but he said everything was fine. It was too early, these were probably just Braxton Hicks contractions. He said I should just relax and breathe, and they would surely go away. He kept saying that right up until my water broke."

Her mouth tightened and anger crossed her face. "And then he showed his true colors. The sweet man I thought I'd married became a cold hard monster. He flat out said he'd never had any intention of my going to the mainland to have the baby. He'd brought the labor on early to ensure that didn't happen, so I might as well resign myself to the fact that I was having the baby here on the island, and stop whining and crying at him. I'd be in labor for hours. Go lie down and leave him alone. He'd check on me later and help if necessary."

"I was young then," Mrs. Dressler said sadly. "And I was shattered by his behavior. I burst into tears and stumbled back to my room and locked the door. And then I decided I wanted that man nowhere near my baby and stuck a chair under it to make sure he couldn't get in." Clucking her tongue she shook her head and added, "And with that one action, I sealed your grandmother's fate."

Sarita's eyebrows rose at the words. "How?"

"Because Maria was in the room," she explained quietly. "I didn't realize it until I finished jamming the chair under the door and turned to see her frozen with the bed half-made, her eyes wide."

Mrs. Dressler shook her head sadly. "If I'd known what my actions would mean for your poor grandmother, I would have moved the chair and ordered her out at once. But I didn't know, and I was grateful to have her there. I was scared and feeling more alone than I had in my life and she was all I had." Smiling wryly, she said, "We weren't exactly friends back then.

While your grandmother knew a few words of English, I knew not a single word of Spanish. There was a bit of a communication barrier there, but Maria was kind and gentle and supportive and helped me through the darkest hours of my life. She is the one who saw Thorne into this world." Mrs. Dressler sighed. "And the moment she laid eyes on him, Maria was doomed to remain on this island for the rest of her days."

"Why?" Sarita asked with confusion.

"Because she saw what I am."

Jerking around, Sarita peered toward the doorway at that grim comment and got her first really good look at Thorne Dressler. The man was breathtaking. With high cheekbones, a chiseled jaw, pale golden eyes, and hair so fair a blond it was almost white where it lay flat against his head. Towheaded, she thought, that was what they called it because it was the color of tow—flax or hemp fibers.

Sarita stared at him blankly for a minute and then shook her head slightly. "I don't understand why seeing you would—"

The words died in her throat as he stepped into the room and out of the shadow that had hidden the humps at his back. Still staring at his face, she'd barely noted the humps when he suddenly swung his arms out and up. Immediately, the two humps dropped and swung out into two huge chocolate-brown wings. They stretched out at least six feet to each side of his back, touching the walls at either end of the room.

"Dear God," she breathed.

Thorne's mouth tightened as if at a blow.

"They're magnificent," she finished and he blinked, looking suddenly uncertain.

"Did you find some clothes for Domitian?" Mrs. Dressler asked gently.

Clearing his throat, Thorne nodded and looked at his mother as he said, "Yes. That is why I came. I thought to tell you he is all set and changing." He hesitated and then said, "I will put on some tea and wait with him in the kitchen for you ladies to finish."

"Thank you, son," Elizabeth Dressler said affectionately.

Sarita watched him leave, her gaze sliding from his pale golden eyes, the sleek, white cap of what she now thought might be feathers not hair, and then as he turned to leave the room, she examined the chocolate-colored wings that had folded back into place behind his back. She also saw that there was no back on his shirt below his shoulders. It had been specially made to accommodate his wings.

"Bald Eagle?" she asked softly once he'd left the room.

"Yes." The word hissed out of Mrs. Dressler on a sigh. "My husband—" the word sounded like a curse from her lips "—apparently drugged me and harvested my eggs on our wedding night. He fertilized them with his sperm and then injected them with various concoctions of mixed DNA from animals he considered valuable. At least I think that's what he told me." She waved a hand irritably and added, "I was a tad distressed at the time."

"I can imagine," Sarita said sympathetically.

"Anyway, while I don't pretend to understand what he did, he did mention gene splicing or something when I confronted him." She shook her head, and then added, "He apparently drugged me again about a week after our wedding and planted one in my womb. My Thorne."

She glanced toward the door where her son had been and then back to Sarita. "The eagle in him shows up the most because of the wings and his eyes. Ramsey always had to wear glasses, so the exceptional vision eagles are known for appealed to him. But Ramsey says there is other DNA in him too. Jellyfish because they age backward. Salamander because they can regenerate limbs, ears, even their hearts, and so on. We don't know what all he has, or what it could mean. Ramsey wanted to test him over the years to see what DNA had taken and what effect it had, but I refused to let him anywhere near my son," she said grimly. "I couldn't protect all those other children he made, but I kept him from Thorne and refused to even live in the same house with him. I threatened to live in the jungle if he didn't build a small cottage for me, Maria, and Thorne to live in, and I would have. I couldn't bear that house after realizing the kind of monster I'd married. I think I would have killed myself long ago if not for Maria and Thorne."

Sarita peered at Mrs. Dressler's face. While she obviously loved and was proud of her son, she was also furious and probably hurt that the husband she'd thought loved her had done such a thing. And she was probably hurting for her son too, because the man could never have a normal life. Were he to show up on the mainland, she had no doubt he'd soon find himself in a lab somewhere, being poked, prodded, and experimented on as doctors and scientists tried to sort out just what he was.

"Here we are."

Sarita glanced to the door as her grandmother rushed back in, and she thought about what Elizabeth had said.

Maria Reyes had been kind and comforting and had been doomed to remain here the moment she'd helped bring Thorne into this world.

Of course, now that she'd seen Thorne properly, Sarita understood. She was quite sure everything Dressler had done was illegal. From harvesting his wife's eggs without her permission to the genetic game of Scrabble he'd played with them and so on. He couldn't risk her grandmother leaving the island and telling anyone what she'd seen.

So all these years, her grandmother had been kept here against her will, while her husband and son had thought she'd abandoned them. Sarita could have wept for her . . . for all three of them really. If her father and grandfather had known the truth, she had no doubt they would have moved heaven and earth to bring her *abuela* home. Not knowing the truth, though, they'd thought she'd abandoned them and had hated her for it instead.

"Do you like it?"

Sarita forced her attention to the skirt her grandmother was holding out and smiled with surprise. It was a lovely slate-blue peasant skirt. Touching the soft material, she nodded. "Yes."

"Are you sure?" her grandmother asked and frowned down at it. "It's probably ridiculously old-fashioned, I know, but we don't have patterns here to make the clothes. We are lucky Ramsey brings in cloth for us at all, and—"

"*Abuela,*" Sarita said firmly, tugging the skirt from her and hugging her tightly. "Peasant skirts will never go out of style. It's beautiful. I love it."

Releasing her, she added dryly, "And I will be ever so

glad to be wearing something more than—as Domitian put it—a hanky ripped into three tiny bits and pasted on."

Her grandmother looked her over in the minuscule bikini she wore and smiled wryly. "I am surprised he complained. You are gorgeous, Chiquita."

Sarita chuckled. "He was complaining that he found it distracting when we were trying to sort out a way off the island."

"Now that I can believe," she said with a grin, and then tilted her head and asked, "He is a good man, *si*?"

"Yes," Sarita answered without hesitation. "He is a very good man."

"How?" she asked at once.

Sarita blinked in surprise, but didn't have any trouble answering. "Well, he's strong and smart and brave. He's considerate too. And he can cook," she added, that was pretty important since she couldn't. "And I think he must be the most patient man I've ever met, and—" Sarita paused and glanced at her grandmother uncertainly when she released a little sigh. "What's wrong?"

"Nothing," her grandmother said quickly.

It was Elizabeth Dressler who said, "I'm afraid your grandmother and I have allowed ourselves to dabble in fantasy a bit more than we should to relieve the boredom here. We had rather built up the hope that someday perhaps Ramsey would die, and we would be free to invite you here. We were sure once you met my Thorne, the two of you would fall in love and we could live happily here with the pair of you producing several grandbabies for us to spoil."

"What?" Sarita gasped, her eyes wide with shock. Turning on her grandmother, she said, "You didn't!"

"Well, Thorne thought you were pretty when he saw

your picture . . . and he enjoyed your letters as much as we did," her grandmother said defensively. "And he is a good man, Chiquita. He is so good to us, but he is so lonely. He deserves to be happy too." She sighed and shook her head. "But if you love this Domitian then . . ." She shrugged.

"I never said I love Domitian," Sarita squawked with alarm, feeling her cheeks heat up with embarrassment. "We hardly know each other. We only met a couple days ago on the little island. I can't possibly love him."

"The things you said about him suggest you know him well, and they sounded like love to me," her grandmother said and then glanced to Elizabeth Dressler. "Did you not think so, Elizabeth?"

"Yes, I'm afraid so."

"Si." Her grandmother glanced back and shrugged. "But if it is not, then bueno. There is a chance still for you and Thorne."

"Er . . ." Sarita said weakly.

"Come on, Maria," Mrs. Dressler said, sounding amused. "Thorne was making tea. Let's go see if it is ready and leave Sarita to dress."

Nodding, her grandmother moved around behind the woman's chair and wheeled her out.

Sarita watched them go and then blew out her breath and shook her head.

"Unbelievable," she murmured. The pair had been marrying her off to Thorne in their fantasies before she'd even met them, let alone the man in question. Wow. So this was what having a grandmother was like?

The thought made her smile faintly. Sarita's grandparents on her mother's side had died while she was quite young. Her memories of them were fuzzy at best.

They consisted of a grandfather who always had a smile on his face and a cigar in his hand, and a grandmother who had smelled of lavender. That was it. It looked like having a grandparent was going to be interesting.

Shaking her head, she began to pull the borrowed clothes on over her swimsuit.

# Thirteen

"You must be tired after swimming all night."

Domitian tore his eyes away from the closed door to Mrs. Dressler's room at that comment from Sarita's grandmother and turned his attention back to the people seated at the tiny kitchen table with him. Mrs. Dressler, Maria Reyes, and Thorne. The table seemed almost too small for the three of them to eat at. He hadn't thought they'd fit five chairs around it. They'd managed it, though. It was tight, but would serve for having tea.

"Yes, I am a bit tired," he said finally, mostly because they would expect any normal person to be tired after such a trek. But while Domitian was tired, he was also in pain. He'd definitely used up a lot of blood with the swim here and needed more. However, he wasn't going to feed off any of the people here at the table. The women were both in their late seventies by his guess, and fragile. Feeding off them could cause a heart attack. As for Thorne—

His gaze shifted to the man. Thorne looked to be in his early thirties, but there was no way he was that young. This house was old and the walls thin, Domitian had had no trouble hearing what Mrs. Dressler had told Sarita about her marriage and her son's birth. If he'd been born eight months after she and Dr. Dressler married and moved to Venezuela, then he knew Thorne was in his fifties.

It wasn't Thorne's age, however, that removed him from consideration as a blood donor. It was the fact that he wasn't wholly human. Domitian had no idea how the DNA splicing had affected Thorne's blood, or how his blood would affect him. He wouldn't risk it.

"Oh well—" Sarita's grandmother began, and then paused as the bedroom door opened and her granddaughter stepped out.

Domitian was on his feet at once, and moving behind the empty chair next to his own. He'd fetched it for her from the living room as they'd arranged the table. It was a straight-backed cushioned chair and he now pulled it out slightly, his eyes sliding over Sarita as she approached in a pure white peasant blouse with a slate-blue peasant skirt. She looked beautiful and he smiled and murmured, "Lovely," as she approached.

Sarita smiled at the compliment as she settled into the chair he held for her. "Thank you."

"My pleasure," he murmured, easing the chair in.

"Domitian was just saying that he was tired from swimming all night," Sarita's grandmother commented as he reclaimed his seat.

"Yes," Mrs. Dressler agreed. "And actually I could do with a little rest myself. I'm not used to getting up this early."

"Neither am I," Maria Reyes admitted and then confessed, "I seem to sleep in later and later the older I get."

"Then I think we should all go to bed after tea," Mrs. Dressler announced. "Sarita, you can have the guest room upstairs. It used to be my room until . . ." She gestured to her wheelchair with distaste.

"Domitian can have my room," Thorne said. "I'm not tired, and someone should keep an eye on the guard on the beach anyway. Make sure he doesn't come up to the house."

"Well, good then. It is all decided," Sarita's grandmother said brightly. "We will finish our tea and then all get some rest. That way we will be bright and well rested when we decide how best to get the needed information to the police waiting to raid the island."

Domitian eyed the old women, noting their satisfied expressions and got the distinct impression they had planned this between the two of them. They obviously didn't want Sarita doing anything as risky as accompanying him to the house to use the phone, and he agreed with them. In fact, they'd just made things easier for him. He could pretend to go to bed, wait until he was sure Sarita was sleeping, and then slip out and go make the call himself . . . stopping along the way to feed on one of Dressler's security men of course. *Or two*, he added, and then noticed that Sarita was eyeing him with concern.

No doubt she'd noticed his pallor, Domitian thought with an inward sigh. Unfortunately, the sun was now climbing the sky and streaming through the windows and there was no way she would miss it. The woman didn't miss much of anything from what he could tell.

"Yes, sleep sounds a good idea," he said now, smiling at Sarita's grandmother and Mrs. Dressler.

Much to his relief, Sarita nodded in agreement and her grandmother then asked her if she'd received her last letter before leaving for Venezuela. As she turned to answer her, Domitian considered his plan. Telling his uncle that the island had been purchased under the name Elizabeth Salter would be helpful in getting them here, but it certainly wouldn't prepare the Rogue Hunters for what they would encounter once they arrived. Part of his coming had been to get as much information as he could about the security on the island and whatnot.

Turning to Thorne, he asked, "Do you know how many security men and domestic workers Dr. Dressler has on the island?"

The man hesitated, but then shook his head regretfully. "Other than a couple of trips to check out where the cameras were and to see if I could not take one of the boats and get my mother and Maria away from here, I stay away from that side of the island as much as possible."

"At my request," Mrs. Dressler said solemnly. "The last thing I want is Ramsey to get his hands on Thorne and experiment on him as he has the others. So he stays here at the cottage for the most part."

"We all do," Maria Reyes said sadly, breaking off her conversation with her granddaughter. "Our whole life is this cottage, the garden, and the beach below the cliff."

Domitian nodded with understanding, but wished it was otherwise. Some information about what the Rogue Hunters would be facing would be helpful, and so far he had very little.

"He has a fair number of people here," Sarita said

quietly, drawing his attention as she began to tick them off on her fingers. "In the house there was the cook, Aleta. She rarely leaves the kitchen so shouldn't be a problem. But there are at least four other people inside the house who help with cleaning and whatnot. There were also three or four men and women working outside in the gardens." She paused briefly and then said, "That's it for domestics. At least at the house."

"And security?" Domitian asked.

"There was a ton of security," she admitted. "He had four men at the front door, two inside and two out, and two more at the back door out to the garden, one in and one out. But I saw a good twenty of them coming from every direction at meal times, so I think there must be a lot of them who walk the beach, the yard, and the jungle. And that's not including the guys in the towers and gatehouse down by the labs."

"Towers and gatehouse?" he asked with interest.

Sarita nodded. "Aside from the guy in the gatehouse, there were four towers. One on each corner of the fencing around the labs," she said succinctly. "There were two men in each tower. But they were more interested in staring at the buildings inside the fence than anyone coming from outside." She paused, and then said, "Now that I know about the people they've kidnapped, I suppose their job is really to watch for possible escape attempts rather than intruders getting in." Her mouth twisted slightly. "I did think when I saw it that the setup looked more like a prison than labs."

Shaking her head, she said, "But while there are lots of men around, like I said, his security is a joke. At least by the labs. The guy in the gatehouse was watching porn. I just walked right past him. And the guys in the towers didn't notice me walking to the buildings until I was halfway to the first one. I was inside before they could climb down the ladder to the ground." She paused and said, "He may have more people inside the buildings, though. In fact, I know he has at least one other person working with him. His assistant, Asherah," Sarita said and then added, "She was a tall blond Amazon, cold as a fish and snarky. Didn't seem to like me much."

"Impossible," Domitian said softly and Sarita grinned at him in response. He smiled back and then said, "Tell me about Dressler's labs."

Sarita nodded. "I only saw the first room of the building closest to the gate. But there are several buildings. From the helicopter I counted six in the fenced-in area and one outside of it. They look like army barracks, long low, narrow metal structures with only one door each on the end facing the gatehouse. No windows that I saw," Sarita added grimly and then said, "I think the one outside the fence is probably the barracks and mess hall for the security guys. A bunch of them would come up at meal times to collect the food, but they took it back to that building to eat and then returned the pans and stuff after."

She paused, thought for a minute, and then shrugged. "That's all I know."

Domitian nodded on a sigh. It would have to be enough.

"But we can't forget to mention the gilled man to your uncle," Sarita added suddenly. "There might be more like him out there. In fact, now that I think about it, there most likely are. That is probably how your uncle and that Santo fellow as well as the others were dragged off the boats and disappeared without your sister and the other pilots seeing."

*"Si."* Domitian nodded slowly. That made perfect sense. They could easily have been shot with a dart and dragged over the side, pulled down into the depths and dragged away by one of the creatures he'd killed on their way here. They could have dragged the immortals all the way to the island without surfacing and not killed them. The nanos would simply have gone into a sort of stasis and then activated again to repair things once oxygenated blood was available again. He doubted that had happened, however. Some of them had been taken so far from the island that traveling back and forth would take too long. There must have been boats around, out of sight, waiting for them to bring their quarry.

"Warn them about winged hybrids watching from the air too," Thorne said.

Domitian glanced to him sharply, but he wasn't being sarcastic.

Raising an eyebrow, the man asked, "Did you think I was the only one?"

"Actually, I did," Domitian admitted with a wry twist to his lips. "There are others, though?"

Thorne nodded. "They only fly at night. Probably because El Doctor doesn't wish them to be seen, but sometimes they fly out quite a distance over the ocean."

"Are there other hybrids I need to warn them about?" he asked.

"I'm sure there are many variations," he said grimly. "However, since I do not go to the other side of the island . . ." He shrugged. "I'm afraid I can't help you."

"Of course," Domitian said and nodded thoughtfully. He'd just have to warn them to keep their eyes open.

"Well, I don't know about the rest of you but I'm ready for bed," Mrs. Dressler announced brightly.

"Me too." Sarita's grandmother stood, hesitated and then bent to kiss Sarita's cheek shyly before saying, "You should sleep too, Chiquita. You have been up all night."

"Yes, *abuela*," Sarita said softly, her hand rising to touch her cheek where her grandmother had kissed her.

"I'll walk up with you after I see Elizabeth to bed," Maria Reyes added with a smile.

Domitian saw the way Sarita's eyes softened and realized quite suddenly that she hadn't had the softer influence and affection of a female in her life for a very long time, not since she was thirteen. This must all be a bit overwhelming for her in some respects.

"Goodnight, Sarita," Mrs. Dressler said, reaching out to squeeze her hand affectionately. "Sleep well."

"You too," Sarita said and then stood to kiss her cheek, before straightening to hug her grandmother and kiss her cheek too.

Both women beamed at her for the affectionate display, and then Mrs. Dressler smiled at Domitian and said, "Thorne's room is the first door on the left at the top of the stairs. You should run along to bed. You look ready to drop."

Domitian nodded politely and stood as Sarita's grandmother began to wheel the woman away. When the ladies disappeared into the room and Sarita turned back, he kissed her cheek gently. "I'll leave you to your grandmother and go get some rest. Sleep well."

"Goodnight," Sarita whispered, and he saw her earlier concern flicker across her face. "Are you okay?"

"I am fine," he assured her and then turned and slipped away before she could ask anything else that might force him to lie.

"Well, this is Elizabeth's old room," Sarita's grandmother said, a little breathless from mounting the stairs. She gestured to the door on their right as they stepped into the upper hall.

"Oh." Sarita glanced at it and then said, "I'll just walk you to your door."

"Don't be silly. It's only a couple feet. Go on in and go to bed. I know you must be tired." She patted her shoulder, then turned her cheek up and Sarita bent to kiss her again, which made the woman beam once more. Turning away, she headed for the door at the end of the hall and said, "Goodnight, dear."

"Goodnight," Sarita murmured and watched her, but then she opened her door and slipped inside when her grandmother reached her own door and glanced back.

Sarita eased the door closed and then simply stood there listening until she heard her grandmother's door open and close. Letting her breath out on a little sigh, she then eased her door open again and glanced out into the hall. Finding it empty, Sarita hesitated, her gaze sliding to the door across the hall where Domitian was. But finally, she slipped out and tiptoed across to his door.

She started to raise her hand to knock, but caught herself at the last moment and rolled her eyes. Someone would hear. She was definitely tired. Giving her head a shake, Sarita turned the doorknob slowly and carefully and then slipped inside.

Domitian was lying on top of the bed, fully clothed and wide awake. He sat up at once as she entered, but remained silent as she eased his door carefully closed. He didn't say anything after that even, but simply watched silently as she approached the bed, Sarita noted as her gaze slid over him.

He was wearing jeans and a backless shirt. She'd noticed that when he'd walked away to go upstairs. But then she supposed she shouldn't have expected anything else. Thorne wouldn't have shirts with backs in them. Still it had startled her and she'd had to bite back a laugh.

She wasn't laughing now. You couldn't see that the shirt was different from the front and this was the first time she'd seen him in anything but boxers. He was sexy in boxers, but she found him just as irresistible in clothes. Domitian wasn't as pretty as Thorne, she supposed, if you took him feature by feature, but there was just something about him that appealed to her.

"Sarita," he growled in warning and rolled off the other side of the large bed as she started to sit on the edge of it beside him.

Straightening, she frowned and walked around to the bottom of the bed as he did.

"You should not be here," Domitian whispered, catching her arms as if to hold her back. "We need to sleep."

"Yes we do," Sarita agreed. "But you need blood too."

"*Si,*" he admitted grimly. "Unfortunately, there is none to be had just at the moment."

"There is," she said solemnly and shifted her long hair away from her neck. Pushing it over her shoulder to trail down her back, she bared her throat to him. Sarita didn't say anything, simply tilted her head to the side, offering him her neck.

"So," the word came out on a hissed breath, and then Domitian pressed a kiss to her throat and murmured, "the impossible has happened."

"What?" she asked with confusion, shivering as his lips ran along her throat.

"Hell has frozen over," he whispered, reminding her

of her words on first meeting him. Hell would freeze over before she let him bite her, she'd claimed.

Before Sarita could respond, his teeth sank into her throat. She stiffened at the sharp pain it caused and then relaxed as that was suddenly gone and pleasure slid through her, a warm wet sensation that settled low in her belly.

Moaning, she pressed closer, her arms sliding around his shoulders, her hands cradling his head as he drank from her. Somehow one of his legs was between both of hers and she gasped as it rubbed against her, and then she shifted, rubbing back and adding to her pleasure as he—was suddenly gone.

Blinking her eyes open, Sarita glanced around with dismay as a loud crash sounded and she saw Domitian slamming to the floor with Thorne on top of him. She gaped briefly as the two men began to roll on the floor, grappling to get their hands around each other's throat, and then some of her good sense returned and she hurried around the pair to reach their heads. Bending, she grabbed each man by an ear and twisted.

"What the hell are you doing?" Sarita hissed when they both froze, their eyes shifting sideways to take her in.

"I did not start this," Domitian pointed out stiffly. "I was just . . . er . . . and then he suddenly knocked me away from you."

"Er?" she asked dryly.

"Is that what you call biting her?" Thorne growled and started to struggle with him again, but froze at once when Sarita gave his ear another twist.

"Dammit, woman, stop that," he growled. "I am trying to protect you from this vampire."

"He is not—"

"Hello?" Her grandmother called through the door, knocking. "I heard a ruckus coming from in here. Is everything okay?"

Sarita bit her lip, and then looked to Domitian and said, "Control his mind and make him tell her everything is fine."

Domitian turned to Thorne and concentrated on his forehead.

"Hello?" her grandmother called again, more loudly.

"What's going on, Maria?" Mrs. Dressler's voice sounded from downstairs. "Is everything okay?"

"I don't know, Elizabeth. No one is answering me."

"I cannot read or control him," Domitian whispered finally, sounding both surprised and worried.

Sarita's eyebrows rose. "Another life mate?"

Domitian gave a start at the suggestion, but then shook his head. "He's not wholly human. Perhaps that is why I cannot read him."

"Hello?" Her grandmother started pounding on the door.

"It is all right, Maria," Thorne said suddenly. "I was just moving my chest for Domitian and dropped it."

"Oh, all right, Thorne dear," her grandmother said, sounding relieved. "Well, don't stay in there too long. Domitian needs his rest after swimming all night."

"Of course," he said grimly and then arched his eyebrows at Sarita.

"It's okay, Elizabeth," they heard her call now. "Thorne just dropped his chest."

"Oh, good. Okay, well sleep well, old friend," Mrs. Dressler called.

When Sarita heard her grandmother's answer sounding farther from the door as she apparently left, she released both men. Backing up she watched warily as Thorne got off Domitian and stood up. He didn't offer Domitian a hand to rise, she noticed, but crossed his arms and watched them both warily in return as Domitian got up as well.

"Let me see your neck," Domitian murmured with concern, immediately moving toward her.

Thorne stiffened and took a step forward, but Domitian cast him a glare and growled, "I am concerned some damage might have been done when you tackled me. If there is tearing she could bleed to death."

Thorne looked concerned at the comment, but didn't try to interfere as Domitian examined her throat. He looked relieved when Domitian said, "It seems all right. I retracted my fangs quickly enough it would seem."

Relieved herself, Sarita nodded, and lowered her head when he released her. She glanced to Thorne then and sighed when she saw his expression. He was going to need explanations.

"I will handle this," Domitian said quietly, taking her arm and attempting to usher her to the door.

Sarita stuck her ground and shook her head. "I don't trust you won't fight."

"We will not fight," he assured her and then glanced to Thorne and said heavily, "Will we."

"Not if she tells me she's okay with you biting her," Thorne growled.

"I wouldn't say I'm okay with it," Sarita admitted wryly, keeping her voice low. "But I came in here of my own free will and without being invited and told him to do it. The swim here obviously left him in need, and there is no bagged blood here like on the island where we were staying."

Thorne shifted his gaze to Domitian. "So that's why El Doctor wanted you? You're a vampire. I didn't think they truly existed."

Frowning, she said, "He's not—"

"*Mi Corazon*," Domitian interrupted. "Please. Go to bed. Thorne and I will talk."

Sarita hesitated, but then sighed and nodded. She was tired, and didn't really want to go through the explanations of what Domitian was and so on. This time when Domitian tried to urge her to the door, she went without protest.

"I will see you when you wake up," he murmured, and pressed a kiss to her forehead before opening the door.

Smiling crookedly, Sarita nodded and slipped out to tiptoe back to her own room, leaving Domitian to explain things to Thorne. She didn't know if it was his taking some of her blood or not, but she was so exhausted that Sarita didn't bother to strip off her borrowed clothes or even crawl under the sheet and duvet. She simply dropped onto the bed, asleep almost before her head hit the pillow.

The moment Domitian woke up, he knew he'd messed up. He'd only lain down for a minute, intending to wait half an hour or so to be sure Sarita was sleeping before slipping out to make his way through the jungle to the big house. His thinking had been that he'd rather take the risk of making the attempt in daylight than take Sarita with him and put her at risk. Fortunately, after he'd explained everything to Thorne, the man had agreed to help by making sure the cameras were out along the back of the house so he could slip into the woods that way. Trying to go the way he and Sarita had approached the house before dawn this morning would have left him visible to Dressler's goon on the beach now that the sun had risen.

Unfortunately, the swim last night had left him exhausted and the little bit of blood he'd taken from Sarita before Thorne had knocked him away from her hadn't been enough to make much of a dent in his appetite. He'd dozed off and the moment that had happened he'd been lost.

Sitting up, Domitian ran a hand through his hair and then rubbed the base of his neck. Shared dreams were common among life mates. While this was his first experience with the phenomenon, he'd heard about them. They never happened when the mates were together and had made love, but when they were near and hadn't sated their needs, the dreams often kicked in.

He'd been told that both parties contributed to the dream whether consciously or unconsciously, and either party could change the dream's setting and what was happening at the drop of a hat. He'd heard that the dreams were hot and all consuming, but differed in that there was no loss of consciousness after sex in the dreams, probably because they weren't conscious to begin with. He'd also been told that, in a way, they could be better than actual life mate sex because the overwhelming need that made life mate sex so fast and frantic was lessened, and life mates could often do those things they never got the chance to do while conscious.

Domitian had found all that he'd heard to be true. He'd apparently joined Sarita in a dream she was already having when he'd fallen asleep. He'd found himself standing on the edge of an outdoor skating rink, watching her whirl and whiz around the ice, leaping and spinning. From the reports he'd received, he knew she'd taken skating for several years after moving to Canada and had watched with fascination, wondering if she could actually perform the moves in real life. It was something he'd have to ask her, he'd thought and then she'd spotted him and stopped to stare with surprise.

As he'd walked toward her, Domitian had consciously changed the setting. By the time he'd taken her into his arms, they were in a wooden lodge with a fire burning to keep them warm and a soft fur rug where he could lay her back and do all the things he never got the chance to do when in the grip of life mate urgency. Of course, Sarita had soon turned the tables on him and he'd found himself tied to a bed while she'd driven him wild with her beautiful mouth and hands, and then his chains were gone and he'd rolled her beneath him and made slow, passionate love to her. And so the day had passed, with him lost in dreams of being in Sarita's arms.

Getting out of bed, Domitian headed out of the room, relieved to see that the door to Sarita's room was closed. Hoping that meant that she was still sleeping, he moved silently down the stairs.

"You're awake."

Domitian stepped off the stairs and glanced toward

Thorne as the other man appeared in the kitchen doorway.

"I was afraid it would be Sarita and you'd have missed your chance," he said dryly.

"She is not up yet then?" Domitian asked with relief. She'd been in his dreams right up until he'd opened his eyes, but might have woken up at the same time and slipped down before him.

"No," Thorne said and then glanced toward the ceiling and said, "but I suspect it won't be long before she is."

"What makes you say that?" Domitian asked with a frown.

"Because she was moaning and groaning like crazy all day, but has finally gone silent. I suspect that means she'll be up and about soon too." He glanced back to Domitian and considered his expression briefly before saying, "You both were. It alarmed the ladies. Maria went up to check on Sarita several times and said she was thrashing around and hollering fit to die and the nightmares she was suffering must be horrible." He quirked an eyebrow. "She made me check on you too. Didn't look to me like you were having a nightmare."

"Why did you not wake me?" Domitian asked with irritation.

"You didn't ask me to," he said with a shrug.

Domitian scowled at him and then turned and headed up the hall next to the stairs, asking, "Did you take care of those cameras for me?"

"I said I would, didn't I?"

"Yes, you did," Domitian murmured. "Thank you."

Thorne gave a grunt of acknowledgment.

"Where are the ladies now?" Domitian asked as he

reached the back door. He was turning the doorknob when Thorne answered.

"All that screaming unsettled them so much they decided to sit out in the garden."

Domitian froze, and then heaved a resigned sigh and pulled the door open. He stepped outside, wholly expecting the women to come at him with a barrage of concerned questions. Instead, a glance around revealed the garden was empty.

"I guess they must have gone around to the pool or out front," Thorne said with unconcern when Domitian glanced back to him.

"Right," Domitian said, heading for the trees that lined the garden. "Keep Sarita here if she wakes up before I get back. And if something happens to me, don't let Dressler get his hands on her."

They had reached the tree line by then. Domitian didn't wait for Thorne to agree, but set off into the woods at a run. He already knew the man would do his best to keep Sarita safe. He had no doubt that Thorne had been there for the reading of Sarita's letters every week too, and that, like the ladies, they had been the bright spot of his life in this gilded prison. Domitian suspected Thorne had been half in love with Sarita before she'd ever set foot on the island. Once he'd seen how vital, brave, and beautiful she was in real life though, Domitian had no doubt the man had lost the rest of his heart to her.

Fortunately, Domitian wasn't the jealous type, and the pinching he'd felt as he'd entered the kitchen and overheard Sarita in Mrs. Dressler's room, saying Thorne was magnificent . . . well that hadn't been jealousy. Nor had the tightness he'd suffered in his chest each time Sarita had smiled at the man while they'd had tea that morning. She'd smiled at all of them several times as they'd had their tea. There was nothing to be jealous of. But it did occur to him as he made his way through the woods that if anything happened to him, Sarita might be stuck on this island for a long time, hiding in the cottage with her grandmother, Mrs. Dressler, and Thorne her only comfort.

"Bastard," Domitian muttered, but it wasn't jealousy.

# Fourteen

Sarita stepped out of her room and frowned when she noted the open door to Thorne's room, where Domitian was supposed to be sleeping. He'd obviously woken up before her, she realized, and she headed toward the stairs just as her grandmother's voice sounded, calling Thorne.

"Coming," she heard him say and the word was followed by his heavy footfalls. Sarita reached the top of the stairs in time to see the man slip outside and pull the front door closed. Frowning, she jogged down to the entry and peered out the window in the door to see that her grandmother, Mrs. Dressler, and Thorne were all out front, talking as they eyed Dressler's goon on the cliff.

Goons, Sarita corrected herself as she followed their gazes to the two men now on the cliff. Dressler had doubled the guard. Did that mean they'd found the gilled man Domitian had killed last night and now suspected they might have come this way? Probably. The gilled man had probably rolled right up on the beach, pushed there by the tide, she thought with a frown. They should have weighed him down or something. Although, they hadn't actually had anything to weigh him down with, she thought with a sigh and turned away from the door.

A glance into the living room didn't reveal Domitian. Neither did a look in the kitchen. Sarita even crossed the kitchen and took a peek into Mrs. Dressler's room, but no luck. The main floor bathroom was the last place he could be, and Sarita didn't even have to open the door to see he wasn't in it, the door was already open.

She started to turn back up the hall, but paused and eyed the back door. Stepping up to it, she tugged the curtain aside and peered out to see a path leading through first a small patch of grass and then a garden before it disappeared into the jungle. It must have rained at some point that day—the path was muddy, and she could clearly make out two sets of footprints heading away from the door. And one returning.

He'd left without her. Sarita knew it as surely as she knew her own name. Domitian had gone ahead without her.

Cursing under her breath, she pulled the door open and slipped outside. She was entering the jungle before it occurred to her to worry about the cameras.

Too late now, she told herself and burst into a run. Sarita was determined to catch up to Domitian. Actually, she *had* to. He didn't know the layout of the house and yard, the routine of the men patrolling the grounds, the path they took to approach the kitchen at dinnertime, or even which set of French doors led to Dressler's office. He needed her.

As desperate as she was to catch up to Domitian, Sarita soon found she had to slow down. While it had still been relatively light when she'd left the house, with the sun setting it quickly became much darker in the jungle. Afraid she'd trip over something and break a leg or that she might even wander off the path she was trying to follow, Sarita slowed down to a quick walk and cursed the need to. She knew without a doubt that Domitian wouldn't have to slow down. The man had great night vision thanks to those nanos of his. He had increased speed as well. Her only real hope of catching up to him was if she arrived at the edge of the woods before the men headed around to the kitchen to get their dinner. He would have to wait inside the woods for that to happen before making a run for the house. At least that was his best bet of success.

The trek through the jungle was longer than Sarita had expected. Long enough that she wasn't surprised to find it was full dark outside the jungle too by the time she reached the edge of the grounds. A quick scan of the area proved she'd missed Domitian.

As well as dinnertime, Sarita saw, stepping quickly behind the trunk of a palm tree as two men drew near, patrolling the edge of the property.

"I don't know why he wants the patrols doubled," one was complaining. "I've already done my shift. Hell if I want to be out here holding your hand while you do yours."

"Hey, I hear ye," the other one said. "And believe me I'd rather be doing this alone."

"Yeah?" the first man asked. "You're not afraid of those vampires?"

The second man gave a short laugh. "I'm not stupid.

I know they're dangerous, but I've got El Doctor's special juice in my gun same as you. Hit him with one of these puppies and it's '*hasta la vista*, baby,'" he said with satisfaction. After a moment, he added, "And frankly I'd rather let the bastard drain me dry than have to listen to you whine and cry about having to walk around a little longer."

As the first man told the other one to do something anatomically impossible, Sarita eased away from the tree and crept along the tree line to get nearer the house. The path came out about two hundred feet in front of and to the side of the house. She wanted to get up about even with it. It would put her in a better position to help Domitian when he tried to leave the house.

He had to still be in there. Sarita had neither caught up to him, nor passed him on the trail. Unless she'd missed another trail that branched off from the main one, he was still in the house. Hopefully, that meant he was on the phone, giving as much information as he could to that uncle of his, and not that he'd been caught in the house and was now unconscious or wounded or just chained up somewhere.

Sarita had just about reached a spot that was even to the front of the house when she spotted movement at the far corner of the terrace. Stilling, she watched, her eyes straining. A moment later Sarita was assaulted by a combination of excitement and concern. She was happy because she was quite sure the head that kept poking around the corner of the house was Domitian. He hadn't been captured or injured. Her concern, though, was because he was obviously considering trying to run across the front yard, despite the two men on front-door duty who would surely see him.

Holding her breath, Sarita watched him change focus and stare at the two men by the front door. Much to her amazement, first one suddenly turned and faced the wall beside the door he was guarding, and then the other did. It was as smooth as clockwork . . . and rather shocking to see, Sarita acknowledged, letting her breath out. She was suddenly very glad the man couldn't read or control her.

Sure that Domitian was going to make a break for the jungle path now, Sarita glanced toward the yard, noting that every man she could see appeared to be looking away from where Domitian was. She glanced up the side of the house next and then sucked in a horrified breath. Two men were just coming around the corner from the back of the house, headed along the side wall toward the front.

Sarita wasn't sure how this mind control business worked, but suspected Domitian had to concentrate to do it. If he were unexpectedly tackled by the two men he couldn't see approaching, he would no doubt lose his focus, and then he would have every man in the yard converging on him. And apparently the men had some special "juice" in their guns. She was guessing a high tech bullet or something. Whatever it was, it would apparently be game over for Domitian.

Sarita considered the situation briefly, and then cursed under her breath and hurried along the edge of the trees until she was about halfway along the side of the house. Now even with the men Domitian couldn't see, she swerved out and charged them. While one of the men appeared deep in the middle of telling a tale about something that needed big hand movements, the other one did glance up and see her just before Sarita reached them. She saw him raise his gun to aim it at her, but it was too late, she was already in the middle of a flying kick. It hit him hard across the face, spinning him and sending him to the ground.

The second man couldn't help but notice her then. He immediately raised his own gun.

Grabbing the barrel of the rifle, Sarita moved her head to the side to avoid getting shot and rammed it back into the man's face as he tried to aim. When he looked dazed but didn't go down, she slammed it into his face again. This time the man's eyes rolled back and his body followed the motion so that he landed flat on his back in the grass.

The third man came out of nowhere. Sarita saw a large shadow out of the corner of her eye and then an iron band was around her throat, lifting her off the ground as the sound of large wings flapping told her it wasn't a human she was dealing with, but one of the hybrids. One who was winged like Thorne.

Gasping for air, Sarita struggled to free herself, clawing at the arm that was around her throat and choking off any access to oxygen. She was also kicking wildly, but dangling under the man as she was, her legs were kicking nothing but air. Desperate to be able to suck in a breath, she redoubled her efforts at clawing up his arm, but he seemed impervious to the deep trails she was gouging into his skin.

"Keep it up," her captor suggested lazily. "If I drop you now, you're dead."

Sarita glanced down then to see that they had gained height quickly and were already above the treetops.

Darkness was just beginning to crowd in at the corners of her eyes from lack of oxygen when she spotted Domitian below. He had reached the trees unhampered and was disappearing into the woods completely oblivious to the fact that she was flying high above him.

"Good girl," the man holding her said approvingly when she stopped struggling. The pressure around her neck eased as he shifted his hold. Sarita found herself suspended in the air with one of her captor's arms across her ribs under her breasts and the other now across her shoulders at the base of her throat rather than choking her.

Too aware that he could decide to drop her at any moment, she merely held on to his arm with both hands and stared out over the island.

"My father will be happy to see you," he announced, turning them toward the labs. "You and that vampire of yours rather ruined things leaving the island when you did. We were on the way to the island to put Father's plan in motion when MacNeil radioed us with the news that the pair of you had left the island, swimming south, and towing an air mattress behind you. He thought you'd headed for the mainland, and we spent many hours last night crisscrossing the water trying to find you."

Sarita didn't comment. That had been her idea. She'd suspected that a man who had so many cameras inside, probably had them outside as well and had suggested leaving by the beach in front of the house and swimming around it to the north after they'd first swum south for fifty feet or so away from the island. Apparently it had worked for a while.

"But when MacNeil radioed in that my brother's body had washed up on shore with his neck broken, we knew you'd come here, so we all headed home."

Yep, should have found some way to sink the gilled man's body, she thought, since that could be the only man he was speaking of. Even dragging it along with them would've been better, she thought grimly. Domitian could have tied the rope from the air mattress around the man's waist and pulled him along, and then they could have dragged his body on shore and into the jungle and left him there under some leaves. At least there was less likelihood he would have been found that way, Sarita thought and then frowned.

"He was your brother?" she asked as what he'd said sunk through her thoughts. Her voice was raspy, Sarita noted with a frown.

"One of many," the man answered indifferently, and then asked slyly, "Afraid I'll want revenge and drop you?"

Sarita stiffened in his arms.

"I could," he said with amusement. "Claim you were struggling and I lost my grip on you."

Sarita peered down at the trees below, wondering what crashing through them would do to a body.

"Fortunately for you, I didn't like my brother," the man added.

Sarita was silent for a minute and then asked, "How do you feel about Dressler?"

He chuckled. "Hoping I hate my father too and could be convinced to help you escape?"

"You might want to consider it. I'm sure the Rogue Hunters will go easier on you if they know you've helped me."

"The Rogue Hunters?" he said thoughtfully. "You don't mean those idiots on the mainland do you? They won't find us here."

"They will as soon as they look up which island Elizabeth Salter owns," Sarita said grimly.

"Problem is they'll never know to look up Elizabeth Salter," he said with amusement. "Is that what you were trying to do at the house? Call the mainland and tell them that? I suppose the vampire was there somewhere and you think he managed to make the call. He didn't," he said with a certainty that struck at her heart.

"The minute MacNeil radioed that my brother had washed up on the beach, Father told him to have the satellite phone removed from his office in the house and locked up in his office in the labs. There's no one coming for you, little Sarita. Your life is here now."

Sarita's mind rebelled at the suggestion and she was about to tell him that her life sure as hell wasn't here now, but snapped her mouth shut when he suddenly swooped downward, dropping quickly toward land. For one moment she thought they were going to crash into the ground between the fence and the labs, but at the last moment he pulled up, swinging his body down and forcing hers with it as he flapped his wings against the wind to slow them. They landed rather abruptly, but on their feet, and then he took her arm in a steely grip and started walking toward the first building.

Sarita glanced around at the yard inside the fence. The towers were all manned with armed men as they had been the first time, but this time they had noticed their arrival at once and were watching them.

"They'll shoot if you make a break for it," the winged man said idly.

Sarita snorted at the suggestion. "I doubt it. Dressler wants me for something. Some kind of experiment."

"Yes, he does," he agreed easily as he marched her toward the first building, the one where the immortal had been cut in half and put back together. "But you don't have to be in good shape for what he wants. Just not dead. They can shoot you in the leg without angering him."

When Sarita glanced at him narrowly, trying to decide whether he was telling the truth or not, he added, "What do you think we were headed to the island for? It wasn't to bring you fresh linens."

Sarita faced forward again, her mind racing, and then asked, "What does he plan to do with me?"

He hesitated and then shook his head. "Father wouldn't like it if I ruined his surprise. You'll find out soon enough. But let me give you a little advice," he said as they approached the lab. "Don't fight him. You can't win and he'll just make things unpleasant for you. On this island my father is God."

They had reached the door and on the last word, he pulled it open and shoved her in ahead of him.

Sarita stumbled inside and glanced swiftly around the lab, relieved to see that the table was empty this time and there wasn't some poor tortured immortal on it cut in half or missing limbs. She was less happy to see Asherah sitting at the desk Dressler had used, writing something in a notebook. The woman glanced up with a start at their entrance.

"I have a gift for Father, Asherah," the winged man announced, pulling the door closed. "Where is he?"

"Sleeping," Asherah said, eyeing Sarita with an odd expression on her face.

"Well, wake him up. He'll want to know we have the girl."

Asherah shook her head and closed her book before standing. "He said not to wake him unless we had them both."

"But—"

"That's what he said, Caelestis," Asherah said firmly, coming around the desk.

"Don't call me that—you know I hate that name," the man holding Sarita snapped.

"Fine. That's what he said, *Cael*," she said impatiently and then arched an eyebrow. "Better?"

"Yeah, but—"

"No, buts," Asherah interrupted irritably. "You know how miserable he gets when he's woken up from sleep. We don't wake him up until the vampire's caught too."

Cael released a resigned breath. "Fine. What do we do with her, then?"

"Lock her in the cells until the vampire is found," Asherah said with a shrug, retrieving a large set of keys from her pocket.

"I thought the cells were full?" Cael commented and Sarita turned slightly, getting her first good look at him in the light. He was almost a dead ringer for Thorne. He had the same high cheekbones, the same full lips, the same pale gold eyes and the same coloring to his wings. He was also just as gorgeous as the other man. But he was on the wrong side.

"They *are* full. I'll have to put her in with Colton," Asherah said absently as she led them toward the refrigerator, sorting through the keys on her chain.

"Is he still alive?" Cael asked seeming surprised.

"Just," Asherah said and paused next to the refrigerator to unlock . . . a door, Sarita saw when Cael urged her closer. She hadn't noticed it the last time she was here because it was hidden by the protruding refrigerator. She should have expected it existed, though. This lab didn't take up a fifth of the building. There had to be a door to whatever lay behind this room, which, as it turned out, were cells from what these two had said.

Sarita glanced around curiously the moment Cael marched her through the door. All there was to see was a hallway with white walls and white tile on the floor like the lab they'd just left. There were also five white doors off it. Two on either side and one at the end. Asherah led them to the end door, unlocked it and stepped in, flicking on a light switch next to the door as she went.

Sarita got halfway through this door and then froze. The white walls and white tile floor were gone, replaced by metal walls and a bare concrete floor. There were also six barred cells here, three on either side, all of them occupied. A wide aisle ran down the length between them, leading to a door at the far end of the room. Since the lab, the hallway, and these cells probably only took up half the length of the building, Sarita suspected the far door led to more cells and more prisoners.

She slid her gaze over the occupants of the first two cells. There were two women in the one on the left. They stood as still as statues, faces expressionless as they watched them enter. A lone man was in the cell on the right. He was huge. Even sitting slumped against the wall, Sarita suspected he was almost as tall as her. Standing, she doubted she'd reach halfway up his upper arm. He was also bald and extremely pale, almost blue. His eyes were closed, his head down, his chin resting on his chest. She wasn't sure he was breathing.

"Move." Cael shoved her forward with his hold on her arm and Sarita reluctantly followed Asherah down the aisle past the first two cells, aware that the women tracked them with narrowed eyes.

"You should have moved Colton to the front cell instead of leaving him surrounded by these monsters," Cael said tightly as Asherah stopped at the second cell on the right and began searching through her keys again. "At least then he would only have had them on one side of him."

Asherah shrugged. "They can't reach him in the center of the cell and he's not moving until we carry him out."

"What about her?" Cael asked, thumbing toward Sarita with his free hand. "They might bite her."

Asherah selected a key and stuck it in the cell door. As she turned it, she glanced at Sarita and her mouth twisted. "Judging by the footage from the island, she seems to like vampires. She'll be fine."

Sarita felt heat rush into her face at the woman's words as she realized Asherah had obviously watched the camera footage of her and Domitian. They'd been careful to not do anything outside the cocooned bed once Domitian had created the little shelter, but before that there had been the incident in the bathroom that first day. There was also their interlude by the pool. It was possible that a camera had been placed in the trees by the waterfall and caught that action. Though she'd been covered by the towel when Domitian had given her pleasure, it wouldn't have been hard to tell what was happening. And there had been no towel covering Domitian's erection afterward, just her mouth.

Her soul shriveled at the thought of this bitch witnessing those intimate moments between her and Domitian, but as Asherah opened the cell door, Sarita raised her chin and asked sharply, "Did you enjoy the show? Or were you jealous?"

Growling, Asherah caught her by the arm, nails digging deep into Sarita's forearm as she dragged her from Cael and shoved her through the open door. Sarita stumbled several steps, nearly stepping on a figure on the floor before catching herself. Freezing, she stared down at the boy she'd nearly trampled. He was young, perhaps six, and he was lying on the cold concrete with only a blanket wrapped around his bulky shape, leaving just his thin face visible.

"Let's go," Asherah snapped as the door clanged shut.

"No. We can't leave her here. If they drain her dry, Dressler will be pissed," Cael said and Sarita glanced over to see him eyeing the inhabitants of the other cages warily.

"Fine," Asherah snarled and pulled a gun from her pocket.

Sarita took an instinctive step back, pausing when she stepped on something. As she glanced down to see that she'd stepped on the boy's blanket, not any part of him, she heard two soft *pffts* of sound, and glanced back to the woman. She then followed the gun point to the cell next to the one she was in as the two men inside suddenly dropped like puppets whose strings had been cut. There were darts sticking out of each of them now, she saw.

"Happy?" Asherah asked Cael tersely.

"What about him?" Cael asked, nodding his chin toward the man slumped against the wall in the first cell on the other side of Sarita.

"He's bloodless. Can't do a thing. Now let's get out of here," she said, heading back up the aisle toward the door they'd entered through. "These guys give me the willies."

Cael hesitated, but then turned and followed Ash-erah out.

By Domitian's guess he was little more than a couple of minutes away from the cottage when something large swooped out of a tree on the side of the path and landed on the trail in front of him. It brought him up short, and he started to crouch into a fighting stance, and then recognized the man in front of him.

"Thorne," he said with surprise, straightening. "What are you—?"

"Did you call your people?" he interrupted, trying to glance around Domitian as if expecting there to be someone behind him.

"No. They moved the phone," Domitian admitted, his voice heavy with disappointment at having failed.

"Did you search for where they moved it to?" Thorne asked with a frown.

"Of course, I searched," Domitian said impatiently. "And then I read the mind of one of the men guarding the front door and learned that Dressler had it moved to the labs the minute he realized we were on the island."

"How did he know you were on the island?" Thorne asked with concern. "I thought I took care of the cam-eras . . . unless the bastard has some I don't know about."

Domitian shook his head. "I do not think you need worry about that. Unfortunately, the man with gills washed up on the shore today. They deduced that his broken neck meant he didn't die of natural causes," Domitian said dryly, and then frowned as he noted that

Thorne was trying to look around him again. Shaking his head, he continued, "They put one and one together and made two. Two being we had made it here."

Thorne cursed violently.

"Yeah. That means a change of plans. I'm going to take Sarita and swim for the mainland or another island, whichever we reach first. I need to get her away from here. From there I'll get the information to my uncle at the villa."

"Your uncle?" Thorne growled. "I thought some special police force was after El Doctor. What is your uncle doing here?"

"Uncle Lucian heads up the special force," Domitian said soothingly. "He's rented a couple of villas in Caracas and taken a couple more on Isla Margarita in the Rancho de Chano area for himself and the rest of the hunters while here."

Thorne grunted and then tried to look past him again.

Growing tired of the game, Domitian turned sideways on the edge of the path so he had a clear view. "What the hell are you looking for?"

Thorne stared up the dark, empty path and then asked worriedly, "Where is Sarita?"

"What?" Domitian asked with alarm. "She's supposed to be at the cottage. You were supposed to be keeping her th—"

"She's not there," he interrupted on a growl.

"What do you mean she's not there?" Domitian snapped. "You were supposed to be watching her. You—"

"I *was* watching her. I sat in the living room almost the entire time you were gone."

"Almost?" he asked grimly. "*Almost* the entire time?"

Thorne winced. "I only stepped out for a minute.

Maria called me, I thought perhaps there was a problem, but she just wanted to tell me that the guard on the beach had been doubled. She feared El Doctor suspected something. The women were upset. I took just a moment or two to calm them and then went back inside to continue waiting. I thought Sarita was still in bed until MacNeil and a bunch of his security men showed up."

"What?" Domitian hissed, glancing down the path toward the cottage.

Thorne nodded. "They barged in, scaring the hell out of mother and Maria and started searching the place. I ran upstairs to try to warn Sarita, but when I opened the guest bedroom door, she was gone."

"Wh—?"

"Just shut up and listen," Thorne snapped. "MacNeil was right behind me and saw the room was empty. He started cussing and swearing and then someone called him on his radio. I didn't hear what was said, MacNeil pushed me out of the room and told his men to take me downstairs to the living room with the women while he took the message and then slammed the door. But he came downstairs a few moments later and said to tell you that they have Sarita and if you want her to live, you are to give yourself up by midnight."

"What?" Domitian gasped with dismay. He then shook his head. "Well, then why the hell did you keep looking behind me? Why did you think she was with me?"

"I was sure he was bluffing," Thorne said on a sigh and then rallied and said, "And I still half think he is. Aside from being a trained police officer, Sarita has years of martial arts training under her belt. Her father made her learn to defend herself after her mother's murder. He was afraid to lose her like he did her mother."

"I know," Domitian said quietly. Aside from it being in his reports, she had mentioned the martial arts training herself.

"And she's smart," Thorne added firmly. "I just cannot see her getting caught on her own. It must be a bluff. She is probably on her way back here right now. You just missed each other on the path. Where are you going?" Thorne finished when Domitian turned abruptly to head back the way he'd come.

Domitian did not pause or slow down, he simply said, "To turn myself in."

"Wait." Thorne hurried after him. "You have a little over four hours before you have to do that."

Domitian paused and thought briefly, and then sighed and nodded. "*Si*. I will look for her first. If I find her I will free her, but if not, I *will* turn myself in at midnight."

"What about getting word to your uncle?" Thorne asked with dismay.

"I have no way to call him and have no idea how long it would take me to swim to Isla Margarita. I will not risk trying to swim there and return with a team in time to save Sarita. I must be here at midnight to turn myself in. We are on our own."

# Fifteen

"**Y**our name is Sarita."

Sarita turned from watching Asherah and Cael leave and glanced warily at the men in the cell across from the one she was in. She was quite sure the man who had spoken was one of those three, but had no idea which one. They all looked very alike. All of them wore identical black leather outfits as if they belonged to a biker gang. They also all had dark hair and similar facial features. They were obviously related, but the two on the ends were a little smaller than the man in the middle. Not a lot, they were all big men, but the two on the ends just had very muscular shoulders, while the one in the middle had *incredibly* muscular shoulders. Sarita dubbed them Biker #1, Biker #2, and Biker #3 in her mind.

"Sarita Reyes," the man in the middle, Biker #2, said now.

"You are Domitian's life mate," the man on the left, Biker #1, said with interest.

"You sacrificed yourself for him," the one on the right, Biker #3, added.

"You—"

"Okay, let's just slow our ponies here, boys," she said finally, interrupting Biker #2. Propping her hands on her hips and using her best constable scowl, she said, "Yes, my name is Sarita Reyes. Yes, Domitian thinks I'm his life mate. But no I didn't sacrifice myself for him." Raising her eyebrows she suggested, "Now how about you guys mind your own business and stay the hell out of my head? Hmm?"

"Domitian does not think you are his life mate," Biker #2 said solemnly. "He knows it . . . and so do you."

Sarita scowled at the suggestion, but before she could comment, Biker #3 said, "And you did sacrifice yourself. Knowing he could not see them, you tackled the men coming up along the side of the house . . . sacrificing yourself so that he could escape."

"I'll take that as a 'no, we won't mind our own business and stay out of your head, Sarita,' shall I?" she asked dryly, and then snapped, "And I did not sacrifice myself." Scowling, she added, "I mean, it wasn't *supposed* to be a sacrifice. I was supposed to kick their butts and join Domitian to head back to the cottage. And I did kick their butts. I just didn't expect Bigbird to fly in and carry me off like an eagle snatching up a bunny," she finished irritably, because, really, that hadn't been fair at all.

"You're more a porcupine than a bunny, lass," one of the two men in the cell on the right of the one holding the bikers commented with a thick Scottish accent. Sarita scowled at the blond man for his trouble.

"Quinn," Biker #2 growled in reprimand.

"What?" the Scot asked innocently. "Ye have to admit she is, Victor."

Sarita stiffened at the name Quinn used to address Biker #2. She was pretty sure the uncle Domitian had mentioned being taken was named Victor. Could this be him?

"Bunnies are soft and fluffy," Quinn continued. "This woman's thoughts are sharp and pointy." Turning to Sarita, then, the Scot smiled charmingly and added, "It's no' an insult. I like sharp and pointy. A lot."

"Dial it down, Quinn," Victor suggested dryly. "Try to romance this woman like you do every other mortal female and Domitian will kill you. She is his."

"I am not!" Sarita protested at once, resenting the way they made her sound like a possession.

"Really?" Quinn asked, waggling his eyebrows.

"Oh, stuff it, Romeo. I'm not interested," she growled, and then glanced down at the boy at her feet when he moaned in pain.

Frowning, Sarita dropped to her haunches to get a better look at his face. While Asherah had turned on bright lights when they'd entered, she'd also turned them off on leaving. The only illumination in the room now came from weak bare bulbs overhead that cast a dim glow. It was enough to see by, though, and she peered at the child's pale face with concern and then felt his cool forehead.

"He doesn't have a fever," she mumbled to herself as she looked him over. The boy was panting slightly, and there was a bluish tint to his lips and ears. Intending to check his fingernails to see if his nail beds were blue too, she tugged his blanket away and then froze.

"*Madre de Dios,*" she breathed, staring at what she'd

revealed. The boy had the head, arms, and chest of a little boy, but from the waist down he was all pony, right up to the tail.

Another one of Dressler's experiments, she thought grimly, brushing the tips of her fingers lightly over one of his legs to feel the coarse horse hair. The boy moaned and shifted restlessly, and Sarita glanced back to his face and frowned. He didn't look well at all.

Sighing, she covered him again, and then brushed the human hair back from his face and peered at him sadly as she asked, "What's the matter with him?"

"He is dying," Victor said solemnly.

"What from?" Sarita asked, glancing around at the man and noting the compassion on his face as he looked at the boy.

"I cannot be sure, but judging by the rapid heartbeat, his shortness of breath, and the blue of his lips and ears, I would guess that he is not taking in enough oxygen to support his body so it is failing."

Sarita glanced back to the boy and thought that was a pretty good assessment of the situation. At least it did match the symptoms. "Do you think it's pneumonia or something? Shouldn't Dressler be giving him antibiotics or other meds?"

"I suspect if that were the case he would," Victor said solemnly. "Since he is not, I would guess the problem has more to do with the boy's physiology than illness."

"His physiology?" she asked, with a frown, lifting the blanket again, a horse's body to the neck where a human upper body began. A whole human torso, head, and arms rather than just a horse head.

"It could be anything," Victor said sounding weary. "Perhaps he was born with only human lungs. They would not be able to supply enough oxygen for the body he has. Or perhaps it has something to do with the fact that he has a human nose and sinuses. Horses have much bigger nostrils and their sinuses run the length of their head. Human sinuses may not be large enough to accommodate his body's needs." He shrugged. "I do not know."

"But if it was physiological rather than an illness, wouldn't he have died shortly after being born?" Sarita asked, not wanting to believe the boy couldn't be saved.

"Perhaps," Victor said. "But from the boy's memories it would seem he has always been weak and gasping for breath. He could manage a sprint for a brief distance, but had no endurance so was unable to run and play with the others. And then as he aged he could no longer sprint or even walk far, and then not at all without losing his breath. He has apparently grown weaker over time as his body grew."

"You can read him?" Sarita asked glancing over with surprise.

"Yes."

"Domitian couldn't read the gilled man we encountered. I thought perhaps they were all unreadable."

"Most of them are," Victor said with a shrug. "I haven't been able to read or control any of the other hybrids we've encountered. Just this boy, which is what made me wonder if from the waist up he is not completely human."

Sarita turned to look back at the boy. He was lying on hard concrete with just the thin blanket beneath him. It didn't look comfortable, she thought. Sitting down, she drew his head into her lap and brushed the hair back from the boy's face as she silently cursed Dr. Dressler to hell.

Knowing that was a waste of time, Sarita glanced to Victor and the other two men in the cell across from her, noting that they'd all moved to the front of the cage and were now leaning against it, watching her. This time when she looked them over, she noted that they not only looked similar to each other, but that many of their features, especially their eyes, were very similar to Domitian's.

"So?" she asked, zeroing in on the larger man in the middle. "You're Victor Argenis? Domitian's uncle?"

"I am Domitian's uncle Victor," he acknowledged, but then added, "However, it is Argeneau, not Argenis."

That made Sarita frown. "But Domitian's last name is Argenis not Argeneau."

"Both are just a variation on our ancient name Argentum," Victor explained. "In old times there were not really last names. It was basically Bob the baker or Jim the smithy. For us it was a first name plus silver, because of the silver in our eyes. As the family grew and spread, different variations of Argentum occurred, Argenis in Spain, Argeneau in France, and so on."

"I see," Sarita murmured, but wasn't sure she did. Whoever heard of someone changing their name to match the country they lived in or moved to? And just what kind of person did that?

"Someone who wishes to not draw attention to themselves," Victor said quietly, obviously reading her thoughts.

Sarita bit her tongue to keep from snapping at him for obviously piddling about in her thoughts again. Though, judging by the amusement that suddenly curved Victor's lips, she suspected he knew she was peeved. Sighing, she shifted her gaze to Biker #1.

"My nephew, Nicholas Argeneau," Victor announced, gesturing to the man she was looking at. Turning next to Biker #3, he added, "And another nephew, Decker Argeneau-Pimms."

Sarita nodded in greeting, recognizing the names of Domitian's cousins. She then glanced to the men in the third cage on the opposite side. Eyes settling on the Scot, she said, "And I know you're Quinn . . . also Argeneau?"

"Sadly no. We are no' *all* Argeneaus, lass," the man said in a tone that suggested he was glad to have avoided that fate. "Fortunately, I'm a MacDonald through and true. And pleased I am to meet ye, m'lady."

He gave a gallant bow, waving his hand around as if doffing a hat, and then straightened and pointed to the second man in the cell with him and announced, "And me cellmate is one Ochoa Moreno, the most recalcitrant Latino I've ever had the pleasure o' meeting. We suspect he and his partner are both hunters for the South American Council, because they did no' come with us. But he'll no' tell us a damned thing about how he and his partner landed here. His partner by the by is Enrique Aurelios, the dark-haired fellow lying unconscious on the floor over there."

Sarita turned to glance toward the slumped fellow in the front cell next to hers.

"No, not him. That fellow is bald, and his name is Santo Notte," he said dryly. "I said the *dark-haired*—Oh, you recognize the name Santo," Quinn interrupted himself to say. "Ah yes, Domitian told you about his disappearing from the boat he was on with the fair Drina."

Sarita turned a glare at the Scot. "Do you think you could just stop reading my mind?"

"I'm afraid not," he said, not sounding very apologetic. "In truth, none of us has to read you. Like all new life mates you're kind of shouting your thoughts at us."

Sarita narrowed her eyes on Quinn and then turned to Victor Argeneau inquiringly.

"He is telling the truth. We are not reading your thoughts so much as receiving them."

Sighing, Sarita shook her head, and glanced to her right now, at the two men Asherah had shot. Enrique Aurelios, he'd said. She eyed the man, noting his dark good looks, and then glanced to the second man lying unconscious on the floor with a dart sticking out of him.

"That is Lucern," Quinn informed her dryly and then added, "Yet another Argeneau cousin of your life mate's."

Sarita merely nodded, recognizing the first name. She then turned her gaze to the last cell, the first one on the other side, across from Santo's cell where the women were. Victor took over the introductions again, saying, "The lovely lady with flame-colored tips to her hair is my sister-in-law, Eshe Argeneau, and the woman with pink-tipped hair is Mirabeau La Roche McGraw."

Eshe Argeneau snorted with amusement. "You could have just said the black chick and white chick, Victor. We wouldn't have taken offense and it would have been simpler."

"I would never deign to define you as simply black, Eshe," Victor assured her.

"But you'd define me by my hair tints?" she asked with disbelief.

"Our skin color is merely something we are born with,

like our hair color and eye color," he said with a shrug. "However, the fiery tint you apply to your hair actually does reveal a great deal about you, and better reflects your personality."

"He's good," Mirabeau—the white chick—said, nudging Eshe's arm.

"Yeah, those Argeneau boys," Eshe said with a slow smile. "All smooth talk and sex appeal."

"Spoken like a woman mated to one," Mirabeau said on a laugh.

"And I'm not the only one here who is," Eshe pointed out and smiled at Sarita. "Welcome to the family, kiddo. I don't know Domitian well, but if he's anything like his uncles, you're in for one hell of a ride."

Sarita felt the blush that suddenly swept over her, but before she could even think of how to respond, the man Quinn had called Santo Notte suddenly issued a roar of pain. Turning sharply, she watched as he suddenly jerked upright and clasped his right wrist in his left hand. It was only then she noticed with some horror that his right hand was missing, cut off at the wrist.

The scream ended as abruptly as it had started, as if the sound had woken him from sleep, and now conscious, he could silence the sound of suffering. He sat panting for a minute, and then leaned back against the wall and took several long deep breaths one after the other.

Sarita swallowed the bile that had risen up in her throat at his suffering and watched with pity as he mastered his pain. She couldn't imagine what he was going through. Wanting to help if she could, she eased the little boy's head back to the floor and stood to move toward the bars between their cells.

"Stop!" Victor barked. When she paused and glanced around with surprise, he added, "Do not go any closer, Sarita. Santo might lose his head and attack if you get close enough for him to grab you."

"I will not attack her." Santo's voice was a weary growl. "But I would appreciate it, Sarita, if you would move back to where you were. Your scent is strong and, frankly, more of a torment than Dressler's pitiful attempts at torture."

"Pitiful?" she asked with disbelief. Cutting off body parts seemed pretty horrific as tortures went to her, Sarita thought as she surreptitiously bent her head to sniff herself by the shoulder and armpit.

"*Si*. Pitiful. I have been tortured by men far better at it than him," Santo said solemnly.

Sarita frowned, both at his words and at the fact that she didn't smell that bad. She wasn't fresh as a daisy, but—

"He means you smell delicious," Victor said, sounding amused.

"*Si. Delizioso*, like Momma's Swordfish a la Siciliana," Santo said on a sigh, and then lifted his head and inhaled deeply.

Her brow furrowing with concern, Sarita ducked her head again, this time sniffing her other shoulder and armpit. She didn't smell anything fishy, but she *had* been in the ocean all last night swimming here and she hadn't had a chance to shower or anything since. Sighing, she moved back to sit down next to the little boy again.

"Is Santo the only one of you that Dressler has experimented on so far?" Sarita asked as she eased the boy's head onto her lap again.

"Experiment? Is that what he calls it?" Victor asked, his voice stiff.

Sarita nodded. "Apparently he's been subjecting the other immortals he has to various and sundry experiments."

"And here we thought he just cut off Santo's hand because he wouldn't tell him how to turn a mortal," Decker said dryly.

"Turn a mortal?" Sarita asked, glancing up with surprise. "Can you do that?"

Victor gave one slow nod.

"And Dressler wants to know how?" she asked sharply. The ramifications of that happening rushed through her mind. The man was brilliant, and as Mrs. Dressler had said, he thought ten steps ahead of everyone else. That was how he had got away with torturing his hybrids, holding people against their will, kidnapping immortals, and probably killing people for fifty years on this island without detection. The one bright spot her grandmother and Mrs. Dressler were looking forward to was the day he died and they would be free. But what if he discovered how to become an immortal and turned himself? God save them all then. The man could continue torturing and maiming people and immortals on this island indefinitely. The thought was a horrific one.

"But no one has told him, right?" Sarita asked anxiously. "Not even the guy he cut in half?"

"He cut someone in half?" Victor asked sharply.

"Who?" Decker gripped the bars of their cell. "What was his name?"

"I don't know," Sarita admitted with a frown.

"What did he look like?" Nicholas asked.

Sarita tried to think back. All she could remember

was his open wounds and how gray he had looked. She couldn't envision his face at all.

"Did you see what color his eyes were?" Victor asked.

"Green," Sarita said at once. Domitian had asked her the same question and she remembered the man's eyes opening as she had when he'd asked. "And he had fair hair, and—"

"It is all right, we can see the memory in your mind," Victor said quietly.

Sarita raised her eyebrows. Domitian hadn't been able to do that, but then he said life mates couldn't read each other's minds.

"It was Davies," Decker muttered with disgust.

"Yes," Nicholas agreed. "Christ, he's just a pup. Barely a hundred years old."

"But he was one of the first to go missing," Victor pointed out. "So if he yet lives, the others might still be alive as well."

"It wasn't the first time Dressler did that to him," Sarita said with a frown. "He said he'd cut him in half and left him for only ten seconds the first time and had worked his way up to two hours. If what Dressler truly wanted was to know how to turn a mortal, well . . ." She shook her head. "Frankly, I'm surprised anyone could withstand that torture and not tell."

"Hmm," Victor murmured, looking troubled, but then he asked curiously, "Would you let Dressler know how to live forever?"

"God no," Sarita said at once. "I'd rather die."

Victor nodded with approval, but said, "The problem is, Domitian wouldn't."

"You don't think he'd die rather than tell him?" she asked with surprise, because frankly, Sarita couldn't see that. She was quite sure Domitian would agree with her and die before giving such information to the man.

"I am sure he *would* die before telling Dressler," Victor said solemnly. "But I do not think he could stand by and let *you* die for any reason. Even that one. He will do whatever it takes to save your life if it comes to that."

Sarita shook her head.

"He is right, Sarita," Decker said solemnly. "All of us would give anything for our life mates. It is our greatest weakness."

Sarita lowered her head, her mind suddenly whirling. These people thought that Dressler's experiments were just an excuse to torture information out of immortals on how to turn a mortal. Or how he could be turned, because that's what Dressler no doubt wanted it for. But she didn't totally agree with their assessment.

Dressler was a scientist, he needed to know how things worked, and she had no doubt he'd want to know how the nanos would affect him once he was turned. She suspected many of the experiments were to see what he could survive, or how long certain injuries might incapacitate him. The man did things ten steps ahead after all. He must know that becoming immortal wouldn't stop the others from hunting him. If anything they'd probably look harder. Knowing what he could withstand and the fastest way to heal, and the like would certainly be useful to a man like that.

But what of her and Domitian? She'd thought they were put on the island as part of an experiment. But this business about turning a mortal and how protective immortals were of their life mates put a new slant on things. The birdman, Cael, had said Dressler was headed to the small island when MacNeil had called with the news that she and Domitian had left it. What had he and his men been coming to the island for? Nothing good she was sure, but . . .

"Dressler probably intended to force Domitian to tell him how he could be turned by threatening your life," Victor said quietly.

Sarita glanced at him, for once not annoyed that her mind had been read. "But why put us on the island at all? Why didn't he just try to force him to do it here? In his lab?"

"Perhaps he thought Domitian would be more likely to give up the information if the two of you had bonded," Decker suggested and then said, "Apparently you did not know Domitian before being thrown together on the island?"

"No. I didn't know him from Adam," she admitted. "But he knew me. He'd known I was his life mate and had been getting reports on me for fifteen years. So are you saying that Domitian would give up that information now, but might not have before our time on the island?"

"No. I am saying Dressler no doubt believed that was the case," he said gently. "You have to remember that he has kidnapped and tortured several immortals in the last couple of years, yet none of them would reveal the information, even though it probably would have saved them from future torture and might perhaps have gained them their freedom. For a man like Dressler, who has no concept of what it means to be immortal or the value of a life mate or even how to love, it would be beyond his understanding as to how a man would not give up that information to save his own life, but would for a woman he had never interacted with. He was probably hedging his bets. Making sure Domitian wanted you badly enough before he carried out his plan."

"So I am the bait," Sarita said grimly. "He'll make Domitian reveal your secret by threatening my life?"

"Undoubtedly," Victor agreed solemnly. "And Domitian will not hesitate to give him what he wants to save you."

Sarita thought about that for a minute, and then glanced to the women and asked, "But Domitian and I are the only life mates he has, right? None of you—"

"You are the only life mates that are both here," Eshe agreed. "Fortunately for us, Lucian would not allow life mates to work together on this hunt. He felt it too dangerous."

Sarita nodded, then eased the boy's head to the floor again and stood to approach the bars between her cell and Santo's again.

"Sarita," Eshe said with concern. "I can see what you are thinking, but there is no need for this."

"Christ, she's going to sacrifice herself," Decker muttered, sounding dismayed.

"Domitian called Lucian with the information about this island, Sarita," Nicholas reminded her urgently. "He will be here soon bringing the other men with him and—

"Santo," Victor growled suddenly in warning when the other man turned his head abruptly, spearing Sarita with silver eyes rimmed with black.

Dressler had said the nanos went into the organs and whatnot to remain in the body when an immortal had been drained of blood, and it seemed a lot of them were in Santo's eyes. Pausing at the bars, she slid her hands through to his side and gestured to Santo like he was a puppy and she had food.

"Come. Feed," she encouraged. "Drain me dry. I don't want Dressler to hurt even one more person."

Domitian was creeping through the strip of jungle between the bluffs over the beach and the fence around the labs when he heard a *pssst*.

Pausing, he peered around until he spotted a woman in a white lab coat, crouched about ten feet ahead, behind a tree. He was sure he'd seen her come out of the labs several moments ago and walk down to the gatehouse to talk to the guard there. Apparently, she'd made her way around here afterward.

Domitian eyed her warily, but when she gestured for him to go to her, he considered his options. He'd searched the jungle for Sarita first. He hadn't been surprised when she wasn't there, but he'd had to make sure and glancing around as he moved through it hadn't slowed him much. He'd reached the edge of the jungle to find the men all gathered on the lawn getting instructions on searching the island for him. Using their distraction to his advantage, he'd moved along the inside edge of the jungle until he was parallel to the back of the house and then had quickly snuck across to the back corner.

A glance through the window in the first door had shown him a kitchen with a woman pottering around, apparently oblivious to or unconcerned by what was happening outside. Domitian had moved on without disturbing her and used a set of French doors that had led into an empty games room. Other than the woman in the kitchen, the house had seemed completely empty. Domitian had searched it quickly, but there had been no sign of Sarita. As he'd feared, she'd been taken to the more secure labs with their towers and gatehouse. He'd spent the last hour or better, moving through the woods that lined the back and sides of the fence, looking for a weak spot, or a place he might enter without anyone noticing. But while he could control the guards in the corner towers and make them look away, the cameras everywhere ensured his approach would be seen.

He'd just been taking one last look around, hoping for inspiration on how to save Sarita before resigning himself to giving himself up to Dressler, when he'd heard that *pssst*. Now he crept to the woman, hoping against hope that the angels had sent a solution to his problem.

"You have to save Sarita," the woman hissed the moment he stopped in front of her. "I can help."

"Who are you?" Domitian asked, eyeing her warily. "And why would you help?"

"I'm—My name is Asherah."

He stilled at the name, recognizing it. Sarita had said the woman had been present when Dressler had injected her with a knockout drug. This woman had done nothing to help her.

"Again," he said coldly. "Why would you help?"

"Because if you don't get her away from here, El Doctor is going to use her to make you turn him immortal," she said grimly.

"And you do not want that?" he asked dubiously.

"Damned right I don't," she snarled, glancing resentfully toward the labs. "He's tortured us long enough. You need to get Sarita out and away from here to somewhere he can't get his hands on either of you."

Domitian glanced toward the buildings again, debating whether to trust the woman or not. Sarita had said Asherah hadn't seemed to like her much, but she might have mistaken the rage obviously boiling under the surface of this woman as dislike of herself. Either way, it didn't really matter. He didn't see a way to get in without help. If the woman betrayed him and delivered him to Dressler, than she was simply doing what he'd just about decided he'd have to do anyway and turning him in.

"How?" Domitian asked finally, still eyeing the grounds inside the fence. "I can control the guards and make them look away, but I cannot control the cameras."

"There's a blind spot between two of the cameras," Asherah said at once, and he turned sharply to look at her.

"Where?"

"Right here," she answered, nodding toward the fence. "If you stay on a straight line from this tree to that third light on the building, the two cameras on this side of the lab will not pick you up."

Domitian eyed the light she was talking about and then glanced at first one camera and then the other on the corners of the building and thought it might be possible they were angled in such a way as to miss a three-foot-wide strip of the grounds. But then he glanced to the next building behind this one and frowned. "What about the cameras on that building? Won't the one pointed this way catch me?"

"It's not angled right," Asherah assured him and then added, "I use this blind spot to slip away from the labs and go down to the beach for a swim when El Doctor makes me stay all night to watch over one of his horrible experiments. I've never once been caught."

Domitian nodded slowly and then eyed the path she was talking about.

"How do you manage the fence?" he asked after a moment. He could climb it quickly and easily, but Sarita might have difficulty with it on their way out.

"There's a slice in the fence that goes up about five feet. I tied a bit of wire around it in the middle and at the bottom to keep it closed between uses."

"And the men on the security team have never noticed?" he asked with disbelief.

"The men on the security detail are useless," Asherah said acerbically. "They don't even patrol along here. I don't know why El Doctor wastes his money on them. Although, I suppose I shouldn't complain since I wouldn't be able to slip away to swim if they were on the ball."

Domitian glanced to the towers. The two men in the tower to his right were talking and laughing as they smoked. The two in the tower on his left looked like they were playing a game of cards. It seemed none of them were too concerned about the search the other men were involved in.

"Once we get to the wall, plaster yourself against it and follow me to the door, but then just wait there. I will get Sarita out to you."

"I will come in with you and get her myself," he announced grimly.

"You can't," she rasped. "El Doctor is working in the

lab. He'd shoot you with a dart the minute you entered and it would all be over."

Domitian's eyes narrowed. "Then how did you get out?"

"He sent me to tell the guard at the gatehouse to gather the men in the towers and go aid in the search. He thinks their absence will encourage you to walk in and give yourself up," she added. "I saw a flash of movement as I came out and felt sure it would be you, so after I passed along the message, I just slipped around to talk to you."

"The gatehouse guard doesn't appear to have listened," Domitian pointed out, motioning to the two towers on their side of the fenced-in area.

"Yes he has," she said and pointed to two men approaching the gate from the other side of the buildings. "He's just slow and lazy. And he probably got talking to one of the men when he called them. Once they all make their way out, we can slip through the fence and hurry to the building. But follow me. If you step outside the blind spot and the cameras pick you up . . ."

Asherah shrugged helplessly, not stating the obvious, and Domitian nodded silently and then glanced again toward the guard towers he could see, noting that one of the men playing cards had stopped to take a phone call. Moments later the man ended the call, said something to his partner and the two men began to descend the ladder to the ground.

Domitian's gaze shifted from them to a third pair of men as they appeared from the other side of the buildings, headed for the gatehouse. That left only—he glanced toward the tower on their right to see the men had stopped talking to each other and one had a phone pressed to his ear. He watched the man end the call and then those two men began to descend their ladder as well, heading to ground. He followed them with his eyes as they trooped toward the gatehouse, wishing he could shout at them to hurry up. It seemed to take forever, although it was probably only five minutes or so. Just long enough for Domitian to come up with another concern.

Spearing Asherah with cold eyes, he asked, "If Dressler is inside, how do you intend to get Sarita out?"

"I have a plan," she assured him.

"What plan?" he insisted.

"She can tell you all about it once she's out. We need to move now," she said and then rushed from the tree to the fence to crouch down and begin removing her ties.

Tense and suspicious, Domitian followed, arriving just as she undid the second tie. Before he could ask his question again, she turned and handed the ties to him. "Make sure you do it up before you follow me. If someone sees the fence torn open they might investigate and block your exit."

Asherah was almost through the hole before she finished speaking. Frowning, Domitian followed, and then paused to do as she'd instructed, slipping one tie through both edges of the fence at about the midpoint in the cut, and twisting it twice to seal the fence loosely, and then doing the same at the bottom of the fence.

When he turned toward the building, Asherah had already reached it and stood with her back flat against the wall, waiting for him. Seeing that she was directly below the light she'd mentioned, Domitian headed straight forward.

Asherah waited until he'd nearly reached her, and

then started to slide along the building with her back still flat to it. Following her example, Domitian turned his back to the wall and did the same.

They paused briefly at the corner of the building while Asherah peeked out to be sure the coast was clear, and then they slid around the corner to approach the door. They were nearly to it when Asherah glanced back and whispered, "Wait here. Sarita will be out in five minutes. Maybe ten. And make sure you take the long way back. Follow the edge of the jungle around the labs and house. They are searching the beach by the boats, expecting you that way."

Continuing forward then, she slipped through the door into the lab and disappeared, leaving him to eye the now-empty gatehouse and the path beside it worriedly.

# Sixteen

Sarita watched as the silver in Santo's eyes completely obliterated the black of his irises. It was as if the nanos were eagerly responding to the offer, but then Santo turned his head away in refusal.

"Goddammit," Sarita snapped furiously. "I don't want to be responsible for Dressler becoming immortal. I couldn't live with knowing he was out there hurting others because Domitian couldn't let me die. Don't force him to make that choice."

"Has it occurred to you that perhaps Santo could not live with knowing he had taken an innocent's life?" Victor asked, his voice sharp. "You are asking him to kill you."

"He's an immortal. You all feed off innocents all the time," she said impatiently.

"To live," Eshe snapped. "But we do not murder people to survive any more than an accident victim or hemophiliac would to get the blood they need. We are not animals, Sarita. He will not feed on you. You are just torturing Santo right now, and for no good purpose. Leave him alone."

Sagging against the bars, Sarita withdrew her arms and then turned to scowl at Eshe and Victor. "I don't want to torture Santo or make him do something he might feel guilty about. But I would rather die than allow Dressler to succeed, and I would rather die than allow Domitian to have to live knowing he'd given Dressler the information he needed to become immortal, and feeling guilty for any deaths and torture that follow."

"I know, but—" Eshe began, and then paused and glanced sharply toward the door when it opened.

They all watched silently as Asherah entered, this time alone.

"Time to go," the woman said, unlocking the cell Sarita was in.

She hesitated, but then noticed the knife Asherah had in her hand and approached the cell door as the woman swung it open.

"Sarita," Victor growled.

"Do not," Eshe commanded hoarsely.

Ignoring them, Sarita stepped out of the cell, mentally preparing herself to kick out at the woman. The way she saw it, she'd either beat the crap out of Asherah, get her keys, and free everyone, or she'd fail and die, blowing Dressler's chances of forcing Domitian to give him the information he wanted. Either way, she won. Although, really, staging a breakout and surviving would be the better ending for her, all things considered.

Smiling wryly, at the thought, Sarita started to turn

toward Asherah and then stiffened and released a startled gasp at a sharp pain in her side. Lowering her head, she stared with amazement at the knife sticking out of her just above the waist.

Well, that was unexpected, she thought, vaguely aware of the shouts and curses coming from Domitian's family. She lifted her head to stare at Asherah blankly.

"You're not dying," Asherah said wearily as the others fell silent. Sliding the knife back out, she caught Sarita by the arm when her legs immediately gave out. Leaning close she whispered, "You should know by now that there are cameras everywhere on the islands. El Doctor heard your plans to sacrifice yourself and decided I should collect you early to make sure you didn't spoil his plans."

Asherah pulled Sarita's arm over her shoulder and turned to half walk and half drag her to the door, adding, "I'll try to get you out of here. But it won't be easy, and he'll kill me if he finds out I helped you."

"Help?" Sarita asked with surprise.

"Do you think I want that bastard living another year let alone hundreds?" she asked in a bitter whisper. "I'd kill him myself if I had the courage, but . . ." She shook her head and opened the door to the hallway, walked Sarita through, and closed it again.

As she helped her along the hall, Asherah added, "He only has months to live. He has cancer. That's why he stepped up his game. Not because he was worried about getting caught. No one will find this island and if they do, they won't make it ashore alive. The flying hybrids circle a two-mile area around the island, watching for anyone approaching. They would sound the alarm and it would be Armageddon on the water with the human security men and the various hybrids all joining in. So we can't count on help. We just have to hold out for a couple months and then we are all free . . . so long as he doesn't find out how a mortal is turned."

"Kill me," Sarita said at once. "That would stop him. Domitian would never tell him without proof I am alive."

Asherah tossed her an exasperated look. "If I can't kill that animal Dressler, what on earth makes you think I could kill you?"

"You stabbed me," she pointed out dryly.

"Yes, but not mortally. And it's just to ensure El Doctor thinks you're subdued and will not be difficult."

"Yeah, well, I'm afraid I believe it too," Sarita said weakly, aware that she was leaning more heavily on the woman with each step. She also felt lightheaded, dizzy, and she was starting to sweat, all bad signs she knew. "I think you hit something important after all."

"*What?*" Asherah asked sharply, and eased her to lean against the wall so that she could examine her side. "Dammit."

"That doesn't sound good," Sarita muttered, trying to keep her eyes open.

"I think I must have nicked an artery or something. Just hang on a minute. Don't pass out. I'll be right back."

Sarita nodded weakly, but her eyes were closed and she couldn't see the woman leave, although she did hear her walk quickly away. A door opened and closed, followed by silence and then the sound of a door opening and closing again. Sarita heard returning footsteps.

"Here. I'm giving you a shot of adrenaline and something to slow the bleeding," Asherah whispered just before Sarita felt a sharp pain in her thigh. "It should start working relatively quickly."

Sarita swallowed, and while she waited to feel better, asked, "How are we going to get out of here?"

"Not we, you."

She opened her eyes at that and peered at the woman with disbelief. "I won't be able to get out of here by myself. I can barely stand."

"You'll be fine once the shot kicks in," Asherah assured her.

"But—"

"Besides, Domitian is waiting outside," she assured her.

"He is?" Sarita asked with surprise.

"Yes. I saw him on the camera earlier, sneaking around the fence, trying to find a way in. So I distracted El Doctor until he was past the camera and then made an excuse to leave and went out to lead him safely through the cameras to the side of the building. There is a blind spot," she explained. "Only one and very small. He's waiting for you."

"What about the men in the towers?" Sarita asked with confusion.

"El Doctor sent them to help search the island for Domitian." Asherah eyed her with concern. "How are you feeling?"

Sarita hesitated and then straightened away from the wall, finding she could hold her own weight again. She wasn't feeling 100 percent or anything, but she could move under her own power at least.

"Good. Now listen, it has to look like you escaped and I had nothing to do with it, do you understand? El Doctor will kill me if he thinks I let you go or helped you in any way."

"How do we do that?" Sarita asked dubiously. "I'm injured and you're no weakling."

"There is a stereo dissecting microscope on the wheeled tray. I put it there earlier. When I walk you past the tray, you grab it and hit me on the head," she instructed. "Make it look good. If he doesn't believe it, I'm dead," she repeated. "Once you've hit me just run for the exterior door. Dressler is old, he won't catch you if you are quick, and you only have to make it out the door. Domitian will be there to get you away. Got it?"

Sarita nodded abruptly, her hands clenching, and then asked, "What is a stereo dissecting microscope and what does it look like?"

Asherah blinked and then cursed under her breath, and said heavily, "Just look for a big thing on the tray that looks heavy."

"Right," Sarita muttered, feeling stupid.

"Come on," Asherah said, pulling her arm over her shoulder again. "Lean on me and look weak. And keep your head down so your expression doesn't give you away. You have to fool El Doctor."

Nodding, Sarita leaned on her and lowered her head as they made their way up the hall the last five or so feet to the door.

"Good luck," Asherah whispered just before pulling the door open and urging her through.

"Ah, there you are. I was beginning to wonder what was taking you so long." Dressler sounded annoyed at the delay.

"I think I wounded her a little worse than I intended," Asherah said apologetically. "She's losing blood fast."

"No matter. It's nearly midnight now. I'm sure Domitian will turn himself in soon and save the day," he said dryly. "And a little urgency wouldn't hurt in helping him make the right decision. Lay her on the table and chain her up, Asherah, so she's the first thing Domitian sees when he enters," Dressler instructed. "I just want to start my notes before the excitement begins."

Asherah squeezed her uninjured side then, and Sarita glanced up to see that Dressler had turned his back to them to bend over the desk and write something in his book. She also saw that they were just approaching the wheeled tray. The only thing on it was something that looked like the microscopes they'd used in high school science class, but more sci-fi-ish to her mind.

Sending up a quick, silent prayer that this would work, Sarita snatched up the weighty microscope and swung it at Asherah. It was heavier than expected and, afraid she'd kill the woman, Sarita pulled back a bit at the end trying to lessen the blow. She still connected with a solid thump and wasn't surprised when Asherah cried out and fell to the floor.

Seeing Dressler straightening and turning toward her, Sarita wheeled the microscope at him and made for the door as quickly as she could. Which really wasn't that quickly, she worried as she staggered forward. Sure she would be stopped by the old bastard at any moment, Sarita put on a burst of speed and stumbled through the door unaccosted. But the effort cost her and she pretty much fell out the door as it swung open.

One minute the ground was rushing toward her face, and the next she was caught up in strong arms and pressed to a hard chest.

"Thank God," she whispered as Domitian's scent filled her nostrils.

"*Mi Corazon?*" Domitian whispered with concern when Sarita went still in his arms. She didn't answer, and the scent of blood was heavy on her. He took a moment to listen for her heartbeat, his own heart stuttering with concern when he heard how weak and thready it was.

"Rest, *mi Corazon*," he whispered. "I have you."

Pressing her tight against him, he glanced around to be sure the way was still clear and the men had not returned from their search, and then he moved quickly around the corner and back along the wall. When he reached the light Asherah had pointed out, he hunched over and ran for the fence, making sure to stay within the dead zone between cameras as Asherah had instructed. Reaching the fence, he didn't bother untying the tie, but pushed his way through, careful to avoid any part of Sarita getting caught by the sharp and broken wire.

Once through he immediately ducked into the jungle outside the fence and then hesitated. It would be faster to cut back on this side of the island and Sarita was injured and needed immediate tending. However, Asherah had warned him that route was too dangerous.

Cursing, he turned and followed the longer route, rushing through the small strip of forest that ran between the fence and the bluffs over the beach, following them around the fenced-in labs and then behind and past the big house. He had to stop only twice to avoid being spotted by the few searchers in this area. As Asherah had said, it appeared they were concentrating on the other side of the island in front of the house, expecting him to try for one of the boats.

Domitian continued on a straight path along the cliffs until he was a good distance through the forest between the big house and the cottage where Sarita's grandmother and Mrs. Dressler lived. He then cut into the forest, avoiding the paths, but making a zigzag trail of his own toward the cottage. Domitian saw a pair of men to his left at one point, but both men were looking the opposite way and he continued on, moving as silently and swiftly as he could, hoping they wouldn't turn and look in his direction until he was well past. When no one shouted or started shooting at him, he was sure he'd avoided detection.

It seemed to take forever to reach the cottage, and Domitian spent the entire trip listening anxiously to Sarita's heartbeat, afraid it would stop at any moment. Nothing in his life had ever terrified him as much as the possibility of losing Sarita did during that interminable journey back to the cottage. He didn't slow as he reached the edge of the clearing, simply raced forward down the path. When the door opened before he reached it, he thought Thorne must have been watching for him, but it was Sarita's grandmother.

"Is she all right?" Maria Reyes asked with alarm as Domitian hurried inside.

"She will be," he assured her grimly in passing and rushed up the hall to the stairs.

Domitian carried Sarita straight up to the guest room she'd slept in earlier, kicked the door closed behind him and settled on the bed with her in his lap. He didn't think about what he was doing, or that he should lock the door or tie Sarita down first, or that he would need blood to help her with the turn, Domitian simply shifted his left arm under her neck so that her head dropped down to hang off it. When her mouth then fell open, he tore into his other arm with his own fangs and pressed the gushing wound to her mouth.

When the bleeding stopped, he repeated the action. Domitian was just finishing doing it for the third time when Sarita's grandmother finally caught up to him and bustled into the room.

"Is she—?" Maria Reyes drew up short halfway to the bed as her eyes telegraphed what they were seeing to her mind. She stared at the blood soaking Sarita's side and hip, the blood smeared on her lips and face, and the bloody wound now stretching from Domitian's wrist to his elbow, and then her eyes rolled up in her head and she just keeled over.

Domitian sat up slightly, craning his head to see the woman, worried he'd killed Sarita's grandmother, and then was distracted when Sarita began to scream and thrash in his arms. Obviously, she'd had enough blood. The turn had begun. Cursing as he realized how unprepared he was for it, Domitian scooped Sarita up, stood, set her on the bed and tried to hold her down.

He could hear shouting from below, recognized Mrs. Dressler's anxious voice, but didn't have time to answer her questions. He was in the middle of a battle royale with his life mate. Sarita was bouncing, thrashing, kicking, and hitting. She was also screaming her head off the whole time, in obvious agony and need and there wasn't a damned thing he could do about it. He didn't have any blood.

After taking a third kick to the groin and having her nails raked across his cheek twice, Domitian, out of desperation, threw himself on top of the wild woman, hoping to pin her down with his weight. It didn't exactly work as he'd hoped. Instead of pinning her down, Domitian found himself holding on for dear life as she bucked and bounced around on the bed like a wild bronco.

"Oh dear . . . What . . . ?"

Domitian wasn't sure if he actually heard those words over Sarita's caterwauling or if Maria Reyes was so distressed she was shouting her thoughts. Whatever the case, he glanced around then to see the woman sitting up on the floor, looking both dazed and horrified as she watched him and Sarita hump around the bed. At least until Sarita gave one great heaving hump and kick that sent them turning and tumbling off the bed onto the floor next to the woman.

Tightening his grip on Sarita, who was now on top, Domitian tried to offer the older woman a reassuring smile, but his head was bouncing repeatedly off the floor, sent there by Sarita's breasts as she thrashed on top of him, and he suspected what he actually managed was a rictus of pain.

Eyes wide, Maria Reyes dragged a golden cross out from the neckline of her dress, clutched it between her hands and began to pray. It wasn't until she started yelling "Out devil! Out foul demon!" that he realized she thought Sarita was possessed.

Domitian closed his eyes and began to pray as well, but he was praying that he would survive Sarita's turning with at least one testicle still intact. He was quite sure that one of them was ruptured.

"What the hell?"

Domitian opened his eyes with hope to find Thorne standing in the doorway to the room with a very alarmed-looking Mrs. Dressler in his arms.

"Oh, *gracias a Dios*," Maria Reyes cried and rushed to stand next to the pair in the doorway, chattering away in Spanish so quickly and frantically even he couldn't understand it, and Domitian had been speaking Spanish for centuries. When she finally wound down, the three of them just stood there watching in horror as Sarita continued to rock and thrash on top of him as if he were a rocking horse. With Domitian's hands locked around her waist, she was now throwing herself forward, smashing his head into the floor with her breasts, and then throwing her upper body back and bringing her knees down, pow, right between his legs. And they were just watching, he thought with disbelief. As if this was some WWF bout.

"Help," Domitian whimpered in a voice he was sure was too low to be heard. Fortunately Thorne seemed to understand. He glanced around a little wildly, and then set his mother on the bed. Maria had followed and settled beside her so that the two women could clutch each other's hands as they watched and prayed. At least he was quite sure Maria was praying, Elizabeth Dressler was shouting advice to her rather confounded son as he tried to sort out how to help Domitian.

"Quick, grab her around the chest when she swings up!" Mrs. Dressler shouted.

Thorne straightened his shoulders, straddled Domitian and Sarita and tried to wrap his arms around her chest as she threw herself up and back, slamming her knees into Domitian's much-abused family jewels. Stars exploded behind his eyes, a buzzing sounded in his ears and he closed his eyes on a groan as he waited for the agony to end. But when he could hear again, Elizabeth Dressler was saying, "Oh dear, Thorne, no I don't think—Oh, that isn't working at all."

Forcing his eyes open, Domitian saw that while Thorne had started out wrapping his arms around Sarita's chest, she was thrashing and bobbing around so much that he now had her only by the breasts, one hand clutching each. It brought a growl from Domitian just before the man muttered, "Sorry," and released her.

"Her legs, Thorne! Try her legs!" Mrs. Dressler suggested.

Nodding, Thorne stepped to the side, and then moved down to grab Sarita's feet as they flew up in the air. That was all Domitian saw before his head was smashed into the hardwood floor by Sarita's upper body. But he soon realized this was not going to work either. With her legs in the air, Sarita's mobility was restricted to a short up and down. Basically, her breasts were playing patty cake with his head on the floor.

"Oh, dear, no that isn't going to work either, Thorne," Elizabeth Dressler said with dismay. "Let go of her legs."

Domitian bellowed when Thorne listened to his mother, released Sarita's legs, and they promptly slammed down into his groin together.

"Out Devil! Out spawn of hell!" Maria Reyes roared in response.

Domitian closed his eyes in misery as he realized he wasn't going to get out with even one testicle intact. He'd felt the second one pop this time. God help him, but he was grateful to be low on blood in that moment. The thought of his testicles healing only to be crushed again . . . Well, it was really more than any man should have to endure, he thought.

"What the hell is going on here?"

Domitian blinked his eyes open and stared at the man now towering in the doorway, and then Sarita's breasts obscured his view. But when she rose up again, and the ringing in his ears ended, he opened his eyes and peered at his uncle once more. All he managed to get out was "She was dying," before Sarita's upper body slammed into his head again. Fortunately, it was a mere bounce this time, because Sarita was suddenly lifted off him.

Opening his eyes, Domitian saw that Lucian had grabbed her under the arms and was now holding her out in front of him as far as his reach would allow as if she were a child with a dirty diaper. Releasing a sigh of relief, Domitian scrambled to his feet, took one unsteady step, and then fell over as the world tipped.

He was quite sure he heard a sigh from his uncle and then the man began barking orders.

"Bricker, run back down to the boat and get the chain we brought! Jo, go with him and fetch the blood! Nephew, stay down!" he added when Domitian opened his eyes and tried to move. "The back of your head is hamburger. You need blood before you try to rise again. And, Basha, please control and remove these ladies so I can set Sarita down!"

"On it," three voices said at once and Domitian watched as the room burst into activity. Justin Bricker and a pretty young woman who must be Jo rushed from the room to fetch chain and blood, and Basha stepped in front of Maria Reyes and Elizabeth Dressler for a moment as Thorne looked on with concern. She then turned to say something to Thorne that Domitian couldn't hear over Sarita's continued screeching and then stepped aside to allow Thorne to pick up his mother. Taking Sarita's grandmother by the arm, she then led her from the room too.

Domitian stared after the woman, trying to focus, and then asked, "Is that—?"

"Yes. Your uncle Felix's daughter, Basha." Lucian nodded.

"I heard she was found," he muttered, closing his eyes again to avoid having to watch the room spin. "Is she a hunter now?"

"Yes. As is her husband, Marcus."

Domitian nodded and then winced when it caused him pain to move his head on the floor. He then pondered the fact that he could hear his uncle despite Sarita's screaming. And then realized the man probably wasn't talking at all, but transmitting his thoughts to him.

Justin Bricker was the first to return with his booty. The rattle of the chains brought Domitian's eyes open again, and ignoring his uncle's orders, he rolled onto his stomach and crawled to the bed as Lucian laid Sarita on it and began to chain her down with Justin's help. Halfway through the process Sarita finally stopped screaming and went silent.

Concerned, Domitian managed to pull himself up to kneel at the side of the bed, and then flinched in surprise when a bag of blood was slapped to his mouth, which was open on a breathless pant.

Domitian raised a hand in thanks, the best he could do with a bag of blood in his mouth, then watched as Jo carried a cooler full of blood around to the other side of the bed and set it down.

"Dani's sending someone with drugs to help with the turn," Jo announced as she straightened. "They found Nicholas and the others. She said most of them are all right, but Santo is in a bad way. His hand was cut off and is partially sealed over and they can't find the hand."

"And Dressler?" Lucian asked.

"No sign yet," Jo said grimly. "They're still searching."

Lucian finished chaining Sarita down, then straight-ened and considered her briefly, before asking, "Is she sending an IV?"

"Yes," Jo said, grabbing another bag of blood and moving out of his vision.

"Then all we can do is wait," Lucian said.

Domitian flinched as the now-empty bag was ripped from his mouth, but raised a hand to catch the next bag as Jo went to pop it on his fangs.

"How did you know where the island is?" he asked, and then popped the bag on himself as he waited to hear the answer.

"A little birdy told me," Lucian said dryly, bringing a snort from Justin Bricker as he finished locking the last chain on his side of the bed and straightened.

"A big damned bird, man," Justin said and then grinned. "Hey, get it? Birdman? Bird, man?"

"Please. Spare us," Lucian said dryly.

"No sense of humor at all," Bricker complained and then glanced to Domitian and grinned. "You should have seen Lucian jump when Thorne came swooping out of the air and perched on the rail of the balcony at the villa like a big damned vulture."

"He is part eagle not vulture," Lucian growled.

"Yeah. Whatever. You should have seen your face, though. That was the first time I've seen you surprised by anything."

"It is the first time I have been surprised in many centuries," Lucian admitted. "Are you saying you were not surprised?"

"Oh yeah, I was surprised all right," Bricker ad-mitted and then glanced to Domitian and told him. "Lucian damned near killed him before we knew he was a friend. Fortunately, Thorne blurted your name and then explained everything. He led us back to the island as soon as we could round everyone up and arm them. About three miles out he made us stop and wait, said he could see hybrids in the air ahead. I thought he was kidding, but Jo pulled out the binoculars and sure enough, there were a couple of them flying around. They were far enough apart Thorne was able to take care of them one at a time. He flew up really high in the sky so he could approach unnoticed," Bricker said, raising a hand upward as far as he could reach. He then brought it swiftly down adding, "And then he swooped down and sucker punched the first one in the back of the head as he flew past." He slammed a fist into his palm with a smack. "The guy was still falling through the air when he swung around and gained height again to go after the next one."

Bricker shook his head. "When he flew out of sight around the island, we didn't know what was happening. Turns out there was one patrol on each side of the island. Ten minutes later he flies back around with a bird hanging from each hand. Literally," he added with a grin. "They were chicks. Both unconscious but alive. Lucian had them locked in the hold of the big boat, and then we picked up the two in the water. One had landed on his wings on his back and was unconscious, but still alive. One landed facedown, though, and drowned before we got to him."

"After locking them in the hold with the other two, we continued forward for another mile, but then Thorne made us stop again, and warned us he could see gilled hybrids in the water about a mile out from the island. Again, I thought he was kidding, but—" He paused to wait as Jo ripped the second bag of blood from Domitian's mouth and replaced it with a third. And then he continued, "Anyway, after some discussion, it was decided Thorne would take Basha up in the air with him. He held her around the waist and flew, and she picked off the gilled hybrids with one of our dart guns. We put them in the hold too, but aren't sure how they'll handle our darts. They're strong enough to knock out rogues, so . . ." He shrugged grimly, not needing to say they might be deadly to the hybrids depending on how strong their constitution was.

At least they'd tried not to kill them, Domitian thought. Although, if these were the ones that Mrs. Dressler had mentioned were loyal to her husband, he wouldn't feel too bad about their deaths. They'd been complicit in Dressler's activities, some of which had been directed against his own people.

"After that, Lucian sent the other boats to raid and search the house and labs, and we followed Thorne around to the cottage to make sure his mother and Sarita's grandmother were all right."

"Because of me." That comment came from Basha as she entered the room and joined the conversation.

"It was not because of you," Lucian said calmly. "Someone had to check on Domitian and Sarita and we had the blood on our boat. If anyone would have needed it, it would have been them."

"We did not even know they were here," Basha argued shortly. "And what we had on our boat was me." Holding up her hand to silence him when he would have argued, Basha asked pointedly, "When before have you ever delegated the battle to others and taken the safer task, Uncle? Never," she answered herself.

"Basha," Lucian began.

"Uncle," she countered, interrupting him. "You really need to let go of your guilt over what you think of as failing to protect me as a child, and stop trying to protect me from everything now. If you do not, I will suggest to Marcus that we move to Italy full-time to be near his family."

Turning on her heel, Basha left the room then and silence briefly reigned.

"Well," Bricker said brightly, avoiding looking at Lucian who appeared to have turned to stone. "Where was I? Oh yes, we followed Thorne back. Of course, flying, he got here faster and . . . well, you know the rest."

Domitian nodded slightly, wincing as the action sent pain radiating through his head. He stopped moving his head in the hopes of ending the pain, but instead it just built and grew, focusing mostly on the back of his skull. The healing had begun, he thought grimly just before he lost consciousness.

# Seventeen

Sarita woke up in the guestroom she'd been given in Dr. Dressler's house and for one moment thought that everything had been a mad, mad dream. After all, who would believe in vampires and winged men? No one, of course, she thought, and then a warm arm slid around her waist, and the scent of the man now spooning her assured Sarita that it hadn't been a dream. All those wild memories crowding her mind had really happened. Including the first time when she'd woken up and Domitian had told her what had taken place after she'd stumbled into his arms outside the lab.

He'd turned her to save her life. Sarita didn't know how she felt about that. She wasn't keen on the whole blood thing. On the other hand, she was even less keen on the whole death thing, so blood won that round, she supposed.

Domitian had also told her that Thorne had taken out four winged hybrids alone, and then had taken an immortal woman named Basha up in the air to use tranquilizer darts on the gilled hybrids. Sarita had much less ambivalence about that. She was glad Thorne was all right and had come through it safely, and while she was sorry for the hybrids who had died, including young Colton who had apparently slipped away during the battle, she was even sorrier for the ones who had fought against the immortals and survived, because their future looked pretty bleak from what she could tell.

Right now they were locked up in cells in the labs where all the others who were now free, had been kept. Rather ironic in her opinion. But there was talk of their being judged by the council. The problem was, no one seemed to be sure which council just yet. Apparently, the South American Council, who had been none too pleased with Domitian's uncle trampling all over their turf, was now delaying talking to him about what to do about the island and its inhabitants. It meant Lucian and a good portion of his people were stuck here until a decision was made. Something he apparently wasn't too pleased about, according to Domitian.

And then there was the something Sarita wasn't too pleased about . . . Dr. Dressler had escaped capture. After Thorne had taken out the hybrids in the air and in the water, the Rogue Hunters had attacked the island. Dressler's security men had put up a bit of a fight and a couple of immortals had been knocked out by darts. But when the locked-up immortals and hybrids had been freed to join the fray, the security men had soon given up. The overriding consensus had been that Dressler didn't pay well enough for them to risk their lives.

It didn't matter, though—it was too late. Dressler had

apparently already made his escape. Despite repeated questioning, no one seemed to know where El Doctor might be until hours had been wasted searching every inch of the island. Only then did MacNeil "suddenly recall" that Dressler had a boat in a hidden cave on the side of the island behind the house.

By that time, the boat was long gone, of course, as was Dressler, Asherah, and an immortal Asherah had apparently gone to fetch after assisting in Sarita's escape. The immortal was Davies, the man Sarita had first seen cut in half. And no one was sadder than her to hear that news. The man had surely suffered enough. What more could Dressler visit on him? No one knew, but Lucian had sent hunters out searching for the trio, hoping to capture Dressler and save Davies and Asherah.

Speaking of Asherah, Sarita was a bit confused when it came to how she felt about the woman. She'd seemed all right in the end. She'd even saved Sarita's life. Well, actually she'd stabbed Sarita and damned near killed her, but then she'd helped her to escape. However, there was something troubling Sarita about that whole escape thing. Domitian had told her that Asherah claimed Dressler had sent her out to talk to the guard in the gatehouse when she'd gone out to help Domitian. But Asherah had told her a different story. She'd claimed that she'd seen Domitian on the camera, distracted Dressler until he was safely past, and then made an excuse to leave and lead him safely to the building. They were two different stories, and Sarita had been trained to look for inconsistencies in people's stories. It was a clear sign of the unreliability of a witness and sometimes a sign of an attempt to cover up a crime.

Sarita was a little concerned about what Asherah might have been covering up.

Pushing that thought from her mind, she snuggled closer against Domitian and sighed with satisfaction. He was such a good man. While he and her grandmother had sat at her bedside as she went through the turn, he'd apparently explained what he and now Sarita were to her *abuela*. Her grandmother had taken it better than Sarita had expected, although she did now wear three crosses and pray a lot for their souls. Other than that, she seemed fine, though.

Sarita stilled as Domitian shifted, his hand sliding to rest over her breast through the sheet. When he stopped there, his breathing deep, she decided he was still asleep and closed her eyes with another smile. As he'd promised, now that the danger was over, he was wooing her as he felt she wanted. She had only been awake a week, but he'd already brought her flowers and candy, and had even taken her on two actual dates . . . with her grandmother accompanying them.

It seemed Grandmother thought they needed a chaperone. For the first date he'd taken them to dinner at one of his restaurants. Sarita had actually enjoyed herself. Talking to Domitian was easy, and the three of them had laughed a lot as they ate. Sarita suspected she wouldn't have experienced that if they'd been by themselves. They wouldn't have lasted through the appetizers before they were rushing out of the restaurant to find the nearest safe spot to have sex and pass out. Instead, they'd stayed for hours, chatting and laughing before flying back to the island in the helicopter. After a chaste kiss under her grandmother's watchful eye, Domitian had left them at the cottage and departed for the big house where he, along with Lucian and some of the hunters, were staying until the situation on the island was resolved.

Their second date had been dancing, an overnight stay at his mainland home, and a trip to visit the graves of Sarita's father and grandfather the next day. It seemed Grandmother had mentioned to Domitian that dancing was the one thing she'd missed most besides her husband and son while a prisoner on the island. Domitian had decided that was where he would take Sarita on her second date . . . with Grandmother as chaperone. It seemed he wasn't above ingratiating himself with the old lady to win Sarita. But she hadn't minded. She'd actually enjoyed it. Her grandmother's presence had forced them to behave and Domitian had spent the night dancing with first one of them and then the other.

Her grandmother had truly enjoyed herself and so had Sarita. But, dear God, dancing with Domitian had been sweet torture. His body pressing against hers, his hands on her, his breath on her ear. He'd driven her wild and there hadn't been a darned thing she could do about it with her grandmother there. Not even once they'd got to Domitian's home afterward.

At first Sarita had been too stunned at the décor to think about her need for Domitian. She'd peered around at the potted plants, the overstuffed light-colored furniture, and the beautiful hardwood floors and had thought this was the home she'd always dreamt of. The one she'd planned to make for herself one day, and here Domitian had created it for himself. It had made her wonder about those nanos. Maybe they really knew their business. Domitian certainly seemed to suit her in a lot of ways.

Sarita heaved a little sigh and peered at the wall across from her as her mind whirled with the chaos that had claimed it for days as she considered all her options and all her wants and needs. She hadn't just been dancing and visiting graves this past week, she'd spent a lot of time helping her grandmother and Mrs. Dressler as they assisted the hybrids on the island. The two women had made it their mission to make sure that as many of them as possible could have normal lives.

For some that wasn't feasible. Like Thorne, their differences were too noticeable and would make their having a life approaching anything near normal unattainable. But for others it was possible, and the two women were determined to make it happen for those they could. It turned out they had the finances to do it too. It seemed the money Dressler had so happily been spending was his wife's. Elizabeth Salter Dressler had inherited a fortune from her grandparents before marrying Dressler, and later had inherited her parents' even more substantial fortune.

Now that Dressler was out of the picture, Elizabeth was taking back her power and her money. She'd reverted to her maiden name and had all her money moved so that El Doctor couldn't access it. She'd then placed nearly half of it in an account for Thorne, and intended to use the rest to help the hybrids.

For Sarita just a week of helping these people had been more satisfying than a year as a police constable, and with not even 1 percent of the stress so far . . . And that was part of her problem and the reason for the chaos in her mind. When she'd first woken up to find she'd been turned, Sarita had felt a little lost and so had instinctively turned to her old life for comfort.

She'd determined she would stay for a week or so and then return to the safety and comfort of her home and job in Canada. Domitian had already said when they were on the little island that he would enjoy living closer to his sister and would follow her and woo her as she deserved, so she hadn't even considered him in the decision. But she had asked her grandmother to return and live with her, and her grandmother had jumped at the chance and seemed really excited.

But that was part of the problem. Now that she was adjusting to the idea of being an immortal, Sarita found she had less interest in returning to Canada and her job. She found helping the hybrids satisfying, and she liked spending lazy afternoon siestas in bed with Domitian. But she didn't want to disappoint her grandmother either, or make her stay on an island that had been a prison to her for fifty years.

A soft snore sounded behind her and she grinned to herself, acknowledging that the truth was, now that he was wooing her as he felt she deserved, Sarita didn't really need it. Something had shifted in her. Or perhaps it was just that everything was blending together to make her realize how much they suited each other, from his home being her dream home to how his sense of humor matched hers, how their taste in foods seemed to be always lining up, and how they had danced together as smoothly as if they'd been doing it their whole lives. While she knew she couldn't possibly love him already, she felt in her bones that she belonged with Domitian.

A soft tap at the door sounded and Sarita slipped quickly out of bed, tugging her clothes back into order as she rushed to answer it. That was one benefit of life mate sex—it all happened so fast and furious they rarely managed to get all of their clothes off, she thought wryly as she reached the door.

"Hi," Eshe said softly when Sarita opened the door.

"Hi," Sarita responded with surprise. She hadn't seen the woman since they'd been locked in the cells. Eshe, along with the other hunters had been out searching for Dressler, Asherah, and Davies morning, noon, and night since they'd disappeared.

"Got a minute?" Eshe asked.

"Of course." Sarita slipped into the hall, easing the door silently closed and then followed Eshe up the hall, her mind whirling with curiosity as she tried to figure out what this was all about.

"It's beautiful here," Eshe commented a few minutes later as she led Sarita out into the gardens. "Hard to imagine the nightmare Dressler made it into for everyone when you look at such beauty."

"Yeah," Sarita agreed, peering out over the well-tended gardens.

"I wanted to talk to you about Domitian," Eshe said, leading her along a path with tall flowers growing on either side of it.

"Oh?" Sarita asked, suddenly wary.

"You know you love him, right?" she asked.

Sarita swallowed and glanced away, her brow furrowing. "I've only known him for—"

"Cut the crap," Eshe said not ungently, and Sarita blinked and turned back to her with surprise. Smiling, Eshe said, "Kiddo, I've been alive for a long time and—"

"How long?" Sarita asked with curiosity. Honestly, none of these people looked over thirty and most of them looked more like twenty-five. Yet Domitian was fricking ancient.

"I was born in 1446 B.C.," Eshe said matter-of-factly.

"Did people exist back then?" Sarita asked, trying to wrap her mind around that number. Was there any history back then? She didn't remember studying anything that old. Wasn't that the ice age or something?

"The last ice age was eleven or twelve thousand years ago," Eshe said dryly, obviously reading her mind.

"Right . . . and you were only born three thousand, five hundred years ago . . . give or take a couple decades," Sarita added sarcastically. "God!"

Eshe laughed at her expression and said, "Look. I just wanted to talk to you before I go because Victor was saying Domitian is worrying that you aren't letting him in and aren't acknowledging your feelings for him."

"I don't know what my feelings are," Sarita said with frustration. "They're all a jumble and I can't think straight when he's around. I mean I know I want him. He's like crack to my crack ho, but—" She shook her head helplessly.

"Hmm," Eshe murmured. "And yet you were willing to die for him in the cells."

"That was so Dressler wouldn't know how to become immortal," Sarita argued.

"No. Actually, what you said, and what I read from your mind at the time," she added firmly, "was that you would rather die than allow Domitian to *live knowing he'd given Dressler the information he needed to become immortal, and feeling guilty for any deaths and torture that followed.* That's dying for Domitian, so he wouldn't suffer guilt."

Sarita stared at her.

"What? You gonna deny it?" she asked and then said simply, "You love him, Sarita. This isn't earth-shattering news to anyone but you. As immortals we know that we'll love a life mate if we're fortunate enough to find them. It's a simple fact. And down deep you know you love him. It's just the mores and traditions of your mortal life that are hanging you up. According to them you can't love him yet and should wait to accept or admit it until a suitable period of time has passed."

Turning, she started walking again and added, "And you're free to do that. But I hope you don't, kiddo, because Domitian has waited a long time for you already and he deserves to be happy. As do you. And it pains me to know you're struggling with this when it's all so simple."

Sarita followed, thinking it really was simple. She had wanted to die that day to save Domitian a lifetime, a very *long* lifetime, of guilt. And she would die for him now to save his life if necessary. He was a special man, so patient and kind and passionate. She'd never met anyone like him. Never dated anyone she respected as much or cared as much about. She did love him, Sarita acknowledged, whether she'd known him as long as society would deem long enough or not.

"Anyway," Eshe said after a moment. "I just wanted to say that before we leave. And to again welcome you to the family, because you're a part of it now whether you admit it today or next year."

Sarita stopped walking and frowned. "Leave? I thought you were all staying until Dressler was found?"

"That boat has sailed, unfortunately," she said flatly. "We've got information suggesting that he's left the country. Lucian's arranging for a couple of Rogue Hunters to stay on the island in case he tries to come back here. They'll be working with a couple of Rogue Hunters the South American Council is assigning to the island and the island will be under both councils' purview, at least until Dressler is caught. But in the meantime, the rest of us are going home."

Breathing out a sigh, she smiled wryly and added, "I was looking forward to seeing my husband, Armand, but apparently that's not going to happen for a while yet."

"No?" Sarita asked curiously.

Eshe shook her head. "Some rogues took advantage of our absence and have caused a good deal of trouble back home while so many of us were away. We have a couple of messes to clean up and some fires to help put out." She shrugged. "Having been a mortal cop, you know how it is. While the cop's away, the perps will play, right?"

Sarita smiled faintly. She'd never heard that one. She'd have to remember to tell it to Jackson.

"Listen, that's something else I wanted to say," Eshe added now. "If you ever get tired of playing cops and robbers with the mortal miscreants, we have some real rotten rogues that need putting down. And every job saves lives. There's no dragging cats out of trees or slapping the wrists of shoplifters. Every rogue is a really bad dude who is killing or controlling mortals. And I already talked to Mirabeau about it. She liked you too and said you could ride with us. Just a thought," she added. "No pressure. And the job will still be there ten, twenty, or even a hundred years down the road if you'd rather stay and help out the hybrids for a bit."

"Did you read that out of my mind?" Sarita asked with amusement.

"Didn't have to," Eshe assured her. "You glow when

you're helping them, just like you do when Domitian is around. It's obvious it makes you happy."

They had walked full circle and were approaching the house again, and Sarita frowned when she saw her *abuela* rushing toward them.

"Looks like I'm not the only one who wants to talk to you today," Eshe said, eyeing her grandmother with interest. "I'll leave you two to it."

"Eshe?" Sarita said as the woman started away. When the older immortal turned back she said, "Thank you."

Eshe smiled. "Don't tell the boys we had this heart to heart. They think I'm a hard-ass and I like it that way."

"Oh please," Sarita said with amusement. "You *are* a hard ass."

"Yeah." She grinned. "But so are you. That's why Mirabeau and I like you. See you around, kiddo."

"Later," Sarita said with a smile and then watched as the two women passed each other. Eshe smiled at her grandmother easily, and Maria Reyes smiled nervously back, eyeing her a little leerily until she was well past her and had reached Sarita.

"She is one of those vampires, no?" her grandmother asked in a whisper, her hand going to the crosses at her throat as she glanced back at Eshe. She was wearing only two today, Sarita noticed. That was progress.

"She is an immortal, *abuela*," she said firmly. "Like me."

"*Si*. A vampire." She turned back to her and shook her head sadly. "So young and pretty to be a vampire."

"Again, not a vampire. And not so young either," Sarita said with amusement. "She's older than you."

"No," her grandmother said, turning to stare at the woman again. "No."

"*Si*," Sarita assured her. She almost told her Eshe's

age, but decided it might give the poor woman a heart attack, so asked, "Did you want to talk to me?"

"Oh, *si*." Maria Reyes turned back to her and said worriedly, "*Si*, Chiquita, I need to talk to you."

"What is it?" Sarita asked, her smile fading. "Has something happened?"

"No," she assured her quickly and then sighed unhappily and blurted, "I want to be a part of your life, yes? But I cannot come to Canada with you, Chiquita. Elizabeth would be alone and she needs my help. These poor hybrids, so abused and imprisoned so long. They need help. And you don't need help. You have your Domitian. But they have no one, and Elizabeth has only me and Thorne and—"

"*Abuela,*" Sarita interrupted gently when the woman didn't show signs of winding down. "It's okay."

"*Si?*" she asked uncertainly.

"*Si,*" Sarita assured her, and then took a deep breath and admitted, "I've been thinking I might like to stay and help with the hybrids too."

"Oh, Sarita!" She hugged her quickly. "That would be wonderful! I know Elizabeth will be so pleased. And then Domitian can stay and keep his restaurants and marry you like he wants and you can make babies for us to spoil and—"

"Yeah, Gran, you maybe want to slow your ponies there," she said dryly. "Domitian hasn't asked me to marry him or anything."

"He asked me for permission to marry you."

"He did?" Sarita asked with surprise. "When?"

"When he took us dancing. He is a true gentleman, that one. He asked for formal permission out of respect. A good boy."

"What did you say?" she asked with curiosity.

"I said yes, of course," she exclaimed as if that should be obvious. "He loves you and you love him and you will make me beautiful little grandbabies to spoil."

It seemed everyone "knew" she loved him, Sarita thought wryly. She was the only holdout . . . and she didn't want to be.

"Oh! There he is now. I will go. You tell him you are staying and will marry him. He will be so happy." Her grandmother rushed off before she could protest and Sarita watched her beam happily at Domitian in passing.

When all he managed was a weak smile in return, Sarita frowned. Something was obviously up, and it didn't look like this was the time to tell him anything. The moment he had passed her grandmother, his smile died and his expression became a combination of anger and concern.

"What is it?" Sarita asked, when he caught her hands and began to urge her farther into the garden.

"I was just talking to Lucian," he said and then announced abruptly, "Dressler went to his apartment when he left here."

"They found him?" she asked with surprise.

"No. They found what he left behind."

Sarita eyed him uncertainly. "Davies?"

"He is alive. He was in a bad way, but they have given blood and he is recovering and talking and told us all he knew," he said, rubbing the back of his neck. Raising his head, he added, "Asherah is dead, though."

"How?" she asked at once.

"Her throat ripped out," he said bluntly.

Sarita stiffened. "Davies didn't—"

"No. That is what they first thought when they got on the scene, but he said no and the information on Dressler's computer backs him up. El Doctor apparently left it in his rush to get out, and I guess it was rigged to record everything the cameras saw . . . *all* the cameras."

"Us on the little island?" she asked and then winced when he nodded. Well, that was embarrassing.

"And us on this island," he said quietly. "Including when I turned you."

"What? But—"

"Lucian sent someone down to search the cottage. There was a camera in every room in the house. The recordings started while Dressler's men were searching the cottage. They were planting and activating the cameras during their 'search.'"

"So he knows how to become immortal," she said with dread, and then realization struck and she glanced at him sharply. "That's why he took Davies."

Domitian nodded.

"He made him turn him," she guessed.

Domitian shook his head. "Apparently he turned himself. Nearly chewed Davies's arm off to do it too."

Sarita winced. "So Dressler killed Asherah."

"He drained them both dry, Davies and Asherah. She died, but most of Davies's nanos moved into his organs. He was suffering until help came, but alive. Poor bastard." He ran a hand through his hair and said, "As for Asherah, she made her own bed. She was never trying to help us when she arranged your escape. That was Dressler thinking his ten steps ahead as usual. His plan was to wound you mortally and let you go so I would turn you in front of the cameras he had placed in the cottage during the search. He did not even stick around until I turned you. Once I had you and was headed back to the cottage, he had Asherah grab Davies and take him to the boat in the cave. They were gone before the hunters made the island."

"Oh," Sarita said quietly.

"Davies says they were on the way to the mainland by the time I got you to the cottage and turned you. Dressler watched it on the boat, and the minute they got to his apartment in town, he attacked Davies. Bit his arm over and over to be sure "it took." I guess he didn't take bagged blood with him. The plan was that Davies would supply the blood he needed."

"But we aren't supposed to feed off immortals," she said quietly. Domitian had been giving her lessons on being immortal since her turn. That was the first point he'd stressed. No biting. Taking in immortal blood was bad. The influx of nanos meant the host's blood was used up at an accelerated rate. Drinking Davies dry would have just increased Dressler's need for blood, which was no doubt why he'd then drained Asherah dry.

"Yes, well, apparently that was one thing Dressler didn't learn from all his experiments," Domitian said dryly.

"I'm sorry," Sarita said solemnly.

He glanced at her with surprise. "For what?"

"That your turning me gave Dressler exactly what he wanted," she said simply. "The knowledge of how to turn himself."

"Oh, no no, Sarita, no," he said gently, taking her hands in his again. "He already knew how an immortal turned a mortal. Davies told him repeatedly in the hopes he would stop when he was cutting him in half.

They have it on the tapes from the lab. Dressler knew exactly how an immortal turns a mortal before he ever put us together on the island."

"What?" she asked with surprise, and when he nodded, she asked, "But then why did he need us? Why go to all that trouble of putting us on the island? And what was that escape nonsense all about?"

Domitian's mouth twisted slightly. "Because he wanted to see what exactly happened before he submitted himself to it. It seems Dressler enjoys inflicting pain on others, but does not care to suffer it himself. He wanted to know if it was painful, and if so, just how painful."

"You mean he had Asherah damned near kill me just to see a turn before he tried it?" she said with disbelief, and when he nodded, she asked, "Didn't Davies tell him it was painful?"

"*Si*. But he thought he was just trying to talk him out of doing it. So he had to see for himself and needed a pair of life mates to accomplish that."

"Us," Sarita growled angrily. "How the hell did he find us?"

"Pablo Guerra, my private detective," he admitted unhappily. "Dressler hired him, explained about our eyes, and said he would pay him a fee for every immortal he reported to him. Well, my eyes fit the description," Domitian pointed out. "So Pablo told him he'd been working for a client for thirteen years who had eyes like that. A strange man, who just wanted regular reports on a girl in Canada. She was thirteen and living here in Venezuela when he hired me, et cetera, et cetera."

"Dressler apparently asked the few immortals he had at that time why I would do that. They guessed, correctly, that perhaps you were my life mate and I was waiting for you to grow up to claim you. So he told the detective he would hire others to find the immortals— Pablo was just to send him copies of the reports I was paying for and put cameras in your apartment. And then he apparently waited for me to go to you, because surely I would do so soon now that you were grown-up."

"Only you were being noble," she said softly.

"*Si,*" he said.

Sarita nodded, and then shook her head. "But why did he keep trying to hire you?"

"I am not sure," he admitted. "He only started eating in my restaurant about two years ago."

"About when he hired Pablo," she commented.

Domitian nodded. "He offered me a job the first night, but said it jokingly, and then repeated the offer every once in a while." He shrugged. "Perhaps he planned to lure you to the island if I did not claim you quickly enough and wanted to be able to use hiring me as an excuse to get us together."

"Which is what happened," Sarita pointed out and then commented, "I'm surprised he didn't wait to turn until he could get his hands on some drugs to ease the pain if he saw what I went through. From what everyone said afterward, it sounds like it was agony." Wincing, she added, "What I remember was agony."

"Ah . . ." Domitian made a face.

Sarita raised her eyebrows. "What?"

"Well, the camera in the bedroom was faulty. There was no sound, and the picture was a bit grainy, and according to Davies, Dressler thought I fed you my blood, held you for a minute and then we had wild sex, so it could not have been so bad."

"*What?*" Sarita gasped with disbelief. "He thought we had sex while I was in the turn?"

"Well, I was on top of you and we were very active on the bed," Domitian pointed out. He then added, "And apparently the camera angle was such that he never saw your grandmother enter the room. And then he only saw your upper torso rising up and down beyond the bed after you rolled us both to the floor. Davies said Dressler stopped watching when that business started, so . . ." He shrugged almost apologetically, apparently able to see how Dressler could misunderstand things so badly.

Sarita stared at him blankly and then closed her eyes and let her head drop into the palm of one hand.

There was silence for a minute and then Domitian asked, "Are you angry?"

She jerked her head up with surprise. "With Dressler? Of course, the—"

"No, with me," Domitian interrupted.

"Why would I be angry at you?" she asked with confusion.

"Because it was my detective who caused all of this to happen to us. If I had not hired him—"

"No," Sarita interrupted firmly. "You are not responsible for Pablo's actions," she assured him and then smiled wryly and said, "So I was worried you'd blame me for Dressler's learning how to become immortal because you had to turn me to save my life, and meanwhile, you were worried that I'd be angry because your hiring Pablo led Dressler to realize we were life mates."

"*Si,*" he said with a crooked smile.

"Hmm . . ." Sarita murmured, then took a deep breath and said, "I guess it must be love."

Domitian stilled, his gaze locking on her face. "Do you think so?"

"I know so," she admitted quietly and then offered him a crooked smile and said, "Actually, everyone else apparently knows so too."

"*Si.*" He gave a solemn nod. "You are an intelligent woman, *mi Corazon*, but in this instance . . ."

"Yeah, yeah, I was the last one to the table this time," she muttered.

Domitian smiled, and then asked, "Does this mean that you will consent to be my wife as well as my life mate?"

Sarita swallowed, but then nodded. "Yes. But . . ." she added, raising her hand between them quickly to prevent him from kissing her when he bent toward her.

Domitian paused, uncertainty on his face. "But?"

After a hesitation, she slid her arms around his waist and pressed her cheek to his chest before admitting, "Grandmother doesn't want to move to Canada."

"I am sorry," he said sincerely. "I know you looked forward to having her with us there."

"About that," she muttered and then took a deep breath and admitted, "Actually, I have been thinking I might like to stay here too."

Domitian stilled and then pulled back slightly to peer down at her. "Really?"

Sarita nodded.

"What about your job?" he asked uncertainly.

"I wanted to help people, Domitian. That's why I became a police officer. But . . ." Shaking her head, she said, "I can't think of anyone who needs help more than the people here do. And I mean, we don't have to stay here forever. I'd just like to help as many as I can get on their feet. But I know you mentioned it would be nice to be closer to your sister and—"

"Sarita," he interrupted.

"Yes?" she asked warily.

"I love you. I am happy to stay here. I like your grandmother and we will be close to her while she is with us. I can keep my restaurants running for now while you help here, and we can visit my sister in the summers. And if you later wish to move somewhere else, we can do that too. We have time."

Sarita snorted. "Yeah, we've got time. Like thousands of years apparently."

"It will pass quickly," he assured her.

"Yeah, I'm not too sure about that," she said dubiously.

*"Mi Corazon,"* Domitian said solemnly, lowering his mouth to just above hers so that his breath brushed across her lips tantalizingly as he spoke. "If there is one thing I have learned in my long life, it is that life passes quickly when you are happy. And you make me very happy. Our life together will fly by in a heartbeat."

"That's so sweet, my love," she said softly and then, grinning, added, "You old guys know just the right thing to say."

Domitian closed his eyes, shook his head, and then silenced her laughter with a kiss.

# ABOUT GOLLANCZ

Gollancz is the oldest SF publishing imprint in the world. Since being founded in 1927 Gollancz has continued to publish a focused selection of bestselling and award-winning authors. The front-list includes **Ben Aaronovitch**, **Joe Abercrombie**, **Charlaine Harris**, **Joanne Harris**, **Joe Hill**, **Alastair Reynolds**, **Patrick Rothfuss**, **Nalini Singh** and **Brandon Sanderson**.

As one of the largest Science Fiction and Fantasy imprints in the UK it is no surprise we have one of the most extensive backlists in the world. Find high-quality SF on Gateway written by such authors as **Philip K. Dick**, **Ursula Le Guin**, **Connie Willis**, **Sir Arthur C. Clarke**, **Pat Cadigan**, **Michael Moorcock** and **George R.R. Martin**.

We also have a strand of publishing in translation, which includes French, Polish and Russian authors. Gollancz is home to more award-winning authors than any other imprint, with names including **Aliette de Bodard**, **M. John Harrison**, **Paul McAuley**, **Sarah Pinborough**, **Pierre Pevel**, **Justina Robson** and many more.

### The SF Gateway
*More than 3,000 classic, rare and previously out-of-print SF novels at your fingertips.*
**www.sfgateway.com**

### The Gollancz Blog
*Bringing you news from our worlds to yours. Stories, interviews, articles and exclusive extracts just for you!*
**www.gollancz.co.uk**

## GOLLANCZ
### LONDON